UBUNTU

UBUNTU

UNCONDITIONAL LOVE

ANITA SCHATTENBERG

Library of Congress Control Number: 2015920655
ISBN: Hardcover   978-1-5144-4391-0
               Softcover   978-1-5144-4390-3
               eBook   978-1-5144-4389-7

Print information available on the last page.

Rev. date: 12/16/2015

To order additional copies of this book, contact:
Xlibris
1-800-455-039
www.Xlibris.com.au
Orders@Xlibris.com.au
728552

FOR PRINCE MANGOSUTHU BUTHELEZI

Acknowledgments

The author wishes to thank Cherry Noel, Ann Porter, Lloyd Griffith and everyone on the team for helping to make this book a reality.

Contents

Chapter 1

The Fundamental Idea

Joshua Mtolo had an idea. He recalled exactly when the notion first struck him. He couldn't forget it because the events that day were so horrific, changing his life in a manner that placed him on the wrong side of the law henceforth.

It happened late in 1989. He was passing through Edendale, near Pietermaritzburg, when it occurred. His actual destination was Durban, where he hoped to attend a reunion of medical students who had graduated in 1976 from the University of Natal. Having won a scholarship to complete his studies in the USA, he had not graduated with them but was invited to join because his work in neuropsychology had aroused interest in medical circles and assured his reputation.

Josh was in no hurry. Following a school bus through town, he daydreamed, looking forward to seeing old friends.

The racket of a volley of shots suddenly hitting the school bus froze his mental images. It careened off the road, scraping to a halt against a lamp post. Josh braked automatically, pulling over to stop while more gunfire shattered the bus windows. Without thinking, he sprang from his car and chased after one of the fleeing guerrillas.

'What in God's name do you think you're doing?' he shouted as he caught the culprit by the arm.

'These are pups of Zulu dogs!' the teenage gunman yelled with fanaticism. Wrenching free of Josh's grip, he aimed the gun back at the bus. 'They must die!'

Josh couldn't believe his ears. 'You gonna kill me too? Look at me, you little shit!' He grabbed the boy's shirt front, savagely yanking him closer. 'I am a Zulu!' With that, he threw two well-aimed punches to the youth's head, which brought him to his knees. His AK-47 clattered on the ground, and Josh took it quickly, pulling the shoulder strap over the stupefied youth's head. It all happened so fast that the teenager needed time to regain his wits. He staggered to his feet. Spitting at his pursuer, he fled. His accomplice was long gone. Only then did Josh hear the cries from within the bus, and he abandoned the chase. Hurriedly locking the assault rifle in the boot of his car, he carried his emergency first-aid kit over to take a look at the victims.

'God, what a slaughter,' he muttered. Of the twelve children in the minibus, four were dead. So was the driver. The rest were too seriously hurt to benefit from his help. What could he do here? How could he perform an intubation on the girl with the collapsed lung? How to stem the bleeding of the worst wounds? Where to get saline drip? It was needed instantly, not twenty minutes later. The children's only chance lay in immediate hospitalization. How long before ambulances arrived? Too long, probably.

While stabilizing the children to some degree, Josh became aware that the vehicle's motor still ran. Would it move again? It was worth a try. He heaved the driver's body away from the wheel. Crunching through the gears, he manoeuvred the bus back onto the road, avoiding bumps and jolts as best he could. Forgetting one does not tamper with the evidence of a crime, he made a snap decision to nurse the damaged bus and its dismal passengers to the Edendale Hospital.

The attendant from a nearby petrol station came running, telling Josh that he had called the police and offering to keep an eye on his car. Speed was of the essence, but the bus had no guts left in it, and the shattered windscreen made for uncomfortable driving. Josh was spared the horrendous, self-imposed task when a police vehicle arrived, followed by two ambulances. He found the children's distressing cries unbearable. Those not unconscious were in pain and shocked beyond comprehension. Only the boy with glass in both eyes sat quietly holding his head.

At the hospital, admission procedures were slow. Staff did the best they could but tried Josh's patience sorely nonetheless. Three youngsters needed emergency surgery, and every minute counted. He helped the doctors, administering drips, injecting painkillers, directing gurney-wheeling orderlies, and speaking words of comfort to the stricken kids and their relatives. He did not leave till he was satisfied with the treatment each child received. Maybe they would survive.

Having missed the reunion, Josh eventually met with his fellow medics two days later. His mood was still depressed. His friends Peter Shabalala and Tom Dlamini listened as he retold his harrowing tale. Both men were married with young families, and the story touched a nerve.

'I can't stand it anymore!' Josh spoke vehemently. 'Our society is rotten to the core. What will happen here in fifteen to twenty years? These gun-wielding youngsters will grow up to be good for nothing. "Liberation before education"—bullshit! I never heard a more destructive slogan. Without education, they can't make use of their liberation. Give me Shenge's dictum any day: "Education for liberation". Doesn't it make more sense that way?'

Wringing his hands in impotent exasperation, he continued, 'That misguided young bloke I cuffed in Edendale should have been at college doing his matriculation. Instead, he only knows how to kill. He has no respect for elders or society as a whole. He hasn't been schooled to understand the concepts. His idols in the United Democratic Front tell him to help make the country ungovernable. What they're achieving is far worse. It's creating a society where barbaric acts are the order of the day, where citizens are afraid of each other, where vindictiveness and hatred rule supreme. A community that's eating itself, where self-respect and consideration for one's fellow beings and morals have all become like foreign customs. It destroys our spirit of ubuntu, our humaneness.

'In the meantime,'—he took a deep breath, reflecting—'how can we help innocent victims like those kids on the bus?' And that was the moment the idea hit.

Excited by the thought, Josh continued, 'Listen, guys, we need a special hospital for cases like those, one with a psychiatric ward because they'll surely need it sooner or later. My fiancée, who's a schoolteacher, says that children as young as six or seven draw pictures of guns, necklacings, and so on during lessons. The poor kids will never erase those grim images of attacks and bloodletting from their subconscious minds.

'Why should those unfortunate children and their families suffer so because we lack the resources to administer to them? The Edendale Hospital opened a new surgical ward for wounded young men last year. If they can do that, we can surely do something for little kids. I can't hack it anymore. I will find money for a clinic the likes of which whites have always taken for granted. I don't care if I have to go begging to De Klerk or fawn to the communists to get it.'

Josh belaboured his friends, who initially couldn't get a word in. He was on a soapbox, and none of his audience could pull him down. Eventually his outburst resulted in a lively debate and, finally, agreement. All wanted to be involved and work together. Two things were needed: money and real estate. Josh desired a site within KwaZulu if their funds allowed it. The money? That was another matter altogether.

Peter was an ANC member, and he spread the word around at meetings via the United Democratic Front (UDF). His suggestion soon reached the ears of the senior echelons of the organization, who proved receptive to the request for reasons of their own.

Amnesty International kept a watch on the treatment of detainees in prison camps such as Quatro, run by the ANC in exile. These camps were located outside South Africa's borders, where ANC dissidents were tortured. To divert Amnesty's attention and play down the allegations, the fortunate survivors from such camps could be rehabilitated in a facility such as Josh and his friends proposed. It offered the commanders of the camps a way out. Cloaking the matter in secrecy, it could be claimed that prisoners who became *unwell* were given first-rate treatment in an appropriate institution, with the ANC footing the bill.

Now Peter had a problem. He was assured of start-up capital, but should he tell Josh the reason for the ANC's generosity? He expected Josh would balk. And so it happened.

'God, man! What do you think I am?' he exploded when Peter tried to explain. 'That's foul money, dirty money, which draws us all into their web of violence and intrigue. We become conduits for other people's suffering.' Josh paced his living room, which was the temporary headquarters of KwaZulu Medical. Two weeks earlier, the friends had thrashed out a partnership agreement in a venture they expected would give them a sense of purpose.

'No, Josh, you look at it the wrong way. We are not the perpetrators of pain. We are the healers. All people deserve to be helped.' Peter spoke with emphasis, gesticulating like a preacher with arms outstretched, embracing his congregation. 'Whether it's shot-up kids on a bus or torture victims and, er, freedom fighters, they all have broken bodies and souls. We are righting a wrong.'

Josh still paced like a hungry lion in a cage. Peter helped himself to another beer and continued, 'Anyway, I clearly recall you saying that you didn't care where the money came from.'

'I did,' Josh agreed. 'The problem is I don't want that much money from any one source lest they gain control over us . . . least of all the ANC. It's like a nation selling its land and industries to foreign interests, a sell-out.'

Peter looked hurt. He was an idealist, still seeing the old, innocent ANC of the early 1950s before they embarked on their armed struggle, which, in his view, had spun badly out of control, resulting in the ruin of civil society. He was a member of their political wing, although he refused to join Umkhonto we Sizwe, Spear of the Nation, the armed faction. Neither had he much time for the UDF, an entity formed in 1983 and directed by the ANC in exile to do the ANC's work at home.

The next day, they met with Tom, the third partner in the business, and voted two to one that the ANC's offer of funds be accepted. Accounts were opened quickly, and the search for suitable premises commenced. Again, by democratic vote, this time unanimous, a property near Vryheid was chosen. The price was right, and the building lent itself to modification. The homestead's original floor plan was ideal for use as administration area. An extension to it became the outpatient clinic and emergency station. Three new buildings were erected for use as a children's wing, a psychiatric ward, and staff quarters.

Josh managed to siphon some of the money to buy shares in gold mines. He hoped to nurture KwaZulu Medical to a stage where it became profitable so the ANC's start-up capital could be repaid. Dependence on the ANC's goodwill made him uncomfortable.

How long ago it all seemed to him now as he evaluated his present position from behind the bars of a police cell, hoping for bail. What would the future hold for KwaZulu Medical? for himself? for the woman he loved?

* * *

Like Josh and his friends, Anna De Bruyn was looking for real estate at about the same time. She required a business premises on the edge of Soweto to house a small computer training centre. Anna was the wife of Hank De Bruyn, a Johannesburg stockbroker who managed De Bruyn Brothers, the family company. Anna worked in the firm, assisting Hank as much as possible. She was not seeking profits now, though. Her action was purely altruistic.

During her lunch break one day, she strolled through Johannesburg's CBD when a young ruffian, about fourteen years of age, snatched her shoulder bag. Anna was too quick for him. She stuck out her leg and sent the boy sprawling. Quick as a flash, she bent down and grasped her bag back. A girl of similar age as the thief stood nearby, laughing as she witnessed what to her was a slapstick comedy. Three other boys tried vainly to appear inconspicuous among the crowd.

'You stupid little sod, aren't you meant to be at school?' Anna accosted the fallen boy as he rose.

He gave her a defiant look. 'What's it to you?' he sneered as he ran after his friends. The girl's effort to vanish failed as Anna caught up with her.

'Do you know these guys?' Anna inquired, furious but unshaken.

The girl nodded.

'Where do they go to school?'

'I can't tell you. They'll bash me up if I do.' The girl turned to follow the boys, but Anna had more questions.

'Why aren't you all at school?'

'Strike . . . boycott . . . take your pick,' the girl replied, shrugging her shoulders. Anna wondered about the truth of that response. Maybe they were playing truant.

'*Niyaganga kakhulu*! You are very naughty.' Anna frowned at her. The girl's eyes widened with consternation. Like her mother who often said the same words, this strange woman saw right through her fibs. Anna scowled as the boys called out from the distance, but she wasn't ready to release the girl.

'Are you going to tell me the name of your school, or do I have to follow you home to ask your parents?' she bluffed. Horrified, the girl stammered something Anna didn't quite catch and ran off.

The kids couldn't have come from too far away, Anna thought, as she walked on, holding her handbag a little tighter. With all likelihood, they came from the Orlando West Secondary School near the Orlando Power Station. Back in the office, the phone book soon uncovered the name of the school Anna thought the girl had muttered. She rang to arrange a meeting with the principal the next day.

'Mrs De Bruyn, what can I do for you?' Solomon Mataka, a tall, striking personage, led Anna into his spartan headmaster's office. 'Please, do sit down.' He indicated an overstuffed old swivel chair, which looked like a relic from government bureaus in the 1950s. It creaked and twisted around at Anna's first attempt to settle. She had to hold the back of it steady and then sit on it briskly before it repeated its cantankerous tricks. Solomon Mataka puzzled as to what she could possibly want.

'Mr Mataka, there was no strike at this school yesterday, was there?'

'No.' Solomon's brow wrinkled. The woman didn't mind coming straight to the point. 'What makes you say that?'

'Then boys as well as girls from your school absented themselves and roamed the CBD yesterday.'

Solomon's back straightened. His chin rose. He took a breath as if to deny the statement. Anna gave him no chance.

'One young chap attempted to take my handbag.'

Inwardly Solomon groaned. What was he to do about crime? Was he a headmaster or a police chief? The sole St George to slay a many-headed dragon? Now this domineering white woman had arrived with her petty complaint. It was about as much as he could take.

'Who were those kids, Mrs De Bruyn?' he asked just to sound concerned. 'You should report it to the police.'

Anna shook her head. 'You know they don't reveal each other's names for fear of reprisals. They were youngsters from your school, and I had to work hard on one of the girls to get that much information out of her. Don't misunderstand me, though.' She raised a hand in caution. 'I'm not here to blame anyone. Neither you nor the kids.'

'Then what are you saying?' Rising, Solomon looked at his watch. 'It is almost time for my mathematics class, Mrs De Bruyn. Perhaps we can talk another time.'

'Yes, I believe we must.' Anna took her dismissal lightly. 'A future must be secured for kids like those, Mr Mataka. I have a proposal.'

Solomon sat down again, looking at Anna with expectation.

'Teach them something relevant for their entry into the workforce. How about computer classes?'

Solomon laughed derisively. He leaned forward over his desk, eyeing Anna with cold accusation. 'Mrs De Bruyn, will the government buy computers for my school? With not one white learner in it?' Emitting a bitter snort, he slumped back into his chair.

'No, Mr Mataka. Not the government, but I, or De Bruyn Brothers, will. We supply the premises and equipment. You appoint the teacher.'

Solomon Mataka remained serious. 'Yes,' he said, slowly milling the consequences over in his head. 'Cindy Khumalo would be the ideal tutor. She loves computers.'

'Good!' Anna rose from the rickety chair, which appeared relieved to be rid of her. 'Then we shall meet again to discuss more details if you agree. Yes?'

Solomon became the personification of a broad smile. It was the most promising news item of his day. 'Very well, Mrs De Bruyn, just ring me when it suits you.' He showed Anna out and steered towards the classrooms, still grinning.

Telling Hank about the attempted handbag theft and her subsequent discussion with Solomon Mataka, Anna needed substantial arguments to convince her husband that spending what he thought 'a great deal of money on a feel-good program' was indeed warranted.

'Oh, come on, Hank. It doesn't cost that much. We buy the building. It doesn't have to be big or expensive. It can be sold again if and when it's no longer required. I was thinking Diepkloof might be a good area. If we select the site carefully, we may eventually sell for a profit anyway.' She stood behind his chair, caressing his shoulders.

'So there's depreciation on the computers, but we don't have to buy them brand-new to begin with. There'll be maintenance and upkeep, power bills, phone, insurance, rates, and that's about it. We don't have to pay for staff. Solomon Mataka will see to that part of the deal.'

Hank reached up to take both her hands in his, trapping her. Anna continued coaxing. 'Think about it. The kids will benefit. It'll keep them occupied, off the streets, and hopefully they'll gain skills to make them employable. We could offer a traineeship to the most promising student as a carrot so they have something extra to strive for.'

'And we get a surplus person on the payroll,' Hank interrupted. He had listened with one ear only. Ms Ethics, as the financial press called his wife, was at it again. The Conscience of the Stock Market, determined to reduce insider trading, instil a sense of social responsibility into the business community, and encourage corporate philanthropy.

'Other firms can employ the more successful students too,' Anna persisted.

'How will you persuade them to do that, my dear?' Hank humoured Anna. He had no intention of forking out one cent.

'You want a crime-free city, don't you? Well, here's a means to convert negative energy into positive outcomes. If everyone played their part in improving this society, we might get there. A start must be made somewhere, and we have the means to do it.' Anna finally had his full attention. Crime was his deepest concern.

'Yes, I see your point,' he replied thoughtfully. 'Crime is bad. I've often thought that one day even the JSE will quit the CBD and move out to Sandton or somewhere to try avoiding it and minimize the risk.'

'Is it a deal then?' Anna asked excitedly, kissing Hank on the cheek.

A provocative smirk spread on his face. 'I must warn my friends never to marry an Australian woman. They are the most incredible schemers and the best at spending their husband's money.' He sighed deeply, resigned to a reduction in his cash account.

* * *

It was Sipho Gwala's lucky day—or night, rather. The day itself progressed in as disappointing and mediocre a manner as many others before. After his ninth or tenth job interview with employers in Johannesburg's CBD, all eventually told him, 'Thanks, but no thanks!' Now, at six o'clock at night, he sat alone on an empty crate by a refreshment stall near a Soweto bus stop close to where he rented the cheapest lodgings money could get, a tin shack with a community toilet and a water tap some fifteen metres away. He exuded such an air of dejection that other commuters steered clear of him, preferring to find the odd stool or box to sit on at the other side of the stall.

Sipho had returned to South Africa from England four years earlier, equipped with a Master of Business Administration degree. He had held a well-paid appointment in Durban for the first two years till HIV caught up with him. For the last two years, he had remained unemployed. Looking ill and down at heel in a crumpled business suit and stained tie, he was going to fish for the last coins in his pocket to pay for his bottle of Coke and fruit when he noticed a tall, broad-shouldered figure move about the bus stop with an aura of calm authority. That man wore a business suit too, an impeccable one. The impressive stranger also bought a bottle of Coke. Finding nowhere else to sit, he headed for Sipho's side of the stall. Sipho's curiosity was aroused. He straightened his sparse frame, contemplating the stranger.

'Still a lot of people at the bus stop tonight. Mind if I sit here?' Joshua Mtolo raised one eyebrow in inquiry, smiling. He grasped another empty packing case and sat next to Sipho.

'Be my guest,' Sipho replied with quiet exhaustion. Maybe he could afford another Coke.

Joshua was in high spirits, having returned from Johannesburg where he had again arranged for a further purchase of gold mining shares for KwaZulu Medical. The dividends from this lot would make repayment of the ANC's funds easier. Only the consignment of state-of-the-art X-ray equipment from America could puncture his fiscal bubble, but he would deal with that when the time came. Now, as he waited for his fiancée, Cindy Khumalo, to arrive, he would not worry about such matters. Cindy was late. She had attended a professional development course to gain extra qualifications in information technology. Solomon Mataka revealed that a donor was providing finance for computer training for his pupils, and he appointed Cindy as instructor.

The suspicion that something was not quite right with the other man eventually penetrated Josh's buoyant mood.

'Is there something I can help you with, man?' He cast a professional eye over Sipho's gaunt, scarecrow-like body, fully expecting to be told to mind his own business.

'I doubt it, but thanks anyway.' Sipho still fingered the coins in his pocket, trying to count out enough for his second Coke.

'I'm Joshua Mtolo. I'm waiting here for my fiancée. She should be on the next bus.' Josh angled for conversation.

'Pleased to meet you. Sipho Gwala.' A tired smile accompanied Sipho's words of introduction, but it was his first pleasurable chat for the day.

'I don't mean to pry into your affairs,' Josh persisted, 'but what do you do with yourself around here?'

Sipho attempted a stuttering explanation, not wanting to confide a bleeding-heart story to a stranger. Feeling too miserable to invent excuses, though, he finally blurted in frustration, 'I do nothing, man, nothing at all. Nobody will employ me.'

'Where have you looked for work?' The stranger intrigued Josh, which made him inquisitive, if not downright nosy.

'All over Johannesburg and further.' Sipho spoke softly, looking down on his dusty shoes.

'So what do you do when you are employed? What was your last job?' Josh felt he had to rouse this dispirited man.

'Hospital finance administrator.'

'No kidding?' Josh laughed. 'I've been looking high and low for one such as you. Tell me more about yourself.'

'Doesn't matter, really.' Sipho's voice was barely audible over the noisy chatter of the other commuters, all eager to get home. 'Nobody wants to work around me anyway. I'm HIV-positive. I've no money for drugs. I'm on borrowed time, I suppose.' He finished counting his change, deciding against further spending before rising from his crate. Joshua stood up as well.

'God! Man, have you eaten anything today?' he asked in alarm as Sipho swayed a little. 'Look here, we have to talk. Sit down. I'm running a clinic near Vryheid.' Josh passed a business card to Sipho. 'I need a hospital administrator like people need their daily bread. Do you want to come with me? Your HIV status needn't be a problem—we don't discriminate. I can get you antiretroviral drugs from America. What do you say?'

The second smile for the day spread over Sipho's face. This was too good to be true.

'Do you live near here?'

Sipho nodded, grinning.

'Okay! See you back here tomorrow morning at nine. Be ready to travel.'

Sipho departed as Sindisiwe Khumalo—Cindy for short—alighted from the minibus which had just pulled up.

'Who was that?' She was as forthrightly inquisitive as Josh.

'Looks like I've got myself a clinic manager.'

'That's good.' She sat on Sipho's crate. 'I suppose he has the right qualifications?' Cindy spoke with a smile, but in truth, Josh's ambitions interested her little. Like him, she loved children but was happier leaving their health care in other people's hands.

Children! That became a difficult topic between them. When would he marry her and start a family? They saw each other less and less. Cindy felt she was no longer Josh's main focus. Since becoming so deeply involved with his hospital project, Josh only came to visit her after a call to his stockbroker. Even now, having met her at the bus stop, he seemed in no haste to drive her home or sweep her off her feet.

'Yeah,' Josh continued, his mind returning from afar. 'Sipho has an MBA and worked as hospital administrator in Durban. Poor chap's HIV-positive, so I don't quite know for how long he'll be able to continue working. At least he was a bit happier when he left. Shall I get you a drink, dear? Then you can tell me about your computers.'

Cindy nodded and sighed. She felt like screaming, 'Just take me home! Home! You know!'

Perhaps they had known each other too long, Cindy thought, while sitting alone. Maybe their love had died over the years. Could it be that it never was real love but only an illusion because their parents had wished to see them as man and wife? Both Josh's and Cindy's parents were dead now, but here they were, still both single, living apart, drifting apart, pursuing their respective careers.

'Cheer up, woman!' Josh grinned, returning with lemonade and sandwiches. 'You must be tired, looking so glum.'

After what seemed like eternity to Cindy, Josh drove her to her little house of which she was so proud. It had running water, electricity, a proper bathroom, and a small garden. Josh finally held her in his arms. For a short while, the old fire flared. No, she was imagining the decline of his ardour. Everything would be fine eventually.

* * *

'What's happening here?' Josh heard the hammer blows sounding from his office as he crossed the courtyard from the children's wing to the outpatient clinic. He had just returned from his fourth trip to Soweto in as many weeks because Cindy insisted on his company at weekends. As was his custom after a long absence from the clinic, he immediately checked the progress of his young patients. At his approach, the hammering resumed. Not the quick, confident *tap, tap, tap* of the trained tradesman but a hesitant, clumsy thumping punctuated by colourful expletives. Josh recognized Sipho's voice. Astonished, he hastened his steps, to be confronted by the comical sight of Sipho wielding a hammer too heavy for his fragile stature, knocking picture hooks into the wall. The effort depleted his strength, but he carried on.

'What have you got there?' Josh turned the picture frames lined up facing the wall. They were his degrees from the Columbia University Medical School and Harvard.

'Sipho, what on earth?'

'You are too modest and retiring, Professor.' Sipho grinned impishly. He had rescued the documents from their cardboard tubes, taken them to Vryheid for framing, and had now hung them where he thought appropriate.

'Anyone surviving three years at Harvard Medical School has a right to be proud.' Sipho stood, pleased with himself, admiring his handiwork. 'I know, because six months at their business school all but killed me. I couldn't hack the competitive pace. Made me run off to England instead.'

It was Sipho's attempt to show gratitude for the new lease of life Josh had afforded him. Not that Sipho harboured any hope about his health. He knew he was going downhill, but what was left of his life, he felt, would be good from now on.

'From this moment,' Sipho announced, 'everyone around here shall address you respectfully by your correct academic title or face my wrath!'

The fierce face on a person barely sufficiently tall to look over the back of a bull amused Josh. He laughed heartily. 'You exaggerate, Sipho.'

'No! I insist that all staff refer to you as *Professor*,' Sipho decreed with the authority of a monarch. By the time Sipho won the dispute, Peter and Tom came in to see what the noise was.

'My worthy colleagues!' Josh leaned on his desk, laughing so much he spoke in gasps. 'Do we have a vacant bed in the psychiatric ward? Sipho has urgent need of it.'

Feeling much stronger due to the comfort of shelter, food, clothes, and medication, Sipho familiarized himself with his new situation at a pace Josh hardly expected. A responsible job and a little money lifted Sipho's morale significantly. He bustled about with total dedication and soon had the administration section up and running. Josh was grateful because it enabled Peter, Tom, and himself to spend more time with patients, who arrived in increasing numbers. The drawback was, however, that many of them were too poor to pay Josh's minimal charges for their treatment. Josh saw his ideal of a small-scale, for-profit private company dissolve. When the shipment of X-ray equipment arrived together with a mind-boggling invoice, the days ahead looked grim. Once the excitement of setting up the machinery subsided, the partners took a sobering look at their budget.

'Shit! We can just pay for this apparatus by the barest margin. We should have leased instead of buying it. It's going to leave us with very little to cover running costs for the next three months. The dispensary needs stocking as well.' Tom had uttered a daunting statement.

Sipho broke the long silence that followed. 'The first quarterly dividend on the Gold Corp shares is due by then. Maybe we can just run up a bit of credit for ninety days or so. It means we'll be behind the monetary ball instead of on it for a while unless Josh agrees to keep the ANC waiting for their repayments. They don't insist on being reimbursed promptly.'

That was not Josh's preferred money methodology, but unless he had a better suggestion, Sipho's plan had to stand. Overseeing a constantly struggling enterprise had not been his intention. More had to be done to address the problem. Fundraising in a community where few people could afford health care was pointless. It also defeated the purpose. He wanted to serve people, not take from them. Obtaining foreign sponsorship was arduous, if not impossible, given the economic sanctions imposed on South Africa. An approach to politicians from the National Party Government and provincial or homeland administrations for grants would only yield peanuts, if anything. The same with the churches. Josh was certain that with Archbishop Tutu as a patron of the UDF, help from ecclesiastic quarters for a KwaZulu cause seemed unlikely because the archbishop and Shenge, the Zulu king's traditional prime minister, held greatly diverging political opinions. Josh needed real money, at least for the initial stages of clinic establishment. He still hoped that once the project ran as he envisaged, it could break even and become self-supporting.

There was one tribe within society whose resources he would gladly tap into—the white business sector. His tentative invitations for their investment in KwaZulu Medical were declined with profound regret. His operation, he was told, was too small, too specialized, or too regional, serving only a narrow area of the country. Never mind the fact that more than 23 per cent of South Africa's citizens lived in the KwaZulu and Natal province.

After much soul-searching, Josh figured that what could not be accomplished by legal means must, of dire necessity, be attempted by illegal avenues. Arms smuggling was profitable but repugnant to him because he was convinced the ANC had brought the weapons into Natal and turned them against Zulus. The action plans he formed in his mind targeted the white business tribe. He would take only Sipho into his confidence. He did not want to involve Peter and Tom in the clandestine undertakings he was about to execute. In the event of possible criminal proceedings against him at a later date, Peter and Tom might be able to keep KwaZulu Medical running.

* * *

Chapter 2

The First VIP

William Rosenberg, CEO of Mineral Enterprises, worked late in his office. He had a little catching up to do because morning phone calls distracted his attention from the reports before him, and later, the extensive lunch with two directors claimed a big chunk out of his day. Now peace had returned and he could get on with his tasks. Or so he hoped, if it wasn't for those faces he saw outside the restaurant. They were there when he entered and still lurked about two and a half hours later when he emerged full of good food and wine. Alcohol had not dazed his senses sufficiently to miss noticing the two young chaps seemingly intent on window shopping. They were well dressed and neat with a military bearing. Could they have been watching him? His mind would not focus on the written sheets but returned time and again to the faces. Who were they, and what was their aim? Was someone out to get him? Had he made new enemies without realizing? Of course, any amount of shareholders always felt deprived of their due while he, in their opinion, cashed in on huge performance bonuses. Had they formed a conspiracy to reckon with him? Or had someone become aware of his purchase of mining shares on inside information? The possibilities were numerous.

It was approaching 2300 hours. William stretched with a yawn. Time to go home. He rose and then halted, remembering the faces. Prudence dictated that he should take a different route to his residence. Breaking with predictable routines became advisable. Tonight he would leave his car in the underground garage, walk a little in the opposite direction to home, then find a taxi to his house in Houghton. Tomorrow a friend could bring him to work. He placed the reports in his briefcase. If he woke up at four in the morning, unable to sleep further, he could read them in bed.

William felt confident as he walked through the revolving door and onto the street. The faces would be waiting in the car park. He convinced himself he had given them the slip. He stopped at a red traffic light even though he could have crossed against it. There were no cars coming.

'Mr Rosenberg! One moment please!'

William turned, surprised. Two men grasped him, each taking an arm.

'Please . . . allow me . . .' One chap relieved him of his briefcase.

'Follow us, Mr Rosenberg.'

William was flummoxed. These guys were polite but meant business. There was no question of 'following' them. They marched him along at a solid pace towards a windowless delivery van. The side door was already open. A driver sat at the wheel, and the motor idled.

'Get in, Mr Rosenberg!'

By now, William's assertiveness returned and he struggled with his captors. After a moment's scuffle during which William shouted for help, he was pushed into the van. One man sat with him. The other climbed beside the driver, who pulled away immediately.

Having regained both voice and courage, William blustered, 'What the fuck is all this about? Where are you taking me? Who the hell are you?'

'Sorry, Mr Rosenberg, we ask the questions,' the man beside him replied. 'You listen and do as you're told.'

William thought the three men were enjoying their evening of adventure. Although William didn't know it, his companions had undergone specialized military training. Driving a flabbergasted business executive through the night was a joyride compared to their normal operations.

William wondered if these were his faces. He couldn't be sure. If they were the same men, they had changed their clothes. They now wore jeans, windcheaters, and knitted hats drawn over their eyebrows. The driver had a baseball cap.

After two hours of driving, William, tired and irritable, spoke again. 'How much bloody longer is this mad ride going to last?'

'Don't worry, Mr Rosenberg, we'll get there presently.'

'Get where?' William was bursting with annoyance and helplessness. He had a revolver in his briefcase, but the polite bloke had not returned it to him.

'No questions, remember!' William heard the laugh in his captor's voice. Heaven only knew what this prank was about, but mayhap he could trick the guy into giving him the briefcase.

'Look here, man,' William tried. 'Could you pass me my briefcase for a second, please?'

'What? You don't want to work now? In the dark?' The man laughed in disbelief. 'We'll keep your case safe for you. That's a promise.' More silent mirth.

'Can we stop somewhere? I need to pee!' That was another desperate ploy William's brain hatched in a hurry.

'Yeah, no worries. We'll stop for a while in about half an hour.'

'Gee, thanks a lot, fellows.' William became increasingly weary and must have dozed for a long time. He woke fully when the van stopped and the door was opened. It felt as if it was almost dawn. William checked his watch and noticed angrily that its face was shattered. He recalled the scuffle during which his left wrist had knocked against the sliding side door. The impact had broken his beautiful Swiss timepiece, a birthday present from Indira Naidoo, his latest mistress. How could he explain the mishap to her? These guys owed him compensation, big time.

'Come on now, quickly, Mr Rosenberg!' He was allowed to take the two steps off the van before they slapped a blindfold on him.

'Bloody hell!' he complained. 'Isn't this getting a bit rough?' Nobody took notice of his discomfort. He felt the grip on his arms again as the two men guided him.

'Careful, Mr Rosenberg, there are four stairs here going up.' He was saved from stumbling. 'One, two, three, four, that's it!'

William relied on his ears and sense of touch for information. He had entered a building. A dozen strides were taken on carpet; thereafter, his and his captors' shoes echoed on linoleum. They seemed to be walking along a corridor. Dishes clattered. 'Watch out!' a grumpy, waspish woman called to someone.

A door was opened. 'There are six stairs going down now, Mr Rosenberg.' They counted again then passed through another door. William was led to a chair and told to sit. He felt intense heat on his face and a light so piercing it penetrated the blindfold. He blinked painfully when his captors removed it for him and departed. William found himself sitting at a table in a cell he thought had the hallmarks of an interrogation room.

'Damn that light!' he cursed, trying to shield his eyes with his hands.

'Mr Rosenberg, thanks for coming.' William's confused gaze followed the sound of the disembodied, brittle tenor voice. He sensed, rather than saw, the man sitting across the table from him for the first time. The spotlight made it impossible for William to note his features, but he appeared to be of rather slight build, the total opposite to the stronger, more corpulent figures he dealt with earlier.

'Where the hell am I?'

'We ask the questions, Mr Rosenberg.'

'Phrase has a familiar ring,' William grunted.

'Let me welcome you as our guest. We will endeavour to make your stay as comfortable as possible. How long you will be here depends entirely on the cooperation of your board of directors. I shall leave you in peace now to settle in. There is a light switch beside the door, and underneath it, you will find a—let us say— room service button. Just push it if there is anything you want by way of refreshments. I can't guarantee five-star cuisine and the wine list is non-existent, but have no fear—we won't let you starve.'

The slight man rose. As he walked to the door, the vile, blinding light went out. He switched on a dim bulb in the ceiling and left. William heard the door lock behind him. He was kidnapped, no doubt about it.

The frail chap had that same laughter in his voice as the men who had driven him here. Hearing it, William became furious again. *Damned kaffirs*, he thought. They think this is a lark while I'm prevented from going about my affairs. He remembered his briefcase. They still had that. He would ask for it at the first opportunity.

Where am I anyway? What sort of place is this? William wondered, scratching his head, trying to think of a way out. He could hear little of the activities above him. The room was well soundproofed. Gradually the blackness before his eyes, caused by the sudden extinguishing of the spotlight, faded, enabling him to see outlines. He was underground. A vent circulated fresh air. At the back of the room was a door and, next to it, a wine rack fixed to the wall. No bottles, unfortunately. William remembered the frail man's lame joke about the wine list. Was he in a hotel? Two hotel chains owned shares in Mineral Enterprises, but William could not recall ever having exchanged words with their directors. It could not have been they who had organized his incarceration. Or could it?

Becoming bolder, William opened the door next to the wine rack. 'A toilet! Hurrah! At last!' he spoke out loud to himself and cackled. What an idea, a toilet in a wine cellar. Someone obviously loved to imbibe. Amusement gave way to serious thought. There was that confounded smell of disinfectant. It had hit his nostrils the minute he was dragged into the building. The place smelled like a hospital, not a hotel. How utterly confusing.

Hospitals? William concentrated. He had no dealings with them. Yet there was something he had heard. It came to him suddenly. A stockbroker had mentioned KwaZulu Medical only two days ago. As a new crowd, they had been buying shares on a minor scale, scarcely worth the broker's time. Nobody expected them to last long. William could safely eliminate them from his list of possible adversaries. He didn't know them. Who could have stuffed him into this hole? Was it political? He had exchanged facetious remarks with Hank De Bruyn about Afrikaners in business. It had failed to impress. Maybe the cunning old fox was exercising a little revenge? *No, not really.* William couldn't imagine it. *Hank's a good man.*

Tiredness overcame him again, and he crossed to the other side of his little burrow, where a bunk provided a sleeping place. He snored as soon as he hit the pillow. When he woke up, he had no inkling of what time it was or how long he had slept. The bulb in the ceiling burned relentlessly. He could have turned it off before lying down but felt too insecure to do so. He was hungry and smelly, needing a shave. Why wasn't anyone coming to talk to him? Faintly the voice of the testy woman he heard earlier in the corridor came to him, but he couldn't understand what she said. The frail bloke had pointed out the button under the light switch. William tried it. He waited. Nothing happened. He was about to push again when someone turned the key. It was the unfriendly woman.

'What do you want?'

William was taken aback. He eyed her from head to toe. 'My goodness, you're a friendly soul.' His expression carried the frustration he felt.

'You want something?' the woman asked again. She was wider than tall, William thought, and quite unsightly.

'What time is it?' he asked, his attitude brash and overbearing. 'I want food, a clean-up and a shave, and I expect to have my briefcase returned.' He pronounced his demands stridently, thumping the door frame with his fist.

The ugly woman, whose name was Margo, nodded.

'Seven fifteen!' she replied with strict word economy.

'Morning or night?' William wanted to know.

'Morning. Breakfast in ten minutes.' Margo turned, locking the door.

'Christ, she loves her job.' He spoke to her departing back.

Margo brought his breakfast exactly ten minutes later if William's watch had worked to time her. After another quarter hour, a man appeared. Who? William had no idea. The guy carried a plastic dish with hot water, shaving gear, and a towel. He put these items on the table and disappeared without a word, not forgetting to lock the door, though. Later, Margo came back. She opened the door a crack, pushed William's briefcase through, and shut him in again conscientiously.

He could now finish reading his reports. No telephone would interrupt him here. He opened his case. The paperwork was undisturbed, but the gun was gone. They had stolen it, he discovered with outrage.

* * *

An atmosphere of shock permeated the boardroom of Mineral Enterprises. An urgent meeting, called to discuss the current emergency, lasted over four hours. Police presence at the director's table kept expressions particularly grave.

William Rosenberg was missing, and a group calling themselves the Economic Equity Movement (EEM) claimed responsibility for his disappearance. Their ransom note was hand delivered, materializing on the managing director's desk as if by magic. He read the few words it contained to the gathering.

> The Managing Director
> Mineral Enterprises
>
> Dear sir,
>
> Your CEO, Mr William Rosenberg, is presently our guest. He is in no danger and well cared for. His release will be secured by your depositing US $200,000 into our Zurich account. (Details on next page.)
>
> We trust this matter can be settled speedily without involving either the press or the police.
>
> Yours faithfully,
> Economic Equity Movement (EEM)

The attached page gave banking details and a contact name and telephone number in Zurich.

'What do you make of it?' the managing director asked, nodding towards the senior detective.

Captain Broadbent from the criminal investigation unit had a new case to solve. In Johannesburg, police officers would never find themselves redundant, he thought.

'We have no file on the Economic Equity Movement,' he told the businessmen. 'It sounds as if a new bunch of miscreants are on the loose. Villains with international connections. They may or may not be home-grown.'

The detective looked over the top of his spectacles out of the window. The view of Johannesburg from the top of its skyscrapers was picture-perfect, without haze casting a film over the horizon. He always enjoyed the spectacle when his duties took him to the heights of the tallest buildings. Some tourists might call Johannesburg a mining dump with its surrounding mountains of tailings, but he had been born here and loved it. If only the crime were under control. He perceived sardonically that the tourist brochures, unlike the investment advice prospectuses issued from some of these offices to advertise their wares, were definitely less misleading.

'Well?' The managing director's impatient tone indicated his vexation. Broadbent's lengthy thought process grated his nerves.

'They are smart cookies, and it would pay to be careful,' the captain warned. 'You see, they don't appear to be your average type of kidnapper. There are no threats or scare tactics. They use no obscene language or political or religious rhetoric. Just a clever group of rat-bag extortionists, I'd say. We have to monitor them closely until they outsmart themselves. At the moment, we have no leads.'

'Should we pay the ransom?' the finance director questioned.

'If you want your man back quickly, yes. We will then hear about Mr Rosenberg's experiences and take it from there. That Zurich account is a worry too. Although the Swiss are changing their confidentiality laws in respect of criminal investigations, their reluctance to cooperate is still evident.'

With that, the meeting closed at last. The finance director showed the police out and, with a heavy heart, ordered the depositing of US $200,000 into the nominated account.

* * *

'We could make the wine cellar available to our VIP guests.' Sipho bore that impish grin again. It appeared whenever he thought he had a splendid brainwave. 'It's already soundproofed, ventilated, fully equipped, and hidden from curious observers.' He shrugged his shoulders with a chuckle. 'What do you reckon?'

Josh grimaced. The wine cellar had a notorious history. When the partners had purchased the homestead, they found the wine cellar under the pantry still stocked with a few remaining bottles. A representative from the ANC thought the little room convenient and commandeered it as 'an office in which recovering prisoners could be interviewed and their future discussed'. The heavy-handed action aroused Josh's ire, but by then, it was too late to rescind on the deal. His paranoia was vindicated when Tom came to him one evening, reporting that something was amiss down below, urging him to see for himself. Peter burst into Josh's office at the same time, his voice unsteady.

'Mandla's finished! Gone! There's nothing we can do for him. And he was recuperating so well. He could have worked again in a few months.'

Josh needed no further explanation. 'I knew this would happen,' he fumed. 'Can't trust 'em as far as you can chuck a heap of elephant shit!' His voice rose. 'That's why I wanted nothing to do with them in the first place.' Cursing, he turned the combination to open the safe behind his desk. 'By god! Shenge's right! The ANC mission in exile is worse than the police. Police brutality is spontaneous, but the ANC comrades plan their actions deliberately, which makes them all the more appalling and reprehensible.' He took his pistol from the safe and, brushing past Tom and Peter, ran down the steps to the wine cellar. 'I'll teach those bastards!'

'Out!' Josh shouted at the two ANC comrades. 'Get out of my hospital this instant!' He approached them, pointing the pistol at their stomachs. 'Remember once and for all that while your men are here, they are patients and, consequently, my responsibility. In future, there will be no interaction between you and patients until they are discharged.'

The comrades edged away from Josh. 'You didn't warn us that he wasn't well enough to receive visitors,' one of them accused, circling Mandla's corpse on the floor.

'Impudent arsehole! This house is a sanatorium, not a torture chamber. You can take your modus operandi back to Angola, Namibia, or wherever, but don't come here unless you want your guts perforated.'

The second comrade overcame his shock at seeing Josh in such righteous anger. With a haughty stare, he hissed, 'Are you threatening us?'

'How astute of you to notice!' As Josh stepped closer to him, still aiming the pistol strategically, the comrades turned to ascend to the pantry, and Josh booted the slower of the two up the stairs. 'And take your fallen warrior with you!' he shouted after them.

Tom and Peter came to reinforce Josh's position. He still shook with cold fury, but their presence had a calming effect. Peter locked the gun back in the safe, and Tom called for coffee.

'Well, that's done it!' Peter mused as he laced his drink generously with brandy from the wine cellar's leftovers and sipped. 'Now the ANC will want their loan back forthwith, and we'll be in trouble.'

'No, they won't!' Josh contradicted, growling. 'Because if they do, we'll go to the press. We'll tell the whole world about what has happened here.'

The commotions of the last ten minutes roused Sipho from the depth of the balance sheets in what he called his bean-counting house. He came into Josh's office. As he caught the drift of the conversation, his eyes twinkled wickedly.

'Er . . . Professor?' He spoke with mock formality. 'Would you agree that due to this recent altercation, a review of the loan repayments to the ANC is in order?'

Like a musical canon, the four men began to laugh, one after the other. 'Do whatever you think we can get away with, Sipho.' Josh consented. 'We've got them now! They wouldn't dare make waves about us defaulting.'

Sipho retreated to his domain, satisfied. As far as he was concerned, the armed struggle was costing the community dearly in terms of lost productivity and general economic health. The ANC had to pay to clean up the physical, emotional, and economic debris their People's War had left in its wake.

As Josh predicted, the expected thunderclap from the politico-military council of the ANC, their approximate equivalent of the government's state security council, never came. Instead, he received a smoothly worded apology explaining that disciplinary action had been imposed on the two individuals who had overstepped their authority. They assured him such an incident would not be repeated. Life returned to normal at KwaZulu Medical. The wine cellar was locked, and nobody mentioned the affair again after Josh obtained a copy of the medico-legal post-mortem report on Mandla from the Gale Street Mortuary in Durban. The nine-page report plus photographs signed by a specialist forensic pathologist indicated unambiguously that Mandla's death had resulted from torture.

Josh looked at Sipho, knowing the man was right.

'So for the present, we have to consider two things.' Sipho held two fingers in the air. 'We must draw up a list of our most desired targets and find out how accessible they are. We have to learn a great deal about them, keep them under observation, and try to anticipate their every move. Next, we must find helping hands. Who would do the work of bringing our VIPs to us? Who has that type of training and expertise?'

'They had better be good because we want no mishaps.' Josh warmed to the topic. 'I want the VIPs to be treated courteously. No rough stuff! When the visitors go back, I want them to have nothing on us. Nor do I want them to know who we are. They can't press charges too easily against people they haven't seen.'

Sipho gave a diabolical laugh. 'Oh, they can talk to me all right! By the time the prosecutors have a court case ready, I'll be cremated. They'll have to appeal to Hades's criminal court.'

'Don't talk rot, Sipho! Just use your calculative brain while you still have it and help us get money for this place.' Josh spoke sternly to hide his emotions. The thought of Sipho's decline saddened him. Each day Sipho's condition got a little worse, but his will to hold on remained strong.

'The ransom money has to go somewhere too. Can you arrange an account in Switzerland, Sipho?'

'Yeah, easy. I know just the person. Had dealings with him during my stint in London.'

Sipho was on familiar ground. Producing his special address book, which he normally showed nobody, he began checking for telephone numbers of his favourite money launderers, Luxembourg and Liechtenstein contacts, and other useful figures.

'Who's going to claim responsibility for the vanishing VIPs?' Josh thought out loud. 'Maybe we could make it look like a new political pressure group. Some economic cause. The communists have handy ideas. Let us say we want a future government to nationalize South Africa's major industries. Imagine that we seek to coerce the government into doing our bidding by holding business executives captive. We shall proclaim our credo to be that wealth must be more evenly distributed. Yeah, I'd say that's it.'

Josh paced Sipho's office just as he had his own living room before the partners established KwaZulu Medical. He found it conductive to creative thought. 'We need a name for this fictitious organization. How about the Economic Equity Movement, or EEM? That would direct suspicion away from KwaZulu Medical. You think that makes sense, Sipho?'

'It might work for a while, Josh.' Sipho still flipped through his phone list. 'Here we go!' He checked his watch for time difference, picked up the receiver, and dialled. 'Give this chap a ring just on the off-chance that he might be around.'

While Sipho spoke to his acquaintance in Zurich, Josh had an interesting thought. 'I know!' He snapped his fingers. 'Caprivi!'

'What was that?' Sipho finished his conversation with a sigh of gratified accomplishment. 'That's done! We won't have any hassles there.' He grinned. 'You were saying, Josh?'

'Caprivi!'

'Co-who?' Sipho wrinkled his brow, not really listening, his mind still on the procedure required for the establishment of the numbered Swiss account.

'The Caprivi trainees! You've heard of Inkatha's crack antiterrorist unit. They are young, eager chaps. No doubt all have girlfriends to impress, so they'll appreciate a little extra cash in their pockets. We can ask them to help us in their spare time. We'll pay them well for each successful mission.'

'Yima kancane! Hold on, Josh.' Sipho held out his right palm like a policeman stopping traffic. 'You're talking too fast. Those Caprivi guys lead a contentious, politicized existence. I doubt they'll risk being seen carrying out unorthodox and unauthorized assignments.'

'Yeah, but there are about two hundred of them, Inkatha supporters, mostly. Surely one or two of them may be swayed to come to our aid. Their training equips them well for our needs. They were recruited by Shenge's personal assistant for training by the South African Defence Force at the Caprivi in South West Africa.'

'Yes, I remember now,' Sipho interrupted. 'Operation Marion, it was called, I think. Shenge needed them because he and members of the KwaZulu Legislative Assembly received repeated death threats.'

'That's right.' Josh cut in. 'The SADF intelligence department organized their training.'

'That they did. And the cost was covered with money from a secret account of the defence budget. Caused a minor uproar, as I recall.' Sipho might have been largely indifferent to such governmental machinations, but he could be counted on to know the financial arrangements.

Josh filled in the details. 'The recruits received weapons training and defensive training. Most importantly for us, their instructions included VIP protection as well as methods of abduction and surveillance techniques.'

Sipho whistled through his teeth. 'I understand why you want them so much. They are exactly what the doctor ordered, aren't they?'

* * *

William Rosenberg had lost track of time. According to his estimate, he had lived in his hole for four days. The true count was two and a half. By this stage, he could recite the contents of the papers in his briefcase from memory. He had considered his responses to them, but what was the use? He couldn't get out. Was anyone looking for him? The frail guy indicated that his release depended on the directors' cooperation. From that, he deduced that a ransom was to be paid before he saw the light of day again. What if Mineral Enterprises refused to hand over the requested sum? Would the skinny chap shoot him then? William shivered. Could his colleagues abandon him to such a fate? He wished he had answers to the numerous questions buzzing in his head like angry wasps, their larvae hatching in his fear.

Before self-pity engulfed him, the door was unlocked, and a man dressed in navy track pants and orange T-shirt entered, carrying ropes. William broke into cold sweat. Was this guy going to tie him up? Hang him? His knees trembled with relief when the man smiled and introduced himself as 'Fernando, the local soccer coach'. William noticed Fernando's gym equipment: weights, scales, and a foam rubber mat.

'Exercise time!' Fernando called brightly, dragging the table aside to clear a space. William eyed Fernando suspiciously. He assumed that Fernando wasn't his real name and that despite his tough, athletic appearance, Fernando was no professional sports instructor. Fernando tossed him a rope, which promptly slipped through William's clumsy fingers.

Fernando laughed. 'Come on! Let's skip. I'll race you. Last one to finish fifty skips is a baboon! Quick! Hop to it, man!'

After the first five jumps, the rope tangled around William's feet, and he came to a stumbling halt. 'Gee, man, what are you?' Fernando frowned impatiently. 'Try again! Snappy now!' Fernando slowed his pace to spare William a little embarrassment, but he still became the baboon.

'What do you weigh?' Fernando pushed the scales towards William. 'Here, stand on that, and let's see. What? Ninety-eight kilos? For *your* height! We'll have to fix that.' He rolled out the foam rubber mat. 'Press-ups! Let me see how you go! Try ten of 'em for starters.'

By seven, William's arms turned to butter, and he stood up humiliated. 'Look here!' William gasped, his face red with strain. 'I'm in this bloody place against my will, and the last thing I need is some shithead of a drill sergeant giving me a hard time.'

'Shithead, did you say? You want to learn boxing? I will teach you.' Fernando approached, fists raised.

William retreated. 'Sorry, man! No offence! Fact is, I'm not as fit as you. I don't do any physical work. I'm the CEO of Mineral Enterprises. You see?'

'I should have guessed.' Fernando's voice bore mild contempt. 'A flop-cock office worker.'

'Flop-cock?' That stung. 'What do you mean? I've got a wife and three mistresses. Isn't that enough activity for any man?'

Fernando grinned sadistically. 'Before you get out of here, I'll have you so energetic you can take on four more women. Isn't that worth a little effort?'

William had no opportunity to gain the aspired sexual prowess. After his session with Fernando, Margo brought the evening meal.

Beans and rice. What did they think he was? Mexican? Exercise had made him hungry, though, and he ate the excessively peppered dish rapidly, coughing and reaching for the tea. The exertion also tired him. He lounged on his bunk, thinking of Fernando's jibe. Would he really be here so long as to be turned into an athlete? He fell asleep. Deep from his subconscious mind, the walls of the room leaned inwards, threatening to suffocate him till the bang of an explosion brought sunlight where the crumbling stones were before. He woke. What had he heard? A noise must have prompted his dream, but all was silent. William still had difficulty estimating the passage of time. His only reliable measurement was the growth of stubble on his chin. It wasn't very scratchy yet, so it could not be morning. There they were again. Voices. William sat up, listening. Something was happening. Preparing for the worst, he pulled on the jeans and checked shirt provided for him as prison garb because his suit had become too scruffy. The sound of the key in the lock startled him. It always did. Two men in similar attire to him entered, their knitted hats pulled down to the eyelids.

'Well, Mr Rosenberg. It's bye-bye, and nice knowing you.'

'What's that supposed to mean?' William had grown weary of the brand of humour cultivated in this place.

'Means exactly what it says.'

William gave up trying to make sense of their talk, but to him *bye-bye* sounded final, like a planned execution.

'Don't forget your suit and briefcase. Here, put your clothes in this bag!'

William packed and was blindfolded as soon as he finished. He couldn't be bothered protesting this time as he was led up the stairs, along the linoleum, over a small area of carpet, and into fresh air. The wind had never felt so good in his hair.

'Hurry, Mr Rosenberg! You don't want to be late for work.'

William was helped into the van. He knew it was the same vehicle as before. It had the familiar feel, and the engine spluttered as if not all cylinders fired correctly when the driver turned the key. His companions had little to say and freed him of the blindfold half an hour into the journey. What could he possibly see from a windowless van speeding through the night? He slumped in his seat to sleep and doze through a brief respite at the halfway mark of the trip. With the dawn, William became alert. Relieved, he thought he recognized the outer suburbs of Johannesburg when he dared to glimpse through a small portion of the windscreen beside the driver's head. He hoped his ordeal would be over soon.

His wish was granted. Time took a quick leap forward, and he found himself standing on the footpath outside the Mineral Enterprises building, feeling forlorn in a city still rubbing the sleep from its eyes in the early morning light. Before his captors hit the gas, the driver leaned out of the window.

'Mr Rosenberg! This is yours!' He thrust a Pick n Pay bag into William's hand and roared away. What had they given him? The plastic shopping bag opened with a rustle as William untied the knot. It was his revolver—unloaded.

'Now what, William ?' he mumbled to himself. 'Can't go in . . . not in this gear. Haven't seen myself in a mirror for days. Must look a sight and a half.'

He discovered he had not been robbed of his wallet as he had feared. There was more than enough change for a taxi home where a good shower and clean clothes would remove his present shabbiness and improve his condition.

* * *

Chapter 3

The Shareholders' Meeting

It was assessment day for Cindy Khumalo's computer class. All students were keen, working hard to learn and pass their tests well. Only Freddie Bonga caused problems. Street-smart like a gutter rat, Freddie attended the class as an escape from other lessons. Freddie appeared to lack drive and self-esteem. Cindy's best efforts failed to kindle even the tiniest spark of ambition. Motorbikes were his one interest, and he often skipped classes to work casually at menial labour, saving his pay for the day he could afford the Harley he desired so much.

Freddie became exasperated when shown that in spite of the additional tuition Cindy gave him, he had failed the course. He was not bright at other subjects either, and his agitation caused him to forget his English grammar entirely.

'Sorry, M-Miss K-Khumalo,' he stammered. 'Not I want to learn this here. It much too hard.' He spoke in English using Zulu syntax.

'There are other programs you can try, Freddie.' Cindy offered, although she sensed it was useless.

'Nah! Not I good.' Freddie gathered his belongings. 'Thanks!' He headed for the exit.

'Freddie, where are you going? Come back!' Cindy rushed after him. 'You can't just leave!'

'Not I can go? Why? I finished here.'

'But what will you do now?' Cindy couldn't fathom what options a poor student like Freddie had.

'I go maybe to my uncle's place in Vryheid. Find work, maybe.' Freddie shrugged, shouldered his bag, and turned away.

Cindy felt stunned. She had never had a pupil walk out of her class. How would she explain this to Solomon Mataka? She pushed the thought to the back of her mind as other youngsters needed assistance. Competition was keen, and two students gained first place equally. The top achiever would be awarded a traineeship by the sponsor. Now there were two. No doubt the headmaster would make the final decision, taking exam results from other subjects into account. Cindy felt sorry for whoever missed out. Perhaps the sponsor was prepared to be flexible. Solomon Mataka never spoke of the donor's identity, but Cindy discovered it was a lady. Maybe she could gain Solomon's consent to speak to her and arbitrate on behalf of both learners. She would suggest the traineeship be shared.

Cindy dismissed the class, telling them how proud she was of their endeavours. Tomorrow she would report to Solomon Mataka and show him the results.

Walking to the bus stop, she saw Freddie attempting to hitch-hike again. *Pity help that boy*, she thought, as he stepped into a stranger's car. Oblivious to danger, it was his normal mode of transport. A knife and a sharpened bicycle spoke was all the weaponry he needed for self-defence.

* * *

'What's the difference between a priest and a whore?' Sipho asked Fernando as they drove towards the outskirts of Ulundi, seeking the address of a rather infamous shebeen, or pub.

'Ha ha ha . . .' Fernando laughed so much the car swerved into the next lane. 'I know that!' His right hand whacked the steering wheel as he corrected the vehicle's course. 'The priest says "amen" and the whore says "Ah, men!"'

Fernando was employed primarily as Sipho's driver and personal assistant. He attended to the things Sipho neglected when, drained at the end of a busy day, he simply stumbled into bed. Fernando ensured Sipho ate nourishing meals, reminded him to take his medications on time, washed and mended his clothes, and ran his errands.

They cracked bawdy jokes to alleviate the boredom of what, for Sipho, was a tedious one and a half-hour drive south-east. Their quest was to make contact with a number of the Caprivi trainees who generally mingled among the shebeen's clientele in their off-time. Fernando knew two men and hoped for introductions to others. Sipho was to arrange a form of gentlemen's agreement with them stipulating that for a handsome remuneration, they might sacrifice a little of their spare time and place their expertise and services at the EEM's disposal.

The Caprivi men proved hard to influence. Shrewd and evasive, their faces as inscrutable as the dinginess of the shebeen. They expressed reluctance to become involved in dubious operations for unknown organizations.

'Look, Sipho,' a soldier said, 'give us one good reason why we should help. We cop enough flack already. It's common knowledge the NP government paid for our training. Public opinion assumes that he who pays the piper calls the tune. That means the ANC is accusing us of forming hit squads against them at the government's behest. As usual, it makes Inkatha look like the bad bloke. We've done nothing wrong, and we're not going to start now.'

It took every last measure of Sipho's communication skills to persuade them. 'Okay, you want a convincing reason?' He looked at each of the indifferent faces around him. 'How about raising money for medical treatment for kids traumatized by the violence unleashed due to the ANC's armed struggle? That's what it's all about. I invite you to come with me to KwaZulu Medical, meet the doctors, have a look around the clinic, and then decide for yourselves.'

After letting much *utshwala*, the local beer, flow freely, Sipho eventually recruited three soldiers. He spelled out that their names and addresses were of no interest to the EEM. The shebeen's phone number sufficed as a contact point. And yes, they would find their efforts financially rewarding. The men were called Caprivi I, II, and III, or C1, C2, and C3. Sipho was SG, for Sipho Gwala I, from the EEM. Fernando became SG2, and for good measure, Josh was SG3. C1, C2, and C3 received their first assignment from SG1 to tail the Mineral Enterprises CEO, William Rosenberg, and report back in three weeks for further instructions.

With the Rosenberg contract completed successfully and US $200,000 sitting in the Swiss account, it was time for another hit. Next, the three Caprivis picked up Paul Fischer from Rand Gold and Diamonds Inc. Paul was less placid than William and prepared to fight. Tact rather than force won the day, however, a lesson not lost on Paul. He tried doggedly to gain Fernando's friendship and almost succeeded. Paul was fit. Routinely working out in his gym, he skipped as fast as Fernando. His weight was perfect, and endless push-ups caused no exhaustion. Fernando respected Paul but refused to answer his questions as to where he was, who ran the place, and what the purpose of his imprisonment was. Paul had to be content with the same reply: 'We ask the questions. You listen and do as you're told.'

When the Swiss account expanded by a further US $200,000, the new Caprivi recruits, C4 and C5, took Paul back to his office. Frank Pinkney from Resource Explorations received similar treatment, as did Geoff White from Reef Mining.

The four victims told similar stories of their ordeals. None could pinpoint with certainty as to where they were taken or by whom. The getaway car was a windowless delivery van. Nobody had the opportunity to note the number. The kidnappers wore jeans, windcheaters and woollen hats pulled down to their eyelids. They spoke only when absolutely necessary. All victims were locked into their prison by a skinny man whose face they could never identify. The abductions were performed with a precision and audacity that left the white business community speechless.

'This cannot be allowed to continue.' Hank De Bruyn told his friends over lunch in an upmarket inner-city restaurant. 'We are in a tight situation,' Hank elaborated. 'If we protest and approach politicians for help, the press will run with the story, and foreign investment, already at low ebb due to sanctions, will dry up altogether, frightened away by crime. So far, it's been cheaper to shut up, put up, and pay up.'

'It's not so great if you are the one commanded to cough up the ransom,' the finance director from Mineral Enterprises commented ruefully.

'My worry is', Hank reasoned, 'that someone will get killed one day. No matter how gently our guys were treated, this may not last. And let's face it, we can't continue paying. We're not milk cows. One day we're going to have to call it quits. What then? Is that EEM—or whatever they call themselves—going to kill hostages if we refuse to comply? Who are they? We haven't a clue who we're dealing with.'

Hank looked around the table at the others, inviting suggestions and theories. Anna sat beside him. She stroked the stem of her wine glass thoughtfully, looking into its deep red contents as if searching for the truth that was supposed to lie there.

'EEM,' she said quietly, as if the others were not there. 'Economic Equity Movement.' She fingered her glass a little longer and took a sip. 'Sounds like a black economic empowerment pressure group. Intellectuals, I dare say. Not common street criminals. They returned

William's revolver, remember? That in itself is extraordinary. There's some communist humbug theory at work, I'll bet. Does anyone know if the victims dealt with white people or exclusively with blacks?' Anna looked at her head-shaking fellow diners. 'We really should get together with William, Paul, Geoff, and Frank. Their nerves will have settled a little by now, and they may recall more details than immediately after their release when the police interviewed them. In my opinion, Captain Broadbent should talk to them again. We could also sound out black business groups. It's significant that as far as we know, not one black business person has been abducted.'

'Your perception is sharp as always, my dear.' Hank smiled fondly at his wife. 'Your thoughts are light years ahead of the police. They haven't got anywhere near your analysis of the problem yet.' To the others he added, 'We must form a self-help group. It's the only way. Let's employ private investigators to find out who carries out the surveillance on us. Someone was watching William. We need to know who.'

Everyone agreed, and the Mineral Enterprises finance director volunteered to approach a private security firm. 'I'll start by having extra security personnel patrol the car parks. Geoff was apprehended as he was about to drive away, and Frank received a phone call from someone purporting to be a parking attendant to come down and view alleged damage to his car. When he did, he was led away. We can't tolerate such crimes any longer.'

* * *

Nkosinathi Zuma scarcely knew whether to be content or apprehensive. His mother and two aunts took the saying 'Dress for success' seriously, pooling their money for the new suit he wore. A tall boy for his almost seventeen years, the clothes made him look like a distinguished young man. He knew it too. Unable to ignore the approving glances from the girls at the bus stop, he straightened his shoulders in pride.

Today the girls were of secondary importance. It was the start of his traineeship, his special job at De Bruyn Brothers. If embryonic tycoons quaked in their shoes with anticipation, Nkosinathi was in good company. His heart pounded at the intimidating thought of entering De Bruyn's plush offices. Mr Mataka gave him a rough idea of what to expect, but did headmasters know everything? How often had Solomon Mataka been in such an establishment? Nkosinathi suppressed the ungrateful thought quickly. Of the two students who gained equal top marks in the computer course, the headmaster chose him because his results in mathematics and English were narrowly ahead of Suzanna Tsedu, his fellow competitor. To be fair to both students, Solomon Mataka ruled that in the following computer classes, the top student must exceed Suzanna and Nkosinathi's average of 97.5 per cent. If not, the next traineeship would go to Suzanna.

Butterflies danced a gavotte in Nkosinathi's stomach as the bus bumped and swayed into Johannesburg. Once there, he had to find De Bruyn's address. His worst fear was to arrive late on his first day.

The glass double doors opened at his approach and closed behind him as if the building embraced him. As instructed, he took the lift to the fourth floor. Watching the numbers glow to indicate each level, he felt he had gone from ground to fourth in half a second. When the lift door opened, he stepped out quickly lest he be trapped in the cabin.

Thick cream-coloured carpet lay everywhere. His feet felt as if they made no contact with the floor but walked on a cloud. An informal array of comfortably inviting chairs stood around a low table near the window to the right. Looking left, he was immediately welcomed by a young, attractive receptionist who appeared to be intensely interested in him. She smiled professionally from behind her desk.

'Mr Zuma, yes?' she purred.

Nkosinathi could only nod.

'Mrs De Bruyn is expecting you. Just take a seat for a minute. She won't be long.'

The receptionist indicated a luxurious armchair beside a large pot plant and Nkosinathi sat down obediently. Astonished at the prospect of meeting the senior partner's wife, he picked up a magazine from the little table and flicked through the pages to disguise his confusion. He expected to be the errand boy, working with the lowest staff members in the pecking order. Solomon Mataka saw that as the most likely outcome. Instead he felt singled out and important, being treated like a prospective client.

'Good morning, Mr Zuma! Nice to see you.' A clear voice and a peal of laughter caused Nkosinathi to look up and rise promptly.

'Come with me.'

'Yes, madam,' Nkosinathi stammered his reply to the lady standing at a little distance.

'This way!' Following her, Nkosinathi thought he had never seen a more glamorous woman on any magazine cover. She was not conventionally beautiful and only slightly younger than his mother, but so very elegant.

At Solomon Mataka's insistence, Nkosinathi had researched the firm of De Bruyn Brothers by going through piles of back issues of the *Star*, Johannesburg's major daily newspaper. The information he gleaned left him in no doubt that absolute commercial power resided here. Six De Bruyn brothers shared an interest in the stockbroking firm that Hank, the eldest of them, managed. Franz, Jakobus, and Gerhard were in mining, merchant banking, and insurance respectively while Jan and Adriaan lectured at Stellenbosch University in politics and law. Together they had their fingers in every financial pie with the ability to alter the ingredients and texture to their own taste.

Anna De Bruyn took Nkosinathi into her office and sat him in a chair facing her desk.

'Welcome to De Bruyn's!' she announced with a grin. 'And congratulations on topping the computer class. What a result! 97.5 per cent! I guess now you're keen to see how everything you learnt in theory is applied in practice.'

'Yes, madam, I am,' Nkosinathi answered self-consciously. From gossip pages in the tabloid press, to which Mr Mataka warned him not to give too much credence, he remembered Anna De Bruyn's nickname: Queen of the Boardroom. The title was bestowed on her because of her gracious manner when talking to the media and the diamonds she invariably wore. Nkosinathi found those fabled rare diamonds disappointingly small, yet they sparkled with a deep inner flame. The ones forming a flower pendant at her throat were cut to perfection and would, if he could but see it, display the precise symmetry of eight hearts and arrows, the pattern used to produce brilliance and fire. Her engagement and wedding rings and her earrings all had double the fifty-eight facets of the traditional cut. They gleamed in nothing more than the dim, curtain-subdued sunlight filtering into her office. In one financial magazine, he read that Anna De Bruyn's diamonds were plotted both for insurance purposes and easier identification in case of theft. It meant that under 10-power magnification, all inclusions, or impurities in the gem, were identified and their positions marked. 'No two diamonds are exactly the same,' Nkosinathi remembered reading. The reason Anna's gleamed as they did was because of their virtual lack of inclusions or flaws.

Nkosinathi wondered about the tabloids' fascination with Anna De Bruyn. To him she appeared too dignified to feature in any of them. She was wealthy, certainly, but nothing about her, not even the diamonds which she wore with natural grace, suggested anything other than a modest security. She was neither ostentatious nor vulgar. Her clothes were plain although well-tailored. She wore a suit of a dusty teal hue, like dry eucalyptus leaves, with a black lace top under the jacket. Handmade Italian black patent leather shoes sporting eight centimetre heels and a fine gold ankle bracelet, accenting peppercorn-coloured stockings on her shapely legs, completed the outfit.

To ease Nkosinathi's nervousness, Anna continued a light, bantering conversation, asking him about the computer course; his teacher, Ms Khumalo; and his fellow students, particularly Suzanna Tsedu.

'Golly, look at the time!' Anna observed. 'I've been up since the crack of dawn, and I bet you have too. Would you like coffee, Nkosinathi? You don't mind me calling you by your first name, do you?'

Nkosinathi did not know which question to answer first, somehow managing to nod and shake his head at the same time, creating a muddled response.

'Betty!' she called her assistant. 'I need my caffeine fix. Could you bring Nkosinathi and me some coffee please . . . and my favourite chocolate biscuits!'

She turned back to Nkosinathi. 'According to Mr Mataka, you like spreadsheet accounting, is that so?'

'Yes, madam. I enjoy formatting spreadsheets.'

'I'll introduce you to Mrs George, our accountant. She can make a start showing you how we record our daily transactions. Our researchers use spreadsheets for statistical data like the rise and fall of share prices, and the financial analysts keep track of the profitability or otherwise of listed companies, entering the information on spreadsheets. They really are an extremely versatile tool.'

Anna picked up the phone. 'Max! Can you and Brad take our new man across the road later? Thank you!' She smiled at Nkosinathi again. 'After lunch, Max and Brad, two of our traders, will take you over to the Exchange just so that you're not bored sitting in the office all day.'

'Thank you, Mefrou De Bruyn. I am very interested in everything.'

Laughing, Anna rose, beckoning to Nkosinathi. 'Come and meet *the boss*!'

Crossing through the adjoining room where Maurice Van Buuren, Hank's personal assistant, toiled, Anna asked in passing, 'Maurice, is Hank in yet?'

'Yes, his appointment with Dr Elbenstein was very early.' Maurice rolled his eyes towards the ceiling. He was always on the verge of exasperation. 'That pesky accountant from Gauteng Electrical is finally off the phone,' he sighed. 'Drives Hank crazy! One minute he wants Gold Corp shares, half an hour later he calls back and asks for Mineral Enterprises instead because he thinks he's heard stories about their explorations. Then he's back on the phone with an order for Diamond Mines. Wish he'd find himself another firm to deal with.'

With a chuckle at the ever-complaining, suffering Maurice's reference to an unpopular but prominent client, Anna winked at Nkosinathi. 'Are you sure you want to work here, Nkosinathi? Look at what it's doing to poor Maurice. His hair is going grey. That's because he's been with us for nearly a decade. You want to be grey prematurely too?

'I'll talk to Mr Indecision from Gauteng Electrical next time he calls.' With that soothing remark towards Maurice, Anna led

Nkosinathi into Hank's office. Hank had altered over the fifteen years of their marriage, Anna thought as she watched him raising his head slowly from his work and laying his pen down. When they first met, Hank had been more like Franz, assertive and unduly competitive. A combination of her influence initially and his health problems in later years mellowed him to become the jovial, debonair man his associates admired. The De Bruyn clan had been wary of Anna when they were newlyweds. Hank's offering her a position within the firm alarmed them. She had no prerequisite qualifications to enter the business world. Anna attained a bachelor of arts degree with honours in politics and a major in journalism at the University of New South Wales. While this endeared her to Jan, who lectured in politics, the others remained sceptical. And as for her seamanship . . . 'That,' they said, 'is superfluous here.'

Anna did not resent their attitude, seeing it as a form of personal challenge to disprove their prejudice. She marvelled at their short-sightedness. Her father ran a prosperous import-export business and shipping agency in Sydney, and her sole reason for coming to South Africa was to seek investment opportunities for him. They both felt a little sanctions busting might go a long way. During the course of making contact with South African enterprises, she met Hank, and they married in love-struck haste.

Hank maintained that Anna should use her skills, making her the firm's public relations and media liaison officer, a position he thought best suited to her degree. It satisfied his brothers, who expected her to be inexperienced in financial matters. They could not have made a greater error. As Hank's haemochromatosis, a condition exacerbated by increased iron absorption, worsened, Anna assumed a wider range of his responsibilities. She studied to attain a diploma in accounting, and Hank taught her the more intricate workings of the stock market.

The clan was aghast because Anna imprinted her personal stamp of ethics on the firm. She avoided any instances of possible insider trading and assured the firm practiced good corporate citizenship. It was news to the brothers De Bruyn.

'How the hell can you make a buck in this game if you don't use every snippet of information to your advantage?' Franz argued with her.

His amazement left Anna unfazed. 'By thinking of your clients and your firm in equal measure, my dear brother-in-law,' she retorted mockingly. 'If you read financial journals from other countries, you will see that foreign investment is cautious about South Africa, fearing they will be taken for a ride.' Her voice had the timbre of a strict schoolmistress. 'Not at De Bruyn's!' she dictated firmly. 'In time I hope our fellow brokers will take my message on board.'

In slow, incremental stages, Anna's ideas filtered through to other firms. It earned her the 'Ms Ethics' tag. Reducing the blatant insider trading did not decrease De Bruyn's profits. The opposite occurred. Their business increased because clients had confidence in the House Of De Bruyn, as Anna christened the firm. Their reputation for clean dealings spread. Gradually, grudgingly, the family agreed she was an asset to the company.

If Nkosinathi was nervous before, his wits all but disintegrated on entering and seeing Hank behind his heavy oak desk.

'Sawubona! I see you, my boy! Sit yourself down.'

'Good morning, Meneer De Bruyn. Thank you for seeing me.' Nkosinathi took great care to make a polite impression.

'Don't thank me, man. What's brought you here is your own good work.'

Nkosinathi found that Hank De Bruyn too was not the type of person he expected to see. Instead of the bombastic, patronizing image he had in his mind, Hank De Bruyn turned out to be a quietly-spoken man inclined to humorous commentary.

'Before we introduce you around and leave you to the tender mercies of our younger female staff, let's have a man-to-man talk about your future.'

'Yes, sir.' Nkosinathi grinned, feeling silly.

'You're taking on a hell of a workload,' Hank cautioned Nkosinathi. 'Two jobs, in fact. The traineeship will be part-time, say, from nine thirty to three. Your other job is your schoolwork, which you'll have to do by correspondence. We'll enrol you easily enough. Preparing for matriculation will keep you out of trouble for the next twelve months or so. By that time, you'll have a reasonable idea as to how this place functions. You can then decide on a course of tertiary studies. And it doesn't have to be commerce. It can be law, politics, geology, engineering, economics, or anything you like, should you decide against accountancy or business administration. Whatever you choose, we'll see you through it. That's our part of the bargain. Your part is to work as hard as you possibly can. Do we have a deal?'

'Yes, sir, I promise to do my best.'

'Good!' Hank rose, amused. He liked ambitious young boys, especially those who could visualize themselves in the role they wished to fulfil. Nkosinathi stood up as well, and they shook hands on the agreement.

'Maurice! Write a letter to Nkosinathi's parents.' Turning to the boy with a grin, Hank joked, 'Now, let's go and check out the girls.'

* * *

After the early morning round of the children's ward, Josh prepared for another drive to Soweto. His heart was scarcely in it these days.

Staying with Cindy in her claustrophobic matchbox house no longer held appeal. It was no fault of Cindy's, Josh conceded. He himself had undergone subtle, imperceptible changes of late, which he had difficulty analyzing. Was it guilt? Could he face Cindy knowing he walked irregular paths on the borderline of legality? Could he confide in her and tell her of his activities? Certainly not. Burdening and involving her was unfair. Like Peter and Tom, who drew their own conclusions from the use of the wine cellar and the sudden availability of money for an operating theatre, Cindy was best kept in ignorance of the facts.

Josh pondered how strange it was that although they both loved children, they had none. While he concerned himself with kids' health, Cindy concentrated on their education. It should have been the ideal partnership. Instead he wondered if it was enough common ground on which to base a union and found their own family. Where could it have gone wrong? Josh refused to believe that Cindy was not involved with other men while he spent so many years in America. He had not been faithful to her either. They made no promises to each other. Cindy travelled to the USA every Christmas break to revive their easy-going, casual friendship. Since his return to South Africa, however, Cindy showed a greater desire to settle down. She goaded him into a betrothal, but was the spark of interest still glowing for them? His life had changed. His patients and the hospital came first, colleagues second, and everyone else a long way behind.

Still, Josh admitted to himself, it would be nice to be a father, have a son or daughter of his own. Yes, he'd love that. And when all was said and done, he didn't have to marry Cindy or any other woman to achieve it. On the other hand, having a child with a very special woman would be emotionally satisfying. He rummaged deep within every crevice of his soul to see if Cindy was that certain woman. They found little to say to each other lately. Furthermore, on the grapevine, Josh had heard that Solomon Mataka was keen on Cindy. He had no way of knowing the extent to which Cindy responded to Solomon's attention, nor had he mentioned it to her. He was afraid she would instantly accuse him of tardiness, keeping her waiting while he played his little games: *I marry her; I marry her not.*

The thought of Cindy's searching eyes noting every expression on his face filled his heart with a dull heaviness. With shock, he realized he preferred to avoid her altogether. He could bypass Soweto and drive straight to Johannesburg, attend the Gold Corp shareholders' meeting, stay with a friend for a day or two, and then return to the clinic. Cindy need never know.

His cowardice disgusted him. With angry force, he threw his spare socks and underwear into an overnight bag. The suit, shirt, and tie for the shareholders' meeting he placed on top more carefully. Still cross with himself, he slammed the car boot on the luggage and drove off, determined to buy an attractive gift for Cindy along the way. Flowers—that was it. Roses, red ones.

He arrived at Cindy's house around about five thirty to find her and Solomon drinking coffee and talking shop.

'Hope I'm not interrupting anything,' he remarked curtly, eyeing Solomon with the unmistakable 'piss off' signal.

Cindy he greeted gently, giving her the roses, which she accepted with undisguised delight.

'For me?' she questioned, surprised and smiling all over.

'Who else, Cindy?'

'How wonderful! Your gallantry melts my heart, Josh.' She hugged him, laughing and forgetting Solomon's presence.

'Gorgeous perfume.' Cindy buried her nose in the flowers while looking for a suitable vase.

Meanwhile Josh's body language indicated more strongly than before that Solomon was free to take his leave. Solomon did so in his own time.

'I'll see you tomorrow, Cindy!' He smiled at her with overwhelming charm. 'We'll have to see what we can do about Freddie Bonga. Heavens, am I glad he's not my son.'

'Yes, see you tomorrow, Solomon!' Cindy returned the farewell absently, still searching for a receptacle big enough to hold the roses. Solomon turned to Josh before closing the door behind him. 'Pleased to have met you, eh . . . Professor Mtolo.'

Joshua failed to notice the biting sarcasm in Solomon's voice. His mind raced ahead to tomorrow's Gold Corp shareholders' meeting and the dizzy world of high finance waiting for him there. Whom would he meet? Removed from his customary academic circles, he knew nobody except his stockbroker, who promised to come along. With any luck, he could cast his eye about for and make the acquaintance of new VIPs to populate the wine cellar. The Swiss account required a cash injection to boost its immunity against the liquidity problem virus.

There was more than twenty-four hours before that event, and they had to be spent mostly with Cindy. To prevent her asking him questions about himself, Josh elected to feign interest in Cindy's work.

'I'll take you to the computer training centre tomorrow,' she enthused. 'You can have a look around.'

Finally the roses were arranged to her satisfaction. 'There, don't they look great?'

Josh had to smile and nod acknowledgement.

'Did I tell you two of the kids had equal results?' Cindy repeated the story at length, giving Josh a detailed account of how Solomon dealt with the situation. 'And guess where Nkosinathi is now? At De Bruyn Brothers, the stockbrokers. At last Solomon told me who the sponsors are. I can't understand why he kept that information so close to his chest. It was bound to come out one day.'

Cindy began preparing the evening meal. She wanted her cooking to be perfect. *Nothing slapdash tonight*, she thought. During her lunch break, she had caught a bus into Johannesburg to buy a bottle of wine and new glasses to add a touch of luxury to her dinner.

To Cindy's dismay, Josh spoke little while they ate. 'You look very tired, Josh,' she remarked with concern.

'Yes, I am rather weary,' Josh sighed. 'That doesn't mean I'm not enjoying your excellent meal,' he added quickly.

'Why the fatigue? You under pressure?' Cindy enquired, dishing out a refreshing dessert of fruit salad.

'I'm lecturing part-time at uni again. KwaZulu Medical needs the money. Also, I help out at other hospitals when the need arises. The consultancy fees go a long way towards employing part-time administrative help for Peter and Tom. The clinic is becoming busier. We need another physician to join the partnership, but I don't know if that will eventuate. Sipho is stretching out the feelers in that regard. Surprisingly, we're attracting increasing numbers of white patients. It gives me some satisfaction because they can afford to pay fully for treatment. It's also a yardstick for the quality of service we offer. It seems I am slowly achieving my goal: a medical facility for blacks of a standard that whites expect and have always had at their disposal.'

It was the most he had told her about his aspirations in a long while. He made every effort to remain on guard. The food and wine must not lull him into comfortable carelessness when thoughtless confessions were likely to slip out. Pillow talk brought similar hazards. Cindy had no intention of sleeping. She kept Josh awake, alternating between conversation and copulation into the early hours.

In the morning, she rose bright and cheerful while he staggered around yawning. He could hardly stay in bed and let her go to work by bus. That wasn't right. Two strong cups of coffee later, Josh drove Cindy to school and promised to meet her at the computer centre in the afternoon. The intervening time he passed catching up with acquaintances such as cardiac specialist Dr Zak Elbenstein. Josh never forgot contacts. It was useful having friends who specialized in other fields of medicine. Their expert opinions were often helpful—if not to him then to Peter and Tom.

Although Josh preferred the workings of the human brain to cyber intelligence, he was impressed with Cindy's equipment. The centre, as she pointed out, used the latest in computer hardware and software. Its layout was more like an open-space office than a classroom, where terminals would normally be four or five in a row across the room. Here students had their own desks, separated sufficiently from each other to enable Cindy to move around easily while helping and supervising. The room was lit perfectly for computer work and well ventilated. Ergonomic chairs prevented students suffering sore backs and stiff necks.

'You see, the donors did not economize too rigidly.' She waved an arm in a wide arc, indicating the whole area. 'The computers were to have been reconditioned machines, but later, they decided to buy new ones. The furniture is as good as new too. The walls are painted in pleasing colours, and the chairs blend with the decor. It couldn't be better.'

'It's quiet in here,' Josh realized in wonderment.

'They double-glazed the windows to eliminate the worst of the traffic noise. The kids can hear me clearly, so there's no excuse for not carrying out my instructions.' Cindy hummed a tune as she prepared the material for the next day's class. She was totally absorbed in her task, Josh noted. And herein lay the source of their relationship problems. He was equally dedicated to his occupation, and neither of them wished to relinquish job satisfaction for a romantic partnership or marriage and parenting. That, at least, was Josh's perception of their current stalemate.

After an hour, which Josh spent reading a newspaper, Cindy shut down her terminal, switched off the lights, and locked the door. As they walked to Josh's car, two young men standing at the curb waved to them.

'Miss Khumalo! Sawubona!' they called loudly. One boy was dressed formally in a shirt and tie while the other wore frayed jeans, a leather jacket, and a bike helmet. At Cindy's approach, he removed his headgear.

'It's Freddie Bonga!' Cindy exclaimed. 'And Nkosinathi Zuma!' She stopped near them. Both appeared to have matured in the short time since they had left her computer class.

'How are you both?' she questioned excitedly. They were an unlikely couple, the best student and the worst. While Nkosinathi had added his efforts to Cindy's in a vain attempt to help Freddie pass his tests, a warm friendship developed between them.

'I see you have your motorbike now, Freddie'

'Yebo. Not the Harley I dreamed of, but I like all the same.' Freddie grinned proudly, showing off his ten-year-old Yamaha. 'My uncle, he help. I work for him part-time in his garage.'

'And how are things with you, Nkosinathi?'

'Good, thank you, Miss Khumalo. I have to work hard, but I'm happy.'

'They treat you well at De Bruyn's then, I take it?'

'Yes. Mr Mataka was too pessimistic. I'm not the errand boy as he feared. They include me as one of the team, showing me everything. Occasionally, Mr De Bruyn asks me questions to ascertain how much I have learnt. I usually manage to answer correctly.' Nkosinathi's shy schoolboy grin bore a new confidence Cindy was pleased to see.

She turned to Josh. 'Meet two of my former students, Freddie Bonga and Nkosinathi Zuma.' Taking Josh's hand, she told the boys, 'This is Joshua Mtolo, my fiancé.'

'Ngiyajabula ukukwazi [Happy to meet you],' the lads replied respectfully.

'Do you want to be a stockbroker yourself one day?' Nkosinathi's keenly intelligent face impressed Joshua. The young chap clearly had high expectations of himself.

'I don't know about that yet,' Nkosinathi replied thoughtfully. 'Mr De Bruyn said I could study anything I wished even if it did not relate to commerce. I like the idea of being a lawyer.'

They said their farewells, turning towards Josh's car. 'And you, Freddie, let me know when you open your own motorbike shop. I want to buy one!' Josh called out while Freddie pushed his helmet on his head, peering through the visor like a television soap-opera *tsotsi* or thug.

'Looks like the apprentice crime gang boss, that Freddie,' he remarked to Cindy.

'He's a problem child for sure, but deep down he has a good heart, I think.' She smiled. It was great to see them again.

* * *

Josh fussed over his clothes as he unpacked the suit he intended to wear to the shareholders' meeting. It was of fine lightweight wool, a beige- or stone-type colour and superbly cut. With it went a cream-coloured shirt and a dark-chestnut tie, which blended with his complexion and emphasized his penetrating eyes. Cindy's heart stopped briefly. Rarely had she seen him so well dressed. The jacket squared his broad shoulders. The trousers were just right—not too tight and not too loose. Josh insisted on running the iron over the creases and gave his shoes an extra polish.

'You look magnificent!' Cindy's eyes lit with admiration.

'That's just as well, Cindy, my dear. I need to attract those folk somehow because I'm still hoping they'll buy into KwaZulu Medical eventually.'

'If it comes to that, Josh, I think you're perfectly adequate without the refinery.' Cindy frowned suddenly, and Josh, although preoccupied, noticed the light dim in her eyes. She had always viewed him as the romantic epitome of the Zulu warrior. He was tall, well-shaped, and strong. Traditional dancing, the only relaxation he allowed himself, ensured his fitness. The clothes he wore now gave him an extra dimension which, although impressive, seemed superfluous.

'You don't understand, my love.' Josh defended his momentary vanity. 'Appearances are everything in the financial world. You could call it artificial, I suppose.' With a last satisfied glance in the mirror, he kissed Cindy good-bye and was out the door.

The Gold Corp building featured a sizeable lecture theatre on the ground floor, which other firms often hired for seminars and conferences. On this evening, their annual shareholders' meeting was to be held in that venue. Josh came with mixed feelings of expectation and uncertainty. He had brought more than sufficient proof of identity with the share certificates to gain admittance. These he showed to two conscientious employees sitting at a table beside the entrance to the room. He noticed with interest that three people ahead of him, two men and a lady, were not asked for documents but were allowed through without comment.

'The De Bruyns are here in force,' one man at the table whispered to his colleague, loud enough for Josh to hear. 'Mark my word—something's going to happen tonight. It always does when all three of them show up.'

'We've got more than the usual four or five journalists here too,' the other agreed.

Anna De Bruyn, reptile-skin briefcase in hand, flanked by Hank and Franz like an aircraft carrier accompanied by two destroyers, entered the auditorium. The appearance of that armada charged the atmosphere within to a degree palpable even to new participants like Josh. He followed the dynamic trio and sat behind them.

Anna, wedged between Hank and Franz, busied herself searching her briefcase for a folder. She pulled it out, snapped the case shut, and stood it under her chair. Josh noticed the lady sat close to the older of the two men, their shoulders touching. He gathered that this gent was the Mr De Bruyn Nkosinathi had spoken of and the lady his wife.

'Are you feeling OK?' Josh heard Anna ask Hank, every nuance of her voice and body language suggesting tenderness and devotion.

'I'll live,' Hank replied with a hushed tone and a reassuring smile.

The hall became still while the Gold Corp executives walked to the front in single file and found their chairs behind a table on the dais. Everyone watched while they sorted the paperwork they carried in. The chairman, seated in the middle, poured himself a glass of water from a crystal decanter and drank. Rising slowly as if arthritic, he lifted his voice and began a wordy speech of welcome.

'Can't that guy cut himself short?' Franz whispered to Anna, who burst into giggles.

'You'd talk a lot too if you loved the sound of your own voice.'

'Anyway, he's only trying to confuse minority shareholders.'

'He better not.' Anna's forehead creased, forming a deep ridge between her eyebrows.

The De Bruyns switched their concentration to the copies of financial statements all shareholders received on entering. Although, unlike the shareholders, the De Bruyns were already familiar with the contents, they read each page again with care. Josh took a glimpse at his also, but it meant little to him. His restricted understanding of the figures did not enable him to unravel the information they contained.

The chairman's voice droned in predictable rises and falls. When he introduced the managing director, Malcolm Price, who was to give the assembled group an outline of the company's activities throughout the year, the De Bruyns' interest revived. For some time, they listened with tense expectation. Josh, behind them, was aware of their alertness.

Franz nudged Anna. 'He's not going to say a word about the sale of the Piccolo mine. The sly prick.' He slapped his left hand on his thigh.

'Give him time, Franz.'

'How long?'

The end of the managing director's oratory was greeted with polite but unenthusiastic applause. Malcolm Price, who had hoped for a generous reception, bent down to converse briefly with the chairman. When he straightened again, he faced the audience, inviting questions.

'Ladies and gentlemen, if you have any questions, the board of directors and I will be very happy to answer them.' Price looked about for signs that someone wished to speak. Anna held her folder high to indicate she had queries. The chairman pointed at her.

'Yes, the lady in the green jacket!' That was silly. They knew perfectly well who she was. Hank coughed to stifle his laughter. Anna stood up, announcing her name.

'De Bruyn Brothers,' she said, her voice frosty.

'Just in case the senile old bastards forgot who we are,' Franz whispered across to Hank.

'Mr Price,' Anna began, 'I think I need your help interpreting parts of your financial statements.'

Coughs, feet shuffles, and craned necks from the press followed.

Anna turned sideways to address the shareholders as well as the executives on the podium. Josh studied her profile. *No, definitely not a beautiful woman*, he thought. Yet she had poise, almost regal. She gave an impression of supreme confidence and power. Was that what attracted men to her? Josh wondered. Couldn't be. In all honesty, he had to admit few men liked powerful, self-assured women as wives. Perhaps it was her aura of feminine mystery, which drew men like Hank to her side. The woman was enigmatic and magnetic. Politically, he placed her in the camp of the archetypal white liberal. Josh thought he had summed her up, not realizing he was already drowning in the quicksand of her unusual nature. He admired her clothes. She wore a navy silk blouse with a shirt collar and a navy calf-length skirt. Over that she had her jade-green jacket, which the chairman had indicated to identify her. It complemented her green eyes and thick deep-auburn hair, which she held up with two combs. A blink of light beamed over Josh's face. It came from her engagement ring as she held the financial reports in her left hand and began reading out loud. Josh looked at Anna's ring, incredulous. The engagement ring he had bought for Cindy was a fine piece of craftsmanship but paled to insignificance compared with the emerald-cut diamond and its surrounding brilliants that this woman wore.

He recalled with wry merriment the near riot Cindy's ring had caused in the Khumalo family. Seeking to negotiate a bride price, or lobola, with her uncle, Cindy became aware of the discussions. With ruffled feathers and bruised pride, she told everyone present that if she were to be traded for cattle, she would never marry anyone. He soothed Cindy's fury and her uncle's embarrassment by offering to buy her a diamond ring instead. Either way, he could never understand what the difference between the two approaches really was. Both methods placed a pecuniary value on human interaction. Josh's thoughts returned to the present when Anna continued.

'I'm looking for approximately R19 million, Mr Price. A bagatelle, I know, but it should be somewhere!'

Ever observant, the press laughed in appreciation of humour with a sting.

The colour of Price's face changed to pink like litmus paper in acid.

'You disposed of the Piccolo mine, the least profitable one, about five months ago. All financial journals carried the story. In fact, I have the clipping right here.' Anna held up the article, which she had enlarged under the photocopier for everyone to see the headline clearly: Piccolo Sold for R19 Million.

'What puzzles me, Mr Price, is that in your reports, you still record the land as a fixed asset.' Mutterings rumbled around the room.

'Mr Price, you don't have Piccolo anymore. The R19 million odd you raised from its sale should be included with the extraordinary items.' Anna spoke as if she were a weary teacher attempting to explain accounting fundamentals to a disinterested class. 'The balance between the R19 million recovered from the sale and the R25 million shown as the value of the land in your fixed assets should be written off. It's a loss in anyone's books.' Her voice hardened in warning. 'Where is that money, Mr Price? I can't find it on your statements.'

All at once, everyone broke into noisy conversation. Price's bald head became radish red as the journalists approached, clamouring for details.

Anna knew as well as Price did where the money was. Three and a half million of it graced Price's own account. The rest was distributed among government ministers as a reward for industry-friendly environmental mining legislation. To herself she wondered why Price and colleagues didn't even have the wits to disguise the missing money as performance bonuses or special payments of one nature or another. She doubted whether the R19 million was the correct amount. Secretly she believed that it was closer to R25 million and both the press and the shareholders were being hoodwinked. They were playing a dangerous game. Tonight she had acted on a tip-off from Jan. As soon as she had concrete proof and Adriaan's advice as to the legal position, she would let the directors have it. As it was, she still wasn't finished with them. She raised both hands to halt the forward march of the journalists who crowded the aisles between the chairs.

'Mr Price, you will appreciate that at De Bruyn Brothers, we wish to give clients the best and most reliable financial advice. It is bad enough if share values fall due to sanctions and economic pressures beyond our control. At De Bruyn Brothers, we do not like to see clients suffering loss because of poor accounting practices within the companies whose shares we trade.'

Anna's comment was a veiled warning to Price that unless he remained within reasonably honest parameters, she would talk Gold Corp's share price down. Her words created uproar among the shareholders, and even Josh realized that KwaZulu Medical may have been adversely affected. When after a pause she was able to make herself heard again, she said, 'I suggest, Mr Price, that this evening's meeting be adjourned until you are able to prepare new financial reports that reflect Gold Corp's position more accurately.'

The shareholders offered spontaneous acclaim and agreement. They rose from their seats, filling the room with perpetual motion. One half of the journalists attacked Price with pertinent questions. The other half stopped Anna as the De Bruyns prepared to leave. Anna knew many from previous encounters, exchanging witticisms while explaining her standpoint. Hank had seen it all happen before. He enjoyed the show each time. This one was particularly rare entertainment.

'It's the changing of the guard,' he remarked to Franz as, one by one, the journalists who finished grilling Price came over to Anna and those who spoke to Anna first moved across to put Price through his paces. Some reporters sought comments from randomly chosen shareholders, and the photographers' cameras flashed at Price and Anna De Bruyn.

Amongst this melee, Anna became conscious of someone watching her. She felt eyes focusing on her, willing her to look up. *Goodness*, she thought astonished. *It's that professor from KwaZulu Medical. What's he doing here?* She recalled hearing other brokers speak of him. What was his name again? Never mind. Didn't matter. For a split second, their eyes locked in each other's gaze. Perhaps it did matter. Her face serene, Anna inclined her head slightly, sending him a quick smile with luminous green eyes. Her lips moved slightly in a quiet greeting.

'*Sawubona.*'

It left him dumbstruck. If that hello wasn't an invitation to trade shares, nothing was. His right hand reached to loosen his tie. The air conditioning must be malfunctioning.

'Anna, my dear, come. I want you to meet the CEO of—' Finding his wife distracted, Hank dropped the sentence. He followed her eyes, interested to find out who had claimed her attention. Hank's eyes met Josh's, but no cordiality issued forth. Keeping his expression bland and deliberately void of emotion, he took Anna's arm and led her to where Franz stood surrounded by friends.

Aiyee! Josh laughed inwardly. *Possessive, Meneer De Bruyn, are we? Not surprising. What is she worth to you? What would you pay to have your woman back safe, sound, and above all, untouched? Half a million? More? Ah yes, she'd be a priceless asset.*

Transfixed by Anna's imposing presence and lured by the shape of her designer-clad body, Josh made two resolutions. An immediate change of stockbrokers was vital. Thereafter he would let the dust storm raised during this meeting dissipate before having her brought to his clinic. That would be a coup worth celebrating. He laughed, pushing the key into the ignition to drive back to Soweto. An asset indeed!

* * *

He found Cindy already in bed waiting for him, wide awake and full of questions about the computer school sponsors, Hank and Anna De Bruyn.

'What impression did you have of them, Josh? Tell me!'

'I don't know them as individuals because I did not speak with them,' he answered cautiously. 'As stockbrokers'—his voice became animated—'I would consider them ultra-efficient. So much so I will change firms as soon as possible. That lazy son of a drag queen I've been dealing with promised he'd be there, but I didn't see a whisker of him. The De Bruyns came in person rather than send a member of their staff. I believe they really care about their clients. They picked the eyes out of Gold Corp's financial reports. All hell broke loose when they spotted irregularities connected with the sale of an unprofitable mine. The managing director couldn't say where the proceeds from the sale had vanished to.' Josh yawned, dreading further questions. He would much prefer to be left to his own bewildered thoughts.

'One reads about corporate bungling in the newspapers. To be a witness to it is so unexpected. Is KwaZulu Medical affected in any way?' Cindy hopped out of bed to hasten Josh's undressing. Unfastening shirt buttons seemed to take him forever tonight.

'I'll buy the papers tomorrow and read through them if I have time. There were numerous reporters and photographers present, all madly snapping away, asking the sort of questions to which small shareholders like KwaZulu Medical would normally receive no answers.'

The battle with shirt buttons and trouser zip won. Cindy dropped her nightie, beckoning Josh into bed. 'Come, my good man,' she whispered huskily while Josh still dallied, draping his jacket over the back of a chair. 'I will give you a taste of women's emancipation. It's woman on top from now on!'

'Cindy, you are wonderful. I submit . . . but just this once! Remember your place in future, woman!' Josh countered with a jest, and they laughed, anticipating delight.

Cindy's appealing voluptuousness never failed to arouse Josh, no matter what. She began a slow, oral awakening of his lust before penetration, after which nothing detracted from the fierceness of her desire. Her burning passion carried him to climax.

'*Sawubona!*'

Anna! Hell, he almost called her name out loud. How could the image of a strange woman's face intrude on his consciousness at such a crucially intimate moment? Had she cast a spell over him? White sangoma, sorceress. Poor Cindy, had she noticed his inattention?

'You are luscious and beautiful,' he murmured, letting his hand run over Cindy's breasts. He covered her body with guilty kisses, hoping the intensity of her own climax had camouflaged his lapse.

To Josh's relief, Cindy fell asleep exhausted, the previous night's exertions creating a cumulative effect of satisfied relaxation. His mind racing, he lay beside her motionless, not wanting to disturb her repose.

Sawubona!

There was Anna again, with eyes green as a ship's starboard light at night. *She should wear emeralds rather than diamonds*, Josh thought. His heart pounded. The lower region of his anatomy stirred anew. Oh God! What sort of virus had entered his bloodstream? Some toxic microorganism, a USB, that's what—an unidentified substance in blood.

Sawubona!

'Woman, lead me not into temptation,' he moaned as the USB virus gained supremacy.

Sawubona!

Alluring female. How the cut of that green jacket she wore drew attention to her breasts and hips. To hell with it. Wasn't there some prophylactic pill against this damned USB?

Spent, Josh gave full rein to his recollections of the evening. When the De Bruyns had risen to leave, he too had stood up. It had given him the first lengthy opportunity to scrutinize Anna's physique. She was not a woman who flaunted her sexuality openly, but discreet indicators hinted at a deep sensuality. For instance, that split in her calf-length skirt, which ended provocatively about ten centimetres above her knee, leaving the rest to tantalize the imagination every time she moved. Her ankle bracelet also pointed to an untamed angle to her personality. Could she be queen of the bedroom as well as the boardroom? Would it be exciting to feel this albino lioness writhe in ecstasy beneath him, hearing her cries of sexual abandon? Or was she the cool, silent type? He'd soon change that.

'Valium, please!' Josh groaned. It was going to be a long night.

* * *

Unwinding after the evening's tensions, Hank and Anna shared champagne in the spa. That is, they had one glass between them because Dr Elbenstein had advised Hank against alcohol. Occasionally, Hank disregarded caution. After all, what was life without wine, women, and song? Especially wine and women.

He looked at Anna, who posed like Venus, relaxed and inviting with her hair pinned high and hot, water-reddened nipples. Insatiable man-eater. She had such a vast capacity for physical love, sex with her could spell instant incineration for a man. During the early years of their marriage, he had kept pace with her, but now? He could subdue her with the help of the gold chain-connected bracelets he bought her as imaginary handcuffs and his trouser belt. She didn't mind the rough play, feeling secure in the knowledge that he loved her and would never hurt her seriously. If anything, the games heightened her lustfulness. She could be so wild. Hank closed his eyes momentarily, thinking. He felt Anna move through the water to his side.

'You are deep in thought, Hank.' She placed an arm across his chest and kissed him.

He suspected she guessed what occupied his mind but replied evasively, 'I fear you made enemies this evening, sweetheart.'

She broke into her silver-bell peals of laughter, splashing him playfully. 'Who, Price? With a head full of lice! We'll fix him yet.'

Hank assumed Price wasn't the only man to endure a sleepless night because of Anna. That warrior-type chap from KwaZulu Medical whose eyes peeled clothing off her might well suffer the same fate. Drat the man. His glance sent shock waves through Anna. What a nerve he had to look at a woman so boldly in her husband's presence. Anna couldn't help but see. With a pang of jealousy, Hank thought it may well be time his lady was reminded of who her husband was. Instantly contrite, he reformed the thought. Mustn't let his insecurities make him unjust. Throughout their marriage, his Anna had been a model wife and would remain steadfast. Although the frequency of their sexual acts declined, he knew she would never be unfaithful. Compassion forbade Ms Ethics to cheat on an ailing husband. Blast and double blast! Damn it all to hell! A groan of regret escaped from his throat. He wanted her desire, not her compassion.

He turned towards her. Reaching for her delicious nipples, he bit them till she cried out with the exquisite agony of it. Her thighs parted instinctively.

* * *

Chapter 4

Benny Shanks's Bistro

'No! Not on your life!'

C1 and C2 shook their heads. 'We're not doing it. That's final!'

Sipho looked at C3, C4, and C5. After the countless rand he had spent on *utshwala* to make them pliable, they were as adamant as ever.

'We are not taking a woman! Full stop!'

Sipho had arranged another meeting with the Caprivi men in the Ulundi shebeen. His previous phone calls requesting surveillance on Anna De Bruyn had been rebuffed. He had no choice but to see the soldiers in person to discuss the matter, but it made no difference.

'Women are trouble,' C3 volunteered by way of explanation.

C2 joined in. 'Yeah! If a guy becomes uncooperative, you can be firm with him, but what do you do with a woman? She'll make work difficult, and there's little you can do about it.'

Indicating to Sipho that he cared for another beer, C4 expressed their thoughts succinctly: 'We are professionals, not cowards who stalk and abduct unarmed women.'

Sipho had to concede defeat. The offer of raising their commission failed to tempt the Caprivis. They were having none of it.

'They're probably right,' Sipho remarked to Fernando as they drove away from the unsuccessful rendezvous.

Fernando nodded emphatically. 'I agree.'

'That De Bruyn woman will be more trouble than she's worth, but I can't get the idea out of Josh's head.' Sipho shrugged his emaciated shoulders. He had said as much to Josh when the De Bruyn project had first come up for discussion.

Josh had only laughed in reply, saying, 'She's going to have to be very obstreperous indeed before she cancels out the half a million her old man will contribute for her release.' Did Josh want the white business community to hunt him like game and wreak revenge when they caught him? Sipho's mind filled with dread. Josh was bewitched by the woman; couldn't get her out of his system. It was bound to end in disaster.

In his mind, Sipho replayed the conversation. 'Anna De Bruyn has got under your skin.' He looked at Josh sharply.

'Nonsense, Sipho!' Josh rebuked him instantly.

'Your denial comes a little too quickly and forcefully.' Sipho's knowing smirk drew further hasty comments from Josh.

'Her husband sits on millions, which he can jolly well share around. He'll pay very smartly, you'll see. And then Anna can go home, and that's it.'

That wasn't it. There was much Josh failed to consider. 'So you are going to lock her in the wine cellar like the other guys, are you? Or do you find that unsuitable for the lady?' He could see by Josh's expression that this hadn't occurred to him.

'Well . . . no.' Josh looked nonplussed. 'I suppose she'll have to live in the staff quarters with us.'

'I thought you didn't want the VIPs to see us? And how do you propose to isolate Anna so that the public doesn't become aware of her presence? She's well known. The recent rumpus she kicked up about Piccolo has brought her name to the forefront again as well as her photo in many newspapers. Remember, we have an increasing number of white patients. She could be recognized by anyone coming in here.'

'I'll take that risk for half a million.' Josh smiled confidently.

Sipho could not share the optimism. Security would be the big problem. The staff accommodation was not accessible to patients, but how could Josh hide Anna? She would have to be confined in the last unit at the end of the passage. Nobody had any business there. The four motel-style apartments were not fully occupied. Josh resided in the first, Sipho had the one next to him, and the last two stood empty because Tom and Peter lived in Vryheid with their families.

The whole affair was going beyond Sipho's capabilities, and now he had to inform Josh that the Caprivis had withdrawn their assistance. He sighed, shaking his head with exasperation. Josh wanted him to contact the De Bruyn Brothers, requesting them to take charge of KwaZulu Medical's investment portfolio. It was a crazy act, considering he planned to abduct Hank De Bruyn's wife, something akin to biting the hand that feeds you. Josh countered that argument by saying, 'It'll be okay as long as nobody recognizes the connection between KwaZulu Medical and the EEM.'

'But one day, someone will. I think you should get out of this extortion game before the link is discovered. You don't need these tactics anymore. We'll muddle through from now on,' Sipho counselled Josh with earnest sincerity.

'Sipho, just visualize it. Half a million! It'll mean we can soon have the CAT scan equipment I've been waiting for. I'm not going to waste that chance.' Josh, as usual, paced Sipho's office. He stopped by the big window, which overlooked the whole front garden and entrance gate to the clinic complex. In the old days, this room had been the homestead's parlour and library. During the conversion to hospital, part of the wall separating this area from the large vestibule had been removed and replaced with a glass partition. It gave Sipho full view of the clinic's constant comings and goings. Outside, prominent signposts directed patients to the emergency section and outpatient areas. They had no need to enter the administration building unless they specifically wished to speak to Sipho or use the payphone positioned there.

Josh turned back to Sipho. 'It'll also give me the funds for my research project into the effects of police brutality on young children or children witnessing violent acts.'

'That's all very well, Josh, but can't you see we're endangering everything we've built up so far? You've come a long way, and now may be the time to keep a low profile and review your progress. Use Anna De Bruyn as a financial advisor by all means, but leave her with her husband.'

Sipho saw it written on Josh's face that these were not recommendations he wanted to hear, not even from a close friend. Josh began to pace again but stopped suddenly, saying, 'Okay, I guess you're right. Anna will be our last VIP guest.'

'You reckon! I've got bad news for you. The Caprivis aren't helping.'

'Why not?'

'To use C4's words, they maintain they are professionals, not cowards who go after unarmed women. I think they are insulted.'

'Right then!' Josh shrugged with a laugh. 'I'll just have to do the job myself.'

'Now I know you're insane.' Sipho sat down at his desk, gobsmacked. With a sidelong glance at Josh, he added in a low voice, 'Or madly in love. It's the same thing.'

'I heard that, Sipho. How often must I tell you it's not so.'

Sipho chuckled wickedly, pleased at having stirred Josh again. 'Anyhow, there's simply no way you can bring the woman here under your own steam.'

Josh turned to face Sipho. 'Have we changed stockbrokers yet?'

'Yes, it's all in hand. I spoke to a Mr Vince Lewis at De Bruyn's. He deals with it.'

'Hm . . . ?' Josh's brain raced. His restless wanderings around Sipho's office recommenced. Door to window, turn. Window to door, turn. Repeat. 'I had a call from Johannesburg General Hospital as well as the Rosebank Clinic yesterday. They want my help with two rather unusual cases, so I'll be up there within the next couple of days. I have to meet with a chap at the Institute for Medical Research too. I might find time to have a brief chat with Mrs De Bruyn. Do you think you could ring and make an appointment for me please, Sipho?'

* * *

Joshua Mtolo could not believe his luck. Standing outside the Johannesburg Stock Exchange, he watched the entrance to the office block directly opposite where De Bruyn Brothers occupied the fourth floor, when Anna De Bruyn emerged unexpectedly.

To Josh's annoyance, it was already 1815 hours when he managed to leave Johannesburg General Hospital in search of a good dinner away from colleagues with problem patients. He had missed the prearranged 11:30 a.m. appointment with Anna because of emergencies and had discounted catching up with her so late. While keeping an eye on Anna, he darted across the street to the accompaniment of car horns and screeching brakes. By the time his foot touched the sidewalk, Anna had moved past the next two buildings and Josh rushed after her.

'Mrs De Bruyn, please wait!' he called when he came within earshot. Anna, it seemed, failed to hear.

'Mrs De Bruyn,' Josh tried again, 'please, I must speak with you!' This time Josh knew she heard him because her steps slowed, although she walked on without turning around. It crossed his mind that the lady was as wary as an impala pursued by a leopard. When she reached the safety of the main doors to the next building where two security guards paraded, she stopped and looked about cautiously.

'Please excuse me, Mrs De Bruyn, we had a number of disruptions to our schedule at the hospital. I could not keep my appointment with you this morning.' Josh was a little breathless. Whether this was due to the chase or the sight of Anna's shining green eyes and pleasant smile, he had no time to guess.

'I'm sorry to be stopping you in the street like this, Mrs De Bruyn, but I need to speak with you. You are obviously on your way home, and I'm a pest, but I really couldn't get away from work.' Josh produced his lengthy explanations still breathing rapidly.

'That's all right, Professor.' Anna gave him her practised winning smile intended to promote good client relations.

'How can I help you?'

'Do not be offended, Mrs De Bruyn, but my clinic manager tells me that your trainee, Nkosinathi Zuma, handles the KwaZulu Medical account. I had hoped that in view of the tender financial situation we find ourselves in, the task would be allotted to someone more senior and experienced.'

Another smile created purely to reassure the public spread over Anna's face. 'I'm happy to be able to ease your mind on that score, Professor.' Her tone became matter-of-fact but still contained that hint of intimacy Josh recalled from their first encounter at the Gold Corp shareholders' meeting. 'Nkosinathi is a very bright young man, believe me. For all that, he is constantly supervised by Vince Lewis, his immediate superior. Furthermore, Hank keeps a close watch on what Nkosinathi does because the boy is such a fast learner and we don't want him to get beyond himself, if you know what I mean. Like he has to learn crawling before he can walk. Rest assured, Professor, KwaZulu Medical's affairs are in safe hands. In fact, the file is on Hank's desk this minute. He scarcely lets it out of his reach.'

Anna watched Josh's eyes as she spoke. 'I can see you don't believe me. How about I show you? Come back to the office with me, and we'll go through your file and discuss your position.' Anna beamed at Josh. She knew a mistrustful client when she saw one. This guy had a big financial chip on his shoulder and would take some convincing.

'Thank you, madam. I wouldn't dare take up so much of your time when you are clearly finished for the day and on your way home.'

'No matter.' She held out her hand pointing in the direction of her office. 'Come with me!' Her green eyes beckoned, shining like traffic lights, Josh thought. *And green is for 'go'! So why not?* He walked beside her, hoping with all his might that Hank would be out.

Maurice showed surprise at Anna's reappearance with Joshua in tow.

'Maurice!' she chided, 'You're still here! You weren't well yesterday. I told you at least three times already to knock off. Workaholics get ulcers. I don't want to see you till eleven at the earliest tomorrow.'

'B-but Hank n-needs—' Maurice stuttered as Anna cut him short.

'I'll look after Hank, don't you worry. What are wives for?' Anna's grin challenged the men to reply, but both declined to comment.

'I'll just finish this before I go.' He pointed to a stack of papers on his desk.

'By the way, Maurice, have you met Professor Mtolo from KwaZulu Medical?' Her hand touched Josh's shoulder lightly. 'Professor, Maurice Van Buuren is Hank's personal assistant.' The men shook hands briefly.

'I'm trying to persuade Professor Mtolo that every client is important to us, be they old, established institutions or newcomers.' Anna looked at Maurice, expecting him to confirm her assertions.

'Oh, yes, that's the De Bruyn recipe for success,' Maurice obliged. 'All clients benefit equally from our attention to detail.'

'Now, Professor, kindly step this way.' With her frequently heard peal of silver-bell laughter, Anna opened the door to Hank's office. 'You see the blue folder on Hank's desk?' She picked it up and held it for Josh to read the name on the cover: KwaZulu Medical.

Josh could no longer keep a straight face. He laughed, relieved that the tension had been dispelled and happy to find Hank's desk unoccupied. If Maurice cleared out as well, conditions, in his view, would reach perfection.

'Please, have a seat, Professor.' Anna invited Josh to the chair across from her desk. 'Care for coffee? Or something more adventurous? Scotch perhaps?'

'No way! I have to get back to work. Coffee will suffice, thanks.'

'Betty! Oh . . . she's gone.' Anna switched off the intercom. 'Excuse me just a second, Professor. I'll be right back.'

With a bewildering mixture of disdain and admiration, Josh saw that this spoilt white madam was about to organise the refreshments herself. The break gave him the opportunity to absorb the overall atmosphere of the De Bruyn Brothers' office. No, not office . . . *chambers* was the more apt word, Josh corrected himself. For starters, Hank's room was opulent. The cost of its furnishings would keep a family in rural KwaZulu fed for many months. Thick carpet, velvet curtains, crystal chandelier, leather-topped oak desk, leather director's chair, and an antique bookcase to name but a few items. The decor represented the unshakable empire white business had built for itself. Hank was the symbolic figurehead of the white financial system.

Maurice's room was no less splendid. It gave Josh the impression that the De Bruyns treated their senior staff like family on an equal footing with the boss. Anna, on the other hand, dispensed with the excessive grandeur. Her office was stylish but functional. She used a pine and glass-topped chromium desk. A bookcase and filing cabinets of the same material stood against one wall. The soft carpet was of a similar colour to the wood, as were the curtains. A pine shelf holding her computer was attached to the left side of her desk, and two comfortable chairs of cream-coloured upholstery filled the centre of her room. A low glass-topped table with a large vase of fresh flowers was placed before the window. On the wall furthest away from the window, Anna hung two Tom Roberts originals of beach scenes around Sydney. They were a wedding present from her parents and her only mementos of Australia. Josh couldn't estimate the value of the heavily insured paintings but felt the room projected friendly vibrations.

Anna returned with a tray, which she placed on her desk. She poured Josh's coffee from a silver pot, indicated milk and sugar, and offered him her favourite chocolate biscuits in a crystal dish.

'I fear this is my drug of addiction.' She grinned as she sipped her strong black coffee and munched a sweet. Between bites, she continued, 'You see, there is no need for you to be perturbed about young Nkosinathi familiarizing himself with your share portfolio. How would you feel if nobody gave a medical student the chance to learn?'

Josh frowned. Wasn't she taking him seriously? 'With all due respect, madam, but in my profession, youngsters practice on corpses.'

'Ha!' Her short, sharp burst of amusement startled him. 'Professor, we too conduct autopsies on cadavers of failed businesses. Nkosinathi has already dissected some and must now have a look at a real live situation. It does not mean that our duty of care to you is lagging. We are not going to see KwaZulu Medical's imminent demise.'

Josh still had not touched his coffee. He watched Anna closely as she opened the KwaZulu Medical file. How well-meaning and sincere was she, really? he wondered.

* * *

It was the first time Anna saw the contents of the KwaZulu Medical folder. When Sipho contacted Vince Lewis, Hank heard of it and retained the account for his particular attention, preventing her from touching the thing. 'Let Nkosinathi Zuma cut his teeth on it,' he suggested with dismissive scorn.

'That's a brilliant idea,' Anna agreed. 'The boy deserves the opportunity. Shows him we trust him. It'll boost his confidence. Vince will oversee his work.'

'I'll keep an eye out as well, dear. I want to see what Nkosinathi would do if given free rein as if he were handling a discretionary account. It's just an academic exercise. You won't have to hassle yourself about it.'

Hank did not ordinarily take a personal interest in a client's account. Normally he would see it as hindering his objectivity and impartiality, diminishing the quality of the advice he offered. Then again, Anna reflected, Hank liked Nkosinathi and felt a fatherly responsibility towards the boy. If he thought Nkosinathi up to the task, why shouldn't the boy have a try?

A second call from Sipho the previous day asking for an appointment with Anna had raised Hank's hackles. 'You have enough work on your plate tomorrow,' he told her. 'I can probably spare the guy a few minutes. Don't concern yourself with KwaZulu Medical.'

Anna found Hank's attitude perplexing, but perhaps he feared laying too great a burden on her. Her workload could be tough at times.

* * *

She flipped through KwaZulu Medical's file, giving each page a cursory glance. Josh finally sipped his coffee. Why was it, he speculated, that in this woman's company he felt tense as a bowstring one minute and quite relaxed the next? He seemed to vacillate between anxiety and calm—up, down, up, down—like a puppet on invisible strings, which she controlled. Was it because here she was ensconced in her habitat? Once in his territory, her security would be blown out the window. He would call the shots. He anticipated that day eagerly. Too eagerly. Maybe contemplation of the abduction caused his apprehension. A troubled conscience before the crime was even committed. Guilt by intent.

Absently reaching for a biscuit while reading, Anna looked up, saying, 'After the recent fuss and bother about Gold Corp, do you want to retain their shares? I must point out, though, that now is not a good time to sell. The abortive shareholders' meeting caused the value to slump by 1.5 per cent. It's probably better to sell them when the furore dies and new buyers push the price up again. What did you pay for them initially?' She turned the pages more slowly. 'Here we are! You bought them at R1,000. They rose quickly to R1,200 then escalated more slowly to a peak of R1,530. Taking the

1.5 per cent decline into consideration, that would bring them back to about R1,507. Let's just check today's closing value and see how right we are.'

Josh watched Anna's faultlessly manicured slim fingers click the mouse at various places on the screen. Rows of figures and dates appeared.

'Oops! Bombed out! They've decreased to R1,504. Rats! They're not likely to rise before next week's meeting.' Anna looked at Josh, who appeared amused by her expressions. 'Do you want to keep them?' she asked, raising one eyebrow quizzically. 'You're not running at a loss.'

Josh scratched his head, wishing Sipho were around to make that type of decision. 'I'd like to stick with gold mines, but I'm open to suggestions,' he answered hesitantly.

Anna leaned back in her chair, twirling her gold pen between her fingers. 'How about something closer to home? Something scientific, closer to your line of business. I'm thinking of pharmaceutical companies. Just for interest's sake, let's have a look at them. See how they're going.' She rose to go to her bookcase. Information on pharmaceutical companies was stowed in a file on the top shelf, a little out of her reach even when standing on tiptoe. Josh saw her difficulty and came to the rescue immediately. Standing close beside her while lifting the pile of literature down, he found Anna diminutive and petite. She loomed big and formidable when she spoke with authority on matters in her field of knowledge, but at this instant, she appeared vulnerable. *Oh man, not that USB again*, he thought as he felt his heart beat.

'Thank you, Professor.' Anna smiled gratefully as they resumed their seats at her desk. For a moment she sat still, looking at the box file without opening it. Her chest felt tight, and drawing breath was not the reflex action one's body performs without conscious effort. Was she nervous? Ridiculous! Why should she be panicked in her own office? Collecting herself, she looked up at Josh, smiling.

'The reason I'm suggesting pharmaceutical companies to you, Professor, is because you would almost certainly know very early on about any new developments or research they conduct that could drive their share value up. You could act instantly. Does that sound good?' She laughed cheerfully with a resonance that began to resemble silver bells in Josh's ears too. In a more serious voice, she added, 'Or would you have a problem with that? Patients may feel you prescribe particular drugs because you have shares in the company that makes them.'

'Mrs De Bruyn, ethics are a luxury I cannot afford at the moment. But no . . . the dividend from such shares would be pumped back into the clinic to help update equipment. It would be very much in all our patients' interest.'

'I'm just a trifle uneasy about you having only gold-mining shares, Professor. It's like carrying all those proverbial eggs in one basket. If gold goes down, you go with it, having nothing else to fall back on. But the choice is yours. And I must warn you that there's an element of a gamble in it at present. With Madiba's release from prison, we are bound to have an election at some stage. How the market will react to a possibly black majority government is uncertain as yet. Foreign investment should return as sanctions are lifted, particularly if a new government can be persuaded to abolish exchange controls and open the banking system to foreign competition. Gold mining . . . ?' She spread her hands wide to indicate all possibilities. 'With hints of conflict to come in the Middle East, it could go through the roof. In that case, you'd want to buy more now to be prepared for that eventuality.' She smiled with the confidence of one who knew her business. Josh's eyes were fixed on her the whole time she spoke. Her chest tightened again, and she swallowed before continuing, 'All these factors need to be considered carefully. Perhaps you would like to think it over before you decide. It's important to keep one's fingers on both the political and financial pulse.'

'I think I'll leave that to Sipho Gwala, my administrator. When I get back, I'll tell him what you said and he can contact you.' Josh stood up to leave.

Anna reached into one of her desk drawers, handing him the information circular. 'Take this with you. It's the fortnightly newsletter we send to clients. I'll put you on the mailing list. Shall I mark it to Mr Gwala's attention? Yes?'

'That will be extremely kind, Mrs De Bruyn.'

'I'll ask our senior analyst to compile information on pharmaceutical companies for the next issue. It might help you and Mr Gwala with your deliberations. Then all you need to do is to let Vince Lewis know. He'll arrange the rest.'

'Thank you, madam. You have been very patient with me.' Josh was about to head for the lift but stopped on impulse. Giving Anna what he hoped was a relaxed smile, he said, 'I came out in search of dinner, really. I've had no lunch, and I'm starving. Would you like to join me, perhaps, madam?'

Her eyelids blinked in surprise. Had she heard right? She rarely accepted invitations from clients unless Hank was included. He had gone to the Rand Club for dinner with the Stock Exchange Committee president. He wouldn't be home before ten. It was seven thirty already. Maurice had finally made a reluctant exit. Anna realized she too needed more substantial nourishment than chocolate biscuits. It was time to shut shop. Returning the KwaZulu Medical folder to Hank's desk, she called to Josh over her shoulder, 'Thank you, Professor. I'd be delighted!' Turning to face him, she added with childish curiosity, 'Where are we going?'

'Have you ever tried Benny Shank's Bistro?'

'No, can't say I have. Who is Benny Shanks?'

'A chap I met at an Inkatha rally. We became good friends.'

Anna was about to turn the light off in Hank's room when she noticed a sheet of paper on the floor. Thinking it had dropped from the KwaZulu Medical file, she picked it up and unfolded it. It was a handwritten draft balance sheet as at the last quarter. The figures were distinct but shaky, obviously written by an unsteady hand. She looked at it closely. These days, even small enterprises like KwaZulu Medical produced computer-generated financial statements. A whiff of suspicion settled on her mind. Some of the amounts were not the same as on the printed version she had read earlier. Vaguely she wondered if the handwritten sheet had found its way into the folder unintentionally. Who had drawn it up? Who had seen it? Was someone cooking the books? Not wishing to keep Josh waiting, she slipped the sheet into her top desk drawer, making a mental note to compare it with the printed statements in the morning.

She found Josh sitting in the same armchair beside the pot plant which Nkosinathi had used on his first day. Seeing her, Josh stood up and pushed the lift button.

'Would you like to go to Benny Shanks?' he asked.

'Where is it?' The lift door opened, and they stepped inside.

'On Rivonia Road in Sandton. I can drive you home afterwards. It's not far from your house in Illovo.'

'How do you know where I live?' This man sure did his homework.

'It isn't hard to guess, Mrs De Bruyn. I can eliminate Orlando, Dobsonville, or Jabavu right away from the list of possible places.' The remark was made lightly, but Anna saw the mildly accusing look in Josh's eyes, as if living in an affluent part of town instead of a black township were a crime against society. She had seen the same expression on Solomon Mataka's features. It felt like disapproval levelled at her personally when he had pointed out the government would not allocate funds to his school for computers. As if she and she alone were responsible for discriminatory National Party (NP) policies. While understanding the sentiments that spawned the unspoken resentment, she wasn't about to apologize for her existence. Furthermore, she didn't want the underlying reproach from Josh. It hurt. He was seeing her in the wrong light. By the time they walked out of the lift and onto the street, unpronounced battle lines were defined between them. If he attacked, she would defend vigorously.

'Until recently, Professor, I would have come into conflict with the law had I wished to live in Orlando. I wasn't allowed to do so. And I did not formulate the Group Areas Act responsible for keeping you in a black area and me in Illovo. Nor was I involved in the implementation of laws that would never have permitted you to invite me to dinner in a white-owned restaurant.' With a disarming smile, she added, 'I would not be so bigoted as to deprive myself of the treat.' To Anna's satisfaction, Josh grinned at her. She had scored first. He acknowledged her simplistic victory diplomatically.

'Yes, at last apartheid will be a thing of the past. We can all breathe a little easier.'

Josh's red Toyota Corolla stood parked around the corner in Rissik Street. His heart sang with triumph as he opened the passenger door for Anna, watched her step in, and then closed it. This was going to be easier than he anticipated, he thought, while sprinting around to the driver's side. At this early stage, events had unfolded according to the logical sequence of his plan. First he had to gain Anna's trust. For this purpose he let De Bruyn Brothers represent KwaZulu Medical in the market. It gave him a legitimate reason to approach her. After two or three further outings together, she would become accustomed to being escorted by him. He would be just another client to her. It should lower her resistance when he eventually took her away from Johannesburg. Perhaps he could even convince her to come voluntarily. He'd hate to use force.

'Now, old man, keep that USB in check,' Josh admonished himself silently, having eyed the split in Anna's skirt, the same one she had worn at the shareholders' meeting. This time she had a hot-pink halter-neck top with it and a lightweight navy jacket over that. Josh wondered if she would feel naked without her inevitable selection of diamonds and gold ankle bracelet, like some people felt undressed without a wristwatch. The diamonds seemed a natural extension to the core of her personality. She carried them without conscious awareness of their value, the way other women wore costume jewellery.

Benny Shanks greeted them warmly when Josh introduced Anna.

'Sorry I didn't book in advance, I—'

Benny wouldn't hear any more. 'There's always a place for you here, you know that.' He led them to a discreetly positioned table for two, partially shielded from prying eyes by a bamboo partition.

'Heard a rumour about you having your own clinic somewhere. Near Vryheid, is it?'

'Yeah, I've been practising there since October last year.'

'Halala! Congratulations!' Benny offered the wine list to Josh, who shook his head.

'No thanks, man. It's not the end of the day for me yet. Have to get back to work soon. I'm the visiting specialist at Johannesburg General Hospital at present.' Glancing at Anna, he said, 'Would you like wine?' He motioned for Benny to pass the wine list to her.

'No thanks. I don't consume alcohol on my own. I'll have mineral water.'

Benny excused himself and instructed a waiter to take the order.

'This place is nice,' Anna said, feeling happier now that Josh no longer censured her.

'Sometimes Benny has a live band here but not tonight unfortunately. I can't believe you've never been in here.'

'Surprising, isn't it? It's the sort of place one looks at from the outside thinking, "I must try that one day," and then you never get around to it.'

The waiter arrived with soup.

'So you met Benny at an Inkatha rally. Interesting! Are you a member?' Anna diluted the spicy pumpkin soup with a mouth full of mineral water.

'No, Mrs De Bruyn. At the moment I am not a member of any political party, although I have considered joining Inkatha.'

'I have been thinking about the probability of an election. I never bothered to vote before because there's been so little choice. I can't relate to the apartheid system. I come from a very egalitarian country.'

'I know.' Josh smiled. 'You're Australian.'

'Hell! What don't you know about me? Fair dinkum!' Anna felt her privacy was violated for the second time that evening. She was on the verge of becoming cross. 'And what's so funny, Professor Mtolo?'

Josh's voice was rich and sensuous, his laughter wholesome. 'It's that expression of yours: *fair dinkum!*' He chuckled. 'I've read it in books by Australian authors but never heard anyone say it. What does it mean?'

For a fraction of a smile, Anna saw real fondness in Josh's eyes. A lump rose in her throat as she realized how easily she could respond in kind.

'It can mean two things,' she explained. 'If something is true, genuine, or real, it is "fair dinkum". Or it can be an expression of exasperation when things fail to measure up and you wonder why. Then it's usually "fair bloody dinkum". And I'm becoming truly exasperated with you.' Her voice rose an octave. 'How do you know so much about me? Have you had me under surveillance?'

'Please, madam!' Josh waved his white serviette in the air. 'I surrender. Don't shoot!' His amusement increased at the sight of Anna's traffic-light eyes, which glowed fiercely as if an electrical surge threatened to explode the bulbs. 'As the astute business lady you are,' he flattered, 'you will acknowledge that I too may inquire into a company and their management team before I entrust my resources to them.'

'Truce,' Anna conceded, mollified, although that was only a temporary state. Renewed calls to arms could sound at any time. 'Nobody is going to vote for the National Party, surely. Their support base will collapse in a heap. I can't help but be wary of the communist element within the ANC. Inkatha's significance lies in their free market-friendly policies. Business is far more comfortable with that. Shenge is demonized in the media at every turn, but I can't believe he's that bad. Sometimes I see the Inkatha president on television and feel that South Africa deprives itself of quality leadership by disregarding the man's advice. I mean, how can they get it so wrong? You can't condemn a man for refusing to join an armed struggle and at the same time accuse him of violence. That's too great a paradox.'

Josh nodded. 'You've hit the nail on the head. Shenge is the real pacifist in this country.'

'If that is how you feel, why hesitate to become a member of his party?'

'Because I want to live, Mrs De Bruyn. I don't see myself as a suitable vessel for ANC bullets.'

The waiter removed the soup bowls and refilled the glasses with mineral water.

Josh continued. 'Maybe it's okay if you don't actually become an office bearer in the party. But what's the use of joining if you can't roll up your sleeves and do a bit of work without fearing for your life?'

The main course arrived, consisting of beef, capsicum, and mushroom casserole. It was simmered with onions and tomatoes and served on a bed of rice.

'Since the mid 1980s, some 428 Inkatha office bearers have been assassinated. One of the latest casualties was a friend of mine . . . shot in KwaMashu on the ninth of February.' Josh took a fork full of rice. It went down the wrong way, and he coughed. 'Poor Mhlongo,' he spluttered. 'He was publicity secretary. A good man who wouldn't have hurt a fly.'

Anna realized Josh had choked on his anger. After quick mental arithmetic, she said, '428? That's an average of about one person a fortnight. How ghastly!'

Josh swallowed with difficulty and grasped for the mineral water. 'The incidents', he went on despite a scratchy throat, 'are even more frequent since the unbanning of the ANC and the return of their exiles.'

'That must be so debilitating for the party.' Anna said sympathetically. 'A man like yourself has so much to offer the organization, but you won't join because it is not safe. How many other people would feel that way? It deprives the party of so much expertise.' She was appalled.

'It's intended to dismantle Inkatha's effectiveness.' Josh had conquered the frog in his throat. His voice was normal again and his sadness reburied at the back of his mind. 'The ANC's commission of strategy and tactics national consultative conference stated as far back as June 1985 that homeland governments should be overthrown to create favourable conditions for the advancement of the peoples' war.'

'I see,' Anna said, absorbed in the topic. 'That would conveniently eliminate Inkatha as a political rival to the ANC. It brings them another step closer to the formation of a unitary state, which is surely their aim in keeping with communist theories.' A flashback brought the television image of the Inkatha president to Anna's mind. His statesman-like demeanour; the conviction in his clear voice; the quick, intelligent eyes darting behind bifocals, missing nothing; the wisdom and sorrow of decades etched in his serious face. Where did he find the tenacity to continue his work, battling continual, undeserved vilification and a hostile press? Where to find the fortitude to carry on when around you people are killed for no other reason than their loyalty to you? What do you say to the families of the dead party members? How do you sleep at night? 'I feel sorry for Shenge,' she sighed. 'He seems to have all the odds against him.'

Anna was not unaware of media coverage of the violence in Natal but had never found the time to inform herself accurately as to what lay at the root of it. It was something that had never really touched her before.

Josh began to explain while the waiter cleared the main course dishes. 'The present unfortunate situation is the result of numerous misunderstandings. The fire of political violence is kept burning by distortion of the truth when their own side stands to gain.' With a barely perceptible grin, he added, 'I guess both sides may be guilty of that at times.'

Benny brought the dessert personally. 'Enjoying the meal?' he asked with a friendly smile and a little bow towards Anna.

'It's great, Benny. I haven't eaten this well for quite a while.' Pleased with Josh's praise, Benny left them to their strawberries and cream.

'I think I know what you're saying, Professor. One thing I've noticed is that when Inkatha supporters are killed by ANC comrades, the newspapers print a small paragraph. When Inkatha's members retaliate, you see a huge headline, but the story makes scarce mention of the fact that the so-called Inkatha attack is a reprisal for violence they suffered at the hands of ANC aggressors.'

'You got it!' Josh was pleasantly surprised to find Anna seemingly on the Zulu side of the fence. 'Inkatha offers membership to whites too, you know. Why don't we both join?' he suggested half seriously. 'Benny is keen to get involved as well.'

'I'll think about it.' Anna said with a laugh.

'You see,' Josh continued, 'Inkatha became very popular when Shenge revived it in 1975. It wasn't a political party then but a cultural movement. Shenge figured that a cultural group could not be banned as easily as a political party. At that time, the ANC and PAC, or Pan Africanist Congress, had already endured fifteen years of banishment.'

'That left the black population without a political pressure group for a good while, didn't it?' Anna was aware of that much at least because Jan had always told her that any black organization walked a political tightrope, needing immense diplomatic skills to avoid banning by the NP on the one hand and branding as traitor by their own folk on the other if they were perceived as cooperating too closely with the white system.

'Yes, Shenge intended to fill that void, and by 1979, people flocked to Inkatha. On average, two hundred new members signed up each day. Their fully paid-up membership reached 350,000. That made Inkatha the largest black body South Africa ever saw. It galled the ANC, I can tell you.' Josh laughed with glee.

'The comrades were peeved,' he went on, still chuckling. 'The crunch came in 1979 at a London meeting between ANC and Inkatha officials. The ANC wanted Inkatha to join the armed struggle and endorse sanctions. Inkatha refused, proposing a multi-strategy approach instead.'

'I guess the ANC viewed that as a betrayal,' Anna surmised.

'Very much so.' Josh nodded. 'They felt that Shenge was concentrating enormous power around himself to push his own agenda. The ANC hoped to use Inkatha for mobilizing citizens into a force for revolutionary change. Shenge ruined that ambition, hence the eventual emergence of the UDF in 1983. The UDF became the ANC's instrument for not only the marvellous revolutionary change but also a campaign of reprisal and vendetta against Inkatha for the perceived slight and betrayal. That's the bedrock for the violence in Natal. Much blood has fertilized the topsoil since then.'

'I get the impression the churches aren't doing very much to stop the violence,' Anna commented with agnostic disapproval.

'Not a thing. Religious tolerance of UDF activities creates a good screen because people don't criticize the clergy. The World Council of Churches turns a blind eye too.' Josh took another gulp of mineral water. He was now wishing he had ordered wine. 'Madiba disappoints me more than anyone,' he said scornfully. 'His remedy is to send the army into Natal to stop the violence. The army is full of ex-MK men. How impartial are former guerrillas, politely called freedom fighters—or bluntly, terrorists—going to be, pray?'

'As for economic sanctions or disinvestment,' Anna reflected, 'that much I do know, it hurts the poorest of the poor. No way could Shenge have agreed to that. The province's unemployment rate stands at roughly 60 per cent anyway.'

The pager on Josh's belt suddenly erupted in shrill electronic beeps.

'Excuse me please, Mrs De Bruyn. Duty calls.'

Benny heard the sound as well and walked towards their table. 'Want to use the phone, Josh? Just over there.'

'Thanks, Benny. I'll have to run. Can you do me a big favour, please?'

'Sure, Josh. What is it?'

'Would you drive Mrs De Bruyn home for me? She doesn't live far from here.'

'No problem.'

Josh looked at Anna, saying with a note of regret, 'I'm sorry about this, Mrs De Bruyn. Thank you so much for giving me your time. I'll be in touch.'

Anna too found the abrupt ending of their dinner disappointing. They had just been getting to know each other. 'Thank you, Professor Mtolo, for the lesson in political history. It has clarified a good many issues in my mind. It was so pleasant to talk to you.'

'My pleasure entirely, madam.' He departed with a smile and a wave of his hand.

'Why don't you stay for a cup of coffee?' Benny sat on the chair Josh had vacated, looking ready for a lengthy chat.

'No thank you, Mr Shanks. I better move on. I'll settle the account if I may.'

'No, no, no!' Benny laughed, throwing his hands in the air. 'Josh is like my brother, and you wouldn't charge your brother, would you?'

Anna stood up. 'Could you call me a taxi, please?'

'No, I'll run you home. It's no inconvenience. Car's around the back.' Anna followed Benny out, wondering about his close friendship with Josh. They appeared to have little in common, so what bound them? Making conversation while Benny drove, Anna prompted him to talk about his connection with Josh.

'Professor Mtolo says he made your acquaintance at an Inkatha rally.'

'Yeah, it's a good while ago now. He just happened to be home from the USA on vacation. Oh gosh, neither of us will ever forget the day.' Benny, whom Anna thought quite talkative, was happy to relate events without further encouragement.

'I'd been following Inkatha's progress for . . . oh, many years, probably since about 1980. Then, in 1985, when the NP abolished the law that prohibited whites from joining black political parties, I started attending their rallies. I felt a bit out of place at first, but other whites gradually showed an interest. One day, they advertised a meeting at Ulundi, and I thought I might drive there, stay a couple of days, and hear Shenge speak. What better town than the party's base for hearing him? That's when I bumped into Josh and we got talking.'

A red traffic light stopped Benny in his tracks, and he asked Anna for directions to her address. When the lights turned green, Benny went on.

'Yeah, as I was saying . . . Josh and I discussed a lot of social justice stuff and the economy and so forth. After the rally, we were walking to our cars when two other chaps came towards us, blurting out a string of abuse. They were pissed to the eyeballs and spoiling for a fight. Giving Josh the evil eye, they said, "Zulu dog turd!" or words to that effect. It was hard to believe that something like that could happen in Ulundi. The creeps were obviously from elsewhere, just coming to stir up trouble. They got stuck into me then. Said that because I was white they couldn't expect any better of me than to go crawling to Inkatha meetings. They blocked our path and called me the Pretoria puppet's friend. "Shenge, the sell-out!" they called. "He's always sucking up to whites! Snake in the grass, that's what he is. Should be hit on the head." Venting their spleen, they then turned their attention back to Josh, threatening him with necklacing. "Wouldn't that Zulu traitor look great with a necklace?" It made me shudder. I once saw a young man perish. Briefly he looked like a walking torch with a petrol-filled tyre blazing around his neck.'

Another traffic light interrupted the recollections. 'It's the second turn to the left now, isn't it?' Benny flipped the indicator.

'How did you rid yourself of those two uncouth louts?'

'We told them to get lost and pushed past them, thinking that was the end of the matter. But no. They attacked us from behind. I had walked a little quicker than Josh and turned around when I heard him call a warning. I couldn't believe my eyes. One of the guys had his arm hooked around Josh's neck and held a knife to his throat. Luckily I had my pistol on me that day. I didn't hesitate. I shot the bloke in the leg. He yelled and let Josh go. By then his companion pulled a gun also, aiming at me. Josh saw him and hurled himself at the guy, grabbing his weapon off him. The scumbags surrendered after that, and Josh patched up the injured rat.'

'What a story!' Anna's eyes were wide with horror.

'That's why Josh and I are like brothers now. We saved each other's lives that day.'

* * *

Anna was in the process of downing her routine cup of morning coffee, a daily ritual she performed as soon as she arrived at work. Insisting that a few minutes of contemplation before the pressures of the day set in helped her map out her work in the best order, she took advantage of the peace before the telephones sprang to life.

This morning, she came to the office in her BMW instead of travelling with Hank. She would have done that yesterday also, except she had forgotten about Hank's dinner at the Rand Club. Foolishly she rejected the offer of his Mercedes, succumbing instead to an urge to have another look at a dress she admired in a shop window before finding a taxi home. And that was when Josh had caught her. She shook her head, disbelieving her carelessness. She had ended up being driven by two strange men in one night. Better not make a habit of that! She grinned, wondering if she could keep her own counsel. Josh said he'd be in touch. She hoped he would. Talking to him was enjoyable and informative despite his being a little prickly at times.

She opened her top desk drawer to pull out a memo pad when she saw the KwaZulu Medical draft balance sheet she had put there before leaving last night. Instantly she recalled her misgivings and remembered to examine the figures more thoroughly. She retrieved the KwaZulu Medical file from Hank's desk, intending to return it before he arrived after his check-up with Dr Elbenstein. She still hadn't worked out why Hank was so strange about KwaZulu Medical. She couldn't think of a suitable word to describe his edginess. *Why?* she asked herself more than once.

Placing both the printed sheet and the handwritten draft side by side, Anna compared where they differed. Identifying the finer discrepancies without the audit trail that referred back to the general journal showing balanced day adjustments made her task more like guesswork. One thing stood out clearly, though: income was grossly understated in the printed, or official, version of the balance sheet. That pointed to the possible intention to evade tax. The dividends from the Gold Corp shares were included in both balance sheets, but the handwritten one showed further substantial interest income from an overseas source—the Union Bank of Switzerland and a number written beside it. Why would, or how could, an insignificant player in the financial field like KwaZulu Medical have need of a numbered Swiss account? If the amount of the interest received was an indication, the deposit in that account was not minute. Whoever compiled the draft—Mr Sipho Gwala presumably—had placed the figure under 'Investments—local, Gold Corp' and 'Investments— foreign, Union Bank, Switzerland'. The Swiss funds were omitted from the computer printout altogether, and the capital figure was altered to balance the statement. 'I smell rotting seafood . . . decidedly fishy!' Anna commented to herself. Total openness and accountability was a two-way street to her. She applied it to the large corporations whose shares De Bruyn Brothers traded and expected it from small clients like KwaZulu Medical as well. Tax evasion was not condoned. And, she pondered, where did the money in that Swiss account come from? Not the ANC. The loan and repayments were shown clearly on both sheets. Perhaps Joshua Mtolo had generous donors in America? If he came back, she would question him a little. Till then, the information was best kept to herself.

* * *

'I'm getting old.' William Rosenberg let the depressing sentiment, articulated with a deep sigh into his shaving mirror, take hold. When a man chose a mistress for the quality of the conversations he had with her instead of the physical temptations, he was ageing rapidly. But the process wasn't quick enough to provide relief from the void he faced without her. Indira Naidoo, the exotic love of his life, was leaving Johannesburg shortly. Visits would become infrequent.

'There's always the telephone,' she tried to comfort him. William thought that a poor substitute for seeing and touching her. His toils and troubles evaporated into thin air in her company. Nothing would ever compensate for one look of smouldering passion from her big dark eyes or feeling the smooth texture of her long black hair, which shone with a lustre William swore he had never seen on other women. She dropped the bombshell of her departure during their regular weekly dinner date. She had resigned from her position at Baragwanath Hospital and accepted a new appointment with KwaZulu Medical, to William a somewhat questionable private clinic near Vryheid. A place where, in William's opinion, her qualifications as a surgeon were wasted. And all in support of a philosophy.

'Why? Indira, why, for god's sake?' William looked at her, his eyes begging her to reconsider. 'I can set you up in your own practice if you've had enough of Baragwanath.'

Indira shrugged her shoulders, giving William that smile that till now had always held the promise of tenderness. 'I know you would, William, because you're a gentleman, but you don't quite understand how I feel.'

Feelings were elusive, abstract products of impractical minds to William. How could she reject his offer? What was the point of leaving Baragwanath and its reliable salary for a new, untested enterprise where her income would be reduced drastically merely to help little kids recover from the brutality that politically motivated violence in black townships inflicted on them? However worthy the ideal, it made no sense to him.

'I'm sorry, William, but I told you before, I've felt like a rudderless ship since my husband's death. I need a new purpose in life, a cause to which I can apply myself, something to give me direction.'

'Can't I help, Indira?' William held both her hands in his across the table. She looked devastating in the aqua-coloured sari, which he adored. He had bought her the gold and sapphire jewellery she wore with it.

'William, you're a married man. How can you possibly offer me the emotional security that a sense of belonging to a good man can give a woman?'

So that was it, he thought. Disappointment fell into his stomach like a brick. She wants marriage. She isn't content to be a mistress, no matter what inducements I offer her. She had not one materialistic bone in her desirable body. What could he do? Divorce Melody? Her name was a travesty. She sounded like a foghorn when she nagged and was all but tone-deaf. Still, she had been a good mother to his sons and deserved respect for that. No, divorce was out unless Melody initiated it. William figured he had to cut his losses. He gave it one more hopeful try.

'But didn't you say you lacked the money to buy into the KwaZulu Medical partnership?'

'Yes, that's true. My late husband's textile business was in debt when he died, and it's left me with very little after the creditors got their money. I cracked my nest egg to pay the staff. But it doesn't matter. The three partners at KwaZulu Medical made no personal monetary contribution towards the business. Their working capital comes from the ANC as a loan.'

'What?' William was surprised. He hadn't heard that story before. 'What's the ANC trying to do? Buy votes for the upcoming election?'

'Maybe.' Indira laughed, her voice deep with eternal unfathomable mystery like the fullness of the deepest blue of her sapphire earrings.

'Indira, you have all the skill in the world as a surgeon. You can't work to your fullest capacity in such a small place. It's substandard.'

She tossed her hair back, laughing. 'Who told you that? You exaggerate both my ability and the inferiority you assume at KwaZulu Medical. Have you ever seen the place? Sure, they have only one operating room, but it's better equipped than Baragwanath. I can make myself at home there quite easily.' She looked past William while thinking aloud. 'I'm not sure if I'll live in the staff quarters or find my own accommodation. Sometimes it's good to keep a little distance from work.'

William became depressed. Indira had taken stock of her future and had crossed him off her emotional inventory. She was building a new life in which he did not feature.

'Where does that crowd get so much money for all their modern stuff?' William muttered to himself, disgruntled. 'I know they hold a very small parcel of Gold Corp shares, but I'd say the dividend from that wouldn't even cover the depreciation on their equipment. It's a puzzle.'

'I'm told they receive donations from NGOs and WHO,' Indira informed William. 'Professor Mtolo spent over a decade in the USA. That's enough time to establish valuable contacts.'

William replied with a derogatory grunt. Both realized their evening together was ruined. Might as well drive home. They said good night outside the restaurant and, without a kiss, walked to their cars. Indira turned around once. 'I'll phone you when I've settled in,' she called after him. William stepped into his vehicle in a cloud of sulkiness, his farewell the slamming of the door.

* * *

Hank De Bruyn entered his office with a thoughtful expression. He lowered himself into his big leather chair just as Anna and Maurice came through the door, wanting to know Dr Elbenstein's latest prognosis.

'He says I should take a holiday.' Hank responded to their urgent questions. 'I know he means retirement, but I'm not ready for that yet.' Hank laughed as if to say 'That man can talk.'

'But', he continued with a smile at his wife, 'the holiday bit doesn't sound half out of place. Feel like seeing your folk in Sydney, Anna?'

'That would be great, Hank. When can we go?'

'The sooner the better, according to Elbenstein. It depends on when Franz has time to come in here and take over for the duration.' Hank saw the excitement in Anna's eyes. As a rule they flew to Sydney every twelve to eighteen months to visit her parents, but the last two years had been so busy that travel was out of the question. Franz could not leave his work either. Also, Rosemary, his wife, had given birth to their third child, another reason for him to be preoccupied.

'You might want a little break too, Maurice. Vince and good old Mrs George can help Franz hold the fort till we return.' Hank's suggestion sounded inviting.

'I'll take you up on that,' Maurice accepted.

They left Hank to start his work. Anna would wait till the evening to discuss Dr Elbenstein's advice at home. Hank needed encouragement to overcome his reluctance to talk about his health. She knew he found some days insufferably long and tiresome, yet he brushed her concerns aside with light comments, his favourite being 'Don't worry, dear. Weeds never die.'

Hank's phone rang. Anna heard him pick it up. Hers sounded next and Maurice's thereafter. The business of the day had begun. She could hear his comments.

'Ah, Captain Broadbent, what news? These EEM fellows haven't stirred for a while . . . What? You're holding two Cape Town men for questioning?' Hank coughed, a little short of breath. 'Are they saying anything? Is that a promising lead, do you think?' As he talked, Hank drew trees and birds on a notepad lying next to the KwaZulu Medical folder. 'No, unfortunately our private investigators have drawn a blank too . . . no idea who these guys are. Yes, yes, I instructed them to pass information to you if they come up with anything useful. Okay, right. Thanks for the call. Goodbye.'

His eyes came to rest on the KwaZulu Medical file while hanging up the telephone. *Miserable little crowd*, he thought. They weren't worth bothering about, just a thorn in his side. From his in tray he dug out the brief report he had asked Nkosinathi to write. Training this enthusiastic youngster was one of his pleasures these days. He turned the pages and laughed out loud as he read Nkosinathi's hypothetical recommendations. In theory, Nkosinathi would have KwaZulu Medical diversify and broaden the spectrum of their investments to include pathology and research laboratories as well as medical benefits and indemnity insurances. By and large, the youngster had sound ideas. Yes, Vince could give it genuine consideration, particularly the insurance part. Might be worth mentioning it to that Gwala fellow next time he phoned. Vince found Gwala easier to talk to than Mtolo. Gwala had the business acumen. And that Mtolo guy was arrogant anyway. The man's body language was cocky, overconfident, his mien haughty and defiant. With a sigh, Hank pushed his chair back far enough to rest his feet on the left corner of his desk. *Might as well admit it, Hanky-boy*, he thought. *You're as jealous as all hell.* That cheeky kaffir, Mtolo. The way his eyes ate Anna! By Christ, yes. That guy took a fancy to her. God, how many men did he know who'd harboured secret affections for Anna? He had never been upset about it before. Why now? Why Mtolo? Was it because Mtolo threatened to become real competition? He's younger—not much. Half a decade or so. Not much, really. Unlike the other overindulged flabby oafs who wanted Anna, Mtolo had intelligence, good looks, and undeniable masculine sex appeal. How long could Anna resist that powerful combination of traits? 'Hope they never meet again,' Hank murmured to himself while lifting his feet off the desk. He straightened in his chair, shaking his head. What an idiot he was, letting unworthy thoughts contaminate the time that may be left for him on this earth. He hoped it was a long while yet. He would take Anna to Sydney and extend their stay twice as long as in previous years.

* * *

Freddie Bonga was growing up. He matured so fast his uncle couldn't contain his astonishment and pride when the boy picked up a second part-time job. Freddie had broadened his horizons. He retained his passionate desire for motorbikes but added another interest to his daily work—cooking. Freddie discovered he enjoyed to cook while his temporarily bedridden aunt suffered a dreadful bout of influenza. The preparation of palatable dishes to tempt her normally not inconsiderable appetite back to its usual healthy level gave him immense pleasure. By the time his aunt recovered, Freddie wondered how best to derive a profit from his new-found skills. He loitered around the back doors of Vryheid's restaurants, approaching anyone he saw.

'You want cook? Apprentice? Me . . . I can do!'

His back-door vigils bore fruit when a kind-hearted proprietor gave him a chance. Managing to become damned near indispensable to his employer, Freddie never looked back. He had come of age in other ways as well. The restaurant proprietor's genuine appreciation of Freddie's help gave him the confidence to go strutting his stuff as his own man. No longer would he head blindly to where a particular bike gang leader dictated. Freddie had ceased being a follower. It sucked. If he couldn't be the gang's boss, they would have to do without him. Freddie was no longer the sheep. Let someone else do the bleating. When the gang dared to park their bikes outside the Zebra, Freddie's restaurant, he would tell them firmly to move away. The gang's taunts that he was doing a woman's job never affected him.

He found fulfilment at the Zebra. True to its name, everything within was black-and-white-striped, from the tablecloths and napkins to Freddie's apron and tall hat. He made good progress. Outgrowing his humble beginnings as gofer, scraping and rinsing the plates before stacking the dishwasher, he worked his way up to cooking simple entrees. Thereafter, it seemed like a short step to the soups and vegetables. Soon the day would come when he was entrusted with the planning of an entire menu.

If there was one thing he lacked, it was a girlfriend. Mostly he was too busy to think about girls. Occasionally when his boss teased him, Freddie realized he was the only young man among his friends who was minus a girl.

'Freddie, why do you save all your money for machines . . . motorbikes? Find yourself a girl. Go out and have fun. You're only young once, lad. Maturity creeps up on you faster than you think,' Mr Bollard, the Zebra's owner, advised. Freddie knew he meant well, but the comments drove home secret longings and a strange aloneness despite him now seeing himself as a man of the world. One day, he knew, he would have a woman in his life. He'd get the girl he wanted soon enough. She would be clever and pretty, like Cindy Khumalo but younger. He already had enough money for three heads of cattle out of the eleven that were the average rate of bride-price payment. If he continued saving his money, he'd be ready to claim his wife.

* * *

Chapter 5

The Anniversary Ball

'Fair bloody dinkum! I hate telephones.'

Hearing Anna's cry for sympathy, Maurice popped his head around the door frame and pulled a clownish face when she lifted the receiver for the seventh time in a row.

'C'mon, Aussie, c'mon!' he sang, bunching his fists like the sporting symbol of the boxing-gloved kangaroo. His antics made her laugh as she said, 'Anna De Bruyn speaking!'

'Mrs De Bruyn! How are you? Has anyone ever told you that you have a very sexy laugh on the phone?'

Anna froze. Her left hand, which held the receiver, trembled. She hoped Maurice hadn't seen. Her reputation for being strong and imperturbable would be in tatters.

'Flattery will get you nowhere, Professor Mtolo,' she purred softly.

'No, regrettably not,' he replied, laughing. 'But maybe another dinner at Benny's will. You'll love this, Mrs De Bruyn. Benny has a string quartet playing tonight, the Khemese Brothers and their friend Makhosini Mnguni. It's an occasion not to be missed. You'll come, won't you?'

'Yes, of course. I'll meet you there. What time?'

There was a brief pause. The mischief had left Josh's voice when he said, 'I'll pick you up at seven.'

'That's very considerate of you, Professor, but I have my car today. I do look forward to seeing you. Thank you for the invitation. *Hamba kahle*. Goodbye!'

She hung up before he could say another word. For a moment he sat, still holding the receiver. Saying goodbye in Zulu hadn't softened the blow. The albino jungle cat had become cunning. She avoided his close proximity by using her own car. Perhaps she wasn't so easily ensnared after all. He would have to restructure his plans to make them infallible.

'Women! How can a man ever understand them?' he remarked to nobody in particular. Two days ago he had arrived at Johannesburg General Hospital in the late afternoon to become absorbed instantly in pressing problems regarding the patients he had seen some weeks ago. He was given so little notice that he had no time to alert Cindy to his coming. Two consecutive evenings now he had called at her house to find she was out. He did not want to ring her at work because to him, calling Cindy out of class was as bad as his receiving non-urgent messages while talking to patients.

What could Cindy be doing? When had he seen her last or spoken to her? Not since his previous stint as visiting specialist in Johannesburg. Their relationship was hardly like that of a betrothed couple, he had to admit. 'Good friends and sometime lovers' was the more accurate term for their exchange.

'But be that as it may . . .' he sighed. Not speaking the rest of his thoughts, his eyes gained hardness and determination. Anna and that half-million US dollars from her old man were his greater concern. How much patience could he afford? Time was passing so quickly. He did not want to see his research project stall due to lack of funds. Hank De Bruyn must contribute—and fast.

Of equal importance was a quick visit to Baragwanath to finalise Dr Naidoo's entry into the KwaZulu Medical partnership.

Indira would be a tremendous help because neither Tom nor Peter had significant surgical skills. Josh himself had none. Her presence would save time in emergencies, and that meant saving lives. Josh looked at his watch. He had paperwork to plough through before going to Benny's. He'd better hurry. A pile of forms needed filling in and completing, but the necessary concentration eluded him.

Anna! He must summon the resolve to steel his heart against her sweet vulnerability and her traffic-light eyes. Damned USB! It jeopardized the whole show. By all that was holy! He wasn't a lovesick schoolboy. Why couldn't he see Anna for what she was? The symbol of the modern-day equivalent of colonialism. Men and women like her who held an African country's purse strings were no better than the colonial overlords of earlier decades. He had to get among them, infiltrate them, because only without their presence in the country or, at the very least, in-depth knowledge of their activities, could complete independence be achieved. The late Robert Sobukwe, founding president of the PAC, described white liberals like Anna and her ilk as beneficiaries of the apartheid system. As such, they would pay lip service to the African cause without doing anything concrete to further it. Could that truly be said of Anna? Wasn't she putting her money where her mouth was? Cindy would have no computer school without Anna's initiative and intervention. Josh threw his pen down. His heart beat too fast. The USB had won for the present. He couldn't wait to see her.

* * *

Josh and Anna converged on Benny Shanks's bistro simultaneously, parking side by side in the guests' car park. Josh stepped out of his Corolla. He watched Anna sweep from her BMW and come towards him with her trademark public relations smile.

'Professor Mtolo . . .' she said in a sultry half-whisper. 'It's so good to see you.'

She was dressed in a figure-hugging forest-green frock with lace-trimmed sleeves. Her make-up was flawless, and her ever-present diamonds sparkled as if reflecting the glow in her green eyes. USB paralysed Josh's tongue. Placing his hand on her shoulder, he led her inside. Benny came towards them, the grin on his face seemingly connecting both ears.

'Wow . . . you're back again! Great to see you, man.' He nodded to Anna. 'You too, Mrs De Bruyn.' Anna craned her neck to watch the four musicians unpack their instruments for the gig.

'It's a full house today,' Benny remarked as he scanned his candlelit tables to accommodate them. 'Don't know where to seat you,' he said with a look of discomfort. 'Do you mind sharing a table tonight?'

'Not at all, Benny. Sorry to put you in such a spot. I seem to have a talent for doing that.' Josh apologized, and they followed Benny to a table for four at which only two guests sat: a man and a lady, talking animatedly. Benny was about to ask them if they minded company when the man looked directly at Anna. Beside her, Josh stiffened. She felt his hand tighten on her shoulder as mutual recognition prompted the man to rise and extend his hand to her. Anna smiled delightedly.

'Mr Mataka! This is a pleasant coincidence. We haven't spoken in ages.'

'No, unfortunately,' Solomon agreed. 'But now is our chance to remedy the shortcoming.'

While responding to Solomon's amicable smile and greeting, Anna noticed that the lady's eyes drilled holes right through Joshua. Did she know him? Josh's hand dropped from Anna's shoulder. Solomon ignored the exchange, saying, 'Cindy, your wish is granted. You always wanted to meet Mrs Anna De Bruyn, and here she is!' Turning his head towards Anna, he said, 'Meet my colleague, Cindy

Khumalo.' Josh stood motionless and perplexed when both women burst into laughter.

'Nkosinathi has told me so much about you.' Cindy giggled, a note of relief in her voice. When Josh had entered with that glittering white doll beside him, she had misconstrued the event altogether. This, she told herself, was the lady whose generosity maintained the computer school. Yet, she wondered, did men generally go out with their financial advisors? A quick business lunch maybe, but the appearance of the two of them here indicated a certain level of intimacy. Cindy found that unsettling. She was about to make a pointed remark to Josh but thought better of it. He too had a right to ask what she was doing here with Solomon. Breaking the questioning eye contact with Josh when she heard Anna speak again, Cindy smiled brightly.

'And Nkosinathi never stops talking about you either.'

'I hope he gave me a good reference.' Cindy's eyes glowed with pleasure at the mention of her star pupil.

'Absolutely,' Anna assured her. 'As his teachers, he is a credit to both of you. He has decided to study law next year, corporate law to be precise. And he will make a success of it, I have no doubt whatsoever. We raised his pay as a reward for his diligence and a carrot to keep on trying.'

'That's really good to hear, Mrs De Bruyn.' Solomon signalled a waiter. 'Let us offer libations to our young generation and pray that all those not as fortunate as Nkosinathi will also find a purpose in life.'

'Well said,' Josh approved and they sat down.

Within a short time, it became clear to Anna that the men treated each other with cool reserve. Why was that? Shouldn't they be friends? Enlightenment came when she overheard Josh speaking quietly to Cindy while the musicians played their first piece.

'Where have you been, Cindy? I called at your house last night and the night before, but you were out. You had me worried.'

'Is that so?' she replied slowly, liquid sarcasm dripping from each word. 'And why shouldn't I be out? Must I sit at home hoping and wishing that my esteemed fiancé can spare me a small fraction of his busy life?'

The music rose to a mighty crescendo, and Anna heard no more of the conversation. Solomon smiled as if about to talk to her, but in reality, Anna thought, probably eavesdropping as well. He conveyed his enjoyment of the music with enthusiastic applause. Anna sat bemused. She often found herself wondering if there was a woman in Josh's life. Obviously there was, although she did not look entirely happy. It was plain to see Josh neglected her and she turned to Solomon for solace. How would Josh stomach that? Anna contemplated the feud resulting from a Zulu and a Xhosa competing for the attention of the same woman. World War Three? The political differences between the tribes were bad enough. Add jealousy to the equation, and the situation could become explosive. Joshua and Solomon were evenly matched adversaries. Equally tall and fit, they were stunning men for any woman to behold. Cindy would find it hard to choose between them.

Anna determined to make the most of the meal and music while maintaining neutrality till she could excuse herself without causing offence. When the string quartet played the last item, the African lullaby 'Ntyile Ntyile', Anna selected the moment as her cue to leave.

'Do I hear a lullaby?' she asked, her head to one side and smiling.

Josh nodded in answer.

'It must be the signal for me to retire home to bed. I have a full day tomorrow.'

'Stay! Listen a little longer.' Solomon placed his hand on Anna's.

'It's a pretty piece of music about two birds roosting in a thorn tree as evening falls,' Josh explained in his deep, melodious voice. 'They lament the sadness of life but find comfort in each other's company. Their conversation becomes a lullaby.'

Anna had the distinct impression both men wished she would remain to stabilize the highly volatile night.

* * *

Disaster! The only correct description befitting the previous evening at Benny's was that of unmitigated disaster. 'A repeat must be avoided at all cost,' Josh vowed as if taking a blood oath. Even Benny noticed that table number 6 was a minefield.

'Listen, man, I'm sorry if I put my foot in it tonight.' Benny drew Josh aside as he left the bistro with Cindy. 'I should never have put you on that table. But how was I to know?' He tilted his head in Cindy's direction. 'You canny old baboon, you! You never told me you were engaged. She's very attractive. Marry her before the other guy gets her. That's what I say,' Benny, the confirmed bachelor, advised like the armchair sportsman who always knows the best angle at which to kick a ball.

Anna had retreated from the embarrassing scene after the meal when the music stopped. Her exit had left the remaining three protagonists with no peacekeeper. Solomon expressed his dislike of Joshua freely. In imitation of the best defence counsel, he twisted Josh's every comment to render its meaning ludicrous, a supercilious attempt to humiliate Josh.

Cindy sat in disgusted silence, disapproving of Solomon's behaviour but even more furious with Josh for bringing Anna.

'There was something in the way you both looked at each other,' she argued on the way home. Solomon, for all his trying, couldn't stop Josh driving Cindy home. 'And what was your hand doing on her shoulder in that familiar pose?'

'That's just an automatic thing with me.'

'Bullshit!'

'Cindy! Such language! I haven't heard that from you before.'

'Well, man, you live and learn.'

'Cindy, be reasonable, please. I've lost count of the many patients on whose shoulders I've placed my hand in reassurance. It's just something I do. I don't think about it.'

'You should be able to invent better explanations.' Cindy opened the car door, got out, and slammed it so hard Josh feared she had caused damage. Before she could open her front door, he hurried to her side, holding her close while she fumbled for the key.

'Cindy, listen! You are imagining things.'

'No, I'm not!' she countered in heated temper, twisting out of his arms.

'Anna's a business contact, nothing more.'

'Pigs might fly!'

'Stop being irrational, Cindy, and try to think calmly. Anna is married, remember? Am I going to antagonize her old man? What would that do for KwaZulu Medical's share portfolio? I rely on both of them too much.'

'Then why didn't you invite her husband as well?'

'He had other business.'

'Yeah, right . . . whatever!'

Cindy unlocked her door. She stepped in, turned, and smiled at Josh with exaggerated sugar sweetness.

'Thanks for the lift home,' she laughed with a pain that surprised her and closed her door firmly, leaving Josh on the outside.

'I'll still be here tomorrow. If you want to go out, leave a message at the hospital,' he called loud enough for her and her neighbours to hear. No reply sounded from inside, but by the next evening, Cindy relented and welcomed him in when he came to take her to dinner.

The long drive back to Vryheid gave Josh time to examine himself. Golly, his private life was a mess, he thought, shaking his head with lack of comprehension. He began to envy Peter and Tom, who enjoyed such blissful family life. So straightforward, so totally uncomplicated—married to warm-hearted women who were excellent mothers, who loved their children endlessly and placed their personal ambitions, if they had any, well behind the interests of the family unit. *What great souls they are.* Josh grinned. *What boring women they are.* Predictably, his zodiac sign's alter ego kicked in. Like many Geminis, he was a prince of ambivalence, unable to make up his mind, causing him to wonder on the other hand where the challenge lay in pursuing such plain women. A man didn't have to work particularly hard to gain their attention, affection, and regard. What reward could there possibly be when they were eventually caught? What games of the mind could be played out with women like those? He did not devalue his friends' wives, but they weren't like Cindy, who indicated clearly that she wasn't playing ball if he didn't treat her well. And they weren't like Anna, whose eyes and voice taunted constantly, 'Touch me if you dare.' Josh knew the answer lay within himself. He was attracted to women who appreciated him as a man, not superficially like a one night stand but a combined appeal to both his psyche and sexuality. Such women kept him on his toes. Josh laughed. He knew himself pretty well, he thought.

As he swung the Corolla off the main road and onto the driveway towards his hospice, he whistled with satisfaction and pride. Sipho was right. They had worked hard and achieved much in a comparatively short time. The place looked neat, surrounded by lawns and flower beds. Sick people needed a touch of brightness and cheer. The buildings were in good repair. A casual glance would not reveal that the clinic was run on a shoestring budget. At his approach, Sipho opened the electronic gate from within, saving him the trouble of fishing for the key card in the glove box. Tom and Peter came out, waving to him from the top step. A strange agitation in their gestures alerted him. They awaited his return. Now what was the matter?

He parked to the left of the stairs in full view of Sipho's window. The area was reserved for the doctors' cars. As soon as he stepped out, Tom came down.

'Glad you're back, Josh.' Tom wasn't smiling. 'We have a problem.'

'Big or small?' Tom's voice set Josh on edge.

'Hellish! A patient came in with what I'm certain is Ebola. I've seen it before.'

'Shit, that's all we need!' Josh flew up the stairs, taking them two at a time. 'Where's the patient? We don't have the facilities to handle such infectious cases.'

'I've got him in the garden beside the outpatient entrance. His cousin brought him about three hours ago. Where the hell can we put him?' Tom looked at a loss.

'Have you contacted the health department?'

'Yeah, first thing.'

'Good, good. We have to get him to Durban, where they have specialists in tropical diseases. Ring the university teaching hospital. They may be of assistance.'

'I did. They're sending help from Pietermaritzburg. Hopefully it'll be speedy because the patient's blood pressure is falling and his temperature is rising by the hour. He's becoming critical. We have to put him somewhere till he can be transferred to a bigger institution. He's got no idea where he picked up the virus. Come and take a look at him.' Tom urged, tugging at Josh's sleeve while he stood looking at the ground, thinking.

'Where's Fernando?' Instead of following Tom, Josh strode into the administration office.

'Sipho! Emergency!' Josh called when Sipho appeared. He didn't have to be told. Tom and Peter's frantic movements were sufficient indication.

'Call Fernando and two helpers. We need the wine cellar refitted post haste. Tell them to get rid of the useless junk in there. Bring a bed down instead of that bunk. Remove the stupid wine rack and replace it with storage shelves. Whatever equipment we use for this patient cannot come out of that room again. It must be destroyed later.' Josh turned to Tom, who still hovered at his elbow. 'Do we have enough protective gear for ourselves? If not, improvise, but be very careful. It's the best we can do for now.'

Slowly Josh followed Tom to where the Ebola patient lay stretched out on a garden lounge with a sun umbrella to shade him. 'This is bad,' Josh said as they walked towards the two men. 'We have to quarantine the patient's cousin as well. Heaven knows how many people he's been in contact with. It could develop into our worst nightmare.' Josh looked down at the patient, a young man of about seventeen or eighteen years of age.

'Have I got malaria, Doc?' the teenager asked, trying to lift his head.

At least he's still lucid, Josh thought while studying the youth's face. He extracted the patient's file, which Tom had written and still carried tucked tightly under his arm. Something about the young man's face struck him as familiar. His name was Samora, age seventeen years, ten months.

'No, Samora, it's not malaria,' Josh said quietly. Turning aside, he murmured to Tom, 'Here's divine justice. It's the young bloke who killed the kids in the minibus in Edendale all those months ago. He must have slipped over the border to avoid a murder charge, and now he's back, sick.'

* * *

Josh heaved a sigh of relief. Leaning back in his chair, he stretched his arms above his head and yawned. Samora and his cousin had been transported away three weeks ago to be treated elsewhere. No other Ebola cases came to his attention during that time or since. The wine cellar was decontaminated and locked. His staff remained healthy. The potential catastrophe was averted. It was time for a well-earned rest. Margo brought him the coffee he requested, and he pushed the paperwork on Samora away to make room for the tray.

Anna . . . The rare, momentary lulls in his daily activities brought unbidden thoughts of her. Somehow he had to make good for the miserable date at Benny's. Would she agree to see him in private again after that fiasco? Funny how he thought of their meeting as a date when that was not the intention. He must let her choose the place for their next get-together. Not only would that indicate his regret about their last tryst but it also held two considerable benefits. Firstly, it would make Anna feel at ease in familiar surroundings, and secondly, she would doubtless select a venue far too exclusive and expensive for that Xhosa peasant Solomon Mataka to frequent. It would be a blessing to know his ugly face wouldn't spoil anyone's appetite. Josh scowled. Why ever did Cindy bother with him? That lamentable excuse for a man had neither finesse nor manners.

Taking a slurp from his coffee, Josh rose and began pacing his office. Next time he saw Anna, he would tell her more about KwaZulu Medical. If he could capture her interest sufficiently, she may ask to come here. She may wish to be shown around. That would play into his hands beautifully. It would negate coercion on his part to secure her cooperation. Then it was merely a matter of preventing her from telling anyone where she was going. That might not be easy. Perhaps a sudden swoop on her, taking her with him before she had time to think, was more effective. The operation required detailed planning, but time was too precious for indecision and procrastination. He needed money. Sipho applied to various NGOs for grants and officials from a number of them visited the clinic but no funds arrived. It left him little choice but to extract money from Hank De Bruyn or anyone else with surplus resources.

He drank the rest of his coffee before commencing his round of the children's wing. It was past the kids' sleeping time already, and the lights in the ward were low. Nodding to the night sister, he walked slowly from patient to patient, shining a torch onto the charts attached to the foot of each bed. The ward was too small by far, but it was the best he could provide. He divided the area in half with ten beds in both the boys' and the girls' sections. He walked the length of the room, checking on the boys and then the girls at the far end. Satisfied that all slept soundly, he turned and walked back again. One boy groaned and cried out in his sleep as Josh passed his bed. 'Skull Cracker again,' he worried as he stepped beside the eleven-year-old boy's bed. The child tossed and turned, throwing off his blanket and twisting his heavily bandaged head from side to side on the pillow. He was dreaming, living through another nightmare.

None of it would do him much good, Josh thought. 'Hey . . . easy, Skull Cracker,' he whispered, covering the patient again. He placed his hand on the boy's shoulder. 'Sandile, *uyalala manje*,' he said quietly. 'Sandile, sleep now.' The nasty dream banished, the child drifted into deeper slumber.

Sandile Duma, alias Skull Cracker, was the living example of Josh's depressing predictions regarding the long-term effects of violence and brutality on the mental health of the young. KwaZulu Medical existed primarily for children like him.

Josh was convinced the hand of fate was at work when Samora had been brought in with Ebola, and later in the week Sandile came, accompanied by his distressed parents. Josh recognized Sandile instantly as the boy in the minibus who had suffered facial injuries from flying glass. He had lost the sight in one eye, and his face bore the scars of his ordeal.

Dr Peter Shabalala was in casualty the day Mr Duma carried his badly concussed son through the door. Sandile had been challenged to a stick fight by a group of older boys and had suffered the consequences.

'Whatever made him think he could win against the bigger boy, I don't know,' his father said, shrugging his shoulders angrily. 'Especially with his poor eyesight, he wouldn't know where the opponent's stick came from. But that's what he's like now, Doctor. He's become so aggressive since the school bus tragedy. He used to be a good pupil but his schoolwork has gone to the dogs. He can't concentrate on anything for longer than five minutes. He picks fights with his friends and argues with his teachers. He's so bad the headmaster threatened to expel him from the school if his behaviour does not improve.'

For once, Peter was glad he had not vetoed the purchase of the costly X-ray machinery. It enabled him to detect the hairline fracture in Sandile's skull where the stick had made contact with his head. It would be useful to have ultrasound and brain scan equipment as well, but that lay in the distant future, at the rate their finances progressed. Sandile would have to be sent to a larger hospital to determine what other injuries he sustained. Sandile's aggression and disruptive behaviour pointed to post-traumatic stress disorder, or PTSD, an affliction Josh usually dealt with.

While Josh kept Sandile under close observation, his convalescence was aided by moral support from friends who visited their one-eyed stick-fighting hero daily.

'Howzit, Skull Cracker? Feeling better?'

'You'll be OK,' they encouraged. 'If you think you're copping it bad, you should see Thabo,' they reported cheerfully. 'He's in hospital too. His nose is flattened, and three front teeth are missing. His arm's in a sling, and he's got a broken collarbone.' Laughter, the most effective medicine, rang throughout the ward.

* * *

Solomon Mataka sat, his right elbow on his desk supporting his head with his hand. His headache and the day's tribulations were both becoming permanent fixtures. Three times this week, members of the public had rung to complain about the misconduct they had witnessed from pupils attending his school. Shoplifting appeared to be their favourite sport, followed closely by purse snatchings in the manner Mrs De Bruyn had experienced. The police had also called to question students about a car theft. It was getting out of hand.

Solomon knew that many kids left home in the morning as if to go to school but boarded taxis and buses into town, going to cinemas instead. Discipline was hard to enforce, and those pupils who genuinely wished to learn were hampered by a lack of textbooks, which the Department of Education and Training apparently saw no need to supply.

What riled Solomon was that some activist teachers furthered the pupils' militant and sometimes lawless acts through the influence of teachers' and students' organizations. Principals often found their authority undermined and sidelined by the combined force of these unions. The teachers responsible for this had themselves been pupils during the Soweto students' revolts in 1976. The civil disobedience of a bygone era perpetuated itself.

'By now they're old enough to have more sense,' Solomon muttered to himself. He expected his staff to be wise enough to realize that 'liberation before education' was no longer applicable. 'Despite Madiba's release, they don't seem to know any different,' he mumbled. Ingrained mindsets were hard to shift.

He pulled a stack of exam papers towards himself, which he felt duty-bound to mark although he knew more than half would probably fail. And where would the dropouts find employment? Solomon saw a socio-economic crisis engulfing the new South Africa's future. Unbeknown to him, he spoke the same words Josh had used nearly two years earlier: 'What will happen here in fifteen to twenty years' time?' Solomon thought he knew the answer. 'Anarchy,' he sighed.

Adding to Solomon's woes, anarchy of a different kind threatened turmoil in his heart. A teacher was at the root of that as well: Cindy Khumalo. When would she wake up to herself and give Josh the flick? Solomon's concentration wandered, and he had to reread two papers to ensure a fair grading for the students' work. He abandoned the task. Maybe a stroll to the staff room for a cup of coffee would help.

Cindy had not spoken to him very much since the evening at Benny Shanks' Bistro. The few words they had exchanged concerned work-related issues. Any other topic became a no-go area. Solomon regretted—but only mildly—the numerous verbal spears he had directed at Josh during the dinner. He felt sure they had upset Cindy.

What other explanation could there be for her silence? She had chastised him for his rudeness to Josh. Solomon couldn't help but grin. He knew she also intended to roast Josh on a spit because of his overtures towards Anna De Bruyn. He'd seen it in her eyes. *Looks like we're both in the doghouse*, he thought as he spooned instant coffee into his mug. Two helpings of sugar followed. *Joshua's an arrogant fool.* Solomon embroidered his mental soliloquy. *Thinks he's God's gift to the female species. Dickhead! Chasing after a married, white woman.*

'Ouch!' Solomon wailed when hot water from the urn splashed on his fingers. Setting the mug aside, he dried his hand with paper towelling from a roll. How could Joshua be so cruel to Cindy, sweet Cindy—keeping her dangling on a string, waiting and waiting, for the day he might feel inclined to marry her? Eventually Cindy would see through his charade. Then she would come to him, Solomon Mataka. He had patience. He could wait.

* * *

Solomon Mataka found his patience was extended to breaking point like an overstretched rubber band. When the elastic snapped, it would hurt someone, most likely himself. His eyes became slits of silent agony as he, like every reveller in the ballroom, watched the only couple on the dance floor.

He glanced at the people around him, particularly the men, their gaze on the gracefully dancing lady. She wore a strapless gown of burnt orange with heavy cream and chocolate-brown beading on the bodice. The straight skirt with its back kick-pleat clung to her hips and buttocks, accenting the outlines of her superb figure. Her hair was twisted neatly into numerous thin plaits with cream and burnt-orange baubles on the end of each. They clacked like percussion to the rhythm of the dance.

'Who's the mesmerizing dancing flame?' Solomon heard a man behind him ask a friend.

Because of her high-heeled shoes, she was as tall as her dashing tuxedo-clad partner. A hush fell upon the room while the guests watched Cindy and Joshua perform a lively samba.

Solomon surfaced from his painful introspection to see Anna De Bruyn heading for him. Here was a lady who could not be beaten for style, he thought. She strode towards him in a dress of heavy plum-coloured satin. The tone matched her auburn hair closely. The princess-line bodice and deep sweetheart neckline flattered her bust. The A-line skirt helped her appear taller. The garment needed no ornamentation. Anna's exquisite body within it brought life to what was a masterpiece created by international designers. Solomon found it hard not to gape a little.

Hank De Bruyn had dug deeply into his pocket for the amethyst-and-pearl choker Anna wore around her slender neck. Solomon compared it with his sports watch. *Its face is as large as that damned centre amethyst*, he thought, amazed. And no, she wasn't without diamonds on this special evening either. Her diamond-encrusted bracelet gleamed as she raised a hand to wave to him. They were undoubtedly the most eye-catching women in the room, he was certain. Anna had sophistication; Cindy, brilliance and flamboyance.

'Mr Mataka, you look sad and lonely.' Anna spoke softly. She knew the reason for Solomon's dejection. 'Hank said no guest must remain in the doldrums on this eventful occasion.' She outstretched both hands to Solomon. 'Won't you come and join our table? We'd be delighted.'

'Why, thank you, Mrs De Bruyn.' Solomon managed a withdrawn smile. 'You are both very kind.' He came to his feet hesitantly to follow her.

'Let's detour across the dance floor,' Anna whispered with a hint of conspiracy.

'Mrs D-De Bruyn . . . ?' Solomon stammered.

'It's all right. Hank consented,' Anna laughed.

Solomon had never heard that silver-bell sound. It resonated in his head, bringing a pale glimmer of understanding for Josh's emotional confusion into his reluctant heart.

'Hank doesn't mind me dancing because it's a festive day.' The silver laughter bubbled from her like champagne foam from a freshly opened bottle. She explained, 'Hank doesn't dance often these days, but I love it so much.'

Inspired by the exuberance of Josh and Cindy's impromptu display of dance steps, other couples ventured onto the floor, showered by a cascade of colour reflected from the mirror-glass ball and chandeliers above. Among them were William and Melody Rosenberg.

'William!' Anna called, waving as she sailed by in Solomon's arms. Looking over Solomon's shoulder, she saw Melody smile and say something to William while he swirled her round and around. Melody wore black, which camouflaged her weight efficiently. The portly William appeared trim in his dinner suit too. They made a surprisingly handsome couple, Anna mused. It was thoughtful of William to bring Melody. His philandering was common knowledge, arousing pity for her among their friends.

When the music stopped, the three couples found themselves clustered in the centre of the floor with other dancers orbiting around them like planets around the sun. Anna was about to introduce this throng to each other when William precipitated her effort.

'Congratulations, Anna!' he boomed. 'You've organized a most splendid function. Haven't had so much fun in a long time.' He turned to Melody. 'Haven't we, dear?'

Before Melody could speak for herself, William continued, 'I must go to wish Hank another twenty-five profitable years in business. It's a wonderful anniversary for De Bruyn Brothers, and success didn't always come easily for Hank either . . . that is, until he married you, Anna.'

Anna, never diffident, took the compliment in her stride, saying, 'William, meet Cindy Khumalo. Cindy's in charge of the computer school we sponsor. And this is Mr Solomon Mataka, headmaster of Orlando West Secondary School, and Professor Joshua Mtolo from KwaZulu Medical.'

William extended his hand to Solomon and then to Josh, whom he eyed peevishly. That chap would be Indira's new boss, he realized with disquietude. A smart, sexy bloke who wore his immaculate evening clothes with panache. *By god!* William swore silently. The guy was a hybrid Harry Belafonte and Sidney Poitier in their younger years. Could Indira keep her eyes off him? *I don't like him*, William determined. *He's a definite danger to Indira.* With a shudder, William feared Indira's affection would turn towards Josh. They had reconciled recently, and William burned afresh with desire. Anger welled inside him, but giving vent to it was impossible with Melody hanging on his arm possessively. Instead, he said as pleasantly as he could, 'William Rosenberg. Pleased to meet you.'

'My pleasure, Mr Rosenberg,' Josh replied with a wary smile as he shook hands with his first VIP prisoner. He thanked his lucky stars for his precaution to remain invisible while William had dwelt in the wine cellar.

The dancers drifted to their respective tables, and Anna steered Solomon towards hers. She introduced him to Jan and Adriaan, who had left the tables they hosted to talk to Hank for a while. Soon the four men were steeped in debate over the inadequacies of Bantu education policies. Anna listened while they abrogated old laws and propounded revised theories for the new South Africa. Her searching eyes found Josh sitting at a nearby table. They had avoided each other so far. Josh had Cindy to hold him fast, and Anna wanted to reassure Hank of her fidelity.

The reason for Hank's truculence over KwaZulu Medical hit her like lightning out of a clear sky. Her dear Hank, whom she thought above such basic sentiments, was irrationally jealous. Discussions about the guest list for the anniversary ball had brought the matter into the open.

De Bruyn Brothers celebrated the anniversary of their founding every year with an exclusive cocktail party in the conference room, inviting a limited number of influential guests. After twenty-four such fetes, Hank determined that 'bash number 25 should be huge. A night to remember. Let's have a ball for all our clients.' Maurice was duly appointed master of ceremonies, responsible for mailing the bulk of the invitations and booking the ballroom.

'I must ask Zak Elbenstein to come. After all, he tries to keep me alive. That lifts him well above the level of a client,' Hank considered.

'Most certainly.' Anna looked up with a quick frown. Hank was not a man for sensationalism. Was he all right?

She resumed drawing up a list of names for the seating. Hank's brothers were each to act as host for a number of tables. 'We should seat Zak Elbenstein together with William Rosenberg,' she pondered. 'I'm sure Mrs Rosenberg and Mrs Elbenstein will find common interests for conversation, seeing as they both have three sons.'

Staff members were informed about the plans and their input welcomed. The next day, Nkosinathi came to Anna, asking, 'Please, Mefrou De Bruyn, would you send an invitation to my teacher?'

'Good idea, Nkosinathi.' Anna made a note. Later she said to Hank, 'Nkosinathi wants us to invite Cindy Khumalo to the ball.'

'Why not?' Hank shrugged with equanimity. 'The computer centre is an offshoot of De Bruyn Brothers. Might as well invite the school principal too. What's his name again?'

'Solomon Mataka?' Anna raised an eyebrow. 'That could be troublesome.'

'Why?' Hank asked, puzzled.

'Are you inviting KwaZulu Medical?'

Hank took a step towards Anna's desk, his brow knitted. 'What's that got to do with it?'

'Well, if you are, be aware that Cindy Khumalo is Professor Mtolo's fiancée.'

'So?' Hank couldn't follow the reasoning.

'You can't partner Cindy and Solomon. Besides, there's a bit of a love triangle—or Bermuda Triangle—happening there.' She gave what Hank heard as an unnatural chuckle. 'Solomon and Joshua have difficulty being civil to each other.'

'Oh, that's their problem.' Hank turned away, and Anna thought he would leave it at that. However, he came back, a touch of anger in his steel-grey eyes. 'You appear to be well informed, Anna,' he said with annoyance. 'Please divulge the source of your intelligence.'

'I hear gossip.' Anna laughed uneasily.

'Has gossip become your new hobby perchance?' Hank asked, an irascible ring in his voice. He hadn't missed the faint trace of guilt sounding in Anna's excuse.

She did not look up from her work when she replied with affected nonchalance, 'No, no, I'm just trying to remember who told me.'

Hank came around her desk and gently pulled her to her feet. With his hand under her chin, he forced her to look at him. 'You're hedging, aren't you, my dear? There's more to this than what you're prepared to tell me.' He left her, returning to his own office.

The lightning bolt came through the closed window, hitting Anna in the chest. Her legs gave way, and she slumped into her chair. Hank was jealous!

'Unbelievable!' she breathed, gripped by sudden panic. Willing her rubbery legs to move, she ran to him.

'Hank! No!' she called. 'You silly, silly man,' she scolded, catching him by the arm before he sat down. 'You have no need to be jealous. I'm your wife. Marriage is forever.' She stood on tiptoe to kiss him. He bent his head a little to make it easier for her.

'Yes,' he whispered wistfully. 'Marriage is forever. Till death do us part,' he added solemnly.

'Hank!' Anna cried, alarmed. Filled with tragic premonitions, she laid her head on his chest, dissolving into desperate sobs.

* * *

Hank lay awake. It was six in the morning, his usual shower and shave time. He had that oft-experienced morning-after feeling resulting from too much excitement and stimulation. He felt as tired as if he'd just gone to bed. Luckily it was Saturday and he didn't have to move. Anna still slept soundly.

'Ah, but it was all worthwhile,' he whispered contentedly into the dimness of their bedroom. Last night's ball had been an enormous success. He had even managed to thrash out a couple of advantageous deals with clients to the satisfaction of all parties. A sizeable commission would come his way by the end of the month. He smiled. The cost of the ball could justifiably be posted to the advertising account.

Anna had enjoyed herself too, thankfully forgetting how deeply he had upset her. He turned his head on the pillow to watch her sleep. 'My god,' he mouthed. In their fifteen years—no, it was sixteen now—of marriage, he could not recall ever seeing her weep, neither with joy nor sorrow. He had thought her a woman without tears. Her loss of control shook the foundations of his soul. Nothing could have convinced him more of her love and need for him. 'Poor girl.' he sighed. He had tried hard to keep the seriousness of his illness to himself, but she knew anyhow. Often, he had caught her watching him carefully. The look she gave him on such occasions revealed her distress. He had behaved like an idiot the day she drew up the guest list, like a stupid, attention-seeking little boy, throwing a jealous tantrum. He hadn't shown the slightest regard for her battles to keep her feelings in equilibrium. It had taken him half an hour to console her. Of course, her tears had saturated the bank notes in his wallet, and he had to extract them in exchange for the pearl-and-amethyst choker and a designer-label ballgown.

Anna stirred and reached for him in her sleep. 'I love you, little sweetheart,' he whispered, gathering her in his arms. She didn't wake.

In retrospect, it hadn't been a good idea to invite the Elbensteins. Old killjoy Zak focused his beady eyes on him all night long. 'Hank, ration your drinks. Hank, only the slow dances, mind! Hank, remember your diet. Cigars? You've got to be joking!' Fussy old woman. Fed up with Zak's well-meant warnings, he had blown caution sky-high. If he couldn't toast the firm's prosperity with his brothers, his life's work was pointless. Not to mention holding Anna tight during a slow waltz and making love later at home. He'd survived the pleasurable exertions. There was life in the old bull yet.

He'd also taken ample opportunity to sit quietly, observing people while they were relaxed, letting their hair down. He learnt much about his clients that way. Often these studies brought rare insights and surprises, like the brotherly manner in which Zak and the black quack, Mtolo, greeted each other, slapping each other on the shoulder, laughing. They were soon engrossed in a work-related conversation. It appeared as if they'd known each other for years. It was gratifying too to see Mtolo with his own woman. She kept him in check. Hank chuckled quietly. He had to hand it to Mtolo. The man had an eye for outstanding women. The temptation to give Mtolo a dose of his own *muthi* became too strong as the evening progressed. The beautiful Cindy oozed lust from every pore of her skin, and he hadn't bothered to disguise his admiration when asking her for a dance—with Mtolo's permission, of course. Consent, he noted, was granted with the barest civility. Cindy was a nimble dancer, and he flirted shamelessly with her in genuine appreciation of her classically sculptured African features. Strangely though, whereas he seethed when Mtolo fixed his attention on Anna, Mtolo remained composed in the face of his interaction with Cindy. Was there no love between them, or did Mtolo detect the farcical nature of the interlude?

Anna opened her eyes and yawned. 'Shit, what time is it? I promised Maurice I'd look at the gold-mining statistics with him. Some areas have shown unexpectedly high yields of late.' She sat up. 'I better get dressed. He'll be here in about an hour.'

'No,' Hank's sleepy voice called to her. 'Relax, dear. I told him to forget about it till Monday.' He pulled her back into his arms.

* * *

'Money, money, money . . . always sunny . . . in a rich man's world,' Cindy sang while washing Saturday's lunch dishes in her tiny kitchen. At the table behind her sat Josh, reading the *Sowetan,* the local newspaper.

She still couldn't believe it. She had danced with a millionaire—a multimillionaire. Few people, Sowetans particularly, would see such a person in their lives, but she had danced with one, talked to him, laughed with him, held his hand. It would probably never happen again. Just looking at Hank knowing he enjoyed her company enriched her spirit. He had a gentle demeanour, which she liked.

Although flirtatious, his conversation conveyed respect for women. She found that fairly unusual. He hadn't danced with her as a formality required by common courtesy. He had sought her out because he liked the look of her as a woman. *Suck on that, Joshua Mtolo*, she thought.

For a long while, an argument had raged as to whether the invitations to the ball should be accepted. Josh had received his and, hoping to smooth over the Benny episode, actually found both time and a telephone to call her asking if she wanted to go too.

'I've an invitation also,' she told him airily. 'Nkosinathi saw to it. It was sent to the school together with a second one for Solomon.'

'You're not going with him, are you?' Josh asked querulously.

'I consider myself very lucky,' she stated with conviction. 'I have a choice of two fine men to take me to a ball. Now who shall it be, I wonder?' Suppressing a giggle, she exploited her opportunity to torment him. 'One is my boss, colleague, and friend who is always available when I have a problem or just need company. The other, although very charismatic, is distant, doesn't have much time for me anymore. Too busy with work and pursuing white ladies. And I don't mean the cocktail by that name either.' She hesitated. 'Hm . . . I think I'll choose my loyal colleague.'

'Like hell you will! Stop teasing, Cindy . . . and the drink is a pink lady, not white,' he retorted hotly, swallowing Cindy's bait whole in one gulp. Collecting himself, he thought a moment. 'Today is Monday, isn't it? Tomorrow I have a lecture in Pietermaritzburg— after that, a meeting with the students. Wednesday I work in Edendale. Thursday I should be seeing Dr Naidoo and her lawyer, but I can defer that . . . Sipho can—'

'Life is so stressful for you, Josh. Don't even try to come here. I'd hate to see you inconvenienced. Solomon will be excellent company for me.'

From the other end came a sound as if Josh had dropped the receiver. She held her hand firmly to her mouth to contain her laughter.

'Cindy, you are an incorrigible tease. Now listen to me, woman. Thursday's the night. I'll be with you at about half past nine, and you better be home. No Solomon, no nobody. Do I make myself clear?'

Cindy couldn't answer immediately for laughing. She eventually spoke the last word on the subject, demanding, 'If I go with you, you keep away from Anna De Bruyn. That's an order!'

'Yes, ma'am!' Josh saluted and clicked his heels, only Cindy couldn't see him.

'Money, money, money . . .' Cindy sang on, laughter ringing in her voice. ' . . . in my mind I have a plan . . . if I found me a wealthy man . . .' She had made the rounds of the wealthy men last night. William Rosenberg was another who'd been sufficiently impressed with her to promise a traineeship for a computer school pupil.

Josh folded the *Sowetan* with a sigh. 'Time flies,' he remarked, 'especially when it's good.' He looked out the kitchen window to where his car was parked. 'Better pack my bag and be off. It isn't fair on Peter and Tom, who always fill in for me when I'm here. They should be able to see their kids at least for part of the weekend.'

'That's one problem we don't have,' Cindy said with quiet regret.

Josh came to stand behind her, stroking her upper arms tenderly. 'One day, Cindy.' He spoke softly in her ear. 'I'm sure it will happen one day. Have you ever considered teaching in Vryheid? Peter and Tom live there with their families, and so could we. Think about it, Cindy.'

And that was the crux of the matter, Josh thought, while driving away. Cindy wasn't interested in coming to Vryheid. She had too many good friends in Soweto, and the computer school proved an even stronger magnet, not to mention that Solomon.

As for himself, he had best see to his own survival. His brush with William Rosenberg had him on tenterhooks throughout the ball. Penetrating the white business community to learn how they ticked was one thing. Leaving himself open to recognition and possible exposure of his extortion racket was another. Should he have kept away from the ball? Or was it better to be out there, be seen, be known and accessible? People never noticed what lay right under their noses. Suspicion was perhaps less likely to fall on him if everyone thought they knew him as a conscientious medical practitioner. Running into Zak had helped to ally people's resentment towards a newcomer. He determined to move more cautiously in future.

* * *

What was to be done about the discrepancy in KwaZulu Medical's balance sheet? Indecision plagued Anna, and she wondered how best to broach the subject with Josh. A good measure of discretion was in order. If she called Josh into her office the meeting would assume the form of an accusation, interrogation even. That was too judicial an approach. She wanted to question him informally because it may have nothing to do with tax evasion. If she wasn't careful, she'd have egg on her face and soured relations with a client. Although Hank maintained Mtolo's business was expendable she had other ideas when it came to helping struggling enterprises. Also, she believed that KwaZulu Medical should be given the benefit of the doubt. Innocent till proven guilty. It may well be that the handwritten statement was a wish list; something Sipho Gwala idled away his time with, attempting to forecast KwaZulu Medical's future potential. That, however, did not explain the date as at the last quarter nor all the other identical amounts on both sheets. Anna found herself scratching her head. She called for chocolate biscuits to help her think. The Swiss account may also be just a component of plans yet to be implemented. Its number, CY52318239, looked genuine enough, though. If it existed, where was the source that fed it? Maybe ringing Mr Gwala would resolve the conundrum. She may not have to talk to Josh at all. It may be weeks before he was in Johannesburg again anyhow.

By the time Anna had devoured four biscuits and drunk the coffee, she felt ready to fax the mysterious draft balance sheet to Sipho Gwala, asking him to explain its purpose.

After a week and a half, his response was still outstanding. Its absence nourished Anna's suspicion of malpractice. Perhaps Sipho Gwala acted alone, drawn into unsavoury schemes without Josh's knowledge. Or was Josh the soloist in this financial Valse Macabre? She needed to discuss the account with him. If his elucidations proved unsatisfactory she would tell him to go elsewhere for advice. That appeared to be the best course to take. Hank would definitely be pleased to see the back of Josh. She picked up the phone with uncommon trepidation.

'Professor Mtolo is unavailable. Is it urgent? Would you like to leave a message or speak to Dr Dlamini?' A soft voice spread the balm of reassurance.

'No, no. Please tell the professor to ring Anna De Bruyn.'

* * *

Vibrant excitement hummed in KwaZulu Medical's children's ward all morning. The word was out! Water! Lots of it. For days, the stronger, fitter kids had their noses pressed against the window watching as the out-door swimming pool received its finishing touches. Now it was ready for its inaugural splash, courtesy of Paul Fischer.

Josh stood nearby looking on as well. He felt the perverse urge to have a brass plaque, Paul Fischer Pool, embedded in the brickwork around the ten-by-twelve-metre stretch. He expected the pool to be of therapeutic benefit for his above-average number of young asthma patients. Air pollution in black townships due to wood smoke from cooking fires brought many youngsters and adults with respiratory problems to the clinic. Coal dust was also to blame. Workers from the surrounding coal mines presented with breathing problems as well.

Josh saw swimming as excellent exercise for young asthma sufferers. The pool would also provide a means of physical training for kids recovering from broken limbs. Without a resident physiotherapist for specialized advice, the children could at least strengthen their muscles by swimming daily.

A whoop and cheers greeted Fernando when he entered the ward laden with two cardboard boxes containing plain, inexpensive kids' swimwear in varying sizes for girls and boys. Josh followed Fernando to observe the patients' reactions. They did not rush towards the boxes like healthy children would but came quietly, chose their bathers, and returned to their beds, waiting for the instruction to put them on. Two little unfortunates were too ill to join the fun.

Sandile Duma swung his legs out of bed. 'Nothing's stopping me getting into the pool,' he announced loudly.

'Sorry, Skull Cracker.' Josh raised a preventive hand. 'Not today. You'll have to wait a bit longer.'

'Shit, no!' Sandile couldn't believe it. 'No way, man. I'm going today.' Waving his hand dismissively at Josh, he pulled his swimmers from the box. Josh intercepted him on his way back to his bed.

'No, Sandile,' he said calmly. 'I can't let you swim yet.' He added more sternly, 'And furthermore, young man, I prefer to be addressed as Doctor Josh.'

Sandile became furious. He was about to take the glass of water by his bedside and smash it on the floor in a fit of temper. Josh expected the outburst and held Sandile's hand before it reached the glass. 'Sit on your bed like everyone else please, Sandile.'

Tom and Peter's arrival was the signal to change into bathers. With a helping hand here and there, the kids were made ready, and Josh said, 'Right! Off you go now. Boys go with Doctor Peter and girls with Doctor Tom.'

The kids did not run out in exuberance but followed the doctors eagerly enough, considering their condition. A quarter of an hour in the pool would be more than sufficient for them, Josh thought as they filed out.

He turned to Sandile, who sat silently with a belligerent look. 'Cheer up, warrior,' he said, coming to sit beside him on the bed. 'We're going to play a game, you and I. We'll pretend we're going to the cinema. And guess what? You're going to be the star in the film.'

'How?' Sandile had question marks dancing around his by now less heavily bandaged head.

'I'll tell you in a minute. First we've got to get us popcorn and a drink. Got your ticket?'

Sandile looked confused while Josh pulled a couple of pieces of scrap cardboard out of his shirt pocket. 'Here's your ticket. Take it,' he said. 'Let's go.'

They headed for the kitchen, where a forewarned Margo had popcorn and orange juice waiting. Provisioned with these goodies, Josh led Sandile to a spare room at the other end of the corridor.

'In you go,' he invited, acting as usher, showing Sandile to a chair in the front row. Josh had prepared the room as authentically as possible with two rows of five chairs each, a screen, and an old slide projector. When Sandile managed to sit still, Josh gave him the popcorn and orange juice. He drew the curtains to dim the room and switched on the projector, its light beaming on the blank screen.

'What are we doing in here?' Sandile asked through popcorn.

'Quiet now. The film's starting,' Josh said, taking a chair next to Sandile. He helped himself to his own share of popcorn and juice, waited a minute in silence, and began the therapy.

'Sandile,' he said, 'you've had scary dreams lately, haven't you?' Sandile nodded, wondering what relevance the question had to the cinema game they were supposed to play.

'We're going to try and stop you having those dreams to enable you to sleep undisturbed so when you wake up you'll be rested and not nervy and aggressive.' Sandile's face showed no sign that he recognized his problems.

'Your parents and your teacher have seen you transformed from a clever boy who worked well at school into a disruptive, aggressive pest who spreads trouble everywhere he goes. We'll have to attempt to retrieve the good Sandile. The Sandile whom everyone likes. Not the Skull Cracker who wants to fight day in, day out.'

Sandile wriggled nervously on his chair. Doctor Josh's talk was boring. It was silly to be sitting in an empty room like this. And there was no movie anyway. Besides, how could he be the star when he'd never had a camera focused on him? He was never on television.

Seeing the doubt in Sandile's one functioning eye, Josh continued. 'You can change yourself back into the clever Sandile, you know. It takes patience and perseverance on your part, but it can be done. You see, you're still the same Sandile deep down. You're in shock because of your traumatic experiences, and that's what changed you. But you can help yourself change back.' Josh knew getting through to Sandile would be difficult. Every time the poor boy looked in a mirror, he'd see the scars on his face, reminding him that he was Skull Cracker the invincible. He had left Sandile, the well-behaved, courteous, and helpful boy, behind many months ago.

Taking advantage of the gap in the conversation, Sandile shot off his chair and headed for the door.

'Where are you going, warrior?' Josh asked casually.

'To watch the others swim.'

'You can do that when we've finished our cinema game.' Josh hadn't looked at the boy while speaking. If the young chap perceived the slightest provocation he'd buck like a colt with its first rider.

'Come on, Sandile. Sit down and look at the screen, because here we go!' Sandile returned, thrusting his hand into the popcorn bucket.

'The film is called "The School Bus", starring Sandile Duma.' Josh spoke in an almost hypnotic voice. He began the narration of Sandile's tragic day according to what he'd been told by the boy's parents and what he had seen himself.

'There is Sandile's house. The camera is showing his front door clearly. Look at the screen, Sandile. Can you see it in your mind? Try.' Josh realized he'd chosen the wrong chair to sit on. He should have gone to Sandile's other side to observe the boy's concentration in his good eye. If he changed now, it would break the sequence of the story, and he might not be able to start it again today, given Sandile's short attention span.

'Look,' Josh continued. 'Sandile's front door opens, and here he comes . . . the star of the silver screen. The camera shows his smiling face as he steps out of his house. He has a backpack for a school bag, and he's heading towards the bus stop. Now the camera shows two of Sandile's friends approaching from the other direction. The boys talk and laugh. Can you remember what they said?'

'Yeah,' Sandile nodded. 'The soccer game on television. We were talking about that.'

He might respond after all, Josh hoped and went on quickly while he had Sandile's ear.

'Here comes the school bus. The camera shows the whole front of it. It zooms in on the windscreen and the driver's face. The camera switches back to Sandile and friends as the bus pulls up. The door is opened. The boys climb in. The camera shows Sandile's face again before he too boards the bus. The door closes and the bus drives away.'

Josh took a sip of orange juice, allowing time for the memories to flood back into Sandile's consciousness.

'Now the camera's inside the bus. It takes pictures through the window in the same direction that Sandile is looking. Along Edendale Road they go. Past shops, past the Edendale Hospital, past houses and trees, till they're almost at Sandile's school. The soundtrack repeats the roaring of the engine and other traffic noise. Then the camera returns to Sandile's face and that of his friend sitting beside him.'

Again, Josh allows a second or two of silence. 'Then, suddenly, *crash!*' He almost shouts the words but immediately tones his volume down again to say, 'The windscreen shatters. The driver slumps over the steering wheel. *Crash* again! The window next to Sandile's friend breaks. He cries. He's hurt and bleeding. Sandile turns to help him when glass assaults his face like hail. He can't see anymore.'

A tear appeared in Sandile's good eye. He sniffed and reached for the orange juice. *This might just work*, Josh thought. Now was the time to give the kid a break before starting the next step of the therapy.

'Okay, it's intermission in this picture theatre. That usually means ice cream, doesn't it?' He smiled at Sandile, who had taken the recollections of his ordeal quite well. 'Come on, Sandile.' Josh placed his hand on the kid's shoulder. 'We'll get ice cream.' At the mention of that most magical food, Sandile's good and bad eye widened together.

'Margo, do you have ice cream for us?' Josh called to her in the kitchen. Looking at Sandile, he asked, 'What flavour, warrior? Chocolate? Strawberry? Vanilla? Or maybe a little mixture of all three?' Margo took the hint, filling two cones to capacity with each flavour.

'The bell's ringing! Come on, Sandile. We've got to get back to our seats or they'll start without us.' Josh urged Sandile to return once Margo thrust the ice cream cone into his hand. Within himself, Josh grinned. The experts who claimed that a sugar-rich diet made kids uncontrollable would be shocked at his method. In Sandile's case, nothing worked better to bribe his cooperation. They sat before the blank screen again.

'Now once a film has been shown, it has to be rewound so that it can be viewed again.' Sandile was too busy licking to talk, so an affirmative shrug of his shoulder had to suffice as reply.

'That's what we have to do now. Rewind the film. Are you ready to do that?' Josh coaxed. Again the shrug of the shoulder, which supposedly meant yes.

Josh began the narration in reverse, starting with Sandile's sudden blindness. After that, his effort to assist his friend, hearing him cry, then the two crashes, the driver collapsing, travelling backwards through the streets, past the familiar landmarks, back to Sandile's bus stop. He ended the rewind with Sandile entering his house, emphasizing that this was where he felt safe, secure, and loved. A place where he could smile.

'Well,' he said, giving Sandile a searching look, 'that's the end of our cinema game, and you've done very well starring in it. What I want you to do now is to repeat the same procedure by yourself tomorrow. You can come in here and do it or just find a peaceful place somewhere. Or you can do it in bed when the others are asleep. Do it every day if possible. If you don't want to do it alone, that's fine. I'm always here to help you. If you can't find me quickly, Doctor Tom or Doctor Peter will talk to you. Remember to look at the film from beginning to end and then rewind it.'

'How can doing that help me sleep better?' Sandile was a little sceptic, the non-believer, the infidel among patients. Josh smiled.

'It will help you to face up to your trauma and in time overcome it. Think of the trauma as a fierce lion that you must kill or it will kill you. You can't run away because it will chase you. It's already scratched you once. That's why you've turned aggressive. Now you have to stand up to it. Show it you're the boss. Make it cower and go away. Then you're free to be your happy self again. Do you understand that?'

'I suppose.' Sandile looked dubious. 'I can try.'

'That's the boy.' Josh encouraged. 'Now we'll see how our swimmers are going.'

Chapter 6

The Swoop

Josh returned to his office, his mind on the Paul Fischer Pool and, of course, Sandile and the exorcism of his trauma devils. He had thought for a long time how best to attack Sandile's problem. Eventually he chose a method devised by Dr David Muss who, like himself, was a graduate of the Columbia University Medical School. Dr Muss's film-rewind technique seemed ideally suited for children because it could be embellished and rearranged to fit the individual patient's needs. Kids usually loved play-acting. He had never tried it before either on adults or children and was keen to see what results it yielded.

He sat down at his desk to write the details into Sandile's file when he saw a slip of paper with a message in Sipho's scratchy hand: 'Ring Mrs De Bruyn.' He rose again and walked around to Sipho's office.

'What's this about?' he asked, holding the sheet towards Sipho. 'Any idea?'

'Yes and no,' Sipho answered timorously. 'No because she didn't say. Yes because I can make a well-calculated guess.' Sipho sighed deeply. 'Sit down, Josh. I can't pick you up if you fall flat on your butt when I tell you.'

'Goodness,' Josh laughed. 'Is it that bad?'

'Yes, I fucked up,' Sipho stated bluntly. 'You're going to impale me when I tell you.' He found his own chair before continuing. 'You remember how we fudged the balance sheets with the computer printout as our official position?'

'Yeah, and?'

'I kept a handwritten record of our real situation for our own use, and somehow that damned piece of paper has found its way onto Anna De Bruyn's desk. Now Madam Bright Spark wants explanations.' Sipho produced Anna's fax and handed it across to Josh. 'I could kick myself for this. My draft must have accidentally got mixed up with the material we sent them when we changed brokers,' Sipho said with basset hound wrinkles on his forehead.

'I see.' Josh rose and began his habitual pacing around the room. Sipho watched with apologetic eyes.

'Settle down, man. I haven't hit the deck yet, as you can see,' Josh joked. He marched the door-to-window distance of the office, talking more to himself than to Sipho. 'Anna's coming dangerously close to KwaZulu Medical's home truths. She's rattling laboratory-closet skeletons. I'll have to create a good cock-and-bull story to get her off our scent. I'll think of something before I call her back.' He retraced his steps, window to door. 'At the moment I have more serious concerns, like converting bumptious and temperamental stick fighters back into pleasant and delightful schoolboys.'

Josh returned to his office, saying, 'Think no more of it, Sipho. It doesn't matter.' The truth was that it did signify. Sipho's blunder had enabled Anna to detect KwaZulu Medical's monetary heart murmur. She would pass critical judgment on how the hospital's affairs were managed. It was imperative that he convinced her of KwaZulu Medical's integrity, not an easy task when much of it was already compromised. Appealing to the Good Samaritan within her may help. He could try pulling her heartstrings, provided they weren't made of titanium.

Of equal enormity was the fact that the generally careful Sipho should commit such a calamitous oversight. Was he becoming forgetful? Was he reaching that phase of the illness when a subclinical involvement of the nervous system could impair his work?

Josh looked at Sipho's message, with his tremulous handwriting telling its own story. Was Sipho heading for subcortical dementia? It was depressing seeing a friend in this state. It wasn't particularly uplifting seeing anyone like that. Much of his time in Johannesburg was spent advising doctors in the caring for patients with HIV-related neuropsychological dysfunction.

If Sipho progressed towards such abnormalities, it might be best if he took over the management of his illness from Peter. It looked like Sipho needed new medication, particularly zidovudine, but getting it into South Africa would be problematic.

Josh drummed his fingers on the edge of his desk. He stared at the telephone. It had a hostile look on its dial. For a moment, he dared not touch it lest it snapped at his hand like a crocodile. Whereas normally he would welcome any opportunity to talk to Anna, this time it necessitated more willpower than a visit to the dentist. Nonetheless, he'd better take the plunge; otherwise, her suspicion would grow, and there was no telling her next step.

'Anna De Bruyn speaking,' he heard her mild but distinct voice.

'Joshua Mtolo here, Mrs De Bruyn. You left a message for me. I'm sorry I haven't been able to return your call earlier.' Why the hell did he always find himself apologizing to her? His job was more vital than hers. His was work of life-or-death importance. She only played Monopoly with other people's money.

'I'm glad you called, Professor,' her pleasant voice seduced, soothing his nerves deceptively. 'I was wondering when you might be in Johannesburg again? Any chance of seeing you? Could we meet somewhere? Have lunch?'

Was that all she wanted? Josh asked himself, half relieved but disbelieving. A meeting. No incriminating questions about faulty bookkeeping? That seemed highly unlikely with her. She followed her agenda. Could she be setting a trap for him? Or was she missing him? That'd be wishful thinking on his part. He wouldn't even go there.

'Unfortunately, madam, I can give you no definite date for that. It depends mostly on how the patients I saw last time are faring.' Suddenly reckless, he added, 'But why don't you come here? I'd be very happy to show you around the hospital.'

'Would you?' Anna asked, surprised. 'I'll keep that in mind for the future.'

'I don't mean the future, madam. I'm talking about the present. Any time you like. Would you care to name your day?' She was silent, and Josh heard pages being flipped in a book.

'I'm just going through my diary. Please bear with me, Professor.'

More rustling of paper sounded before her voice came back. 'It will have to be soon because we're going on holiday shortly.' There was Gogo's big party in Cape Town on the weekend too. They dared not miss that. 'No . . . I don't think I can make it. It will have to be afterwards.'

Josh wondered if she mistrusted him as much as he feared her power to destroy him.

'Oh, well,' Anna sighed. 'I would have liked to see you before we depart for Sydney, but it can't be done now, I suppose.'

She sounded disappointed, and for the briefest instance, Josh felt she meant it.

'I will let you know when I'm in your vicinity again, Mrs De Bruyn,' Josh said kindly before hanging up.

Sipho entered with a weird look on his face. Had he been listening? Josh wondered.

'Man, your reputation spreads like the pox. Read this fax that's just come in, will you!' Sipho passed the letter to Josh with awe. His crass announcement did not disguise his pride at being part of the busy and bustling establishment into which KwaZulu Medical had evolved.

Josh took the note. It was a request from the Pretoria Academic Hospital for his assistance with AIDS patients. There was no end to their inexorable increase in numbers. Pretoria Academic expressed the hope that he could find time soon. A hire car, accommodation, and expenses were compensations offered in anticipation of his help.

For the patients' sake, Josh responded immediately, making the appropriate arrangements for the trip. It occurred to him that Pretoria was only fifty kilometres from Johannesburg. That meant seeing Anna was a real possibility. He intended to deal with her before she flew off on her vacation.

* * *

Gogo De Bruyn entered her richly furnished dining room. Her shimmering grey satin dress rustled against her walking stick, which the matriarch of the clan carried like a staff of office.

'Congratulations!' the assembled family erupted in happy unison. It could have been a birthday party, but it wasn't. Gogo had ceased celebrating birthdays when she reached fifty. This was a graduation dinner. At the age of seventy-six, Gogo had at last attained her life's secret ambition, an academic degree. One by one, in order of seniority, her sons embraced her.

'Well done, mother!' Hank kissed Gogo on both cheeks, followed by Franz, Gerhard, Jakobus, Jan, and Adriaan. Gertrude De Bruyn was never happier than with her brood gathered around her—sons, their wives, and grandchildren. It made for a crowded house, but that bothered her little. What did disturb her as she looked at her sons in turn was how much her normally closely knit family began drifting apart. The grandchildren were the first to miss out on family companionship. They scarcely knew each other as cousins; so little did they see of one another. Franz and Rosemary, with their two boys and the new baby girl, lived in Johannesburg, close to Hank and Anna, but the women communicated infrequently. Rosemary was first and foremost a mother and architect second. Anna was all stockbroker and partner to an increasingly ailing Hank. Not much common ground there. Jakobus and Gerhard spent most of their time in Durban with their families and only travelled to Johannesburg on business. Their spare time was absorbed fully guarding with eagle eyes the small but highly profitable diamond mine started by their late father, Walter De Bruyn. The De Beers had licked their chops for years at the thought of acquiring De Bruyn's, and the continuous vigilance to ward off takeovers took its toll on the brothers' family life. Jan and Adriaan, the family academics, were still unwed and probably had the easiest time. Adriaan sometimes overtaxed himself running a law practice in Cape Town as well as his responsibilities as a lecturer. Jan too was kept busy with university and frequent calls to Pretoria to sit on parliamentary advisory committees. Personal life went on the back-burner.

Gogo feared that a major crisis had to occur before she saw the family close ranks again. Inevitably, the rare occasions when she had everyone under her roof were precious moments for her. Family visits were a luxury, and Gogo found with utter horror that life was passing them by so quickly she no longer knew her sons like she should. She had little idea how, for instance, they felt about their work, the fading of the old South Africa, the slow evolution of the new or the country's economy. She missed the Sunday dining room table discussions which dominated the weekend in Walter's days and wondered if they did too. How distant and estranged they were showed in the way they reacted to Gogo's graduation. None knew of the desire to study, which had consumed Gogo since they were children. When Jan and Adriaan had begun tertiary studies, Gogo had read their textbooks with single-minded zeal. But to the young men, she was still the mother who cared, worked, guided, and occasionally advised. That she had visions for herself, thwarted goals that gnawed at her soul, would have flabbergasted them, particularly her husband, Walter. Gogo was never asked what she wanted out of life for herself. Expected to find happiness in her family's achievements, her inner self remained unrecognized. Upon the birth of her first grandchild, Gertrude was christened with the nickname Gogo, Zulu for 'grandmother', and to her own mind, it closed the lid on that chamber of her heart that longed to utilize opportunities she had missed as a young woman.

'Too late now,' Gogo often told herself till fate intervened. Shortly after her seventy-first birthday, Gogo had travelled home from a symphony concert when a drunken motorist slammed into her vehicle. Her driver was killed, and Gogo suffered a fractured hip and broken legs. She spent three months in Groote Schuur Hospital before being fit enough to take one daily walk around her house. Gogo became dispirited and bored. Her daughters-in-law took turns to keep her company and ward off depression.

Late one evening, when Anna entertained Gogo with stories about Australia, Gogo did what for her was a most unseemly and shocking thing. She asked the butler to bring two bottles of wine. 'We're going to polish these off tonight, Anna. I'm going to get drunk!' She said with emancipated determination.

'Gogo!' Anna protested, surprised and alarmed. 'Alcohol will diminish the effectiveness of your painkillers.'

'Pah!' Gogo shook her head and waved a hand in disregard. She never swore. 'Pah!' was her strongest expression. 'When I'm drunk, I'll sleep well and won't feel any pain.'

Raising glasses and toasting Gogo's recovery, Anna said, 'Getting drunk can have monumental consequences. Did I ever tell you about the time my father drank himself senseless with his mates in the yacht club and entered the *Coomelong* in the Sydney to Hobart race? Mother had kittens at the thought of it. So did Dad when he sobered, but he was committed and not keen to lose face.'

'Great man, your father, Anna. Salt of the earth. I hope he visits me next time he's here.'

'I'm sure he will, Gogo. I'll make him.'

Gogo pushed her glass towards Anna with a wordless request for a refill. One bottle had already bitten the dust.

'What does *Coomelong* mean? It's a very musical name for a yacht, I think.' Gogo looked agog with curiosity.

'I believe it's Aboriginal for *possum*,' Anna giggled, feeling the effect of the wine. 'Anyway,' she went on, 'when Boxing Day dawned, the weather looked perfect but nobody was fooled. Veteran entrants in the race know how unpredictable and spitefully changeable conditions could become. With the starting gun, the race began under a moderate north-easterly breeze, just right. By late afternoon, it had swung north-west and freshened. There was no cause for alarm in that. At midnight it blew steadily north-west with three-metre waves. Nothing Dad and his crew couldn't handle. As the boats worked their way down the coast, the wind became wilder and seas rose to four and a half metres. Still, Dad wasn't worried. *Coomelong* did well.'

'Then what happened? Did he win the race?' Gogo asked, enthralled.

'Coming level with King and Flinders Islands on their way south, they were suddenly confronted with the Roaring Forties, strong west, south-west winds, which rapidly whipped themselves into gale-force fury. Many yachts were caught off guard, sustained damage, and limped back to safety in Victorian ports. Mum and I had the radio and television going day and night. We were really scared of the ominous weather reports coming through by then. One boat had overturned, and a rescue helicopter was ready to swing into action. And then we heard that Dad wasn't turning back. Mum all but fainted. 'It's Hobart town or the devil and the deep blue sea!' he told us later. He saw no purpose in turning around only to cop the gale's broadside to port instead of starboard, so he kept going. He remained at the helm till the end of the race. Mum and I flew to Hobart to join him. We thought he'd be upset about finishing fourth in his category, but we found him in good spirits—literally. Sitting on a bollard beside the *Coomelong*, gulping champagne straight from the bottle, he simply worshipped the boat. It had remained intact while a number of others had lost masts and equipment overboard in the rough weather. He thought crossing the finishing line in fourth position wasn't bad for a drunken wager.'

Gogo's eyes glittered with vicarious enjoyment of adventure at sea. The second bottle was nearly empty. She called for a third. 'You're not drinking, Anna,' she admonished.

'Like I said,' Anna continued, 'the Bass Strait weather gods are anti-yachtsmen. They reserve their most churlish moods for the Sydney to Hobart entrants. Their perversion is legendary and, as you might expect, for four days after the race, the weather was divine. It was so sunny and calm Dad let me sail back to Sydney and alternate taking the helm with him.'

Gogo yawned and chuckled. 'Wish I could do that!' Her cheeks were flushed and the sharpness of her bird-of-prey eyes accented by their glitter. Although unaccustomed to alcohol, Gogo was still coherent. While Anna and the maid escorted her to bed, she suddenly slurred, 'Had'n idea! Gonna shtudy at uni. See'f I don't! Show 'em what'n old woman can do!' When Gogo's head hit the pillow, they still heard her mumble, 'Gonna get m'self a bashelor'farts d'gree. You'll see!'

* * *

Maurice Van Buuren was a worried man. He hadn't slept all night. His face was ashen. The nervous tick in his eyelids and left corner of his mouth drove him to distraction. He needed a cigarette, although he hadn't smoked for six months. Where was that emergency packet and lighter he kept in his bottom desk drawer? He had hidden it there in case dire events struck. His shaking hand reached as far back as possible till it hit target. He lit up, tried to relax and think straight. It wouldn't do to lose his head. Hank, his boss and best pal, had been away for five days now on a speaking tour addressing business forums in Durban, Cape Town, and Pietermaritzburg. It was costing Maurice every morsel of moral fortitude to ring Hank telling him to cancel any further engagements and return to Johannesburg instantly. 'Merciful heavens!' Maurice sighed, blowing a perfect smoke ring, which would have amused him under happier circumstances. 'How will this crisis affect Hank?' With all probability, Hank would throttle the last breath of life out of him. Hank had expected him to look after Anna during his absence, but he had failed. Anna was gone. Her welfare depended on Captain Broadbent's skills now.

Maurice's unease began with Anna's phone call from Pretoria telling him that a yellow VW Golf had followed her all the way there. She had seen it parked diagonally across the road from her home when she returned from work the previous night. At that stage, she thought it belonged to the neighbours' visitors. In the morning, it was gone.

Anna came to the office, checked her messages, collected papers and material of interest to the clients she was seeing in Pretoria, and left in a hurry.

'I'll be back at about five, if not earlier,' she told him. 'I'm having lunch with Mrs Odenthal, and I'll be talking to Mr Pienaar as well.'

On that note, she departed. If it were possible, she was dressed with even more chic than usual, Maurice noticed. He hoped she was having a good day till he heard her voice on the phone.

'Call the cops please, Maurice. I got the number of the car. The driver has vanished.' She laughed at that. 'Not much of a spy if I become aware of him that easily. But I don't like it, Maurice. Best to be cautious. Could be some psychopath stalking me.'

'Stay with Mrs Odenthal.' Maurice warned. 'I'll come and pick you up.'

'Oh, no need for that, I shouldn't think. I'll be okay when I'm in my car. If the guy follows me back, we'll have him right where we want him: in Captain Broadbent's grasp.'

Maurice admired Anna's cool level-headedness. She tackled the most threatening situations, not a trace of hysteria in her voice, but now she was gone, and Hank would hang him for it.

Anna's deadline for her return to the office came and went. Six o'clock passed. No traffic disruptions between Pretoria and Johannesburg were reported on the news. Seven, eight, nine; Maurice waited till ten before leaving for home, gravely concerned. He rang Captain Broadbent again from his house.

'There's a chance Mrs De Bruyn may have become too apprehensive to stay at home and has gone to join her husband,' Broadbent suggested. 'We'll be checking that.'

Maurice wondered angrily if Broadbent thought him stupid. As if he hadn't tried ringing Anna's residence. The housekeeper had answered, saying Anna hadn't come home. Franz, Jakobus, and Gerhard knew nothing. Hank couldn't be reached. He was in a meeting, and Maurice left a quick message couched in language that wouldn't alarm him unduly. A plausible explanation for Anna's delay may still emerge.

The sun had barely risen when the anxious Maurice came to the office the following morning to be there in case Anna arrived. She didn't. He had to call Hank. There was no shirking the duty. Broadbent would have prepared him for the worst by now.

By late afternoon, Hank arrived back in a state of exhaustion and shock. Franz supported him. Fortification with brandy relaxed nerves and lubricated tongues, which enunciated theories for Anna's mysterious disappearance. Broadbent knocked quietly and was admitted into Hank's office by Franz. The offer of brandy was a godsend for an all-too-human police officer who was suddenly expected to perform miracles. Could he produce a crystal ball to find Anna?

'Bet I know who's behind this outrage,' Franz postulated grimly as he handed a crystal brandy balloon to Broadbent. 'It's that Malcolm Price arse-hole. He wants Anna out of the way because she's about to nail him for bribing government ministers.'

'Could be the honourable members themselves,' Maurice added, sneering.

'Price has always hated Anna,' Hank confirmed. 'He calls her the Australian goody two shoes.'

Broadbent remained silent. Sniffing the brandy, he looked into the crystal glass as if it were the ball he wished for. He listened, watching their faces. It was too easy to attach this crime to one person. There was every indication that the three men were on the right track, though. Darren Thompson, the driver of the yellow VW Golf, had made comments that fit the hypothesis. On the other hand, the guy claimed to have given up following Anna after she saw him. That, according to him, was around about one in the afternoon. From that point on, nobody knew Anna's movements. He had talked to her clients who were unable to provide further information. Her burgundy BMW was found half a block from Mrs

Odenthal's law firm. It had not been tampered with. The worst scenario was that someone had killed her for her diamonds. They might never find her body. Broadbent did not mention that fatal possibility to his audience. It would dawn on them without his prompting. He said instead, 'I've talked to the driver of the VW Golf.'

'And who would that perverted swine be?' Franz demanded.

'He gave his name as Darren Thompson and called himself a retired mercenary operating as freelance private investigator.'

'Oh yeah, Mr Nice Guy! I know the sort.' Franz smiled thinly.

'His story checks out. He confessed to being well paid in cash for keeping an eye on Mrs De Bruyn,' Broadbent said. 'He claims not to know his client specifically but suspects he's a businessman who sent an intermediary to negotiate the contract. We have Thompson in custody and I'll be accompanying him when his next pow-wow with his client is due. We'll use him as a decoy to catch the big fish behind the deal, provided news of Mrs De Bruyn's absence hasn't filtered through to him.'

'Man, we can't wait that long,' Hank shouted in despair. 'Anna might be dead by then.'

'Her diamonds!' The words burst from Maurice like a cannon shot. 'Someone abducted her to rob her of her diamonds. Maybe the Thompson crook works with an accomplice.'

The thought had occurred to Broadbent, although Thompson swore he had nothing to do with Anna, hadn't approached or touched her.

'We'll get those diamonds if they show up somewhere for sale. They are too well documented to be disposed of easily. Isn't that the case?' Broadbent looked at Hank, who nodded in numb agreement, his eyes drawn towards the KwaZulu Medical folder still lying on his desk.

'EEM?' he said, barely above a whisper. 'Those EEM guys . . . could it be them again?'

Broadbent cast doubt on the suggestion. 'They are renowned for dispatching prompt ransom demands. If they are the perpetrators, expect a request for money within the next twenty-four hours. Or do you have one already?' They shook their heads.

Captain Broadbent ran his eyes over the shocked group of men, studying their body language. Franz De Bruyn was hopping mad. His white-knuckled fists clenched and unclenched. He was ready to thump every remaining blob of excrement out of Thompson or whoever was responsible. Maurice Van Buuren's nerves were red raw. He tried vainly to be the rational, analytical one among them, but give him a gun and he may not be accountable for his actions. Hank De Bruyn was shattered, barely able to take in what had happened. He slumped in his chair with his shoulders rounded as if a rock had crushed him. From time to time, his right hand touched the centre of his chest. He rummaged in his desk drawer then searched his pockets when he couldn't find what he wanted.

'Where the hell . . . ?'

'You left your pills in the car,' Maurice surmised. 'I'll get them.'

Jakobus and Gerhard pushed through the door just as Maurice left to fetch Hank's medication.

'God, what an awful tragedy to hit us so soon after our anniversary ball. I've been thinking we ought to check the guest list to see if we had people there who might have been less congenial than we thought.' Jakobus's fingers scratched his head with agitated little movements. He seemed unaware of them, as if they had a life of their own.

'Coming to think of it,' Gerhard agreed, 'I thought I noticed at least two gatecrashers from Gold Corp. There could have been more. It was a bit hard to tell without offensively going around with a list and ticking off names.'

With silent appreciation and gratitude, both took the brandy Franz still distributed.

'If anyone from Gold Corp is responsible for this, I'll see their share price drops below the level of dirt.' Franz laughed with sinister undertones. 'Then Mineral Enterprises can have them for just one note of a song.'

'Shit!' Gerhard blurted out his thoughts. 'Maybe the Gold Corp board thinks we supported Mineral Enterprises's hostile takeover bid. They might be seeking to teach us a lesson. What a cowardly way to go about it. It reeks to high heaven.'

Hank rallied, cutting through his brothers' anxious voices and taking Broadbent in his sights. 'I want a full-page notice in every major daily newspaper with a photo of Anna and an R100,000 reward for information as to her whereabouts.' Hank found it hard to sit still. Talking was fine, but it had to be underscored by action. He was already searching for numbers in the phone book when Captain Broadbent intervened.

'No, I wouldn't advise it, Mr De Bruyn. It's too early for that.' The others looked at him blankly. Jakobus thought it a good idea.

'Why?' he asked critically.

'Because', Broadbent answered, 'if Mr Van Buuren is right and some scoundrel is holding Mrs De Bruyn for her diamonds, he may panic and kill her if he sees her picture in the paper.'

'Do you mean I'm supposed to sit here and do nothing?' Hank said, leaving his chair and stepping to the window as if to watch for

Anna's appearance. He turned back to Broadbent. 'I don't need to tell you what unspeakable perils can befall a lady at the hands of criminals,' he said, pointing a finger at the captain and raising his voice. 'Find her!'

Broadbent felt helpless. How could he calm Hank when he was no wiser as to where Anna De Bruyn might be? Thompson was his only slim lead, plus the few facts he gleaned from his conversation with the De Bruyn men. Particulars of their animosity towards Malcolm Price and Gold Corp generally would bear investigation. Gold Corp may not be the only enemy. Who knew what would crawl out of the woodwork when he probed?

When Jan and Adriaan entered Hank's office, the De Bruyn clan repaired to the conference room for their emergency summit. Meals were ordered from a nearby restaurant to sustain them, particularly Jan and Adriaan, who had arrived on a domestic flight from Cape Town. They were running on empty and eager for the amber super fuel Franz poured out liberally.

Taking his leave, Broadbent declined food and drink. He had work to do. He could gain no more from talking to the men. They were in overdrive and needed a day or two to come to terms with the atrocity.

After a further hour of discussion and speculation, Hank became restless. He wanted to be home in case Anna tried to contact him. He rejected Franz's urging to stay with him, but the brothers did not want to leave him alone. After a brief debate, Adriaan brought Hank's car to the front of the building and, together with Jan, drove him home and remained with him.

* * *

Anna De Bruyn glanced in her rear-view mirror, annoyed. The yellow VW Golf followed two cars behind her. Dashing through amber lights in an attempt to shake it off hadn't worked. Her frequent lane changes failed to confuse the driver. She indicated right but did not turn. Half a kilometre further, she indicated left but changed into the right lane. All to no avail. That yellow vehicle hung on. For safety's sake, she stopped her dangerous road-rage-like manoeuvres. She would soon reach Pretoria. Maybe she could lose him there.

Anna had become aware of the yellow car the previous night when she saw it parked on the opposite side of the road from her house. She thought nothing of it. The neighbours had visitors for dinner, and it probably belonged to them. She laughed at it because it was yellow and parked under a tree. During her student days in Sydney, a friend drove a yellow car.

'Never buy a yellow car,' Virginia had warned. 'I swear the birds favour them. The colour inspires their creativity.' Every day Virginia cursed the feathered graffiti artists for pasting her automobile with a fresh layer of white paint. Virginia always parked under a tree.

When Anna reached Mr Pienaar's business consultancy the yellow car was not in evidence. She sighed with relief. She spent two hours chatting with Mr Pienaar before making her way to Mrs Odenthal. And there it was again.

'This is ridiculous,' Anna said under her breath, watching the pursuing car with narrowed eyes. She couldn't find a parking spot closer than half a block from Mrs Odenthal's office, and that yellow creep had the cheek to move into an area marked No Parking a mere fifteen metres away from her. She gave the driver a menacing look when he climbed out. He smiled as he walked past her. 'Nice day!' he commented cheerfully.

Unable to digest his effrontery, Anna turned on him.

'You're standing in a no parking zone, did you realize?' She pointed to the glaringly obvious sign.

'Oh, I'll take pot luck. I won't be long,' he replied.

'Man, you drive as if your license came out of a cereal packet,' Anna said with disgust.

He laughed loudly. 'No, lady, I won it in a raffle.'

'Well, keep off my tail. I'm warning you!' Anna snarled. The man shrugged and walked away. Anna memorized his car number.

Maria Odenthal welcomed Anna and settled her comfortably in a big chair. Over the years, their friendship had matured and the broker/client relationship became an incidental part of their discourse.

'Do you mind if I call Maurice please, Maria? I had this lunatic following me all the way from Johannesburg in a yellow VW Golf. Quite scary!'

'Go right ahead. We can call the police if you're worried.'

'Thanks, but I think Maurice should ring because the car's been parked near my home too.'

Maria looked pensive. 'Are you on someone's hit list?'

'Christ, I hope not. Why would I be?'

'You stockbrokers aren't the only ones with professional grapevines. Lawyers have them too.'

Anna grinned at her friend's comment, but Maria remained serious.

'I have my own personal cutting of the plant. It tells me stories about fearful cabinet ministers who have been caught like naughty boys taking money in return for passing particular legislation. Do you get my drift?'

'Keep going.' Anna thought she knew where this was leading.

'From what I hear, the party who suborned the parliamentarians is unhappy. In fact, the vindictive old bastard is looking for an opportunity to hit back at whoever is bringing the matter to court.'

Anna smiled now. 'What else does your wonder vegetation tell you?'

'It wouldn't be you and Adriaan, would it? My plant thinks so.'

'Scandal photosynthesis, Maria, that's what your plant is up to.' Anna chuckled at the tale of corruption. 'We'll get them. It may take time, but we'll get them.'

'Be on your guard for reprisals. They can take any shape or form.'

She shrugged off the warning. 'Someone has to keep the pricks honest. I think I have some experience in such matters.'

'Just be watchful, Anna.'

'Are you telling me the yellow VW Golf may be playing a part in this?'

Maria's dark eyes opened wide as she nodded. 'I wouldn't rule it out.'

'Ah . . . to hell with it.' Anna refused to be daunted. 'Let's go to lunch.'

* * *

'What fuckin' rotten luck.' Sitting on the can in his police cell, Darren Thompson swore to himself. What right had the pigs to keep him locked up, preventing him from doing his job? That was all he was about—his daily work, like thousands of other people. Just a job. The type he'd performed countless times already. Only this last one had a slight twist.

Observing a man or woman at the behest of their spouse to ascertain if their loving partner went astray was his mainstay, his bread and butter. His present assignment was similar except it wasn't the husband who wanted to know. It was a third party who, Thompson suspected, required the information as a tool for blackmail or a smear campaign. He wasn't silly. He read the papers and knew of Anna De Bruyn's sparring with Malcolm Price.

He thought he'd discovered something too when she came out of the Pretoria Academic Hospital accompanied by a tall, well-presented black man. There was one for the book!

Thompson shook his head sadly. 'Fuck me dead, I must be losing my touch.' He cursed again. 'Getting too bloody old for the job.' Never before had his prey spotted him. He shouldn't have stopped outside her house, pretending to be next door's dinner guest. She would have been alert to strange cars in the neighbourhood. He had followed her too closely to Pretoria too. Boy, could she drive. Like the living devil. Spunky lady. Speaking to her was a mistake, but something made him want to hear her voice. Christ, he went all jelly-kneed when she got out of her car. Damned attractive woman.

He knew he had to quit tracking her after she'd had a good look at him. He'd need to change his clothes, slap on a false moustache, spectacles, and hat and take up her trail in a hire car. Thompson grinned as he imagined his mirror image wearing a disguise. Out of sheer curiosity, he'd watched her and the Odenthal woman go to a restaurant and, later, when they parted, followed De Bruyn to the hospital. After about twenty minutes, she reappeared with the black bloke. Afraid to push his luck, he'd returned home to find two pigs waiting for him. He thought he had been assigned a welcoming party because of his unlawful parking earlier in the day, but no. The pretty woman ran scared and complained to the police about being stalked. To make matters worse, by late evening, her employees reported her missing and the pigs refused to believe he had nothing to do with it. 'She might have shot through with the black guy.'

Thompson chortled. Be blowed if he'd tell the pigs any of that. Let them do their own dirty work.

* * *

Anna De Bruyn hated hospitals. They contained too much suffering. No matter how modern the building or how sunny the day, hospitals felt infected with despondency, and she preferred to keep away from them. Most hospitals resembled rabbit warrens to her, full of corridors, passages, and side doors. As the taxi approached Pretoria Academic, she felt this place would prove no exception to her rule. Its street address, Dr Savage Road, spoke for itself. How was she to find Joshua in there? Fair dinkum, the man was crazy.

Joshua gave her instructions how to reach the small office allocated to him when they arranged their Pretoria meeting on the phone two days earlier. Setting her briefcase down, she pulled the sheet of paper with her scribbled directions out of her handbag. Hoping she had jotted down the right room number, she walked on resolutely. Following Josh's guide to the letter, she found herself knocking on his door. She didn't like the fluttering feeling inside her as she did so. Some strict, humourless matron or sister might pop out like a cuckoo from its clock and tell her Professor Mtolo was busy. She didn't need that. The day had brought her enough hassles already.

'*Ngena!* Er . . . yes, come in!'

That was Josh's voice, Anna thought, relieved. He must be totally involved with his work to automatically call 'Enter' in Zulu and then remember to say it in English. Anna felt a little guilty for disturbing him, but he had asked her to come. She turned the doorknob timidly, startled when Josh opened from within.

'Mrs De Bruyn!' He smiled broadly. 'I thought it must be you. Nobody else around here knocks so softly.' His eyes ran over her appreciatively. Her clothes were faultless, as always. A cream-coloured linen suit with a violet silk shirt emphasized her youthfulness. The violet blouse clashed with her traffic-light green eyes, but the effect was not unpleasant. It brought freshness to her face.

'Please, come in.' He beckoned her into a cramped broom cupboard of a room filled with a desk, two chairs, filing cabinets and medical paraphernalia like books, skulls, skeletons, and appalling stuff in jars.

'Have a seat,' Josh invited, his voice hoarse with USB. The urge to embrace her came naturally. He restrained it because she was about to throw the book at him. For this encounter, he was thankful to have her sitting on the other side of the desk for a change. It meant he was in the dominant position. He noticed with satisfaction that Anna looked mildly disconcerted. She found the altered circumstance less than ideal. He smiled to himself because her body language betrayed how unaccustomed she was to lack of command. He was, however, unprepared for the onslaught of Anna's feminine weaponry on his sensibilities.

She placed her briefcase and handbag on the floor beside her, leaned back in the chair, and crossed her legs. Her skirt split revealed her thigh in exactly the right amount; not too much and not too little. Her gold ankle bracelet shone with provocative lustre.

Barely able to look elsewhere, Josh fingered his ballpoint pen nervously, picked it up, put it down, sorted his paperwork, then restacked it. She wrenched authority back to her side by driving him into heated confusion. He determined that she must not succeed. Gathering himself, he sat up straight, saying, 'What was it you wanted to see me about, Mrs De Bruyn?'

Anna took the KwaZulu Medical file from her briefcase and handed him a photocopy of Sipho's handwritten balance sheet. 'What is that?' she asked with a puzzled frown.

'I haven't a clue, Mrs De Bruyn.' Josh looked at her searchingly, wondering what she would say next.

'Look at it closely, Professor.'

Josh did so to please her. 'Balance sheet?' He looked up and laughed. 'Mrs De Bruyn, you know that type of stuff escapes a financially illiterate being like me. You're going to have to tell me.'

'Read it again. It's not just any balance sheet. It says "KwaZulu Medical, Balance Sheet" . . . it's yours. Do you know who wrote it?'

'Sipho Gwala,' Josh replied, his voice faltering a little. 'It's his writing.'

'Right!' Anna leafed through the file to find the computer printout. 'Now please compare it with this.' She passed the computer sheet to Josh. He shrugged his shoulders.

'What am I supposed to be looking for?'

Anna knew Josh played dumb. He feigned ignorance, laying the papers aside as if what she showed him was inconsequential. Any minute he would tell her to stop wasting his time. She had to forestall that. Armed with a green highlighter, she leaned forward and circled the capital figure on each sheet. Changing to blue, she underlined the investment income figures on Sipho's personal sheet.

'And what does that tell us?' Josh had become strangely serious.

'Professor, are we agreed that the computer sheet is KwaZulu Medical's official financial statement?'

'I believe so, madam.'

He's getting worried, Anna thought, glancing quickly at his sombre face.

'In that case, why does the printout not show the interest received from your foreign investments?'

'I can't tell you, madam. All I can say is that I have faith in my finance administrator. He knows what he's doing, I'm sure.'

Anna laughed. 'Yes, I expect he does. He will also know that what he's cooked up here gives every impression of tax evasion.'

'Mrs De Bruyn, you jest. I didn't think we made enough money to pay much tax.'

Smoothie, Anna thought. 'On the contrary, Professor. Do you know anything about that Swiss account? Looking at the interest you received, I would venture a guess that you must have between seven and eight hundred thousand US dollars there. Am I right?'

'Yes,' Josh agreed. 'We receive regular donations from various sources. They deposit US dollars straight into that account.' This was wishful thinking posing as truth.

'Depending on your arrangements,' Anna went on, 'the donations may be tax-free, but the interest you derive from them will not be. Remind me to recommend a good tax accountant to you.' She smiled with a twinkle in her eye. *He's feeding me crap and fibs all the way and hopes I believe him*, she thought.

'Do you have any idea why Mr Gwala failed to include interest income from the Swiss account in your official statement? As a matter of fact, he doesn't mention Switzerland at all . . . as if the account did not exist.'

Josh gave a long sigh and struck a relaxed pose, leaning back in his chair. It was an act to impress her. In reality, he felt he was being pushed through a wringer. What could he tell her? He had to think fast.

'Mrs De Bruyn, Sipho Gwala is a very sick man. His condition concerns me greatly. I'm afraid I have to admit that he is becoming forgetful. That is the only explanation I can give you. He may have forgotten about the "interest income", as you call it.'

'An honest mistake then?' Anna asked with a cynical smile. She looked directly into Josh's eyes.

'I'd say so.' He returned her scrutiny without flinching.

'Can I rely on you to tell him to change it for the end of the next quarter?'

'Of course, madam.' He relaxed visibly, happy to have come through the interview unscathed. Yet one look at her face told him she didn't believe a word he said. She was prepared to let it ride for now, pending further developments. And she wasn't as discomfited about sitting on the opposite side of his desk as he had hoped . . . the little hellcat.

Anna closed her briefcase, flashing Josh a conciliatory smile. 'Thanks for talking to me, Professor. I won't hold you up any longer.' She rose to leave.

'You're not holding me up at all. I'm finished here. I only have to tidy these papers away to leave the room in an orderly state for whoever uses it next.' Josh pulled open a filing cabinet drawer and dropped sheets into hanging files. 'I'm still faced with the long drive back,' he went on while throwing pens into a drawer. 'I'd like to unwind a little before I attempt that. Why don't you join me? I know a delightfully intimate little wine bar you'd probably like. We won't drink much, seeing we're both driving. The driving was my own choice, so I can only blame myself. They wanted me to fly, but by the time I get from Vryheid to Durban, I might just as well drive all the way, considering I'd need a car from Johannesburg to Pretoria too. It's just more convenient this way.' He became conscious of his garrulity but looked hopefully at her, wishing she would come with him.

Anna laughed, shaking her head as she replied, 'I still have two more clients to see. I'd love to have a drink with you, but—' she hesitated.

'Please!' Josh smiled, giving her a fiery look of the variety Hank called *eating her*. 'Your charming company would improve my day beyond recognition.'

Anna emitted her silver-bell laugh. 'Flattery and more flattery. You do try hard, Professor.'

Taking her laughter as agreement to accompany him, he said, 'Come on, let's go now.' With his hand on her shoulder, they walked to the doctors' parking area.

'Hop in,' he prompted, opening the passenger door of the hire car.

'Where's your red car?' Anna fastened her seat belt.

'Left it behind this time. The hospital hired this one for me. I dare say it's more powerful and comfortable than my poor, rickety, coughing Corolla. That's travelled more kilometres than it cares to remember.' Josh reversed from his parking bay and nosed into the mainstream traffic, driving along Hamilton Street.

'How did you get here?' he asked with interest. 'Where are your wheels?'

Anna giggled. 'Standing outside Odenthal Partners' law firm. I had lunch with Maria, and we drank half a drop too many. I wasn't going to risk being picked up by the cops. I've moved around on foot and by taxi since lunch.'

Joshua drove on, seeking the wine bar. He turned right into Church Street. They passed Odenthal Partners again, and Anna said, 'There's my car, still waiting for me. It's good to know nobody has stolen it yet.'

'The place we want can't be very far,' Josh said, driving slowly, surveying both sides of the road. 'I can't remember if it's one or two intersections further on.' After gathering speed again, he braked suddenly a short distance past the next crossroad where Church and Du Toit Streets intersected.

'I knew it had to be here somewhere.' He reversed into a convenient parking spot, locked their briefcases in the boot, and led Anna into the bar. It was long past lunchtime, and only a hand full of people sat chatting over coffee and liqueur.

'Just what I could do with,' Josh remarked, looking towards the patrons enjoying their drinks. 'How about you?'

'Yes, that will be fine,' Anna replied, turning towards a small table by the window.

At one end of the bar stood a display rack of postcards for tourists; beside it, a basket with sprigs of violets and roses. They caught Josh's eye. He selected a particularly pretty spray of violets to compliment Anna's blouse. Grinning, he stepped towards her and, without ceremony, pinned it to her jacket.

Momentarily astounded, Anna said nothing. She felt as if a mist of pure, undiluted masculine sexuality enveloped her. It emanated from Josh as if he had stepped out of a hot shower with his body still steaming. Involuntarily, she took a little step backwards.

Josh's smile died. Had he overstepped the mark? Was he taking liberties, invading her personal space? Of course he had stood too close to her. He couldn't help himself. His heart imploding, he thought sadly, *She doesn't want such deliberate attention from a black man.*

Anna saw doubt on Josh's face but had no idea why. She laughed and stood on tiptoe to catch a glimpse of herself in the bottle-filled mirrored shelves behind the bar.

'That's beautiful.' She smiled so happily Josh forgave her initial awkward reaction. Perhaps he misread her gesture. 'Thank you, Professor. What have I done to deserve this?'

'Just for being here with me.' He walked back to the bar to ask for coffee, spirits, and snacks. Anna watched him return with a glass in each hand. He sat down.

'They'll bring us coffee and a bite to eat in a minute.' He lifted his glass, smiling. 'Good health!'

Anna followed suit. 'Success!' she replied, enjoying the burning warmth of the brandy. Catching a whiff of Josh's bourbon, she grimaced.

'How can you drink that concoction?' she asked with a shiver.

'Bad habit I picked up in the USA,' he laughed. 'Perhaps I should have asked for a bottle of Backsburg for us to share. Do you like reds?'

'I do, but I'm content with my brandy and coffee.'

They smiled at each other, and their eyes locked for a moment. Anna winked. Lowering her voice, she became secretive and conspiratorial.

'You must tell your Mr Gwala to get out of Gold Corp, you know.'

'Why's that?'

Anna looked around to ensure nobody else listened. 'The talk has not reached into the wider business community yet, and the media don't know, but Mineral Enterprises is making a takeover bid for Gold Corp. It will be a pretty hostile affair, and Gold Corp will slump. We've given as much detail as we dare in our newsletter and Vince Lewis is tipping off our clients by phone. He's probably rung Mr Gwala already, but if not, at least you're prepared. Keep a close watch on the matter.'

'Thank you, madam. I'll tell Sipho.'

'You see, Gold Corp's share price never recovered from the repercussions of that meeting you attended a while back and'— Anna lowered her voice still further—'their managing director did bribe two MPs. It's an ugly situation, which causes uncertainty in the market. Mineral Enterprises are being quite opportunistic with their takeover bid. It's like dog eats dog.' She took another sip of brandy. 'For the moment, you'd be safer with Mineral Enterprises. Act quickly before the takeover talk hits the news.'

Josh nodded his thanks for the hint while downing his bourbon. The mention of Mineral Enterprises reminded him of William Rosenberg. He enjoyed the irony of acquiring shares in William's company using William's ransom money. It was an amusing turn of fate. A quirky smile spread slowly over his face. His eyes gleamed with mirth known only to him.

'Tell me, Professor,' Anna went on. 'You said your administrator is ill. What's wrong with the man?'

'AIDS,' Josh answered simply, drawn away from his thought of Mineral Enterprises shares.

'Oh dear!' Anna's sympathetic tone encouraged him to continue.

'Yes, poor Sipho! I met him in Soweto one night, sick as a dog and stone broke. I badly needed administrative help for the clinic at the time, and Sipho was hospital finance director in Durban, so I took him on. He's an excellent worker despite his illness, but sometimes I fear he's reaching his limits. I'd hate to pension him off. He's a friend who plays a large part in fleshing out my dream.'

'Dream, Professor?' Anna tilted her head, questioning. 'Tell me about it, please.'

'I'm not sure that you'd really want to know,' he replied quietly. How could the origin of KwaZulu Medical interest this pampered dame? he wondered, watching her slender, diamond-ringed fingers encircle her glass. What did his desire to provide a quality medical service for his people mean to her? The excellence of South Africa's medical care had made world news when Professor Christian Barnard performed the first heart transplant in Cape Town's Groote Schuur Hospital on 3 December 1967. What did not hit the headlines was that such first-rate standards were not for the benefit of blacks. But this stockbroker lady wouldn't understand. She had no idea how the majority of South African citizens, the blacks, were forced to exist. The unemployment, resulting poverty, rudimentary housing, inadequate education, and insufficient health care were unknown concepts to a millionaire's wife.

'I do want to know, Professor. Dreams, visions, goals, and ambitions are important. Where would we be if nobody had them? Goodbye, productivity and enterprise.'

Josh smiled. 'All right.' He looked at her almost tenderly. 'I'll tell you on one condition.'

'And what would that be, Professor?' Anna's green eyes glowed, looking at him with unabashed interest.

'That you stop calling me *Professor*. It may have escaped your notice that my name is Joshua. My friends call me Josh, and my juvenile patients refer to me as Doctor Josh. You can call me any one of these but not *Professor*.'

Anna began to bubble with laughter. 'All right, Doctor Josh,' she giggled, her eyes sending him a message of affection of which she was unaware. 'I'm Anna, by the way, not *Madam*.'

Josh shared her laughter. 'This *Professor* business gets on my nerves. Sipho started it at the clinic, and it goes on all the time. It makes me feel like Figaro in that . . .'—he snapped his fingers—'you know, that *Barber of Seville* opera. Figaro here, Figaro there—Professor here, Professor there, Professor everywhere.' He gestured to his right and left with quick theatrical movements of his hands.

Anna burst into her full silver-bell laughter, causing people to turn their heads, staring.

'But you were going to tell me about your dream, Josh.' Anna leaned forward a little, indicating he had her full attention.

A profound sadness touched Josh's eyes. 'It's not much of a dream, really—nightmare's more like it.'

'How so?'

Josh became solemn, as if he bore more grief and responsibility than was humanly possible. His mood swing was total and in vivid contrast to a moment earlier. Anna took his hand in perturbed silence. 'Go on,' she encouraged.

'KwaZulu Medical is a brainchild we nurture with the greatest care.' Josh began hesitantly. 'That is, my friends and I. We're all in it together. Peter, Tom, Sipho, and other indispensable helpers and volunteers. We started the clinic after I witnessed a school bus shooting near Edendale. There were twelve kids in the bus. Four were killed. The others suffered horrible injuries. I'm always concerned about the mental state of very young victims of politically motivated violence. They don't understand what goes on. Cindy told me of kids she'd taught who drew ghastly images of guns, necklacings, machete attacks, and such like during lessons. Their bodies and minds won't recover for a long, long time. It struck me that we needed a hospital for such cases. My friends agreed and have supported me ever since. As you know, our financial problems seem insurmountable, but we don't let it deter us. At the moment, I'm working on a research project on the effects of violence and brutality on the young. That's coming along very slowly, partly hindered by lack of funds.'

Josh stopped speaking when he felt Anna's hand on his arm.

'We can do something about that,' she said with certainty.

Josh couldn't imagine what and said so. 'What do you mean, Anna?'

Her cynical smile was back as she replied, 'Our mates, the pharmaceutical companies, think it's time they revealed themselves as good corporate citizens. We should test the strength of their resolve by asking them for a grant.'

'Oh, no! No, no. Not those rapacious hyenas,' Josh objected, with hands raised to ward off the suggestion. 'Not for me, thanks.'

'Josh, I remember you telling me you couldn't afford ethical considerations. I expect that encompasses ideological aspects as well?' Absent-mindedly, Anna ran her fingers gently over the back of Josh's hand. 'Your research should whet their appetite. It is bound to demonstrate a need for specific drugs and medications, which they could develop and eventually derive returns from . . .' Her sentence trailed off when Josh gave her a distasteful look.

'Yes,' he said severely, 'drugs and medications which they will test among the poor in the developing world before they are even fully aware of how such drugs will affect people.'

Anna sighed, feeling Josh's verbal slap acutely. 'I know, I know.' She hid her face in her hands for a moment. 'It is one of the world's greatest problems. You are the only one who can decide, but why not think positively and consider the public good? Think of the benefit your work can bring people. Weigh public health against your ideological qualms and see which side tips the scales. Nobody's health will improve if your research remains in your desk drawer because you are too careful about whose help you accept. Also, should you acquire a sizeable parcel of shares in the pharmaceutical industry, it will give you more leverage to dictate the terms on which your research is used. That won't happen for a long time yet, I admit. You don't have the funds. You could start slowly, though, by buying into companies who are major shareholders already. Their support could help you spread your influence.'

Although Josh found the idea tempting because Anna had somehow made it sound acceptable, he laughed at her. 'You have it all worked out, it seems.'

'Yes, I think I can help you overcome some of your financial constraints if you are prepared to trust me.'

Trust, Josh thought, was the key word. Could he believe in her? Would she stay loyal, or would she assist him till KwaZulu Medical became viable and then stand back, watching while a white business consortium bought it lock, stock, and barrel? Even if she proved genuine, how would her husband and his brothers operate? Although Sipho disapproved in the strongest terms, Josh thought his own plans posed less danger for KwaZulu Medical's independence and the furthering of their dream. And his steps were simple. Hold Anna captive for a time, extract money from Hank, and then part company with her and De Bruyn Brothers. She was too exacting and far more thorough than he imagined. Already she had suspicions about KwaZulu Medical, smelling at least a dozen rats. He'd find someone else who was prepared to ignore little accounting glitches, and he'd intimidate Anna into silence about everything she knew.

No such thoughts reflected in his eyes as he smiled at her, wondering if he had the ability to be severe enough. Those green traffic-light eyes beguiled a hapless, USB-suffering male.

Anna suddenly became aware of the time. 'Oh, ye gods!' she exclaimed. 'I've got to be off. I told Maurice I'd be back by five. Hank's away on a speaking tour, and Maurice and I are sharing his workload.' Taking her handbag, she stood up saying, 'You've locked my briefcase in your boot.' Before her haste marked her as impolite, she added, 'Thank you for everything, Josh. It's always so wonderful to see you.'

Josh rose as well. Pulling his car keys from his pocket he said, 'Yes, I should be hitting the road too. I'll be greeted by a mountain of work when I get back.'

They left the wine bar, and Josh persuaded Anna to accept a lift to her own vehicle.

'I can walk,' she protested. 'It's only three blocks or so.'

'Ah, come on, Anna. It will save time for you,' Josh said reasonably.

Anna recalled her adventure with the yellow VW Golf. She might be safer going with Josh. He opened the passenger door for her.

'My briefcase, please, Josh. I'll probably forget it later,' Anna reminded him. He unlocked the boot with a good-natured shrug and handed the case over. Belting himself into his seat, he looked at the dashboard clock.

'I won't be home before ten if I stop somewhere for dinner.' He turned the ignition key watching the fuel gauge. 'This machine drinks more than I do. My Corolla is a sober customer in comparison.'

The car hummed softly at the turn of the key, and Josh eased into the traffic. He drove around the block to turn right into Church

Street again. They encountered green lights at the next two intersections. The third showed amber, turning to red. Josh floored the accelerator. The car shot forward like a dog kept too long on a leash. It gained speed, and Anna had a momentary vision of a collision.

'Joshua, stop! You've driven right past my car. We're way beyond Odenthal's. You better let me out here and I'll walk back.' Josh drove on.

'Joshua! Please do a U-turn or let me out here.'

No reply came from him. He looked straight ahead. If anything, he was going even faster.

'Did you hear what I said?'

He glanced at her. Anna thought she perceived a gleam of triumph in his eyes.

'Let me out, please, Josh.' She repeated her request firmly.

'No, you're coming with me,' he said with finality.

'I what?' Anna's traffic light eyes widened with a warning glow.

Seeing her stunned face, he laughed. 'You wanted to visit my clinic at some stage, didn't you? Now's as good a time as any.'

'I can't, Josh. I've got to get back to Johannesburg. I've got too much work there. Besides, I want to see your place at leisure when I can give it the time and attention it deserves, not a rushed trip on the spur of the moment.'

'You'll have time, don't worry, plenty of it.' Josh grinned vaguely.

A seed of disquiet sprouted in Anna's mind while she studied Josh's profile. Something was wrong. It felt surreal to be driving away with him. Why didn't he let her out or take her back to Odenthal's?

'At least stop somewhere so that I can phone Maurice. If he doesn't hear from me, he'll think I've been kidnapped.'

Josh looked at her piercingly but said nothing. Steering well clear of the Johannesburg direction, he tore along Church Street, turned right into Festival Street then left into Pretorius Street, merging with the N4 towards Mpumalanga.

'I had this jerk follow me all morning in a yellow VW Golf. Maurice will think that psycho's got me.'

Josh half turned to look at her. 'Anna,' he said, shocked, 'tell me what happened.' His eyes were soft again, filled with caring and concern. 'It must have been frightening for you,' he said, his voice warm and comforting.

'It didn't exactly thrill me,' she admitted. 'Maria Odenthal thinks Malcolm Price may be planning some form of vendetta against me, trying to scare me because of his company's continued poor share performance. Nor would he like me to inform the press of his and certain government ministers' malfeasance.' She added with bravado, 'Little does he know Anna De Bruyn cannot be threatened or intimidated.'

Josh frowned. 'And you think the VW Golf man was sent by Price?'

'Maria seems to think so.'

'In that case,' Josh said slowly, 'it might be just as well for you to be out of town. Nobody will come near you where we're going. You can rest easy.'

They drove on in silence for many kilometres while the sun set and darkness dropped like a curtain, obliterating the delusion of their unsubstantial togetherness.

* * *

'Mr De Bruyn, have you received a ransom demand yet?' Broadbent was on the line, keeping Hank abreast of developments.

'No, Captain Broadbent. Nothing!' Hank replied, each word costing him a supreme effort. He was bone-weary. He hadn't slept for two nights, spending his working hours alternately on the phone, raising all hell in an effort to find Anna or standing by the window, looking down onto the street as if expecting to see her approach at any time. At home, he also sat by the phone non-stop, willing it to ring.

The House of De Bruyn became a bleak place. Hank, who normally kept his office door open to be accessible to all staff, was morose and closed himself in. Seniors like Maurice, Vince, and Mrs George had long faces and spoke in whispers as if someone had died. Maurice did Hank's work because Hank had no will to communicate with anyone. Nkosinathi was promoted to assist Maurice. That brought him into frequent contact with Hank. It tore at his heart to see his boss and role model grieving, and he hatched ideas that might help to locate Mrs De Bruyn.

'So nobody has claimed responsibility for your wife's disappearance?' Broadbent continued questioning.

'Not that I've heard,' Hank yawned.

'We persuaded Mr Thompson that it's in his own interest to tell us a little more of what he knows,' Broadbent said with a sardonic inflection. 'It appears that the reason he was paid to carry out the surveillance on your wife was to find out whether she met other men during your absence. Thompson believes that his employer hoped to either blackmail her or besmirch her name.'

'Oh, Christ!' Hank cursed, but the words lacked force. He was too exhausted.

'Mr De Bruyn, please pardon my offensive, next question.' Broadbent paused awkwardly. 'But is it possible that your wife may have left with another man?'

'That wouldn't be like Anna at all. She'd never do that,' Hank answered defensively. The suggestion angered him. 'Isn't it time you discovered the identity of Thompson's employer?' Hank shouted aggressively into the telephone.

'We're working on that, Mr De Bruyn. I'll keep you informed. We have to keep the lines of communication open between us. Don't hesitate to call me at any time for whatever reason.'

Franz, who had listened to the call on an extension in Anna's office, came over to Hank when Broadbent hung up.

'Isn't that just a bucket of slime?' he roared. 'It's got Malcolm Price's hallmark all over it. Nobody else would stoop into the gutter like that. We're gonna get the shithouse rat for that, brother. See if we don't.'

'We can't be sure if it's Price,' Hank cautioned wearily with a wave of his hand.

'Then tell me who else is currently feeling sufficiently desperate to fight so dirty?'

Nkosinathi, who sat at Maurice's desk feeling like a man of influence, heard the conversation with revulsion. He left the room and headed for the library. Searching the filing cabinets for scrapbooks containing the latest newspaper clippings, he found the ones with photographs of Anna taken at the last Gold Corp shareholders' meeting. Of the three available pictures, he chose the clearest and made a number of photocopies. Trimming them down to size, he put them in his pocket. Freddie Bonga would know what to do with them. Freddie travelled around and still had connections to bike gangs. Nkosinathi hoped that these shady characters might know Mrs De Bruyn's kidnappers. And Mrs De Bruyn was a clever lady, Nkosinathi knew. She wouldn't disappear without a trace. She'd leave a deliberate trail for interested parties like Freddie to pick up. He would ask Freddie to distribute the photocopies among his motorcycle cohorts on Saturday when he came to Soweto to visit his mother. Satisfied and cheered by his positive thoughts, he tidied Maurice's desk and went home.

* * *

Chapter 7

KwaZulu Medical

Anna stood in the middle of her room, displeased, measuring the extent of her living space at KwaZulu Medical. Josh had told her to make herself comfortable. What a comedian he was, she thought moodily. The place was no architectural showpiece and more like a budget, no-frills backpacker hostel. On opening the door, she was confronted by an old kitchen table and two chairs. Beyond that, a door led to a tiny bathroom. To the left was a double bed of the same vintage as the kitchen furniture. A low chest of drawers served as a bedside table. Of more recent date was a narrow wardrobe with a mirror door, which stood against the far wall. The window beside the bathroom door revealed the garden when Anna drew the cheap curtains aside. In the darkness, she saw only the nearby shrubs.

'So much for that,' she muttered to herself. 'Thanks for nothing, Joshua.'

With the friendliest display of his best bedside manner, he had suggested that she should go to sleep. Tomorrow they'd talk about everything.

'And don't forget to look under the pillow,' he prompted with a grin. 'There could be a surprise for you.'

Anna hadn't gone to bed. Nor had she bothered to investigate what lay under the pillow, her apprehension cancelling curiosity. She was too stunned to be interested. The hours spent on the road from Pretoria to Vryheid had passed uneasily with a sporadic, stilted dialogue of monosyllables between them. Every time he refused to break the journey to enable her to telephone Maurice or Hank, she lapsed into brooding silence, studying the man beside her who was fast becoming her adversary. Their interaction became ugly when Josh stopped for petrol at Middleburg. She wanted to get out of the car as well to find a telephone, but Josh grasped her wrist hard when she reached for the door.

'You will remain in the car,' he commanded threateningly.

Pain travelled up her arm, preventing her from pulling free of his hold. Enraged but wary, she came to understand that this was no longer a joke. Her pride took a hit below the watermark. Nobody dictated to Anna De Bruyn.

'You have no right to treat me this way. This is assault and deprivation of liberty. Both are indictable offences.' She spoke quietly and as calmly as she could, her face averted so he could not see her pain, although her voice trembled.

Josh hadn't missed Anna's slight stammer. He pressed home his advantage, tightening his hand on her wrist further, saying, 'This is just the beginning. Don't make it unpleasant for both of us. We can be friends or deadly enemies. It's up to you.'

Slowly, fearfully the enigma dissolved in her mind. By the time they reached Vryheid via Ermelo and Volksrust, she became convinced she knew his other identity.

The very fact that something had been deposited under the pillow proved that her presence at KwaZulu Medical was not a random, impulsive event but a premeditated abduction of the sort William Rosenberg and others had been subjected to.

Anna wouldn't sleep till she had made contact with Hank or Maurice. There was a public telephone in the foyer. She had noticed it on arrival when Josh took her through before showing her to her room. She rarely carried much cash and hoped the few coins in her purse would suffice for a quick call. Holding them tight, she ventured into the corridor but closed her door quickly upon hearing footsteps. She waited five minutes, took off her shoes to eliminate clicking heels, and crept out. Walking stealthily, she passed the next room and then the one marked 'S Gwala' on the door. The next door had a name plate also, 'J Mtolo', and light shone from the crack at the bottom. Hurrying past, she turned sharp right and moved on till she reached the foyer to her left. The hallway ran past the administration office, and further down, at its end, another office door stood ajar with a slice of light escaping from it.

Anna did not explore that far. She headed for the telephone and was about to drop her coins in the slot when she saw the Out of Order sign on it. She lifted the receiver but heard no dial tone. The thing was dead.

At the extreme end of the passage where the light shone from the open office door, Josh thought he sensed movement and came to see who was afoot. He walked slowly, noiseless without shoes. *So,* he thought, when he saw Anna by the phone, *the albino feline prowls her new surroundings.* He knew better than to think she would sleep.

'Anna!' he called, a little over a whisper. She jumped, startled. In the dim night light of the foyer, she saw Joshua stepping towards her. He had changed his dapper light-grey jacket, black trousers, shirt, and tie for KwaZulu Medical's uniform of blue jeans, white shirt, and stethoscope. In the semi-darkness, he looked fatigued with eyes wide as if hydraulic jacks held them open forcibly.

'Can't you sleep, Anna?' He spoke as if to a patient.

'Not before I've contacted Hank or Maurice.'

He smiled. 'Tired but defiant,' he sighed a silent rebuke, shaking his head. Pointing to the phone, he said, 'That thing doesn't work. You better come to my office.' Anna followed him, hoping he would let her use his phone. After the sparse illumination of the foyer and passage, Josh's office was very bright, and it took a moment for her eyes to adjust.

'Sit down.' Josh pointed to the patient's chair beside his desk. He had a cup of steaming strong black coffee beside his work Anna noticed, sniffing it longingly. He should offer her a cup also, he thought, but that would keep the little hellcat awake. His heart softened when he saw her look at it with obvious craving. He was about to fetch some for her when it struck him that she would use the opportunity to pounce on the telephone.

'I can see you're after my coffee,' he laughed with jaded cheer. 'Come with me and I'll show you the kitchen.' He took her hand as if to safeguard her presence. This woman needed constant monitoring. She was a cunning schemer and bound to escape unless he exercised caution.

'The kitchen is right opposite, which is why I chose this office. I like being close to a source of sustenance.' He opened the door, switched on the light, and followed the quiet bubbling noise and wisp of steam from the hot water urn. He had no need to ask whether she wanted sugar or milk, remembering well his first visit to her office and her joke about her drug of dependence.

'Here you are, addict,' he chuckled as he gave her a cup.

'Thank you.' She laughed despite herself. 'I'll feel normal in a minute.' She turned back to his office, sipping along the way.

'Joshua, please . . . I must use your phone,' she began again when seated. 'It is most important that Hank knows where I am. You understand that, don't you?'

'Of course,' he said with a sly grin. 'I see your problem. You must tell Hank . . . but not yet.'

'Why, Josh?' Why can't I call him now? What are you afraid of?' Her voice rose with impatience.

'We have to talk first,' Josh mumbled without looking at her.

Anna drank more coffee while watching Josh carefully. The puzzle pieces came together in her mind. That Swiss account, the misleading balance sheet, the approximate amount in the foreign account, which equated to roughly four lots of US$200,000 from William, Paul, Frank, and Geoff. And now she herself was Josh's prisoner. What ransom would he ask from Hank? She shuddered.

'What's wrong, Anna? Are you cold?'

'You!' she shouted in disbelief, her eyes narrowed. 'It's you! It was you all the time!'

'Me . . . ? Me what?' Josh asked hesitantly, noticing a change in her eyes that was new to him. The traffic lights no longer beamed brightly. Nor did they burn with rage. They adopted a dull bottle-green sheen, like the dusty glow when the sun shines directly into them and a driver has difficulty seeing whether they are functioning.

'E . . . E-E-M,' she stammered. 'You are EEM!' Their eyes locked in mortal combat as both realized the cardinal error they had made, a fundamental mistake with far-reaching consequences to bind them forever.

Anna saw too late she should have remained silent. Telling Josh that she knew of his crimes assured her indefinite incarceration. He would not let her go lest she informed the police. He might even kill her. The thought chilled her heart, and she looked away to hide her fear.

Josh recalled Sipho's warning that the link between KwaZulu Medical and the bogus Economic Equity Movement would be revealed. Trust Anna to be the one to do so. He knew he could never release her. Even if he intimidated her into silence, her husband and his brothers would not be deterred from bringing him to justice. He was indifferent to the threat of jail. His political activities as a student had acquainted him well with that style of accommodation. However, a criminal conviction could see him struck off the Health

Professions Council of South Africa or HPCSA's list of authorized medical practitioners. Although, given the shortage of doctors in South Africa, he had reason to hope for leniency. The De Bruyn clan wouldn't stop there, though, he imagined. Nothing short of KwaZulu Medical's destruction would satisfy them.

'Anna,' he sighed, searching her face for any sign of malice when she looked at him. Finding none, he said quietly, 'Go to bed. We'll talk later. Take your coffee with you.'

When she rose, shaking with weariness and shock, he remembered that neither of them had eaten since they consumed the snacks in the Pretoria wine bar. He headed for the kitchen again and gathered a small plate full of Margo's maize cakes.

'Here,' he said, 'in case you get hungry.'

'Thank you.' She took what passed for refreshments and walked to her room deep in thought. Josh watched her go, a mixture of desire and regret scorching his soul. Sipho was right again, he thought. He should have left Anna alone. They would ruin each other's lives. He shrugged in resignation. She was here now, and the ironic curse of it was that he no longer had a use for her. The longer he deprived her of liberty, the more she would lose her contacts to the outside world and thereby cease to be of value as a financial advisor. He might still demand money from Hank but could not return Anna. Her menfolk would question and pester her till she revealed everything about KwaZulu Medical. He could not take that risk. To how many people had she already shown the two differing balance sheets? A chill ran down his spine. The only way to prevent her talking further was to kill her. He dismissed the thought instantly. Murder was a last resort. Anna would still yield benefit as a hostage. She gave him an avenue to avoid exposure by threatening to harm her if anyone informed the police. In the meantime he'd persuade her to join him in more pleasant pursuits. He thought of the split in her skirt as he returned to his office. A little sexual servitude may be better for her than trading shares. He'd make the queen of the boardroom earn her keep. An added bonus was that she'd be disease-free, something that could not be taken for granted with other women. Sipho was the living reminder of that disastrous fact.

Joshua shook himself awake. What was he dreaming? His brain, he told himself, had degenerated into loathsome, putrid sediment, fermenting ideas to shame the toughest Mafia godfather. Shocked by his turpitude, he wondered if there was a side to his personality he never knew existed. 'Now is not the time for self-doubt and soul-searching,' he reprimanded himself aloud. What he had told Anna was true. KwaZulu Medical was his brainchild, and he would protect it with whatever means he found necessary, and if that meant disposing of her? He had no answer.

* * *

Nkosinathi had not seen that worried look on Freddie's face since the distant days when he had feared failing his tests in the computer course. The young men agreed to meet outside the computer training centre for old times' sake, and Nkosinathi sensed his friend was troubled.

'What's the matter, man?' he asked, ready to share Freddie's difficulties again. He began to think that maybe it wasn't the right time to ask a favour from a friend so obviously upset.

'Ah . . .' Freddie waved a hand irritably. 'My mother and the comrades, they fall out.'

'What happened?' It had to be serious, Nkosinathi thought, for Freddie to be so downcast.

'Have your parents paid rent yet?' Freddie wanted to know.

'I'm not sure.' Nkosinathi tried to remember if his father mentioned it.

'My mother,' Freddie went on, 'she want to pay rent, but the comrades turned on her. They told her she must observe the rent boycott. The comrades, they tell her the same old story that she was aiding and supporting apartheid bureau-bureaucratic str-structures'—he could hardly pronounce the words—'by paying rent. If she pay, she is a traitor and will be dealt with, they said.'

'That's terrible, Freddie. Do you want my father to go with her?'

'My mother, she try again next day, and same thing happened. Comrades outside the office tell her to go away. Not she can send cheque. Not she with cheque account.' Freddie shrugged in despair.

Nkosinathi placed a comforting arm across his friend's shoulder. Poor Freddie was going to pieces judging by the way he talked.

'Just a little while ago when I arrived, I found comrades loitering outside my mother's house. They said, "Your mother's very proud of her house, we can see. She keep it neat with flowerpots in the window and all . . ."' Freddie paused for breath. 'I wonder what they want, and I say "Piss off." They laugh and say, "Tell your mother to watch her house. We don't want no arson, do we? No rent! No traitors! No collaborators!" I tell them to go fuck their grandmother. They hit me, but I pull out my knife so they left.'

'We'll have to alert the police to the possibility of a riot, Freddie. Who else has been prevented from paying rent, do you know?'

'The whole street my mother lives in. The street committees watch everyone.'

'Such threats should be reported to the police,' Nkosinathi insisted.

'Only if we can be sure about whose side the cops are on,' Freddie warned.

'Yeah, you're right,' Nkosinathi had to admit, anger spreading through his own system as well. It was the helplessness that burnt his guts. How could it be fair that gangs with a particular ideological and political bent could terrorise whole neighbourhoods with impunity? The De Klerk government was dismantling apartheid. Why wasn't that good enough for them? They'd get their free—and hopefully fair—democratic election eventually, and the communists could field candidates like all other parties. Why this anarchy in the townships? Maybe it was Madiba's fault. While he travelled the USA and urged America not to lift sanctions against South Africa yet, no progress towards an orderly civil society could be expected at home. Nkosinathi talked of such matters only with his father. Few of his friends understood. They would deride him with snide remarks about his having fallen victim to too much white influence.

Having poured out his woes to Nkosinathi, Freddie felt more optimistic. 'Okay, man,' he said, pulling his baseball cap back to front. 'Fuck the cops. Self-help's the go.' He rummaged in the pockets of his leather jacket, coming up with a hand full of money.

'Is the phone booth on the corner open today?'

'Don't know. What're you gonna do?'

'Make phone calls, of course, twit.'

'I get it,' Nkosinathi laughed. 'You're rallying the troops. Calling on your bike gang fellows for help.'

'See how the comrades like doing battle with my impi. When I hit the telegraph poles, like so,'—he picked up a stick to demonstrate the signal—'my army will surround my mother's house. If the comrades make strife, we're ready.'

Nkosinathi agreed it was a sound strategy. He waited till the induna, or commander, Freddie, summoned his warriors on the phone and then invited him home for a meal, where they discussed the incident with Mr and Mrs Zuma. Before Freddie left late in the evening, Nkosinathi said, 'You know Mrs De Bruyn's gone missing?'

Freddie stopped short. 'You mean the lady who sponsors the computer school?' he asked wide-eyed.

'Yeah, her, the wife of my boss.'

'Shit, man. She been abducted, mugged, or what?'

Nkosinathi shrugged. 'Don't know really. Some bloke followed her on her last trip to Pretoria, and nobody's seen her since.' He pulled the photocopies of Anna's picture out of his pocket and showed them to Freddie.

'That her?' Freddie looked at the pictures for some time.

'Yeah. Do you reckon you could pass those photocopies around among your friends? Mr De Bruyn's promised a R100,000 reward for information as to her whereabouts. That's an incentive for your friends to keep their eyes peeled.'

'Man, you bet they will. Can't promise we turn up anything, but we sure as hell try.'

'Thanks, Freddie.' Nkosinathi would sleep better from now on.

* * *

Anna placed the maize cakes and coffee mug on the kitchen table in her room. Sleep would be elusive, so why go to bed? She pulled the curtains open to let the moonlight flood in. Pushing a chair to the window, she turned off the light and sat in desolate and anguished contemplation, awaiting a helpful sunrise.

How could she get out of this mess? It was the one question, together with anxiety for Hank, that circled round and round in her head like a spinning top, making her dizzy. Hank would worry himself sick. She had to let him know she was alive. Any signal would do. What, though? How? Mentally she ticked off a checklist of necessary procedures.

Hank had to be told. For that, she required either a phone or fax. To gain access to those communication devices, she had to study the routine of the place. She wanted answers to questions like who worked where and when? When did the staff take breaks? When was communication equipment left unguarded? Could she create a diversion to cause a lack of vigilance? It remained to be seen. Security couldn't possibly be foolproof, and Josh had already said that Sipho was forgetful. Friendship with such a person may prove advantageous.

Of equal urgency was the search for an escape route. That necessitated the observance of everyone's movements to and from the clinic, not just the staff but outsiders who called regularly as well. Bribery might be another method. Who could resist the temptation of a cheque waved invitingly before their eyes? Anna sighed deeply. It was going to be so time-consuming when ideally she wanted to be gone immediately. Her head drooped in despair like the violets Josh had pinned to her jacket. Their perfume brought a momentary illusion of hope. Josh couldn't be an unreasonable man, she hoped, rubbing her painful wrist. He was too intelligent. Maybe she could coax him into adopting a better course. Above all, she must demonstrate to him that his trust in her, such as it was, was not misplaced, even if she had no reason to have faith in him. It was important not to get angry with him or lose patience and composure. And—this was vital—she must never, never let him recognize her fear. Under no circumstances must he have the upper hand.

She sat up straight, looking at the moon. Wasn't Josh gaining ground already, breaking her spirit, having her sitting here like a prisoner on death row? If she acted like one, she'd become one. She had to change her outlook now and completely. It was the best means to counteract the damage he inflicted on her psyche.

She would stage a many-pronged assault on her oppressor, just like Shenge's proposed multi-strategy approach to defeat apartheid. As Josh explained to her, Shenge believed that many different methods to counter apartheid should come into play. A passive, civil disobedience campaign, intelligence-gathering to gain knowledge of thine enemy to facilitate hitting the foe with his own weapons, particularly diplomatic weapons and negotiation, which should form the linchpin of all efforts. Negotiation should be the first, not the last resort, with armed struggle used sparingly, carefully, and only if all else failed.

Anna thought her predicament contained similarities in reverse. It was black oppressing white. She required a verbal ordinance arsenal to fight for her life if need be. Was she here, she wondered, because Josh wanted money, or was her abduction his solitary protest against white dominance, particularly superiority of an economic nature? Most likely it was a combination of both factors. Josh had a complex mind capable of running in numerous directions at once. Could she build safeguards to arrest his sedulous journey into catastrophe?

For now, her civil disobedience would take the form of seeking escape routes and formulating plans to that end. Assaulting Josh with his own weapons meant discovering how the clinic worked and using any loopholes in his routine to aid her escape. Diplomatic negotiation served to attempt influencing Josh's thinking with her own better philosophy. If that proved ineffective, the armed struggle would begin with active defiance, such as seeking to use phone or fax and establishing contacts outside. More radical measures could be employed later if compromises and diplomacy failed. What these actions would consist of, she could not say at this early stage.

Having thus compartmentalized her reactions to every facet of her abduction like documents in a filing cabinet, Anna felt calmer. She could start expediting her war plan right away. The violets on her jacket were drying and dying. They needed water. She removed them and ventured out of her room again to fetch a glass from the kitchen into which she could stand the dainty flowers. On the way, she explored the layout of the clinic further. The light in Josh's quarters was still on when she traipsed past on stockinged feet. Reaching the foyer with the malfunctioning phone, Anna looked through the glass partition into what she recognized as the main administrative office. There was an opening in the partition like a sliding window with *Enquiries* written on the glass in red paint. She ran her hand along the panels. They did not move. She felt along the centre strut of the window and touched what appeared to be a lock. Peering in, she noted the position of the desk, computer, phone, and fax machine.

Thinking of locks and keys revived the memory of her arrival and the recollection that Josh had not taken his car keys with him. Anna turned towards the main door and looked out at Josh's red Corolla parked close by as if to taunt her. The hire car in which they had travelled from Pretoria stood next to it. She descended the stairs and examined Josh's own car and then the hired vehicle. Both had the key in the ignition. How convenient was that? Before Josh's casual handling of the keys excited her, she knew another hurdle had to be overcome in the form of the electronic gate, which operated by insertion of a plastic key card. She checked the hire car glovebox and found it empty. Josh had definitely taken a key card from the glovebox. Next, she headed for the Corolla and searched its nooks and crannies. *Jackpot!* The key card lay on the dashboard near the steering wheel. Now for the exit! Move, girl!

Quickly but quietly, she hurried back to her room to fetch her handbag and briefcase. She turned the ignition key with crossed fingers, hoping nobody would hear the car start. Driving slowly, without lights, she inserted the card in the slot when she reached the gate. It failed to respond. She tried pushing the other end into the opening with negative result. Turning the card around and trying both ends again brought no success. 'Open Sesame!' Anna screamed inside herself, stamping her foot. Feelings of defeat outlawed, she steeled her soul upon discovering the power was disconnected. Here, she thought, was mission number 1. Find the power switch. It must be somewhere in the front office. Dejected and scared, she reversed the Corolla back to its parking spot.

Anna slipped the key card into her skirt pocket and walked back into the foyer. Heading left towards the kitchen, she tried the knob of the administration office door. Locked. While passing Josh's office, she tested that door as well. It too was locked. That, she thought, concluded her first adventure. There was no more she could do now except take her belongings back to her room, go into the kitchen and seek a glass or vase for the violets, and try to relax. She found a small earthenware dish, filled it with water, and put the grateful violets in it. Placing the dish on the chest of drawers that doubled as bedside table, her next step was to hide the key card in a side compartment of her handbag. It approached three thirty in the morning, and Anna felt she needed rest. Lacking a nightie and toiletries, she faced the prospect of sleeping in her underwear or nude.

'Fair bloody dinkum, how am I going to clean my teeth?' Anna muttered and cursed. 'Jesus, I've never been so desperate in all my life.' She opened the bathroom door in disgust, turning on the light.

'The bastard! The sneaky bastard!' she whispered to herself in spitting fury when she found towels, soap, and toothbrush laid out neatly on the edge of the washbasin. 'He has this room in readiness as if he was certain I would arrive today.' How long had

Josh spent planning her abduction? she wondered angrily. There was even a white towelling bathrobe hanging from a hook on the door. At least she could shower, she thought, weariness resigning her to her fate. Cleanliness and sleep may bring fresh inspirations in the morning. She would sleep in the bathrobe, and her underwear could be washed in the basin. That left her with the task of hanging her clothes in the wardrobe. There she found more evidence of Josh's meticulous preparation. Her personal version of the KwaZulu Medical prison uniform awaited her. Two pairs of blue jeans, one denim skirt, and three white tops of varying styles hung side by side with spare hangers for her own clothes. Anna arranged her linen suit and silk blouse carefully before finally collapsing on the bed. She shot up again, startled when something rustled under the pillow.

'Christ!' she swore, her heart pounding in fright. 'Oh yeah, it's his surprise.' She'd forgotten about it. Breathing deeply, she calmed herself before lifting the pillow. The rustle was caused by a layer of tissue paper, which she unwrapped slowly.

'Oh, no.' She held her breath when the contents was laid bare. A silky, soft, and luxurious ankle-length nightgown of animal-print pattern with a most revealing décolletage. If she wasn't so tired she'd try it on. Yawning, she hung it in the wardrobe, experiencing a medley of conflicting emotions.

'I know what you're trying to tell me, Josh, but it's all wrong. Your approach to this whole situation is impossible—you're dreaming,' she sighed as she drifted into fitful sleep.

* * *

'I have a note from Anna!' Hank spoke excitedly, phoning Broadbent with the news. The sun streamed through his office window, filling his morning with hope and energy.

'It's a short message in her handwriting,' he explained, 'and it is firm and clear as if she is in control of her situation. You can't imagine how glad I am to see it, Captain.' Hank turned the paper over and over.

'What does the note say?' Captain Broadbent asked sceptically.

'Just that she has decided to go into hiding for a while to escape from the man in the yellow VW Golf.'

Hank's enthusiasm waned slightly. 'She must be in some predicament because she wrote a sentence in German at the bottom of the sheet to say she is trying to extricate herself from a difficult situation.'

'That sounds confused,' Broadbent grunted. 'If your wife decided to leave town because of Thompson, she would not necessarily find herself in trouble, and she'd be free to let you know where she is.'

'Yes, I hadn't thought of that,' Hank admitted, crestfallen. 'I must say that relief at knowing her to be alive has impaired my appraisal of the letter.'

Broadbent muttered sympathetic words. He could imagine Hank's nervous agitation. 'What's the postmark on the envelope? Where and when was the letter mailed?'

'Oh, it didn't come in the post. It was hand-delivered earlier today by a rough and rumpled-looking teenager off the street.'

'I see.' Broadbent believed nothing in Anna's communication. It didn't even guarantee that she was alive. Someone could have forced her to write it before murdering her. He said nothing of the sort to Hank, knowing the adverse impact it would have on his health. Deep down, he still harboured the hunch that Anna may have left Hank for another man.

'Was the envelope addressed to you, Mr De Bruyn?'

'Yes, but here's a strange thing—the writing on it is not Anna's. It looks masculine.'

Broadbent saw the formation of a pattern. Mrs De Bruyn and whoever—Mr X—had formed a conspiracy to confuse Hank and the police. He did not reveal his theories to Hank, who had already protested that his wife would not leave him. On the other hand, the pattern did not explain the sentence written in German. That indicated instead that Mrs De Bruyn wished to tell her husband something of which a third party had to remain ignorant. She was afraid of someone. Would she leave her husband for a man she feared? Not without coercion. That brought the incident back to a possible kidnapping.

'And you still have no ransom demand?' The only similarity this case had so far shown with the EEM crimes was the hand-delivered messages, which may or may not signify anything.

'No, Captain, nothing of the sort.'

'May we have the note and envelope for further assessment please, Mr De Bruyn?'

'Yes, of course. I'll get one of our lads to bring it to you straight away.'

'And, by the way,' Broadbent concluded, 'we had to let Thompson go. He has nothing to do with your wife's disappearance. He was just in the wrong place at the wrong time. As you suspected, a Gold Corp executive is behind that, and I expect to know who very soon.'

'That would mean Anna can come home,' Hank said quickly before Broadbent put down the phone.

'Mr De Bruyn, your wife doesn't know that Thompson poses no threat. I fear we're looking at something quite serious here.'

Broadbent was right, Hank thought, deflated. Anna wouldn't run away from Price. She'd spit in his eye. How he wished he could help her. That German sentence told him someone had imprisoned Anna and she was trying frantically to come home. Obviously the kidnapper's censoring of her note stopped her writing in detail. If only he knew who, where, and why. Hank left his desk and returned to his almost-permanent position by the window. He could only hope Anna was being treated kindly. The unaccustomed feeling of powerless futility placed him under unendurable stress.

* * *

Anna awoke to the slamming of a door and a raspy tenor voice hollering in the passage.

'Margo, can't you bring my breakfast quietly?' the voice called with acerbity. 'Have a little consideration for my nerves, you stupid old woman. You frighten me to death.'

'Go back to bed, Sipho! You're crotchety!' Margo shouted back unsympathetically as she approached Anna's door.

Anna yawned and looked at her watch. Breakfast time: seven thirty. A good time if one had slept soundly and sufficiently. Neither applied to her. Her head hurt. She sat up rubbing her eyes which felt like golf balls. Did every morning at KwaZulu Medical begin on such a discordant note? 'I'm not going to be here long enough to find out.' The words came from her as if sworn on the Bible.

Margo twisted the knob and kicked Anna's door open, her arms full with breakfast tray and newspaper. She offloaded her cargo onto the table and turned to leave.

'Thanks, Margo! I'm Anna!' She hoped for a response, which was denied. 'By the way,'—she accosted Margo—'do you reckon you could knock next time? Bet you wouldn't just walk into Professor Mtolo's room without warning.' Margo ignored her.

Anna had already learnt the previous night that privacy was not a high priority here, as was indicated by the absence of a lock on her door. Perhaps insecurity had prevented her from sleeping properly. With Margo's departure, reality flooded her mind, and she became fully conscious of her deprivation of freedom. Recounting the resolutions she had made in the early hours of the morning, she forced herself to be positive.

The breakfast tray offered no grounds for optimism when she examined it with indifference. Maize porridge and a lukewarm swill purporting to be coffee. Feeling a greater need for sleep than food, she took a quick glimpse at the *Natal Witness* headlines and flopped back on the bed. She dozed off almost instantly, still sleeping at nine thirty when Josh had finished attending to the children. He became concerned when she failed to show herself and thought to check on her. *She hasn't escaped already? That would be all but impossible.* He smiled, talking to himself. With Anna he'd never be certain of anything. He opened her door softly.

Anna lay on her side facing the door, a peaceful smile on her lips. Enveloped in her favourite recurring dream of the approaches to Sydney Harbour on a sun-drenched morning after a party on her father's yacht, she bore the look of defenceless vulnerability, which always touched Josh. He entered on tiptoe, leaving the door ajar. She hadn't eaten her breakfast, he observed when he sat on a chair. The coffee was cold. Margo had to organize something fresh, fruit juice maybe. She laughed in her dream, and Josh noticed the length of her hair without the combs which usually held it up. The bathrobe's belt had slipped, and the collar gaped, partly exposing her breasts.

'Dolphins,' she mumbled, turning onto her back. The bathrobe parted more to reveal a flawless thigh.

A USB-related panic attack gripped Josh. If Anna awoke and found him sitting, watching her, she'd at best scream and at worst consider him a lecherous voyeur. Neither reaction was desirable. Josh stood up to go. He wanted to linger, stroke her long, auburn hair, kiss the dark bruising on her wrist better, and wait for her to open her traffic-light eyes. He dared not.

What had he done to this woman? he asked himself, examining more closely the angry bruise caused by his own hand on her wrist the day before. She was so gentle and lovable. She even cared about the insignificant violet blooms he had given her, putting them in a dish of water. How easily he could open his heart to her. 'And that's no euphemism for opening my trouser zip either,' he attempted to convince himself. He meant his real heart, every living beat of it. He found it impossible to reconcile this unprotected sleeping woman with the stock market vixen who could wipe out a faltering enterprise like his with one word from her delectable mouth.

'I'd better leave,' Josh reminded himself again. Any minute she would wake up, her ethereal aura evaporating like droplets of mist in the sun, making way for the harsher angle of her personality. The side with the curved claws, which gave rebirth to the hellcat holding sway over KwaZulu Medical's life or death.

He took one last look around the room, feeling certain she would complain about its austerity. With the curtains shutting out the morning sun, it looked neither inviting nor restful.

Once, he had driven past her home in Illovo to satisfy his curiosity about where she lived. He found the house hidden from view by a high brick fence, but what was visible through the tall, ornamental wrought-iron gates told him enough. The building was a stretched white rectangle with French windows opening onto a covered portico. Six Greek revival columns supported its roof. Running parallel to the length of the house, a rectangular fountain spurted six jets into the air, equidistant to each of the columns. The villa resembled a small nation's seat of government rather than a private residence. He had occasion to travel past again that same night. A party was in full swing. The French windows were open, releasing music to which couples danced on the portico by the fountain's floodlights. He imagined the clink of champagne glasses as he passed.

Cindy's beloved Soweto cottage compared unfavourably, he thought grimly, offended again by the large disparity in wealth distribution within South Africa's society. Cindy's place with its kitchenette, cramped living area, and shoebox bedroom looked like a cardboard dolls' house. Josh closed Anna's door behind him and headed for the outpatient section, where Peter and Tom needed him.

* * *

Anna's dream became disturbed. The *Coomelong* broached in heavy seas. Albert Henry Cumberland shouted to his daughter above the tumultuous waves, 'She'll never right herself! Get the life raft, quickly!' But Anna clung to the lurching deck. As the roaring water mass came aboard to crush her, she awoke with a cry. Frightened by her unfamiliar environment, she jumped up as if a mamba hissed in her bed. Seeking a semblance of normality, she walked to the window and pulled the curtains open to admit the sun. At the same time, she became aware of an almost familiar scent in the room. What was it? Aftershave? 'Yes, it's Josh's aftershave,' she remembered, having smelt a slight trace of it when he pinned the violets to her jacket. 'The bastard has me so jittery it's no wonder I've got that sinking feeling,' she confessed to the morning sun. 'He must have been in here while I slept.'

The wardrobe mirror reflected her dishevelled image with the gaping bathrobe revealing much of its wearer. Acutely embarrassed, Anna realized Josh would have had a similar view. 'This won't do.' Whoever the maintenance person was around here, he'd have to fit a lock to the door.

She opened the wardrobe. 'Which leisure wear shall I don today?' Refusing to call the garments prison clothes, she mimicked before the mirror as if strutting a catwalk. 'The choice is overwhelming. Denim, denim, cotton, and denim. One couldn't ask for more.' She settled for jeans and a shirt, leaving its top three buttons unfastened and tying the bottom in a knot around her waist. Shoes? There were none. Barefoot was the KwaZulu Medical fashion.

'Ready to look the world in the eye?' she asked her mirror double before heading for the galley to hunt for a belated breakfast.

Searching the benches and larders, she found bread rolls, margarine, and honey. That looked good enough, she thought. Margo sprung her while making herself fresh coffee.

'What you want in here?' Margo barked. Anna knew of Margo's charms. William had told her about the 'ugly old frog' and her idiosyncrasy. 'You're going to be a nuisance, helping yourself at will and making a mess. Keep out of here and stick to mealtimes.' Margo waved both arms at her as if she were a pet animal. 'Get out, go on!' she squawked, stamping her foot.

'Easy does it, Margo. Just let me get my coffee.' Anna took her time filling the mug. 'I thought helping myself to what I want would save you the burden of looking after me. You should be pleased.'

'You could have brought your breakfast tray back if you're so helpful,' Margo grunted, unimpressed.

'I could have, but I didn't. Anything else you want me to do? Wash up for you?' Anna took her provisions and left, saying airily, 'I might do that one day if I get bored enough. Then you'll be out of a job. How would you like that?'

'Hmf!' Margo sniggered.

'Don't give me shit, Margo, you'll regret it.'

She wasn't making a friend there, Anna realized. It was probably the wrong approach at a time when she needed all the friends she could get. Who cares? She found the homestead's original back door, which led into a courtyard providing access to the new extensions. A garden seat outside the children's ward appeared an ideal place to devour her breakfast. Some youngsters came out for a swim with one of the doctors. She followed them, coffee mug in hand, munching the last bite of bread. She sat on the edge of the pool watching an assistant unlock a shed at the far end from which he emerged with buoyancy aids, hoops and balls. What else was stored in there? It would merit investigation. The young patients only had twelve minutes in the pool before returning indoors leaving the floating toys in the water. Anna hoped the doctor would go with them, enabling her to check out the shed.

'Hello! Haven't seen you around here before.' Dr Peter Shabalala smiled a welcome as he approached. 'You must be Tom Dlamini's patient.'

'No, my name is Anna. Anna De Bruyn. I'm not a patient. I'm the financial advisor.' Her emphatic reply silenced Peter for a moment. He looked uncomfortable.

'I'm sorry, madam. I mistook you for somebody else,' he explained awkwardly. 'I'm Peter Shabalala. You'll find me in outpatient if there's anything I can do for you.'

'Thank you,' Anna giggled. 'I don't even know how to get there yet. Where do I have to go?'

'Through the lobby, past Sipho's office, out the front door, and turn left. Just follow the arrows after that.'

'Thanks, Dr Shabalala. I might pay you a visit one day if Josh will let me.'

'The old despot's laid down the law, has he?' Peter asked, frowning, but his eyes laughed.

'Let's say he doesn't want me to be overwhelmed by too many new faces before I get my bearings.'

Peter departed smiling and leaving Anna to wonder if he might help her escape. He knew or suspected more than he revealed, judging by his clumsy attempt at conversation. His meaning lay between the unpronounced words rather than his spoken sentences. From the stories Josh had told her, she gathered his friends offered him unquestioning loyalty, but how far did that stretch? Would they cover up his crimes? Pervert the course of justice to save his skin?

When Peter was out of sight, Anna stole into the shed. A long pole shaped like a paddle at one end lay on a workbench, presumably to fish the toys out of the pool. She could do that. It gave her a logical explanation if someone should ask what she was doing there. At a quick glance, she saw the shed contained tools of all varieties and many other implements besides. Some of them could be useful in the event that her armed struggle became inevitable. Two items in particular attracted her attention, and she determined to give them a new storage place in her room very soon. She took the paddle to try retrieving the toys from the water. The balls were the hardest to get. They twirled out of reach.

'Here, let me do that! I'd hate to see you fall in.'

The assistant returned, and Anna saw he wore an orange T-shirt and navy track pants. Must be the bloke William called Fernando, the self-styled soccer coach.

'Hi!' Anna called back to him. 'Is your name Fernando?'

'Yep, that's me!' He came to take the paddle from her.

'I can do this,' Anna offered. 'I've got nothing else to occupy me, so if you're busy, I'll fix this for you.'

'Thanks, lady. I'm flat out this morning. What's your name, by the way? How come you know mine?' Fernando asked, intrigued.

'I'm Anna, and Dr Shabalala just told me your name,' she lied.

Fernando handed her a key. 'Here, lock up when you finish, and thanks for helping.'

'Where do I put the key?'

'Give it to Sipho.' He hurried towards the psychiatric ward.

It took Anna another ten minutes till she cornered the balls and lifted them from the pool. She tossed them into an empty box to stop them rolling about and searched the shed more thoroughly.

'Just what I need,' she breathed with delight upon finding a number of latches in individual plastic bags with self-tapping screws in each. She chose the sturdiest of them, took a screwdriver from a rack on the wall, concealed both in her shirt, and locked up.

Returning to her room, she made quick work of screwing the latch onto her door. 'Perfect job! Pat on the back!' she praised herself, feeling secure now that she could sleep without men observing her and leaving traces of aftershave in the air like a calling card. She hid the screwdriver under the mattress. It was too good a weapon to relinquish.

Anna wasn't rushing to return Fernando's key to Sipho. Twice already she had walked past his fiefdom without seeing him. Josh's office was closed as well. During the day, with numerous people passing, she was reluctant to test if either door was unlocked, but she'd try the front office anyway. The toolshed key gave her a motive. First though, she'd finish reading the *Natal Witness* in case somebody else was waiting for it. That done, she took both the newspaper and the key and set out in the hope of meeting Sipho Gwala, the balance sheet wizard, master of creative accounting. His office door and the enquiries window stood open, but Mr Clever Tricks wasn't around. Anna homed in on the telephone without delay. She didn't reach it.

'*Sawubona Nkosazana*! I see you, madam.' Anna turned at the Zulu greeting called by a shrunken, wizened little man who seemed like a transparent shadow of the person he had been once.

'Mr Gwala! Nice to meet you!' Anna applied her public relations smile, more to remind herself of her true role than to impress Sipho because KwaZulu Medical added nothing to De Bruyn's turnover to merit particular courtesy.

'You're Mrs De Bruyn, aren't you?' Sipho shuffled towards Anna, who had come close to his desk, directing sly glances at the computer screen. 'Can I do anything for you?' Sipho asked, finding her nervous and tense.

'Fernando asked me to give you this key.' She held it out to Sipho. 'Also, I've brought the paper back. Somebody else may wish to read it.'

'The newspapers are for you.' Sipho gave an obliging smile. 'The professor is most concerned about your comfort and insists that you should have all possible conveniences.' He took the key and hung it on a board with others.

'Sit down and talk to me,' he suggested, rolling a second chair to his desk. 'You're the only person with whom I'll be able to talk business. The others wouldn't know a quarterly profit or loss if it bit them.'

Anna smiled at Sipho's quip. 'Joshua would have a fairly clear idea where the clinic is headed, don't you agree?'

'He likes to think he does,' Sipho cackled. 'Nobody has the heart to disillusion him by telling him it isn't so.'

Anna sat down with Sipho, who reminded her of a tokoloshe, or an African type of leprechaun. The physical appearance of these chaps was open to one's imagination, and to confuse the issue, the little imps were capable of changing their shape and looks to suit whatever mischief they choose to carry out. Sipho came in the guise of an accountant. According to African myth, tokoloshes were mostly of malevolent disposition, but Sipho appeared to have broken with tokoloshe tradition. Anna thought him friendly and kind. She looked at Sipho as if about to paint every detail of his portrait on canvas.

Mistaking her attentive observation for unease, he said jovially, 'I think you need a cup of coffee. We both do. The problem is, though, that you'll have to make it. I'm dreadfully clumsy, and Margo goes off her tree whenever I come near the kitchen.'

This brought an outburst of laughter from Anna. 'She's already thrown me out this morning.'

'Ah, then you have met the Gorgon.' Sipho grinned impishly. 'I'll show you where she hides the good coffee,' he confided. 'What's more, on the professor's instructions, an assortment of chocolate biscuits was procured and now resides in the pantry somewhere. Maybe we can flush them out.'

Anna followed Sipho to the pantry where, like a magician, he conjured up chocolate biscuits from the depth of a plastic storage bin, and behind that lurked a jar of good Kenyan coffee.

'Ha! Got it!' Sipho held his trophies high.

Together they invaded the kitchen, where in high-spirited good humour, they made coffee and ripped into the biscuits.

Margo's tekkies squeaked on the linoleum behind them.

'God! She always knows when someone's in here,' Sipho whispered, annoyed.

'What?' they heard her screech. 'You too scared to come on your own now, Sipho? Need Anna here for moral support . . . hm?' Margo sniggered at them as if they were mice caught in her newly set trap.

'Shut your face, tetchy old woman,' Sipho replied, his words harsh but his tone mocking and good-natured.

'And you got the chocolate biscuits too, you absolute glutton,' Margo shrieked in high-pitched staccato.

'They're not for me and you know it. The professor ordered them especially for Anna,' Sipho defended himself.

'New kind of medicine, eh? Just for one woman! Unheard of!' Margo muttered under her breath. She turned angrily towards Anna. 'What you do here? You're not sick.'

'She will be if you talk to her like that,' Sipho couldn't resist commenting.

'I'm here in the capacity of a financial advisor,' Anna said calmly, hoping to make peace with Margo.

Margo guffawed till Anna thought the rotund woman would fall over and roll on the floor. 'I've heard it called by other names before,' Margo shouted, 'less genteel ones.' She gave Anna a smutty sideways glance.

'Watch your tongue, old woman!' Sipho warned sternly this time.

Swallowing her rising anger, Anna broke into the chatter. 'It's true, Margo. And I'll tell you something for free. You're lucky I'm not an economic rationalist or neo-liberal economist because I'm here to explore more avenues for cutting costs to make the clinic profitable. You know what that means, don't you? It means staff reductions.' Anna frowned at Margo, relishing the effect her words had on the grumpy woman. 'I wasn't joking when I said I'd wash the dishes and you'd be out of a job.'

It was too much for Sipho to retain a serious expression. He retreated to his office with the biscuits while Anna followed, balancing the coffee cups on a tray.

'Don't make me laugh so much, Anna. I'm losing my trousers.' The skeletal Sipho arranged his clothes and sat down at his desk.

'Laughter is good for you, Sipho. I hope I can administer more of such an inexpensive remedy.'

Without realizing, they had dropped all formality and conversed like old friends. Sipho was in the middle of filling Anna in on the details of the ANC's loan when Josh thrust his head through the open-enquiries window.

'I expected it wouldn't take you two long to get your heads together.' He smiled benignly. 'Coffee and chocolate biscuits, eh? Living in high style, I must say. Can I join the party?'

'Yeah, sure. If you hurry, we might leave you half a cookie,' Sipho called back, stowing the biscuits in his desk drawer. Joshua came in presently with a mug of coffee and, perching on the edge of Sipho's desk, looked around for the biscuits.

'All right, where are they? I know you couldn't have eaten them all. Bring 'em out, Sipho.'

Sipho was about to deny having any such delicacies when a buzzer sounded, and both men looked out of the window towards the gate. An ambulance had arrived, and Sipho opened the gate by pushing a button on a small console beside his desk. The first ambulance was soon followed by a second, and both vehicles steered towards Casualty.

'Must be a road accident somewhere,' Josh said, still watching. 'I better go and help. Tom and Peter have their hands full today as it is.' Josh slid off Sipho's desk, leaving his coffee mug behind.

'When's Doctor Naidoo coming again, Sipho?'

'Next week, as far as I know.'

Josh was halfway out the door when he turned back, asking, 'Sipho, have you seen my key card? I can't find it anywhere. Do me a favour and ring the hire-car crowd. I might have left it in their vehicle.'

Anna hoped her face was deadpan when Josh gave her a poignant look before he left.

* * *

After lunch, which consisted of baked sweet potatoes, Anna returned to her room with an arm full of paperwork she offered to process for Sipho. There were invoices to write and receipts for payments to be mailed.

'It's very kind of you to help me,' Sipho said, 'but you must do it in your room. The professor doesn't want you coming into contact with the public. I can't let you sit in my office.'

'Joshua is a pill,' she flared up in reply. 'What does he think I'm going to do? Shout for rescue from the rooftops? As if anyone would care about what happens to me!' She threw the hospital stationery and cash receipts journal back on Sipho's desk, ready to storm out. Sipho stopped her with a pleading look.

'I appreciate your help enormously. You've no idea how tired I get. Joshua will be grateful too.' Sipho held onto her arm. It felt like a moth had landed on her skin. The lack of strength shocked her. Relenting, she picked the bundle of papers up again.

'Anna,' Sipho implored, 'you must understand that none of us condone the manner in which you were brought here. I think it is the height of folly, and Peter and Tom have strong reservations too. We love to have you among us, preferably at your own volition. On the other hand, we also recognize why the professor acts as he does. We are with him all the way because he is trying to do good even though his methods are risky. I think you can see all that for yourself.' Sipho's sunken dark eyes begged Anna for tolerance. She nodded.

'Yes,' Sipho continued, 'I think you do appreciate our circumstances here far more than the professor believes you capable of.' Sipho laughed suddenly. 'Why else would you call yourself the financial advisor instead of the kidnap victim you really are? You are protecting Josh as much as we are. All we have to do is convince him of it. I think that may be the only way you can regain your freedom.'

Sipho's reasoning was half right, Anna thought. She called herself a financial advisor to save her sanity. Surrendering to victim mentality would see her in the psychiatric ward. She had to live in denial of the truth. Yet Sipho was correct in guessing she had no wish to expose Josh to scrutiny from the law. Already during her first morning, she had learnt enough about KwaZulu Medical to appreciate the hard work everyone contributed to keep it running on its meagre resources. To have come as far as they did required sound economic management. Credit for that had to go to Sipho. He fell into self-conscious silence when Josh charged through the door.

'We'll have to call Dr Naidoo, Sipho. That wasn't a road accident. We've got two teenage boys with a body temperature as high as a skyscraper, suffering infections from botched circumcisions. Curse those irresponsible initiation procedures,' Josh fretted while he dialled Indira's number.

'Yes, I've got them on antibiotic drips, but that doesn't reduce the danger—' Anna heard medical jargon pour from Josh as he impressed the urgency for surgery on Indira.

'Xhosas,' he said, shaking his head as he hung up. 'King Shaka, in his pragmatic wisdom, forbade this nonsense. Recovery from circumcision struck about three months of military training from a warrior's career. King Shaka saw no need for initiation ceremonies. The battlefield soon sorted the men from the boys. A teenager could prove himself a man facing the enemy.'

Anna left Josh and Sipho to dwell on their disapproval of circumcision. She tossed the pile of papers on her kitchen table and sat down to work. Concentration was in short supply, and she soon found herself attempting another hazardous journey to the kitchen for coffee. Josh and Sipho were still discussing various matters, and nobody bothered her.

Carrying a mug and more biscuits she passed Sipho's tokoloshe guardhouse and foyer in time to see a white Mazda pull up and a beautiful Indian woman alight from it. She was dressed in a KwaZulu Medical uniform. Blue jeans, white shirt, briefcase in one hand and stethoscope in the other. Indira Naidoo the surgeon had arrived. She set off towards Emergency at power-walk tempo. Josh dashed out to intercept her, almost colliding with Anna, who spilled coffee on her jeans.

'Anna,' he said hastily, 'do us a favour and stay in your room till Sipho calls you.'

Anna gave him a withering look from under her long lashes. She felt like a naughty child being sent away to contemplate improving her behaviour.

'Stinker!' she mouthed under her breath. For that indignity, she would punish him by not doing any paperwork. She had hoped to meet Indira, thinking that a woman confidant would act like a tonic on her disrupted life. Josh had dashed her longing to alleviate her loneliness. She couldn't do a thing or speak to anyone without his consent. She tramped back to her room angrily, shutting the door with a wall-shaking crash. With the coffee mug and biscuits set on the bedside table, she threw herself on the bed to stretch out with her hands under her head.

Why was Josh afraid of her meeting Indira? Anna wondered with eyes half closed. Of course she couldn't talk to her before the patients were seen to, and after that, Indira might be too weary for conversation, but a quick introduction would have sufficed. Indira was new at KwaZulu Medical, and Josh may be uncertain as to her reaction when she discovered Anna was not a patient.

On the whole, she was not disappointed with the day's progress. She had found out how to open the gate. That was of paramount importance. The key card was still in her handbag. Right now, with the circumcision emergency occupying everyone, she could drive away from here unseen. It was the type of situation she needed, except for the tokoloshe sitting in his guardhouse observing everything. Could she distract him? If Sipho fell ill suddenly and had to leave his office, she could get clean away. She intended to be alert for just such an event. Furthermore, she had identified a number of useful gadgets in the shed and knew where to find its key should she need them, and she installed a latch on her door. Except for her inability to get a message through to Hank, the day had been productive so far. 'And it hasn't finished yet,' she grinned.

Hoping to hear the talk and activities in the corridor, Anna rose to open her door wide. She drank her coffee, demolished the biscuits, and upon counting her blessings because Josh had not locked her into the wine cellar like poor William, resumed the paperwork. Not for Josh's sake but for the ailing Sipho.

Chapter 8

Ransom Negotiations and the Bad Dream

For a long time, nobody came to speak to Anna. Daylight was fading. She had finished Sipho's work a good while ago and fidgeted impatiently, reading entries in the cash receipts journal from months earlier. As she fully expected, there was no reference to grants from NGOs or donations of any sort. The Swiss account was stoked with unrecorded ill-gotten gains. She'd try taking a look at the general journal tomorrow but did not anticipate startling revelations. If she carried out a trial audit of all books in the place, it would not unearth one trace of US dollars. Speechless, she wondered for how long they hoped to conceal their secret slush fund. Chafing at her enforced inactivity and convinced she'd been forgotten, she took the bookwork back to the tokoloshe guardhouse. Sipho, becoming increasingly weary as the day passed, sat stooped like the Hunchback of Notre Dame, reconciling ledgers. He looked up, almost too tired to smile when she approached.

'Thanks, Anna,' was all he managed to say. Fatigued, he jerked his thumb in the direction of Josh's office.

'The professor wants a word with you.'

'You look spent, Sipho,' Anna said, overcome with pity. 'Is there anything else I can do for you?'

'No, it's okay. I'll lock up in a minute.'

Anna turned towards Josh's office, tapping on his door which, like the day before, was slightly ajar.

'That you, Anna?' She heard him shuffling papers. 'Come in! Sit down!' He was writing furiously. After a number of sentences, he looked up.

'Thanks for helping Sipho. Heaven knows he can do with assistance.'

'How are the two new patients?' Anna asked thoughtfully.

'They'll recover, I hope.' Josh sorted documents into manila folders. He took his time, checking his work all over again.

Anna thought their interview had ended. While he may not care to speak, she had plenty to say to him.

When Josh laid his pen down, she remarked casually, 'You concentrate so intently on your notes. Are you composing a ransom demand to Hank?'

'I haven't even thought about that yet,' he replied while going through his files. 'I've been so busy.'

'Could you make it your first priority, please? I'd like to get home.'

Josh chuckled. 'Why, don't you like it here?' he quizzed with affected disappointment. 'I thought you were settling in quite well, making friends with Sipho and threatening Margo with redundancy.'

'How much money do you want from Hank?' She would not be thrown off the point by his frivolous remark.

'I haven't figured that out yet either,' he said with a shrug. 'but half a million US dollars sounds inadequate for a lovely, talented lady like you.'

Josh still sorted papers on his desk, not looking at her. He thought he heard her brains whir while she calculated if Hank could raise such a huge sum without running into deficit.

'It's too much,' she said without hesitation.

He laughed. 'The amount is not negotiable. It's half a million in full or you stay here.'

Josh was in no position to drive such a hard bargain, Anna thought. Eventually his crimes would come to the attention of the police, forcing him to face the music. She said nothing to Josh while wondering how the money could be brought together. They had little spare liquid cash. Their private capital was tied up in property and gold mines. De Bruyn Brothers ran smoothly, observing trading rule 163 without fail. Under that regulation the partnership's assets must exceed liabilities at all times. And that meant mostly cash. Property didn't count because of the fluctuations in its value. If not, De Bruyn Brothers could be hammered from the stock exchange. That was unthinkable. The idea of De Bruyn Brothers going under because of a ransom payment to an irresponsible individual was outrageous. No way would she let that happen. Josh could do his worst.

'How much time would you give Hank to pay?'

'Sorry, what did you say, Anna?' Josh thought he hadn't heard right. Here she was, in his office, sitting beside his desk, speaking to him in a businesslike manner as if he was buying a parcel of shares. Where was her agitation? fear? hysteria? tears? Wasn't she cowered by the power he now had over her? Amazing woman. Only her eyes were different. Opaque, bottle-green. What did that mean? Was it an alarm mechanism he should take note of?

'I said, Joshua, how much time would you give Hank to pay up?'

'Don't be so hasty, woman. I haven't sent a ransom demand yet.' Finished with his work, he sat back, looking smugly at her. 'To be quite frank, I enjoy having you here. I'm in no hurry to see you go.'

The remark failed to register on Anna's mind, which was still busy with thoughts about finding money. Her father would definitely pay half of the amount, although Hank would loathe asking him. Scratching together a quarter of the sum would cause Hank no problems, and his brothers could lend the rest. That way, nobody had to sell any assets and De Bruyn Brothers remained untouched. Or was there another option?

Josh pondered Anna's failure to react to his comment when her mysterious opaque eyes stared at him coldly. 'Will you accept a donation of US $800,000 over four years and let me go?'

'Didn't you hear me? I said no negotiation.' He became recalcitrant. 'I will not bargain with you, Anna,' he said, as if that meant lowering himself to the level of a woman. 'EEM operatives may approach your husband—'

Anna interrupted his sentence, a sign of disrespect in his macho estimation. He glared at her.

'Joshua, we can't pluck half a million out of thin air.'

'My heart bleeds for you.' He grinned mirthlessly, and against her better judgment, she couldn't resist pulling him off his chauvinistic high horse.

'So it should! Call yourself a man, victimizing an unarmed and defenceless woman. Why not abduct your equal? Try the minister of finance or a top police officer.'

She expected a combative response, but Josh laughed.

'How do I extract half a million from them? Crazy woman! Don't talk such unintelligent stuff. Besides, I'm not victimizing you. You are here because, as a leading stockbroker's wife, you epitomize all that is oppressive, exploitative, opportunistic, and socially irresponsible. It's payback time, Anna. Reparation is due. Wealth must be more evenly distributed. I need money to keep this clinic afloat and to help lighten the burden of disadvantage for my people.'

Anna bristled at his voluble accusations. 'You are forgetting, Joshua, that wealth is like respect. It doesn't fall into one's lap like manna from heaven. It has to be earned. Wealth has to be created, not stolen.'

'You whites can talk,' he half-shouted, half-laughed at her. 'You've all but stolen the whole damned country from us.' He rolled his eyes towards the ceiling impatiently.

Ignoring his obvious signs of annoyance, she continued, 'What you're doing here with KwaZulu Medical is a step in the right direction, especially now that South Africa is on the brink of change. It is a time of opportunity for you. Be a Voortrekker, a pioneer. Be the first black business listed on the stock market.'

Josh stared at her as if he should take her to the psychiatric ward. 'KwaZulu Medical stands no chance, you know that!' he said, aggrieved. 'No more than ten corporate enterprises control just on 90 per cent of shares listed on the JSE. That's a monopoly situation by anyone's name. How's a new player supposed to break into that?'

'Don't be discouraged. It's not as bad as it looks. What you're seeing as a monopoly is caused largely by South Africa's isolation due to apartheid era sanctions. In any case, the world's markets are a little incestuous. I'll give you examples. Take Britain—about fifty institutions own some 45 per cent of all British shares. So South Africa's performance is not too bad, given we're the world's outcasts. Also, the top five hundred companies in the world transact 70 per cent of direct foreign investment. A third of all that global trade consists of deals between the dominant transnational companies.'

'You may be right.' Josh conceded with a note of doubt. 'Even so, after the coming election, blacks expect to have more representation, but it will not be good enough. White business magnates will brook no interference, and even a black-majority government will have to come to grips with white industrial and financial interests holding the purse strings.'

'Your outlook is too bleak, Josh.' Anna exhaled with an air of defeat. 'Think about what I've said. I want to help you, but there's nothing I can do while you hold me incommunicado. Remember, I'm offering more than half a million over four years. Let me go. Bring this ignoble phase of your operation to an end.'

He was about to say something, but Anna cut him off again. 'I promise I will take no legal action against you.'

'Your husband and his brothers will,' Josh remonstrated.

'No, Josh. I guarantee it.'

He gave her a deprecating smile. 'How can you prevent it? What influence has one woman over six powerful men?'

It was Anna's turn to chuckle. 'I have dealt with them since the day I married Hank. I know how to persuade them.' She told him how she had vanquished the family's prejudice against her. How she had shaped De Bruyn's company policies vis-à-vis insider trading, and how, by example, she encouraged her brothers-in-law to accept her doctrines.

Brushing her polemics aside, Josh looked at his watch, saying, 'It's getting late. Time I checked on the kids. Why don't you come to my quarters and have dinner with me in about forty-five minutes?'

'Don't change the subject please, Josh,' she demanded, placing her hand flat on his desk as if to detain him. 'If you don't want to talk money, let me at least write to Hank so he knows I'm alive.'

'Yeah, okay! Here's paper and an envelope.' He tossed a pen in her direction. 'Write!' He instructed. 'Only make it quick because I've got to look at the kids and then we'll have dinner.'

Anna held her breath. She hadn't expected Josh to agree so readily. What was his game? There had to be a catch.

'No doubt you'll be vetting every word I write,' she said with a sour smile.

'Wrong!' he protested. 'You're on your honour not to betray me. I don't want to read the letter. I'm going to trust you, although that may be foolhardy. We'll soon see.'

Anna put the pen down again. Her eyes, as dull as traffic lights switched off, fixed on Josh's face. 'You make it sound as if I were the criminal. I resent that.'

Josh smirked. 'Poor innocuous victim. I'm testing you, that's all.'

'Well, that's a pointless exercise,' she said dismissively. 'Tell me,' she insisted, 'if you found yourself a prisoner of war, would you not feel obligated to escape and rejoin your impi? If only to maintain your self-respect. I'm no different. I am a prisoner of war in your hostilities against the white business community.'

Anna began to write. 'Hank, darling . . .' Josh watched her keenly but turned away when she looked up.

'All right,' she sighed. 'Without a show of goodwill, we're not going to achieve much. Let's be honest. We trust each other as far as a fish can ride a bicycle. Because I suspect you will read this letter behind my back irrespective of what you say, I'll tell you what I'm going to write.'

'You don't have to,' Josh replied, needled by her directness. 'I meant what I said.'

She expressed her scepticism with a fake cough. 'Remember the VW Golf driver I told you about?'

Josh nodded. 'Come on, Anna. I'm running out of time.' He tapped his fingers on the desk.

Refusing to be hurried, she wrote slowly. 'I'm going to tell Hank that I've gone into hiding for a while because I fear Malcolm Price may have sent that man to harm me.'

'What you tell your husband is your affair,' Josh said, his voice indifferent but his eyes alight with approval.

Anna knew Hank would realize something untoward had happened because Price's threats alone would never drive her to seek cover. To clarify the treacherous fate that had overtaken her, she wrote a sentence at the bottom of the page to say she was trying to extricate herself from a difficult situation. She penned the sentence in German so that Josh could not read it. '*Ich versuche einer schwierigen Situation zuentkommen,*' Anna wrote, blessing her German immigrant grandparents who had taught her their language. Hank was good enough at German to decipher the words. If not, Jan and Adriaan could give him a word-perfect translation.

'Finished?' Josh demanded curtly, trying to hide his relief at her sidestepping of the truth. Maybe Sipho was right, he thought. With typical male chauvinism, Sipho had stated, 'This albino lioness of the financial jungle is a harmless pussycat. She derives her power from her husband's position. Hank and his brothers use her as the human face of the firm while they remain the powers behind the throne.' Josh had his doubts. Anna's celebrated ethics, compassion, and fairness were not necessarily synonymous with feminine weakness. Sipho was deceived by her occasional look of vulnerability and her gentle fussing over him. Josh knew how susceptible he himself was to her periodic displays of warmth.

Wondering if Josh had the decency to send it, Anna flicked her letter across the desk to him with an imperious movement of her left wrist. Taking umbrage at the gesture, Josh gave her a warning look. No woman had gotten away with treating him offhandedly. She needed training in deference towards a Zulu man.

He said brusquely, 'For obvious reasons, this cannot be sent in the mail, but it will be delivered, I promise.' He wrote Hank's name on the envelope, folded the sheet, and placed it inside. A split second's glimpse at the letter aroused his misgiving about the German text at the bottom. The word *Situation* stood out, clearly referring to her current circumstances. What was the rest? He would copy it down later and, inventing a story of sorts, ask Zak Elbenstein.

'It's too late for dinner now.' Josh banished Anna, upset over her high-handed manner. 'You have taken too long over this matter. I must check on the children and look in on the teenagers. Go to your room now.' His desire for her company had taken a battering. She must be put in her place. Loneliness would teach her humility.

Unconcerned about Josh's wounded masculine pride, Anna left him. Surely he didn't expect her to feel indebted for letting her write to Hank. For the second time, she wondered who the innocent or guilty party was in this crime. Josh had a way of twisting the facts as if she were the one at fault. He wanted the moral high ground, to which he was not entitled.

Satisfied, Anna thought her first full day at KwaZulu Medical well spent. Finally she had what she wanted—contact with Hank. That is, if Josh dispatched the letter promptly. She had to take his word for it.

There was still a little time to take advantage of what daylight remained, and defying Josh's command to go to her room, she went outside for fresh air and a walk around the garden. Tomorrow, she promised herself, she would check its perimeter centimetre by painstaking centimetre for possible outlets, any hole to slip through or fence to climb without being seen.

The last glimmer of twilight was extinguished so quickly that she found herself walking in darkness. She had slipped out the front door because Josh would use the back exit to go to the children's ward. The tokoloshe had also retired in the meantime, leaving his guardhouse illuminated by the night light. She tried the office door. Locked, as usual.

Stepping outside, she saw that Dr Naidoo's car was gone, and apart from Josh's Corolla, there was no other vehicle in the doctor's parking area. For a hospital, the place was quiet at night, deserted. Keeping on the grass to save her bare feet from scratches, she followed the arrows Dr Shabalala had told her would lead to the outpatient and casualty sections. Lights blazed in that area, staffed by medical student volunteers who would call Josh if anything urgent occurred. She skirted around the prefabricated buildings and walked to the back, which brought her into closer contact with the shrubs she had seen from the window of her room. She really had been quartered at the tail end of the place, she thought.

Her enjoyment of the balmy evening was marred drastically by a nagging feeling of culpability settling on her spirit. She had lied to Hank. She wasn't hiding from Price. Why had she written that? Did she have a choice of wording? Yes? No? Could she reveal her imprisonment at KwaZulu Medical and expose Joshua Mtolo, the driving force behind the EEM? As if! Joshua would simply love having such accusations broadcast. Not! She had her comfort and safety to think of as well. She didn't want to end up stuck in the wine cellar or provoke him to such an extent that he might kill her. She sighed with frightened despair. Would Josh really go that far? Wasn't there just the slightest hint of affection for her in his voice and occasional smiles? She wished it so . . . desperately. Was it totally impossible to build on that small cornerstone of love? Imperfectly moulded as it was and mixed from equal and opposite parts of understanding and mistrust? Or was Sipho right? Was she protecting Josh? Was she raising a structure of justification on that malformed cornerstone? It was hard to work out.

Hunger drove her back indoors, and she sniffed around the kitchen for something to eat.

'I'll fix you up soon,' Margo promised in her customary gruff attitude. 'First I have to take this tray to the professor. Then I'll get you something.'

'I can take Josh's meal to him if you like,' Anna offered impulsively.

'Right, if that's what you want. Here!' Margo passed a tray of food to her. Beans and rice, the stuff William was fed on, she grinned. Fresh fruit for dessert and strong coffee. The good Kenyan beans Sipho showed her. Josh obviously still had work ahead of him and wished to stay awake. She took the tray and tapped on his door.

'Anna!' He sounded surprised. 'Come in!'

He pointed to the coffee table on which she could place the tray. His quarters were larger than her prison cell, she noticed. He had two rooms. One was a living area with the obligatory desk and bookshelves by the window and a two-seater couch with two matching chairs around the coffee table. A television and Hi-Fi system were placed opposite the couch for convenient operation and viewing. An open archway led to his bedroom which, like the living room, was furnished simply but comfortably.

'It's so sweet of you to bring me my dinner.' Josh beamed at her with delight.

'Sorry, Josh, I must confess ulterior motives.' Anna laughed, setting the tray down. 'Margo said I'd get nothing before she had catered for you, so I thought I'd hasten the process by helping her.'

'Hau!' he exclaimed. 'Here I was thinking you were doing me a special favour.' His shoulders sagged with disappointment.

'What about Sipho?' Anna asked quickly to give their talk a different direction.

'He's fine. Fernando looks after him.'

Leaving the door open, Josh sat on the couch, beckoning her to sit beside him. When they heard the squeak of Margo's approaching shoes, Josh called out.

'In here, Margo! Bring Anna's dinner in here please.' Margo did so and closed the door quietly, which Anna thought made a pleasant change.

'You're grinning, Anna. What's the joke?' Josh studied her profile while she ate.

'Beans and rice,' she said with mouth full.

'So? It's good for you.' Josh professed while taking a forkful.

'I know, but I just remembered William Rosenberg's evaluation of it. He thought he was being mistaken for a Mexican.'

'Did he now?' Josh frowned, although a trace of mischief glowed in his eyes. 'He was damned lucky to survive his serving of the meal. He called Fernando a shithead, so for revenge, Fernando threw extra pepper on it before Margo took it down. Rosenberg must have the digestive system of a scavenging seagull. Eats anything.'

Leaning against the backrest of the couch, Anna threw her head back and laughed. For an instant, Josh saw her traffic-light eyes shine with fun before they dulled once more.

'I think Margo's bean and rice mix is very tasty,' she complimented.

'Yeah, she's a good cook. That's one reason why I employ her. The other is because she loves kids. She has a very warm heart and much empathy with traumatized children.'

'You could have fooled me.' Anna looked dubious.

'I know she's a grim woman. She has no people skills, and she can't change her obnoxious ways. It's a birth defect, a congenital problem. She just can't help herself. Deep down she's a genuine soul, though.'

'Maybe one day I'll be pleasantly surprised when Margo shows me her better characteristics. She shut the door silently before. That's a hopeful start.' Still laughing, she managed to relax a little.

They finished their repast in apparent good form, chatting idly. Josh stretched comfortably beside her, placing an arm on the backrest behind her shoulders. Imperceptibly, he had moved closer to her. Their thighs almost touched.

'Anyway,' he said more seriously, 'I can't talk about Margo's faults. I'm cranky at times. I'm sorry I was rather abrupt to you before.' He looked down at her bruised wrist. The contusion was changing from a deep purple colour to yellow. 'I regret that too,' he whispered, taking her hand gently and kissing the sore imprints of his fingers on her skin.

His touch sent her heart rate soaring, while her brain warned that she was like the fly in the spider's web. The spider closed in on her. Soon he would spin binding threads around her. Already she felt paralysed, neither moving nor speaking.

'You see what happens when you do not do as I ask?' Josh lectured, pointing to her wrist. 'It causes difficulties.'

Then we will have difficulties galore, she thought but said nothing.

'I never want to be nasty to you again. You must help me by not doing anything to make me cross. You may not realize it, but I do lose my temper quickly, especially with wilful and obstinate women.'

She sat with downcast eyes. His chauvinism was the perfect antidote for her paralysis. She could lash out at him for painting her as the guilty party yet again. The wiser option by far, she knew, was to play meek and let him believe he convinced her. Released from her trance by his irritating preaching, she rose to take the dishes back to the kitchen. Unable to keep the ice from her voice, she said, 'Good night, Joshua!' and left.

* * *

Anna returned to her room, placing the latch across her door. Peace. No disturbances. Relieved that the end of her first day at KwaZulu Medical was nigh, she stretched out on the bed for a while. The need to be constantly observant and on guard had made the day strenuous. Many unconnected thoughts criss-crossed her mind. She wanted to unwind and ease the colossal tension within her. At home, she would have sat in the spa. Here she had little more than a lukewarm shower. Would that help her to sleep? A better-quality soap and shampoo were needed too before her skin broke into blemishes. She had none of her favourite cosmetics with her. How could such items be procured? Who would help? Josh would not be agreeable to allowing her out for a shopping spree. Life was going to be cumbersome here. With a sudden jolt, she found she prepared herself for a lengthy sojourn at KwaZulu Medical. That couldn't be. She had to get back to Hank.

She rose from the bed with a depressed sigh. 'Better a lukewarm shower than none at all,' she mumbled. She didn't stay under the shower for long. It wasn't satisfactory; wasn't what she was used to. While towelling her hair dry, it occurred to her that she had no blow-dryer either. 'Shit!' Things were going from bad to worse. With a towel wrapped around her, she stood by the basin brushing her teeth when someone rattled her door.

'What are you doing, woman? Open the door, Anna!'

It was Josh. 'What do you want?' she called with toothpaste around her mouth.

'What have you done? Will you open up!' He sounded angry.

'I'm not dressed!' She shouted, dropping the towel, flinging the bathrobe around her, and wiping her mouth.

'*Anginandaba*! I don't care' came his petulant reply. His voice carried frustration, and she hurried to the door.

'Anna, what the hell . . . ?' Josh examined the latch. 'Did Fernando screw that on for you?'

She looked past him while thinking about a response. If she said yes, she would be lying and Fernando would be hauled over the coals. If she admitted having done it herself, she would very likely be banned from the toolshed. And there were things in there that she needed. She decided to go on the offensive.

'I don't want men watching me while I sleep,' she said, circumventing his question.

'I think you have been dreaming, and you haven't answered my question.' Josh reminded her firmly.

'The smell of your aftershave was not in my dream,' she shot back. 'It still hung in the air when I woke up.'

Defeated, he groped for a quick retreat. 'I just popped in to see if you were okay. I do that with everyone here, including Sipho.'

'I'm not sick, so you needn't bother about me.'

'Are you going to reply to my question any time soon?'

She had to confess but not without pushing moral barbs into him. 'I put that latch there because privacy is the smallest courtesy you owe me for disrupting my life.'

Josh ignored the pin pricks. 'In future, my dear lady,' he argued with a blend of exaggerated severity and fun, 'if you are going to make major modifications to the building, do you mind asking my consent?'

'And would you have given your hallowed blessing, my dear Doctor Josh?' Anna retorted swiftly.

'No.' Josh smiled as a little of the old glow returned to Anna's eyes.

'You see what I mean? What's the point of asking you?' Their vexation with each other had given way to joviality, although Josh spoke seriously again.

'And I'll tell you why not. I don't like locking anyone in, not even the psychiatric patients. In case of fire, how do you think they can get out? The same goes for people locking themselves away.'

'I am not a patient, Josh.'

'No, but while you're here, you will follow my safety rules.'

The explanation, although convenient for him, was sensible. She should have thought of it herself, but she wasn't going to let him win easily. 'William Rosenberg must have enjoyed a special exemption from your regulations down in the wine cellar.'

'Never mind Rosenberg,' Josh grinned. 'He's not as exquisitely beautiful as you.'

She gave him a shove towards the door. 'Go on! Be off with you!'

He didn't budge half a step. Turning towards her and thrusting some papers in her hand, he said, 'I thought you might be interested in this.'

She hadn't realized the folder he carried was for her. 'Bedtime reading material. Great.' She took it eagerly.

Josh explained its contents. 'A short time ago, Inkatha and the ANC had a meeting at the Royal Hotel in Durban, its purpose being to kiss and make up. This folder contains transcripts of both Madiba's and Shenge's speeches. You may find it informative.'

'Thank you. I will read it before I go to sleep.'

'You'll see that there is a culture of violence towards Inkatha, which originates at the top level of the ANC hierarchy and trickles right down to the grass-roots membership. It will help you understand what lies behind the fracas Benny and I ran into, as well as the school bus shooting, which inspired us to build this clinic.'

'Thank you, Josh,' Anna said again, beginning to skip-read before he was out the door.

'My god!' She took him by the hand and sat him down at the table. 'This is so hypocritical.'

'What is?'

'Madiba! He says, "The ANC believes that the efforts of our people have brought about a situation in which apartheid can be eradicated by peaceful means."'

Josh interrupted. 'Pretty rich, isn't it, coming from the leader of Umkhonto?'

'What a way to disguise the fact that their armed struggle failed.'

'Of course it had to,' Josh affirmed. 'With the collapse of communism in the USSR, the ANC lost their material and ideological support base. They can't continue the armed struggle without Soviet aid. Therefore, it's best to aim for a negotiated settlement, isn't it? But we mustn't admit that Inkatha was right in the first place. Oh, no. We can't lose that much face.' Impassioned, Josh's voice rose. 'It would be too much to ask of the ANC leadership to apologise to Shenge for the hurt their vilification caused him.'

'I can't believe this,' Anna said, shaking her head slowly. 'They condemn Shenge for his pacifism. Ridicule him for saying that negotiation will win the day and then proclaim apartheid can be ended peacefully as if that was their opinion all along. One would think that Umkhonto or the UDF never existed.'

'Yes,' Josh said while Anna turned the pages. 'They should know better. Shenge's been in politics all his adult life, and his experience is vast. What he says comes true eventually. But read on. You'll find many such discrepancies.'

'I think I need a drink to wash down this flagrant backslide.' Anna looked about, confused. 'Gosh! If you were my guest at home, we could share a drop . . . but I'm not at home, am I?'

'That doesn't mean there's nothing to drink. Give me five minutes.' Josh headed for the door. 'I'll be back.'

The wine cellar's remnants still offered marginal temptations. Maybe the bottle of Backsberg he had noticed last time he took stock was still there, or perhaps the Bollinger. Although the collection was stored in a cabinet in his office, Peter and Tom were free to help themselves to anything they fancied.

Grasping the bottle by the neck, Josh took it to the kitchen for uncorking. He searched for two glasses and, gathering his trophies on a tray, added chocolate biscuits to the spoils. Feeling well equipped, he walked back to Anna's room. Halfway along, his hands began to tremble, threatening the stability of bottle and glasses. Anna wasn't wearing a stitch under that securely belted bathrobe, he realized. Had she tried on the nightgown yet? She hadn't said anything about it. Maybe it didn't fit her. Throughout the day, she had worn the rather sheer cotton shirt tied invitingly around her slender hourglass middle to emphasise her bust. It drew disturbing attention to the outline of her bra. Couldn't she deck herself out in other gear to spare him the debilitating USB attacks? 'Dumb prick!' he cursed himself under his breath. The woman had nothing else to wear but what he provided for her. Anyway, he thought, she would still look sexy wrapped in a potato sack with a string of teabags around her neck.

In Anna's presence again, he had problems controlling his state of nervous arousal. She noticed his unsteady hands, taking the tray from him to ensure its safety. With relief, she remembered Indira was the surgeon, not Josh.

'Are you okay?' she asked, becoming worried.

'Yeah . . . yeah, I think so. I'm fine . . . just getting a bit tired. I should have coffee instead of this stuff,' he said, indicating the bottle.

'Do you ever relax?' Anna asked, prompting him to sit down again.

'Not at night,' Josh replied with a meaningful look and half-smile.

'No, seriously, you just keep on going and going. I've not seen you take a break all day.'

'I prefer to keep alert at night because Peter and Tom go home. I'm the only one here. I can't afford to get too comfortable.'

'But you must rest sometime.'

'Occasionally I'll have an afternoon nap to compensate.' Josh poured wine into the glasses without spillage. He saw that as a fair accomplishment, given Anna's effect on his system.

They clinked glasses. 'To Shenge!' Anna said, tapping her finger on the sheets of paper. 'If a real multiparty democracy is to evolve in South Africa, we need leaders like him who offer voters a choice.'

Josh nodded agreement. He found Anna a fast political learner, and her obvious pro-Inkatha stance was one of her redeeming features in his view.

She went on with a faraway look. 'But citizens must learn to appreciate choice. They must come to see it as democracy's lifeblood, every drop of it as precious as the purest drinking water from pristine springs.' She cupped her wine glass in both hands as if it were a priceless antique chalice filled with the source of life itself. 'And just as surely to evaporate if we become careless and blasé with its use,' she warned. 'People cannot go about killing others who have different affiliations.' She shrugged with a sigh. 'Africans must change their DNA to rid themselves of their fondness for one-party governments. If they fail to do that, the ANC will win the upcoming election. The ANC's centralist, 'all or nothing' rhetoric sweeps the people along with them. Under such ideological pressure, constituents don't think for themselves. They can't see that a choice exists between the ANC's drive towards a unitary socialist state and Inkatha's push for federalism, provincial autonomy, and an appropriate role for traditional leaders.'

'That's where voter education comes in,' Josh opined. 'The ANC are experts at indoctrination, but education is something different.'

'You are confirming what I suspect, Josh. People can't grasp the democratic model. Or perhaps they have no wish to do so.'

'You forget, Anna, our people have never voted before, and the ANC runs a spectacular propaganda machine to impose its agenda onto them. Propaganda is an art they acquired from their Soviet as well as Vietnamese teachers. I would say the pupils surpass the tutors. Part of the propaganda machine's function is to coerce the people into a submission born from gratitude to the comrades for liberating them from apartheid's yoke.' With a sinister grin, Josh added, 'And there's always intimidation for the thankless traitors.'

'As in killing Inkatha's officials?' Anna asked, perturbed.

'Exactly!'

Anna continued reading while Josh's gaze swivelled from her face to the bed and back. Could he pick her up and lay her on the bed? It was only a matter of two or three strides. Imagining unfastening the bathrobe, he nonetheless dreaded the ensuing scene if she was unwilling to participate. Of course, he could beat her reluctance and fighting spirit out of her, but despite his rugged thoughts, brutality was not his line. He preferred her to meet him halfway. Would she?

'This is dreadful, Josh.' Anna's voice tore him from his illicit reverie.

'Right here, on page 9!' She picked up the sheet and shook it as if to make the words fall from it and break up to resemble fly specks. 'The *Times* in London has, in the past, reported none other than Chris Hani, secretary general of the South African Communist Party and chief of staff of Umkhonto, as making no apologies for his support of selective killing of black collaborators like policemen, township councillors, and other minor public servants. Hani is quoted as saying "Targets for assassinations included members of Inkatha's Central Committee" and "The ANC's policy was to politically isolate and destroy Inkatha's leaders and the KwaZulu chief minister." That's Shenge they're talking about!' Anna gave the paper another disgusted flip. 'Now I really need a drink.' She picked up her glass, found it empty, and refilled it before reading on.

'That Alfred Nzo chap . . . who is he?'

'Secretary general of the ANC.'

'Says much the same thing: "Necklacing was an acceptable means which the people at home have devised to deal with collaborators."'

Anna pushed the sheets from her. 'This is repulsive. I can't read any more of this today. What sort of society is this? What people are spurred on by such misguided, criminally minded leaders?'

'Very desperate people, Anna,' Josh said sadly. 'In their desperation, they forget they fight against their own brothers. These people are without hope and feel they have nothing to lose. The most dangerous person is always the one who has nothing to lose.'

'But . . . but this is a carte blanche for mass murder,' Anna said, revolted. 'It's genocide. It amounts to a declaration of war.'

Josh nodded emphatically. 'And make no mistake, it's the ANC's war against Inkatha. Don't ever let anyone tell you it's the other way around.' Josh couldn't sit still. He rose, but there was nowhere for him to pace in Anna's cell. His movements restricted, he turned back to her.

'Do you know what happened to Steve Biko's Black Consciousness followers?' he asked, not at all surprised when she said she had little idea. Josh's face set in a scowl. 'The UDF used them as targets on whom to practice their killing campaign before lunging at Inkatha supporters in the same manner. I'll give you Ryan Malan's book *My Traitor's Heart*, which deals with the unhappy demise of Black Consciousness,' he offered 'To take an anti-violence stance is taboo in the ANC. They immediately stamp you a traitor. They say if you're not for them, you must be against them. Therefore you have to go. It's as simple as that.'

'Is this the way to a healthy civil society? to liberation? to democracy? to a new South Africa?' Anna asked softly, taken aback by the horror, which had, up till now, left her life largely untouched.

'No, it isn't. That's why we should help Shenge and the Inkatha Freedom Party as much as we can.'

'You mean finance Shenge's election campaign?'

'Yes, that's a vital part of it because the ANC has millions to splash around and Madiba travels the world with a begging bowl. Inkatha's funds are sparse in comparison. They have to make every Rand stretch as far as possible. Shenge is too dignified and proud to go begging.'

'It shouldn't be too hard to convince at least part of the business sector of the merit. They have serious doubts about the ANC comrades' command economy. They want South Africa to be competitive in a free market.'

'That may be true, Anna, but they also need the assurance that Inkatha is for all South Africans, rural and urban. If they believe what's printed in newspapers, they will shy away, thinking Inkatha only works for Zulus. That's the impression the media conveys, but it's incorrect. Shenge says that we should strive to become "a truly African and yet truly modern state". Does that sound as if it concerns only rural Zulus? I don't think so.'

Josh pushed his chair under the table. 'You'll have to excuse me now. We can talk about this in more detail tomorrow perhaps.' He shrugged. 'I've been saddled with updating and rewriting course material for Uni. I'm way behind schedule, and it's becoming urgent. It's an ongoing task, but I tend to leave it to the last moment. Unless I spend a solid four hours on it each day for the next three weeks, I won't get it finished.'

'Can I be of assistance?' Anna saw an opportunity to kill time.

'How quick are you at word processing?' Josh asked hopefully.

'Respectable.'

'Good, I may call on you for help.'

Josh bid Anna good night. 'Sweet dreams.' His smile embraced her. 'Not about aftershave though, unless it's mine.'

* * *

William Rosenberg rubbed his hands and smacked his lips. This was good. Gold Corp shares in the bargain basement at R7-98. Soon Mineral Enterprises would have a controlling stake as disenchanted investors dropped Gold Corp like a hot potato. He already saw himself as managing director of the combined entity, which they would rename Mineral Explorations Corp.

He had to thank the De Bruyns for the wondrous opportunities that came his way. Anna, that wily damsel, had set the ball rolling at the shareholders' meeting. Soon thereafter, a tale circulated that Malcolm Price had misappropriated company funds. Someone— De Bruyns maybe—leaked information about legal action against Price for corruption. Shareholders lost confidence. They pulled their money out of Gold Corp by thousands of rand. While the Gold Corp building trembled with financial aftershocks from the rumour mill earthquake, William jumped to offer R9-00 per share in a takeover bid. That was R0-65 more than their true market value immediately before the shareholders' meeting. *Quite generous*, William thought. Gold Corp rejected the offer, preferring to ride out the storm, but the shareholders insisted on another meeting, urging in a non-binding advisory vote that the R9-00 be accepted. The Gold Corp directors wouldn't hear of it. They countered by relieving Price of his duties and buying back their own shares at R9-15. Then the crunch came. Price was arrested for fraud. Anna De Bruyn vanished, and suspicion of a vendetta fell on Price. It sent the share price tumbling. No amount of buy-back could save Gold Corp, their management unable to follow the speed of events. By that time, fantastic stories had spread that Anna's father and her husband were buying a controlling stake in Gold Corp. Nobody held their breath to wait what would happen next. Investors bolted, leaving a demolished Gold Corp with its finances in disarray like a wrecker's yard. Enter William Rosenberg to pick up the pieces at R8-75.

Ah, he deserved that glass of port, to be sure. William laughed, his ample girth shaking. Still, there was no resting on his laurels. The current price of R8-35 was way too low. Mineral Enterprises would make use of the chance to buy enough for a 65 per cent interest. Then the value must rise again. They didn't want to feed a dead duck. But that was tomorrow's worry.

Today had been excellent. Nothing could dampen William's spirits. Almost as soon as he settled at his desk this morning, the phone rang. He didn't want calls so early but picked it up anyway, his heart leaping at the sound of the voice from the other end.

'Indira! Gee, it's nice to hear your voice. Music to my ear . . . it's true!' he said when she laughed at his clichéd compliment. 'How's the new job?'

'Really good, William. I can keep my hours down to part-time, which gives me freedom to study. I want to go into neurosurgery.'

'Ambitious, aren't you?'

'Yes, of course. What do you think? I'm surrounded by male colleagues. I have to prove my worth.'

'You're worth ten of them at least, Indira.'

'You should come and see the place, William. I've already managed to make improvements, which I thought my men here would never agree to.'

'You've charmed them.'

'No, I hit them with common sense. They think it's a miracle taking place.'

'Don't be too hard on them, Indira. You begin to scare me.'

'You have to see this place. It's really good, considering their lack of financial backing.' Indira's excitement rang in her voice. 'I've asked for the best anaesthetizing equipment. Josh consented without argument. It arrives next month. You've no idea what this machine can do. It shows you everything about the patient's functions during the operation.' Indira laughed softly. 'It'll tell me what the patient is dreaming, I swear,' she joked. 'It's the latest of its kind.'

Indira talked about her operating room for a substantial time. William let her. He wasn't about to offend her by cutting her short. She was hell-bent on showing him the place. A guided tour of an operating theatre. Yuck! His skin crawled. Still, why not visit the place? KwaZulu Medical was one of the first businesses to discard their Gold Corp shares before the price went into a tailspin, he recalled. They immediately bought into Mineral Enterprises, gaining a neat windfall when all the hubbub and speculation that followed drove Mineral Enterprises up. One could almost suspect Mtolo had inside information. William determined he should go and see for himself. There was evidently more to KwaZulu Medical than met the eye. Unfortunately he couldn't give Indira a firm date for his coming. It was a matter of time and opportunity because Melody took a lively interest in his movements of late.

* * *

Another morning at KwaZulu Medical dawned for Anna. It was Thursday, but that didn't matter. The routine was no different to Wednesday's. A lukewarm shower, Margo's unappetizing breakfast, the same choice of denim and cotton to wear. Still no shoes unless she used her own high-heeled ones, which weren't practical. Then it was time to help Sipho and avoid boredom as much as possible.

Sipho was effervescent all morning because Fernando drove him out to meet with a friend for lunch every second Thursday.

'We're going to the Zebra today, Anna,' he announced excitedly.

'What do they serve, Sipho? Game?'

'No, very ordinary dishes, I'd say, but the place has such atmosphere. It's all black-and-white-striped, soft furnishings, napery and all. I like it there.'

It was good, Anna thought, that Sipho still had friends who cared about him. It gave him strength and upheld his morale. She watched him tidy away his paperwork while Fernando waited outside, ready to go. Sipho jingled the office keys in his pocket.

'My wallet!' He returned to his desk and pulled his money out of a drawer before locking the enquiries window and the door.

'Why do you lock everything around here?' Anna queried. 'Is that your normal procedure, or is it because I might wish to ring my friends? Not to mention my husband, relatives, and colleagues.'

Sipho hated to see Anna frown. He found her questions awkward to answer and disliked his role as virtual mediator between her and Josh. Josh made the policies regarding Anna, and he, Sipho Gwala, had to implement them—a Herculean task for one such as himself. He was the administrator, not a prison guard and devil's advocate rolled into one. He tried to smile bravely. 'The professor thinks it necessary to stop you from . . . eh . . . becoming too involved and searching around unsupervised,' he explained, feeling way out of his depth.

'Yes, I understand. I enjoy his confidence. It's a heavy responsibility I'm unable to live up to.'

'Anna!' Sipho exclaimed, exasperated and wanting to be off. 'Either he locks up the offices or he locks you up. And he doesn't want to do that.'

'So much consideration is heart-warming. I'm touched.' Anna turned away from Sipho to go to her room, disgruntled.

'Don't be impossible, Anna. The professor loves you. We all do.' Sipho gesticulated helplessly to add emphasis to his words because Anna would never believe his incongruous claim.

She thought he resembled a stick figure like Sherlock Holmes's Dancing Men. A chuckle escaped her. If anyone in this place could cheer her, it was Sipho. Was there a lesson in this for her?

'Ah, Sipho,' she smiled. 'What do you know about love? Hm . . . ?' She raised an eyebrow, daring him to reply. 'What does Joshua know about love? One does not imprison the object of one's affection. That is only manipulation, selfishness, expediency, not love.'

A loud cough sounded from Josh's open office. Neither Sipho nor Anna realized he had overheard them.

'You're wrong about that love bit, Anna.' Josh's voice carried clearly in the corridor without him leaving his office. 'Why do people keep caged birds or fish in tanks? Do you think they hate them? Of course not! It is to have them near, the better to admire their beauty and enjoy their company.'

Anna's laughter broke off. 'Thanks, Josh,' she said bitterly. 'I've always wanted to be someone's household pet.'

'Good! I'm glad you're mine and not somebody else's.'

'Some pets bite and scratch,' she cautioned.

'Is that a threat or a promise?'

'Wait and see.'

The suggestive chit-chat brought a grin to her face, which Sipho saw with plain relief. He didn't have to feel so bad for taking Josh's side. He turned to join Fernando and Anna headed to her room with Josh's voice following her along the passage. The man always had to have the last word.

'I look forward to it, Anna.'

In her room, she toyed with the thought of carrying out the intended border patrol she had contemplated the night before. She could only walk along the back fence because Josh, like Sipho, had a commanding view of the front gate from his office window. She didn't want him to see her checking the boundaries of the hospital grounds for a means of escape.

A knock on her door startled her. *Fair bloody dinkum*, she thought. Was that Josh again, wanting to come in under some spurious pretext? He probably wanted to deliver another lecture about what she must or must not do, appending warnings of unpleasant repercussions if she failed to heed his explicit instructions.

She opened the door to see a tall, moderately attractive girl.

'*Sawubona!*' she greeted Anna. 'You're Mrs De Bruyn, aren't you? I'm Felicity. Can I talk to you for a minute?'

Anna asked the girl in, pointing to a kitchen chair.

'Sit down, Felicity. What can I do for you?'

'It's what I've been instructed to do for you that we need to talk about,' she laughed.

'Explain yourself!' Anna demanded with asperity, her eyes distrustful.

'Have I come at the wrong time?' Felicity looked doubtful, ready to withdraw.

'No, no. It's okay . . . I'm not myself around here. Don't be repulsed by my temper,' Anna comforted her visitor. 'Can I get you a drink of fruit juice or coffee?'

'No, please don't bother. Mum's already given me plenty.' Felicity giggled at Anna's bewildered expression. 'You know my mother, don't you? Margo, the cook!' she added when Anna shrugged with lack of comprehension. 'My cousin, Mark, is a volunteer here too, like me. You'll meet him soon.'

'Now I understand!' Anna smiled and relaxed. Felicity wasn't going to depreciate the modicum of freedom granted to her.

'You need extra provisions, I'm told.' Felicity launched into her cause. 'The professor said to buy whatever you want.'

'Well!' Anna marvelled. 'I didn't expect that! You're right, I'm short of many necessities. A change of underwear and a pair of sandals is just the beginning.'

'Let's make a list,' Felicity suggested.

Anna wrote everything down, including her cosmetics, toiletries, and hair care products.

'That's quite an order!' Felicity ran her eyes down the sheet. 'It'll be costly. I can't imagine the professor intends spending money on expensive make-up and skin lotions.' Felicity appeared critical and judicious.

'Heavens, Felicity!' Anna exclaimed. 'I don't expect Professor Mtolo to pay. I'll give you a cheque.'

'No, I'm not allowed to take it.'

'Why ever not?'

'The professor insisted that I ask Sipho for the money.'

'Right!' Anna realized Sipho wouldn't cash her cheque because the police could use banking records to trace her.

'Maybe I can come to some arrangement with Sipho. I'll talk to him when he returns from lunch. Does that suit you, Felicity?'

'Sure. It's just that I don't always have time to go shopping. As I said, I'm here as a volunteer at irregular intervals. You might have to wait for your delivery.'

'I'll survive. I'll give this list to Sipho and talk to him about the payment, and he can pass it to you. If I have to wait, so be it.'

'Okay! I'll be around till six this evening.' Felicity rose to go.

'Thanks for dropping by, Felicity.'

Alone again, Anna pondered briefly over the difference between Felicity and Margo. They were total opposites. Felicity was tall, slender, and eloquent; Margo short, ugly, and bellicose. The contrast couldn't be greater. Felicity had the potential to become a good friend with contacts to the outside world, exactly what she needed. Perhaps her cousin, Mark, could eventually be helpful too. At present, Felicity was taciturn, but time and pleasantness could change that. Anna determined to work on it.

* * *

Sipho and Fernando returned at 1430 hours, singing and making an undignified spectacle of themselves.

'Shame on you both,' she scolded, straight-faced. 'You've been drinking.'

'Yes indeed,' they repented as if it were true. 'We're full as boots.' They performed a convincing pantomime of the ataxic gait induced by excessive alcohol consumption.

'Take care, Fernando!' Sipho warned with a staged hiccup. 'The queen of the boardroom is not amused.'

'I'll leave you to deal with her.' Fernando grinned and slipped through the rear door.

'Chicken!' Sipho called back while unlocking his office. He turned to Anna. 'You've got something on your mind, I can see that. Come and sit down for a minute.'

He took off his jacket and hung it over the back of his chair. From its bulging pocket, he produced a plastic bag, which he handed to her with a bashful smile.

'Just a little token to express my appreciation for your help.'

Anna opened the bag, releasing a soft toy zebra. She burst into silver-bell laughter. The sound brought Josh from his office to find out what Sipho had said or done to draw her out of her shell. Be dashed if he could make her laugh like that. Since the day they had sat in the Pretoria wine bar together, all he had gotten were doleful looks.

'Isn't it cute!' Anna smiled, enchanted. She sat the zebra on her knee. 'It's adorable. Thank you, Sipho. I shall call him Xavier. Because he's a zebra, he's allowed to spell it *Zavier*, with a *Z*.'

'Sipho, where did you buy that?' Josh interrupted their tête-à-tête, feeling like the spare tyre in the boot of the car, disregarded and rarely needed.

'Old Bollard at the Zebra sells them as a fundraiser for the Royal Natal National Park.'

'Great idea.' Josh watched Anna's slender fingers run over Zavier's spiky mane. She appeared as content as a child. Could he emulate Sipho's tactics to please her? It wasn't possible. He could never have the light-hearted relationship with her that Sipho enjoyed. Sipho hadn't abducted her, and he didn't crave her body every minute of the day. In a singular flash of honesty, Josh admitted to himself he was smitten with Anna. The USB had become a terminal illness. He could no longer envisage his life without her having a part in it, be that experience pleasant or painful. He returned to his office sullen and circumspect.

'What's up with him?' Sipho puzzled. 'Reticent, isn't he?'

Anna shrugged. 'He's lost for words for a change.'

'Now'—Sipho returned to business—'I bet I know exactly what you're going to ask me.'

'Try guessing.'

'You hold a list of stuff you need to make you feel a little more at home here. Let's have it.'

She handed him her shopping list, and Sipho whistled as he estimated its price.

'I know it's not modest,' she pointed out. 'What if I give you a cheque? I won't date it yet. You can do that later at a time that's convenient when I'm home again.'

Sipho was not about to cast a shadow over her optimism by telling her that wouldn't be for a long while.

'No.' Sipho's face broke into his impish grin. 'Let Josh pay. It'll give me pleasure to take it out of his salary.'

'You wouldn't! You can't! I won't let you,' she protested, aghast.

'Just watch me.'

Anna witnessed the daylight robbery of Josh's allowance as Sipho first debited 'petty cash' and credited an account he called

Domestic Supplies and then purposefully debited 'Salary, J. Mtolo' and credited 'petty cash'.

'There we have it!' He sat back with another wicked-tokoloshe cackle of accomplishment.

* * *

Anna awoke with a sob and a heartbeat fit to burst her ribs. Her hand trembled as she reached for her watch. Five fifteen. Friday. What a nightmare she had had! Was the dream a warning? Was Hank well? She had dreamt of discussing business with him, but he had remained mute, not answering her questions. Instead he had hung in his chair with his upper body slumped lifeless over his desk. 'Horrible,' she wept, her whole body shaking. She couldn't sleep anymore. In an effort to steady her nerves, shake off the dream, and calm herself, she belted her bathrobe around her and opened the window. The morning felt fresh, much less languid than the previous ones. Maybe a walk around the garden would distract her and blow the cobwebs away. Perhaps she could sit somewhere and listen to the birds pipe the morning aboard. She was bound to find that soothing. Leaving her room, she slipped noiselessly along the passage, heading for the main entrance. Josh's door was open. Was he in there? If he noticed her, he'd call out. She wished to avoid the encounter. Thinking to make use of the early morning tranquillity, she retraced her path along the front fence. Maybe she'd find an opening she overlooked previously. No such luck. The wire mesh fence was overgrown with thorn bushes and designed to keep anyone lacking a chainsaw and bolt cutters within. She gave up.

Desire for coffee flooded her system. Seeking an instant fix, she went back in, steering for the kitchen, but changed her mind halfway. Opening the back door, she strolled towards the swimming pool, intending to sit on the lawn behind Fernando's shed for a while. Rounding the shed corner, she stopped suddenly. A male figure, perfect as a god descended from Mount Olympus, practiced traditional Zulu dance steps on the grass. His clothes lay in a heap nearby. Joshua! She ducked back behind the shed too late. He saw her, beckoning to her with an extended arm.

'It's a great morning,' he called. 'Come and dance with me.'

Averting her eyes from the intimate splendour of the scene, Anna made a halting move towards Josh's shorts on the grass. She picked them up, giggling. 'Put your clothes on,' she said, blushing.

'No, you take yours off.' He grinned back, thinking she was about to drop his boxers and flee—but no. Hesitantly, she unbelted her bathrobe. Little by little, it slipped from her shoulders with every step, as she tiptoed towards him.

Josh reacted instantly to Anna's sexual piquancy, the USB virus multiplying unchecked in his vital organs. He moved away from her to conquer his arousal, dancing by himself for some time. Anna watched, hypnotized by the unparalleled vision.

In control of himself again, Josh said, 'Come, I'll teach you the steps,' holding out his hand to her. She took it, following Josh's footwork as best she could, unable to say what embarrassed her more, the nakedness or her clumsiness at dancing the traditional routines.

'Do I have to leap into the air with legs outstretched like you?'

'No, ladies are not expected to perform so strenuously.'

Although inept, she began enjoying herself, and Josh showed no irritation when she stumbled. After twenty minutes, they were breathless with exertion and laughter. The birds had done their duty coaxing the sun to rise fully, and the dancers were hungry for breakfast.

Picking up his shorts, Josh stood on Anna's bathrobe, preventing her from covering herself. The more she tried pulling it from under him, the harder he stamped on it while simultaneously attempting to get his shorts on. Anna pushed him over while he stood on one foot, but in spite of his handicap, she failed to retrieve the garment. Their boisterous frolic ended when Josh finally had his boxers on. He grasped the bathrobe and draped it around her shoulders, holding her close. She tried to disengage, but he held her tighter. Smiling down at her, he brushed his lips over her hair. 'Mornings like these are gifts from heaven.'

Her hands, which she had pressed over her breasts in subconscious modesty, rose tentatively to caress his bare chest and came to rest on his shoulders. Invigorated, her eyes glowed as she returned his smile with a kiss. Their arms around each other's middle, they walked back inside. It was time for a shower, breakfast, and work. The seriousness of the day demanded Josh's energy.

'Come out to dance again tomorrow morning, Anna,' he invited.

She shook her tousled auburn hair. 'I'm not usually awake early, so I can't promise to be there.'

'Then what brought you out today?'

'I had a bad dream.'

Josh watched her green eyes dim again like lights lowered in a theatre at the start of a performance.

'What worries you? Tell me about it.' He tried holding her again, but this time, she avoided his touch.

'I dreamt Hank was dead . . . or he might have been just ill . . . it's hard to tell in a dream.'

'Would you like to write him another note?' Josh offered to ease her fear.

'Yes, please . . . and would you do me a favour?'

'If I can, certainly.'

'You are good friends with Zak Elbenstein. You were both at our anniversary ball. Hank's been Zak's patient for four years. Please ask him if Hank is all right.'

'Zak wouldn't tell me anything about Hank. Not without Hank's consent. You know . . . it's that doctor–patient confidentiality.'

Josh watched Anna pull at her hair in agitation. He held her hands to prevent the destruction. 'You never told me Hank was ill. How serious is it?'

'Bad enough for Zak to suggest retirement sooner rather than later.'

'Okay! I'll try probing for information, but I can't be certain of success. In the meantime, you can write another message, and I'll attempt getting it to him via the same route as the last one.'

Josh entered his quarters when Margo came with his breakfast. Anna held his arm, pleading.

'Please let me go home, Josh. My absence is going to kill Hank, I know it. I can feel it. Remember the offer I made? It still stands. It will always stand, and we'll be friends. Please, Josh.'

Josh wondered if her story about the dream was true or a devious plot she had masterminded to get away.

'No, Anna. I have told you already that even if you are helpful and cordial, your husband and his brothers will take a different view. You can't go back.'

If looks could kill! Her black dagger eyes charged him with murder. 'If Hank dies, you are responsible!' She flung the accusation at his feet like a challenge to a duel.

'Anna, take note of this one point,' he retorted, his tenderness for her blown away by her insinuation. 'In the bigger scheme of things, the fight for black economic empowerment in which you have become enmeshed, the life of one white businessman is of no importance whatsoever.'

She blinked a tear away. 'Aren't doctors supposed to help prolong life rather than hasten its premature expiry? Or am I misinformed?'

Josh slammed his door, leaving her standing in the passage. Where had the romantic morning of birdsong and dance gone? He showered and rubbed himself down vigorously, but his appetite for breakfast failed to return. He switched on the radio to listen to the news but flicked it off again.

Damn Anna, he thought, unnerved. *It's those eyes of hers*. The depth of them unsettled him. They stripped him of his defences, causing him to overreact to whatever provocations she pronounced. Accusing him of murdering Hank! If that wasn't pure melodrama. He would check the veracity of her claims. Woe to her if she told him lies. The little hellcat played cruel games, flirting with him in order to beg concessions. He should have raped her on the spot behind the toolshed. She didn't deserve consideration or sympathy.

He listened to his favourite CD before starting his morning's duties. It calmed him sufficiently to eat half of his breakfast and swallow the coffee. With a fuller stomach, different thoughts entered his mind. Her voice rang in his head. 'You make it sound as if I were the criminal. I resent that.'

'Yes, Anna,' he sighed with an air of capitulation. He had severed the orderly flow of her life. He couldn't expect any better. She'd never love him. What was in those opaque eyes? A melancholy disconsolateness, a pity for the human race, which was harder to take than if she spewed hatred like a fire dragon.

Chapter 9

The Plot Thickens

Josh put the phone down slowly, his mind dwelling on his conversation with C5. What C5 didn't know wasn't worth knowing, and what he couldn't find out didn't exist. He was a luminary among the hunter-gatherers of intelligence. C5 enjoyed delving into mysteries and was capable of blending chameleon-like with every setting. Josh had watched him in action, selling vegetables by the roadside, regaling shoppers with droll humour while watching and waiting patiently till his target appeared. At other times, C5 played the toff, mingling with the KwaZulu administration's top brass or, in a total about-turn became the thug who bullied his way among the instigators of political unrest and violence. C5 was clearly multiskilled. Dressing respectably and offering his best smile plus a gift of chocolates for Zak Elbenstein's receptionist, he extracted a great deal of data on Hank De Bruyn from her.

Anna hadn't exaggerated Hank's cardiac problems. Josh didn't know whether to laugh or kick himself when confronted with the evidence. He had given her hell last Friday. For what? It had ruined their pleasant morning behind the toolshed and made her cry. According to Sipho, she'd had 'a gut full of him' and didn't venture from her room till he departed for Soweto at one in the afternoon to spend the weekend with Cindy.

The envelope containing her letter to Hank lay before him. He should check its contents. She'd had three days to scheme and scribble messages, which would inevitably reflect the defiant mood in which he left her. Given half a chance, she would concoct daring plans to escape his clutches. He picked up the envelope, tapping its edge on the desktop, undecided. She hadn't betrayed him last time, but that day, he stood over her looking on till she became annoyed and changed to writing in German. And even then, she hadn't revealed anything.

'Go on, man! Open the damned thing!' Josh prodded himself. Why the hesitation? Was his conscience jabbing him with a strong dose of shame? Telling himself that he simply couldn't take the risk and that common sense alone demanded that he examine her possibly treacherous epistle, he slit the envelope with his penknife.

'Here we go again,' Josh sighed. 'Dearest Hank, blah, blah, blah, etc.,' he read, whispering the words as he went.

> I am in good shape and am generally treated with adequate courtesy.

Adequate courtesy? I'll be damned! Josh felt an uneasy qualm settling on him. 'What does she expect?' he muttered, confused.

> I try my utmost every day to persuade my new friends to let me come home.

Greatly relieved, Josh realized Anna was extraordinarily fair and cautious. He needn't have worried. In fact, he should have shown her the adequate courtesy of forwarding her message unopened. She made no mention of his name, KwaZulu Medical, or EEM. Her note was watertight. It was a letter of comfort to Hank, just as she had promised. Dash her! She had a way of humbling a man.

Josh stood up and pushed Anna's letter into the back pocket of his jeans, its delivery another job for C5. It was time he tackled the numerous tasks left undone during his absence, but a quick look around the children's ward came first. It was Tuesday, he noted absently as he glanced at the calendar on the ward sister's desk. Sandile Duma had another appointment in the late afternoon, and a new group of medical students would come for their induction as volunteers. The place was becoming a pseudo teaching hospital. He also intended discussing with Sipho Anna's suggestion to rent out underutilized space to other practitioners, such as a dentist, optometrist, physiotherapist, or whoever wished to hire consulting rooms. She said it made the clinic a one-stop medical shop, which would attract more people to the outpatient section while generating rental income. Any money-spinning idea was welcome.

He should try making peace with Anna sometime today. Surely she would have simmered down by now. He had regretted his callous remarks about Hank long before he left for Soweto and firmly intended apologizing but lost his nerve to knock on her door when he heard sobs from within. One part of him would have willingly sacrificed all other worldly pleasures to hold her in his arms. His pragmatic side, which usually gained the right of way, expected, however, that she would repeat her request to return home. That wasn't on. Torn asunder, he walked away from her door while his soul reached out to the weeping, which filled him with clammy unrest.

He decided there and then that the long weekends in Soweto must stop. It was inconvenient for Peter and Tom to juggle their time trying to cover his absence. Josh saw that rostering staff around Anna was unworkable. Sipho always had weekends off. He needed the time to gather his strength. Volunteers manned the front desk on Saturdays, and a local woman was paid to come in on Sunday afternoons. These helpers did not know Anna. She could easily hoodwink them into calling her a taxi to freedom. Fernando couldn't be everywhere at once, needing breaks like everyone else. Felicity, who cooked on Sundays, was too gullible to be entrusted with keeping Anna confined. As it happened, Sipho felt less well this weekend than he normally did. He elicited Anna's sympathy, keeping her occupied seeing to his comfort. It enabled Fernando to enjoy a respite. Josh concluded that security was far too haphazard on weekends. It was only a matter of time before Anna took advantage of the slack and absconded. And what would he do without her?

The thought struck him with unexpected force. No more Soweto weekends for him. He needed to be with Anna.

Breaking the engagement with Cindy would mean hurting her and offering more apologies. His stomach turned. What was wrong with him? Was there ever a man who had so much need to assuage offended women? What could compensate Cindy for the wasted years during which she had hoped to be his wife? Not his miserable utterances of propitiation, that was certain. Cindy would be crushed and angry. Not for long, though. Solomon conveniently waited in the wings.

'Doctor Josh! Look!' He was reminded of his tasks when the ward burst into life at his approach. The kids had missed him, his jokes, stories, and tricks that brought smiles to their sombre faces. They sat up in their beds, waving toy zebras in the air while calling greetings.

'Well, what have we here?' Josh looked at each child in turn. 'You guys been out poaching wildlife, have you?' Josh saw with surprise that the zebras were the same breed of cuddly creature that Sipho had given Anna.

'Mine is called Zebbie,' a girl named Nozipho announced.

'My word, he's a fine fellow,' Josh encouraged.

'No, she's a girl. She's Zavier's girlfriend,' Nozipho explained.

Josh stood corrected. Zavier? Wasn't that what Anna called hers? Obviously she was behind this and, together with Sipho, had some explaining to do.

Nozipho had a basket of quality fresh fruit beside her bed. Josh wondered how she had come by that. He found his answer immediately when she pointed to it and offered him a plum.

'That's for being a nice doctor.' She smiled sweetly.

'Thanks, Nozipho. Did your cousins bring you fruit?' Josh asked, although he doubted whether anyone in her family had the means to buy a gift hamper of delicious treats.

'No, I won it,' Nozipho said with pride.

'Won it?' Josh's mystified look made her laugh.

'There must be some mistake. It looks to me as if Father Christmas has come in here about four months too early.'

The kids grinned at this assumption, and Nozipho explained what happened. 'We had a competition to see who could think up the most names beginning with *Z* for the zebras . . . or any name with a *Z* in it, like mine. The prize was a basket of fruit, and I won it.'

'Aren't you lucky, Nozipho? Tell me, who organized the contest?'

'Nkosazana Anna.' Nozipho looked as if she had let slip the biggest secret of her eight-year-old life. The children appeared as happy as could be expected. Josh left the ward, satisfied.

The first of the new medical students arrived, and Josh introduced him to Peter and Tom. That done, he returned to his office to reread the notes he had taken on Sandile at the last appointment. Passing Sipho's door, he called in.

'Sipho, what's with the herd of zebras in the kids' ward?'

'Don't blame me,' Sipho replied defensively. 'They are the result of Anna's foray into the children's wing on the weekend.'

Josh came into Sipho's office, seating himself on the spare chair. 'Mind filling me in on the details?'

'Very long story.' Sipho turned away as if he was too busy for extensive explanations.

'I'm listening.'

'You upset Anna dreadfully,' he reminded Josh.

'Yeah, I guess I did.'

'She was still pretty cut up Saturday morning. Tom and Peter found her sitting by the pool when they brought the kids out. She had Zavier with her. Heaven knows why a grown woman should take so dearly to a toy animal. I suppose she loves it because she's lonely.'

What was Sipho implying? He wasn't backing out, taking Anna's side, was he? Josh looked at him searchingly.

'Little Nozipho spotted Zavier, and Anna let the kids play with him.' Sipho absently flipped pages in his ledgers while speaking. He picked up a pen, switched on his calculator, and turned to Josh.

'Of course Tom had never met Anna, so Peter introduced them, and they had a chat. Tom told her much of the children's family backgrounds. Rather too much, I'd say . . . about Nozipho in particular because her parents and uncle and aunt all died of AIDS. She's lucky not to be HIV-positive herself. Now the poor girl relies on her cousins' charity. Not that they have much to give. You can imagine the effect such a story has on an already-depressed woman.' Sipho's voice bore disapproval.

Josh frowned. Why did he get the impression Sipho held him accountable?

'Anyway,' Sipho went on, 'Anna looked after me all weekend with more charm and gentleness than Fernando could muster in a hundred years.' A slight grin played around his face. 'I dare say I prefer her ministration.

'She expressed a desire to cheer the kids, badgering me till she wore me down, and I agreed for the sake of peace to let Fernando go and buy a zebra for each child. Mind you, she'd already decided to break the kids' routine by holding the naming competition. "I want to make their day," she said. So a prize had to be bought for the winner. Margo's maize cakes were too mundane.'

Josh made a sound, which was part laughter, part sigh. 'Sipho, that woman is becoming too expensive to have around. Felicity still has her shopping list, and I've noticed you reduced my account to cover that. Now all these damned zebras!' This time Josh did laugh out loud because there was no way he'd deprive the children of their amusement.

'Don't ever buy Anna another present like that,' he chuckled. 'The flow-on effect is too costly.'

'Don't get your boxers in a knot, man. I paid for the zebras and the fruit basket.'

'Sipho, I wasn't criticizing you.'

'I know, it's okay.' Sipho began tapping on his calculator. 'An Irishman I met in London said to me one day, "You can't take anything with you, my friend. There are no pockets in a shroud." What do I want money for, Josh? Tell me that.'

Josh felt he'd been read a lesson, the gospel according to Sipho. He stood up and said with a smile, 'The kids are happy. That's the main thing. Thanks, Sipho.'

He returned to his office, chastened. Flinging himself into his chair, he opened Sandile's file. The little chap had gone back to school with what for Sandile represented a minimum of fuss. He had joined the ranks of the outpatients, visiting regularly for progress assessments. Yet somehow Josh felt that wasn't good enough. It seemed like a job half finished. He should do more for the boy. Sandile's PTSD was controlled with the rewind method and mild medication. While that was great, Josh thought it left the boy in an emotional no-man's land. It took care of Sandile's immediate needs but may leave a vacuum in the long term. What came after post-traumatic stress disorder? There had to be post-traumatic stress growth, a process of learning from the bad experience once a patient had left it behind him, a means of gaining strength through adversity. This approach was missing from normal trauma debriefing and counselling.

He had told Sandile to look upon the trauma as a fierce lion, which he must kill or be killed by. Sandile handled the lion well so far. It adhered to his command. Once he killed it, what would he do with its body? Skin it? Turn it into a rug or wall hanging? Sandile should be steered towards making use of his traumatic experience in a positive way. He harboured guilt about his failure to help his friend who died later in hospital. That destroyed much of his self-worth. He had to find it again. He must be helped to see his own strength. Once he recognized it, he could be encouraged to share it with others. Getting him to relate successfully to other people again was the main game.

A brisk knock on the door interrupted Josh's thoughts. Fernando reported difficulties in the psychiatric ward. Two patients currently occupied the ward, both trying to overcome drug dependency. Josh tut-tutted as he made his way there. The ward was meant for afflicted kids. He didn't want adults there.

He had barely finished dealing with that when one of the patients in the children's ward took a turn for the worse. The medication wasn't working. A trip to the dispensary produced a suitable alternative, which would have to suffice till the appropriate product he had ordered arrived. Josh was about to leave the ward when Nozipho called out, 'Doctor Josh, is Nkosazana Anna coming to talk to us today?' It seemed the kids had taken to her. There was probably no harm in her entering the ward from time to time.

'If you guys take your medicines without protest,' Josh replied, 'I'll tell her to read you a bedtime story tonight.' Yes, Anna could spread motherly warmth here. Many of the young patients missed their homes, homes destroyed by internecine strife to which they could never return. Their parents were sometimes killed in the fray.

Walking back to his office, Josh pondered the irony. Cindy was the schoolteacher. She should be here, reading to the kids and keeping their minds occupied. Instead, he had press-ganged a hard-core businesswoman into staying who wouldn't hesitate to shower the kids with affection. Was that the second gospel reading for the day? Was he really so ignorant about human nature?

* * *

The rest of Tuesday flew past Josh at supersonic speed. He couldn't recall having had lunch. Judging by how hungry he was, he probably hadn't. Margo was dishing out dinner for the kids, and he could no longer postpone approaching Anna because the youngsters looked forward to their story. Why had he made such rash promises? What if she didn't want to read? Would she even talk to him? Steeling himself for a hostile reception, he knocked on her door.

'Anna, may I come in?'

'Yes.'

He opened the door and was riveted by her reflection in the wardrobe mirror. The nightgown he had given her on her first evening at KwaZulu Medical fitted her to perfection. She swished around at his approach.

'You're back again.' She smiled. 'The kids really missed you, you know. Sipho and I tried to distract them but we're only second best.'

'You look ravishing.' Josh took three strides towards her, and she was in his arms. Laughing, she tried to disentangle herself from his grasp, but he saw her eyes flash with underlying lust. He wouldn't release her.

'Not cross with me anymore?' he asked, his voice thick with USB.

'Not right now,' she grinned. Josh thought he heard a tone of uncertainty but chose to ignore it. Kissing her was better than talking while she yielded. He felt a tremor of response run through her body. *Later*, he thought. It would have to be later or the kids might not get to hear their story today. Reluctantly he relaxed his grip, and she stepped back.

He noticed Zavier standing on the bedside table. His head was bowed towards the dish that once held the long-since-discarded violets, as if facing a watering hole. He looked funny with his head in the empty dish, seemingly drinking. It made him chuckle in that deep, seductive way of his.

'You're not second best around here, Anna. You need to remember that.' He turned towards her. 'You're quite a hit with the kids yourself. They want you to read them a bedtime story. Would you do it for them?'

'Of course. Do we have any books?'

'Not educational children's books, if that is what you mean. It's only home-made material of the sort their own parents would tell them. Will you try?'

'Yes, I'll just get changed.'

'Take your time. The kids are still eating. I need to feed myself too. I can't remember if I had lunch. I suppose Margo will show up with something for both of us soon enough. Want to come and eat with me?'

'Okay!'

Josh left, and she changed back into her jeans and cotton top. Trust him to come in just when she tried on the nightie. She had to admit she liked her flattering mirror image.

It wasn't hard to hear Margo coming with the evening meal. Today she wore ankle bracelets with bells, which heralded her progress along the passage like a herd of goats being driven home in the evening. Josh made a big scene when she arrived carrying his tray.

'Margo, my god!' He opened his door wide. 'What have you got for me? I've missed your cooking like you would not believe.' She glowed with satisfaction.

'It's good to have you back, Professor.'

In her room, Anna whispered, 'Did you get that, Zavier? That's the first civil comment I've heard from the old bag since I've been here.' She flicked his mane. 'She should keep her voice down, though, so Sipho can get some sleep. The walls in this place are so thin you can hear a flea sneeze.'

Anna's private exchange with Zavier was broken when her door flung open.

'Your stuff's in the professor's room. He wants you now.' The tinkling bells receded.

Expecting that the 'stuff' Margo referred to was her dinner, Anna waved 'bye bye' to Zavier and removed herself to Josh's quarters. He had made inroads into his plate already.

'Sorry I started without you. I'm too damned hungry.'

'No worries. What's on the menu? Not beans and rice again?'

'No, we're lucky. It's chicken casserole, corn, and pumpkin. Sit down. Eat before it gets cold.'

They dined quietly, only glancing at each other occasionally lest one careless word fomented renewed resentment. When Josh demolished the last scrap on his plate, he rose and extracted a hand full of typewritten sheets from his bottom desk drawer.

'Is that the story for the kiddies?' Anna reached for the manuscripts. She read the title. 'Shaka and the Mamba Warriors! Okay, let's go and see if we can capture their attention.'

'I thought we might introduce life and drama to the story if you are the narrator and I'll read the parts King Shaka is saying. What do you think?'

'Sounds good to me.' Josh took Anna's hand as they walked to the children's wing.

'When we finish, we can have coffee together,' he suggested with unusual reserve.

The kids called enthusiastic greetings when Josh and Anna came in. 'Story time, story time!' they chanted. Josh borrowed the ward sister's chair for Anna, placing it in the middle of the room. The fitter patients sat on the floor in a semicircle.

'Just a minute,' Josh said to Anna before stepping to the bed of the three-year-old whose medicine he had changed earlier in the day. The fragile girl managed a smile when Josh lifted her up and brought her to a closer bed to let her join in the fun.

Anna sat down and the kids hushed with expectation. Josh stood behind her, looking over her shoulder.

'This is the story of Shaka and the Mamba Warriors,' he announced before Anna began.

> They arrived long before sunrise and assembled noiselessly on the crest of the hill. There they crouched, still as stones, hidden by tall grass, waiting for the first signs of life in the village of Izinkomo below.

They had come from far away, running in single file throughout the night. Four hundred men formed a long snake, which slithered over the ground they crossed. That's how they got their name. The Mamba Warriors. Their reputation was fierce, their blood cold like that of the reptile embossed on their shields.

The Mamba Warriors planned to attack Izinkomo because the fattest, healthiest cattle grazed there. The Mambas intended to occupy the village and confiscate the cattle. They thought the success of their evil venture was assured because their scouts had reported that the villagers who tended the animals appeared harmless and peaceful.

Their Induna felt certain that bringing so many soldiers was overkill for the type of engagement they faced. Quietly he detached a group of fifty men, giving them the order to strike as soon as the first soul stirred in Izinkomo.

What the Mambas didn't know was that the choice Nguni cattle did not belong to the villagers. The herd of close to a hundred beasts was the property of the king. The penalty for harming them was death. The Mambas would face horrific retribution for their greed . . .

The children listened wide-eyed, their imagination fired by a tale of do-or-die as the Izinkomo peasants, who were in reality well-trained and armed King's Guards, overran the Mambas and sent them limping home without as much as one hair from a cow's tail.

The story carried two mottoes: 'Crime doesn't pay' and 'Brains win over brawn.' Although the King's impi were outnumbered, given the reinforcements streaming down from the hill, the Guards' clever disguise as peasants gave them the advantage of surprise when attacked.

The audience clapped and burst into song at the end of the presentation.

'Okay, maidens and warriors. Into bed, the lot of you! Quickly!' Josh ordered. The children sought their beds reluctantly, the boys making spear-throwing motions as they went.

'Can't we hear another story please, Doctor Josh?' they begged.

'Maybe tomorrow,' Josh replied kindly. 'You guys still have much recuperating to do.'

Anna picked up the lethargic three-year-old who was almost asleep, gently putting her back into her own bed. Josh watched. Even Sipho wouldn't have guessed what lay behind the expression on his face as he returned the ward sister's chair to her desk.

'Damn.' Josh muttered a profanity in Zulu under his breath when they left the ward. 'I just remembered I still have course material to write for the students. There goes our coffee time.'

'I offered to help last time you mentioned it, Josh.'

'Yeah, I'll hire a PC for you. We can install it in your room.'

'You don't have to spend money on renting one. Cindy's got plenty. A whole classroom full.'

'And they all belong to you, so I'll have to decline the offer.' Josh grinned sheepishly.

'Go and start working. I'll make your coffee provided Margo lets me near the sink.'

'Yeah, thanks. I'm in my room, not my office. I prefer to keep the Uni stuff separate from the hospital paperwork.'

Anna made coffee and plundered Margo's maize cakes, which she had learnt to judge with qualified approval. She set everything down on Josh's coffee table, preparing to take her share and depart.

'Don't run away.' Josh dropped his papers and left his desk.

'No, I mustn't deflect you from your task.'

'I haven't started yet. It's not going to take long to drink coffee.'

'All right, ten minutes.'

They sat on the couch. Josh, peckish again, took to reducing the maize cakes.

'I loved the Mamba fable,' Anna said, sipping coffee. 'Where does it come from? Is it folklore?'

'No, it's pure fiction. The plots are just figments of my imagination. I jot them down to distract the kids when they feel low.'

'You mean you wrote it?' Anna asked, surprised.

'Yeah.'

'You're a genius, Josh. Do you have more of these imaginary legends stashed away?'

Josh smiled at Anna's eagerness. 'See that deep drawer in the bottom of the desk? It's full of 'em.'

'You must have them published. Royalties are another earnings potential for you.' Anna crossed to the desk, pulling open the drawer Josh indicated. 'Let me read them.'

All thought of coffee vanished as she sat balancing an approximately twenty-centimetre-high stack of papers on her knee. And that was by no means all. She hadn't emptied the drawer. Josh revealed himself as a prolific author of children's short stories. While she read, laughing occasionally at the witty humour Josh brought to his writing, he began work on his course material. Absorbed, neither realized how late the hour was. When Josh yawned and stretched, Anna rose stiffly, gathering the remaining unread manuscripts to take to her room.

'I know a publisher for this,' she told Josh. 'Shuter and Shooter's Pietermaritzburg office would be very interested. I know the people there. Adriaan can hammer out a favourable contract for you.'

'Not so fast, Anna.' Josh gave her a cautionary smile. Full of exuberance, she had forgotten herself. She was a prisoner, not a free woman. She could no longer negotiate business in her accustomed manner.

'Well, Sipho will need to contact them. I'll keep out of it. It's just that I know them, you see. And they'll have to . . .' Anna's voice trailed off as she realized she could not use her influence. She shrugged with exasperated resignation. 'Joshua, can't you see? I can do so much more for you if you just let me go. You're clipping my business wings keeping me here, and it's to your detriment. Not to mention that every extra day you incarcerate me, your lawyers will find it harder to defend you when the police eventually get wind of your activities.' Inhaling deeply and throwing her arms in the air, Anna chided, 'You're your own worst enemy, Joshua Mtolo. And', she added as an afterthought, 'what about Inkatha? How can I help raise money for the party if I'm stuck in here?'

Disappointed and unable to understand his intransigence, she said good night and left without the manuscripts. What was the use? Josh wouldn't listen to her.

'Unpredictable female,' he grunted. Why was she leaving him? Had he said something wrong? As if he didn't know the problem. Before long he would have to come to a decisive conclusion about Anna. Should he send a ransom note to Hank? Should he take up her offer? These two options necessitated parting with her. His desire for her precluded that possibility. Could he forgo the money and keep Anna? Was there a path towards having both the money and the woman? It was worth developing that idea further. Anna had a disparaging way of pointing out that the current state of affairs would come to a bitter end, suggesting police involvement. Who would inform the police if not she herself or her six guardian angels? That brought him back to square one. He couldn't trust her. As yet she had done nothing to merit his misgivings, but her abduction created a labyrinth of dangerous emotions he found increasingly difficult to navigate.

* * *

'Dammit, Broadbent. Why can't you find Anna?' Hank's style of dealing with the police became progressively demanding and assertive. 'She's alive, for Christ's sake!' he shouted into the phone. 'If her captors deliver her letters to me, why the hell can't you track her down?'

Hank, roused by Anna's latest note to him, felt it should be comparatively easy to follow the message back to its source.

'I notice, Mr De Bruyn, you made no attempt to freeze her bank accounts as I warned you to do.' Broadbent countered the question he least wished to hear. 'We will step in and do it if you won't.'

'I told you why I didn't do it, and don't interfere,' Hank responded angrily. 'Anna is somewhere, possibly not very far away. Who knows what difficulties she faces? She may need money to bribe her way out of imprisonment or aid her escape in some way. I refuse to cut that avenue of hope off for her.'

'Her captors will run up enormous withdrawals and purchases on her credit cards. You realize that, don't you?' Broadbent pointed out the obvious with veiled schadenfreude.

'That's a risk I take happily, Captain. In any case, it hasn't happened yet. I almost wish it did. It would give us a clue where to look for her, but the bastards appear to be too smart for that. They haven't even sent a ransom demand. There is something strangely benign about this whole thing. It's somehow weird.' Hank, plagued with worry and wretchedness, comforted himself, saying, 'Anna is a good negotiator. She would try reaching an agreement with the other party, I'm sure.'

'Mr De Bruyn, don't be tricked into illusions. Your wife is in danger, perhaps not so much physically but certainly mentally. Do not think for one minute that what she writes to you are her own words.'

'I believe they are.' Hank was adamant. 'I know Anna too well.'

How can I counter so much blind faith? Broadbent thought, scratching his head.

He said, 'Let's recap on what we do know. Point one—your wife is alive. That's almost certain. She's also, if her claims are correct, well treated. Point two—the criminals are not holding her for immediate financial gain. Point three—they appear prepared to imprison her indefinitely. Four—her diamonds have not appeared on the market. That rules out robbery, more or less. Five—like you say, she may be nearby. The kidnappers have not taken her out of the country. We monitored the airports, conducted vehicle checks at the borders, and inspected cargo vessels in the ports. Six—Malcolm Price is clean.'

'I could have sworn he had a hand in it,' Hank ruminated, suspecting chicanery on Gold Corp's part.

'So we'll have to look further. If this is not a domestic matter like Mrs De Bruyn leaving with another man and money is not the motive, then what? Revenge? Axes to grind? I believe two of your clients lost money recently on deals you brokered. Are they upset enough to go to extremes?'

'No way!' Hank stated forcefully. 'Our clients never suffer loss. We don't allow it. We restructure their investment portfolios in such a way as to avoid that. Our clients receive due attention at all times.'

'Can you think of any other way your wife may have made enemies?'

'No, she hasn't. And it's high time the public was involved. Offer a reward for information. Publish a hotline in the newspaper, that kind of thing. You've done it to solve other crimes. Why won't you help Anna?'

'It's not a matter of not wanting to help,' Broadbent replied, insulted, but he continued his explanations patiently. 'We must work in a manner that will not endanger your wife further. We don't know who her captors are. They may be unstable and given to panic. Or they may be ruthless and fight like cornered rats if they perceive us on their tails. That would not bode well for your wife's safety.'

To Hank it sounded like police inertia. He threw the phone down, clicking off in Broadbent's ear and thinking hard. EEM! They had to be the culprits if Price wasn't involved. What was it Anna had said about the Economic Equity Movement? It came back to him slowly. She suspected they were a new black economic empowerment pressure group. She called them 'intellectuals, not common street criminals'. That could explain the deceptive amiability of the crime— if a crime could ever be described in those terms. It was almost as if Anna knew her captors, Hank thought. Police statistics indicated that this was often the case. And if Anna was right and the EEM guys were black, what black people did she know? He ran his hand over his eyes to aid the process of elimination. Their domestic staff? That was laughable. Nkosinathi Zuma and Cindy Khumalo? Equally ridiculous. Solomon Mataka? He lacked the imagination. Who could have . . . ? KwaZulu Medical? Joshua Mtolo? Now here's a likely candidate. Why hadn't he thought of that daredevil Mtolo earlier? It might pay to have someone keep an eye on his Vryheid premises.

Unlike Broadbent, Hank was certain Anna's letter was not dictated to her. Her words flowed on the paper as if she spoke to him directly. They were neither stilted nor artificial. Yet her 'new friends' had evidently intimidated her sufficiently not to drop hints as to their names or location. But what the hell did they want? What was their motive? Frustrated and antagonistic, Hank sighed. The deep breath left him hunched over his desk with tears of indignation stinging his eyes. Whoever the villains were, he'd get even with them. Why hadn't the bastards asked for money? Did they want Anna for her own sake? Mtolo probably did. Why was that incompetent Broadbent continually implying Anna had gone with another man? Not Anna. She'd never . . . It was just Broadbent's way of covering his ineptitude.

Yet what if Broadbent was right? Hank's mind spun like a turbo prop at the idea. Once awakened, that awful, gut-churning notion would not die. The instant attraction between Anna and Mtolo at the shareholders' meeting was too obvious to ignore. Would Anna really leave with that guy? Without a word to anyone? It wasn't her style. If she was with Mtolo, would she ever come back?

'Oh, Christ!' Hank wrung his hands in misery, muttering. What would she come home to? A man advised by his doctor to retire. A man unable to compensate her for the relentless work she invested in the family business. She was not on the De Bruyn payroll. She had never received the minutest remuneration for all her years of work. Like many of his friends' wives, she was allocated a budget to cover the household's running costs and nothing more. Was that fair when he more or less relied on her to carry the place?

He should have taken more care of her. How long was it since they had an enjoyable evening together, free from the intrusions of work? God, she was his wife, not an employee. Why did he expect her to sacrifice so many of her pleasures?

She hadn't seen her parents in ages. She'd had no opportunity to go sailing for over a year. The delightful chamber music concerts she had once organized regularly became rare. The piano had been neglected. Her cat had taken to sleeping on it. When was the last time he heard her sing?

The pressure of work had broken her, and he should have been alert for the warning signs. Her running away, if that was what she had in fact done, was a form of subconscious protest. If only she had expressed her feelings of exhaustion rather than trying ever harder to stay on top of the demands, but she loved the work, Hank tried reasoning. The exciting world of high finance gave her a buzz, and she always kept her eye on the firm's welfare. It wouldn't have occurred to her to seek personal gain from it. He was in the fortunate position to know Anna had not married him for money. She had enough of her own.

He struck his desk with his fist. Why had he been so blasé about her feelings? His treatment of her was the same as his father's patriarchal attitude towards his mother. She was part and parcel of their lives. Her individuality was unimportant. If the family was happy, she as part thereof must feel contented too. Well, time had moved on, and father's methods were best buried with his generation. He came to recognise his wife as an independent modern woman with new-generation ideas. Was it too late to make changes? Pulling a notepad towards him, he began drawing up a list of necessary improvements.

Top priority went to his health. For some time, he had harboured doubts about Zak's treatment. Suggesting retirement was the limit. Convinced Zak's medications clashed, producing too many side effects, he threw them in the rubbish and immediately made an appointment with a naturopath.

Zak advised exercise. That was an idea worth following up. His staff, he knew very well, worked their butts off and needed stimulus other than statistics and money talk. He couldn't have them burning out as well. If he hired a spare room in the basement, had it fitted out as a gym which he and his employees could use, it would be a good long-term investment. He needed a personal trainer. The same man could coach the others as well if they wished to participate in regular exercise.

Staffing levels were next on the to-do list. If, as had recently been revealed, he was to take over from Michael Tripp as stock exchange council president, it would place extra pressure on Maurice. Someone has to be trained to help him. Vince Lewis hadn't been well and should only work part-time. Another person was required to step in and assist. What if Anna wasn't coming back? 'Oh hell, I'm doing it again,' he chastised himself fiercely. 'I'm automatically counting Anna as staff. It has to stop.' His hands trembled as he wrote. He turned the page.

The new leaf only bore two words in large capital letters: FIND ANNA! And when he did, they would start doing things together that would make her happy.

For that to happen, he required more information. Talking to William Rosenberg, inviting him to dinner, and sounding him out thoroughly about the EEM may prove helpful. Comparing William's EEM experiences with his own information on KwaZulu Medical might throw light on the puzzles. What if the two groups were one and the same? Adriaan should come too. He could ask straight questions and analyse the answers. If Broadbent wouldn't investigate Anna's disappearance properly, the De Bruyns would.

* * *

Sipho's muscles resisted lifting him from his chair for fear of an accident. His heart beat wildly, and black spots danced before his eyes momentarily. Intuition warned him before he placed his finger on the green button to open the electronic gate. He knew he shouldn't, but how could he not? The place was a hospital after all, and any person seeking help had to be admitted even if he arrived in a gleaming, silver Jaguar, parked presumptuously in the doctors' area, and came pushing his generous, solid frame through the glass double door. With an effort, Sipho pulled himself together.

'Yes, sir, can I help you?' He shuffled to the enquiries window, his brain switching to damage control. Where was Josh? Fernando? Anna? God! Sipho panicked. Anna, especially, had to be kept the hell out of sight.

'Yes,' the big man's deep voice rumbled. 'I'm looking for Doctor Naidoo. Where can I find her?'

Sipho had the presence of mind to display a caring smile, but the visitor saw the wariness in his eyes.

'I will direct you, sir.' He walked back to his desk, picking up the internal phone. 'I'll let her know you're coming if you would give me your name, sir.'

The big man's face became pale, his expression dazed, as if thinking back, attempting to relive formless, undefined recollections, like trying to remember an indistinct dream. If Sipho hadn't recognized him right away, he would have thought the caller suffered amnesia, unable to remember who he was. Slowly, glancing past Sipho, his eyes vainly searching for familiar focal points, the man replied, 'William Rosenberg's the name.'

That voice! William thought, shocked. I remember that skinny man's voice. He half expected Sipho to say, 'Thanks for coming, Mr Rosenberg.' Now that he could see Sipho properly, he thought the guy looked and sounded like death warmed up. The disinfectant smell too jolted his memory back to the uncomfortable blindfold and the piercing light on his face which had brought beads of perspiration to his brow. He had to be in the same place, he figured, almost convinced. While Sipho spoke to Indira, William paced the foyer, counting the steps from the door to the beginning of the linoleum-covered corridor. The glass door? Did it slide open, or did someone hold it open when he was pushed through blindfolded so many months ago? He couldn't recall hearing the door slide like automatic doors do, so it must have been held open by one of the men guiding him. He closed his eyes and tried to remember in which direction he had been taken. Unerringly he headed to the left of Sipho's office, past the kitchen and pantry.

Alarmed, Sipho came out and stalled William's advance towards the wine cellar. 'You are going in the wrong direction, Mr Rosenberg. Come with me. I will show you to Doctor Naidoo's office.' Sipho removed William as quickly as he could before Anna should happen to make another of her frequent pilgrimages to the Holy Grail of coffee and biscuits. While she was occupied typing Josh's teaching modules, she was out of harm's way. 'Let busy women well alone' was Sipho's philosophy.

'Mr Rosenberg, if you follow these arrows, you will reach the outpatient section, and Doctor Naidoo's rooms are just beyond that.' Sipho pointed to markings on the narrow walkway outside, which nobody could miss. 'You may wish to take your car to the other parking area further on, as that is much closer to where you need to be.'

Sipho thought he had diplomatically told William to get his car away from the doctors' parking lot and take it to that designated for patients and visitors. William got the hint but replied unfazed, 'Oh yeah, I wasn't thinking. I just saw Indira's car there and parked beside her automatically.'

'We haven't seen you here as a patient, Mr Rosenberg, so I take it Doctor Naidoo is a friend?' Sipho asked, making a guess at the most probable nature of their relationship.

Inquisitive little bone sack, William thought. He didn't bother answering the question. He increased his pace, impatient to see Indira. Sipho trotted behind him, falling back.

'That's right,' he puffed. 'Just keep following the arrows. You can't miss. Ask for Doctor Naidoo at the desk.'

'Thanks,' William called over his shoulder. Sipho stood watching till William disappeared from sight. He had to warn everyone to stay out of reach till the coast was clear again.

William found Indira already waiting for him. 'William,' she smiled cheerfully. 'So glad you could come. You arrived at an opportune moment too when I have a little spare time. Come into my office. Let's have coffee.'

She sat him beside her desk, fetched the drinks, and made a quick call asking reception to hold all messages for her.

William looked around Indira's office while she sorted paperwork, gathered preprinted forms, and put them under a paperweight of a sort he had never seen before. He did not find the gadget particularly tasteful or ornamental. 'What is that?' he asked, pointing to a carved wooden head with lines drawn on it in blue and red like a road map.

Indira followed William's pointing finger. 'Oh, my paperweight? It's a phrenology bust.'

'Speak English, Indira.'

She couldn't help but chuckle. William was so out of his league here. She explained, 'I see it as the medical equivalent of a globe in Christopher Columbus's era. You know, the one that shows Australia as the great unknown continent in the south merely because a land mass had to be there to balance the world. This little guy is similar in a way. You could call it an early chart of how eighteenth-century medics thought the human brain was divided.

'Crikey!' William had a closer look. Despite himself, he became interested. 'And who devised this map of the brain?'

'A Viennese doctor called Franz Gall, back in 1758. I suppose you want to know how he did it?'

'Yes, I'm kind of curious.' A shadow fell over William's face as he wondered how much of Indira's new interest in neuroscience was directly attributable to Joshua Mtolo's influence.

Indira saw no dubiety in his eyes. She prattled on, 'Gall thought the key to finding out which sections of the brain were responsible for which activities lay in the bumps on the surface of a person's skull.'

William began to laugh, shaking his head at such primitive assessments.

'Gall made a skull cap,' Indira went on. 'In it were movable pins which the bumps on the person's skull displaced. When the pins pushed upwards through the paper around the cap, Gall thought he saw a reading of the person's character.' William was still laughing, and Indira became mildly annoyed.

'Of course, today we know the brain does not work in clear-cut compartments, but all areas interact to produce a specific result, be that movement, speech, or whatever.' That was as far she was prepared to speak in lay terms. When William kept laughing, she said, irritated, 'Stop it.'

Wiping the grin off his face, William thought he might as well get the grisly part of the visit behind him and let Indira show him her operating room. With an enthusiasm he didn't feel, he said tactfully,

'I'm interested to see your operating theatre. Do you have your new equipment already?'

* * *

After William left Indira, promising faithfully to call at her house and take her to dinner, she wondered why he had been in such haste to be off.

'I mustn't monopolize your time,' he said. 'Your patients need you as much as I do.' This was said with a meaningful grin.

What was driving him? Indira thought she had explained the workings of the OR in sufficient detail and layman's language, but William wasn't really focusing on what she showed him. It wasn't lack of understanding on his part. He asked a number of intelligent questions. Still, his attention was flighty. Something bothered him. Maybe he would tell her over dinner.

Josh and Sipho acted out of character as well when she finished work and bid them goodnight. They talked briskly in a whisper. At her approach, their conversation ceased altogether. Instead of their usual question, 'Have you had a good day?' they stole mortified glances at her like teenage boys caught with pornographic videos. What was wrong with everyone today?

* * *

'Hank!' Anna screamed out of control as the bomb went off, reducing the JSE building to rubble. She awoke to Margo's kicking her door open and setting her breakfast down with predictable ill humour. A further morning at KwaZulu Medical progressed in the customary way. *No, not really the same*, Anna thought. Something was different. The place was eerily quiet. Apart from Margo entering with her usual bull-in-a-china-shop crash, causing her to dream of bomb blasts, there were no other sounds. Margo hadn't even indulged in her verbal morning fencing exercise with Sipho. No swords clashed today. How could she neglect a practice which was second nature to her?

Anna reached for her watch although she knew the time. Margo brought her tray with unfailing punctuality each day. Looking at her watch had become a nervous habit, like a small child might clutch a security blanket. To Anna it was a tracking of the hours she spent in captivity. More and more she found herself thinking back or having to look at a calendar to calculate the duration of her imprisonment. 'Nearly five weeks,' she complained mentally.

'Good morning, Margo.' Anna attempted elementary politeness.

No reply. That was normal, but Margo's eyes seemed quite moist, and Anna could have sworn she saw a tear on the cook's cheek. *Goodness*, she thought. Did Margo have sore eyes or was she upset? Anna rubbed her own eyes, flabbergasted and wondering what was happening. She rose to look at her breakfast. It was more unpalatable than on previous mornings. As always, the *Natal Witness* came with the breakfast, and she picked it up, thinking the cause for Margo's distress might be found among the usual diet of reported crimes and politically motivated violence. This morning, the newspaper's commentary proved unremarkable.

Margo wouldn't talk. Anna had to find the reason for the ominous silence herself. She belted her bathrobe and began the investigation. Sipho's door was closed. He was probably still asleep. Josh's room was wide open, but nothing stirred in the dimness within. He had yet to open the curtains, but there was no sign of him.

Turning right, Anna looked into the spare room. This was Sandile's cinema, and a woman sat on a chair, weeping. A man, sobbing himself, tried unsuccessfully to comfort her. Margo served tea and maize cakes for both. The atmosphere was heavy with grief.

The back door burst open, and Peter entered, followed by Tom talking in rapid Zulu. Anna understood nothing except 'Abantwana abafuni ukuhlamba namuhla ekuseni.' The children didn't want to swim this morning, Tom had said. That was uncharacteristic. They normally followed the doctors with sufficient alacrity. Had someone had an accident in the pool, or did the kids feel the gloom too?

Peter and Tom headed for Josh's office. All three began speaking at once when Josh came out. From the resulting gush of sounds, Anna recognized the word *file*. Dead! Had someone died? 'Not Sipho, please!' Anna pleaded silently. Was it one of the kids? Could it be that the delicate, feeble three-year-old girl Josh had worried over had slipped her life ring during the night and drifted on? Were the couple in Sandile's cinema her parents? There was nobody she dared to ask, not wishing to intrude on anyone's private sorrow. Nor did she feel overly stoic herself with the memory of the child's tiny drawn face, so marked with suffering, painfully clear in her own mind.

The best she could do was to retreat to her room, start the computer, and finish Josh's modules. At least she was being useful. She had no idea what awaited her when she offered to help with the input. The material was way over her head. She understood none of it. Now she saw how Josh felt when she rattled off her finance speak. It left him as baffled as she was with the medical terminology. Luckily the reference material was on discs and she only needed to change the wording according to the alterations and amendments Josh had marked on the hard copy. Anna thought herself in a time warp, like yesteryear's copy typist.

By lunchtime, a mortuary ethos had penetrated every corner of KwaZulu Medical like dense fog. Nobody moved or spoke. No requests for midday meals sounded. The kids had lost their appetites along with the adults. Margo had vanished, and Sipho's 'bean counter cave' was still closed. Its occupant couldn't be found either. Josh sat brooding in his study.

At three o'clock, the place resembled a mausoleum, and Anna became concerned about the kids. They should be hungry by now. Sipho, she noticed, had found his way into his office, giving off an air of industry.

'Sipho, are the kids okay? Do you know? Have they been fed?' she asked, concerned.

'Yeah, I think so. The sister's with them. We're expecting a grief counsellor in about an hour. Little Mary Ngubane's death has hit the others hard.'

'So it was the three-year-old who died?'

'Yes, it was.' Sipho looked away. He couldn't say much more.

Anna sneaked into the kitchen, took a basket, filled it with apples, and walked to the children's ward, convincing herself that she wouldn't cry. Greeting the children cheerfully was no use. Pretending nothing had happened wouldn't wash. The kids turned their heads towards her but said nothing. Anna walked solemnly from bed to bed, giving an apple to each child. As she thanked the sister for accompanying her through the ward, Nozipho made herself heard.

'Nkosazana Anna,' she said sadly, 'we don't have our zebras anymore.'

Anna noticed then that the toys were gone. 'What happened to them?'

'We gave them to Mary to take with her.'

Anna swallowed. It was hard to keep the lump in her throat down.

'My father and big brother used to tell me stories about Egypt. You know, in the north of Africa, when a pharaoh—that's their king—', Nozipho clarified, 'died, they used to bury his horses, chariots, weapons, and stuff with him so he could use them in the next world. We thought Mary might like the zebras.'

'That was thoughtful and very kind, Nozipho. It will make Mary happy.' Anna left the ward, giving the basket with the rest of the fruit to the sister for distribution.

Entering the administrative building again, she saw Josh standing by the double glass door, eyeing a package in his hand. He shook his head angrily.

'Too late,' he swore loudly. 'Too damned late.' A chain of Zulu curses sounded amidst the English. His voice rang with desperation when he turned towards her, showing her the parcel. 'Just twenty-four hours,' he said, his normally melodious voice ragged. 'A day too late, not even that. Twelve hours would have been enough to save Mary.' He was as distraught as if Mary had been his own child.

Mr Tough Guy has an Achilles' heel, Anna observed, looking at him with new awareness when Josh faced her with forsaken helplessness in his eyes. Sir Ruthless battled to keep tears at bay.

Becoming conscious of Anna's regard, he handed the parcel and invoice to Sipho through the enquiries window. 'Give it to Tom or whoever is on dispensary duty,' he said before turning towards his quarters, his shoulders hunched with fractured confidence. Anna was about to follow, intent on offering what comfort she could, when Sipho called her back.

'Anna!' He beckoned to her. Josh was best left alone when the professional blues struck him down. There was nothing she could do. Then again—Sipho's eyes sparkled with his own cleverness—maybe she could.

'Do you think you can liven Josh up a bit?' he asked without revealing his innermost thoughts. 'He punishes himself too much.

It's not good. Life goes on, especially for the other kids who depend on him.'

'I don't know what to say to him,' Anna confessed. 'I'm not a doctor, so I don't know how it feels to lose a patient. In his present state, Josh would misconstrue every word from me.'

'I don't think so, Anna.'

She couldn't conceal her chagrin when replying, 'Don't you know, Sipho? I'm supposed to be the rich bitch, the indulged white woman who is unfamiliar with deprivation and suffering. Many underprivileged children perish daily, but their deaths do not touch me or cause any ripples in my life. I'm not meant to care, Sipho. That's how Joshua sees me, the only way he sees me. He told me I represent everything "oppressive, exploitative, opportunistic, and socially irresponsible". Anything I say would sound insincere to him.'

'Words aren't necessary, Anna.' Sipho's look spoke volumes. 'You shouldn't torment each other like that,' he added.

She turned on her heels. It crossed her mind that Sipho had chosen an odd time to play matchmaker. Silly man. He knew she was married. He had far too fertile an imagination, but he was right about Josh. It was cruel to leave him at the mercy of his depression. The late arrival of Mary's medicine was not due to his shortcoming. He had ordered it in good time. No effort had been spared to save Mary. Josh shouldn't blame himself, but that was easier for her to say than for him to do.

Unsure how to deal with Josh while he was under the influence of his despondency, she resolved to put her best foot forward by knocking on his door and hoping the moment was not too importune. When no invitation to enter came, she opened the door quietly, stepped inside, and closed it without a sound. She saw Josh lying on his bed with his face buried in the pillow and felt that he was racked with the excruciating pain of abject defeat. In the face of his anguish, her indecision returned. She'd done the wrong thing coming in. She knew no words to express the right balance of empathy and encouragement. She could offer no support. What Josh needed, she decided at length, was emotional warmth, and that she could give aplenty.

He hadn't stirred and, by the look of him, was unaware of her presence in his bedroom. Anna sat on the edge of the bed, stroking Josh's shoulders very much like she would pat her pet cat. If she expected him to purr, she was disappointed. He said nothing. Not about to give in, she realized Josh needed company now more than at any other time. Without much ado, she came to lie down beside him, placing her arm across his back in a protective gesture.

Their silence lasted about half an hour, Anna thought, maybe more. Josh eventually raised his head, looking at her questioningly, wondering what she was at. She wanted to start him talking and assumed the topic foremost on his mind, the children, was the best for thawing his numb heart.

'You know Nozipho told the others to give their zebras to Mary,' she began.

'Kids can be astonishing. That's their charm.'

Delighted to hear a reply, she pushed on. 'Nozipho is a clever girl. She displays leadership qualities already.'

'She's smart for her age,' Josh agreed. 'Her parents were teachers. They used to live next to Cindy's folk for a while. She came to know them quite well.'

'Sipho says Nozipho's parents are dead, but I heard her say something about a big brother, if I understood her correctly.'

'Her brother lives in New York. He's only nineteen but headed for a stellar career in computers.'

'Why don't you marry Cindy and adopt Nozipho?'

'Got any other benevolent ideas, Miss Ethics?' Josh scowled, his face dour.

She changed tack instantly, suspecting she had hit a sore spot. Perhaps her statement was a little undiplomatic.

'Don't send Nozipho to one of those impersonal charities for AIDS orphans. She likes you. When she gave you the plum the other day, she said you're a nice doctor. Sipho told me about that. He thinks she needs a new family.'

Josh sighed, giving Anna a look that suggested her chatter disturbed his peace. She ignored it, continuing in a mellow, persuasive voice, 'Nozipho's right. I agree with her. You are a nice doctor.' He rewarded her with a sad, lopsided grin. She went on provocatively, 'Well, apart from a minor technicality or two, which we need not mention now.' He laughed at last. It was the sound she wanted to hear.

'Anna De Bruyn,' he said, looking at her with what almost amounted to respect. 'Sometimes I curse the day I met you and then loved you. Your sense of humour always surfaces despite my causing you so much harm. I'm not easy on you, I know.' Anna had grit, courage, and pride. These attributes he appreciated greatly in people. No matter how unhappy she was or how frightened and insecure she felt, she would not bow her head. She was a fighter. Determined not to show weakness, she kept her tears to herself. And cry she did. He had heard her, standing at her door, debating with himself whether to enter and enfold her in his arms. But how could he alleviate her pain when he was the cause of it? It made so little sense sometimes.

It was the first indication of an apology Anna had heard from Josh, but she skirted around it, saying, 'That's not what we're talking about. We're discussing Nozipho, Cindy, and you.'

'It's a romantic notion,' Josh replied with the hint of a shrug, 'but Cindy and I are no longer an item.'

'What? I don't understand,' Anna said, looking at Josh, puzzled.

'We've drifted too far apart. We have separate interests now. And as you know, Solomon's been courting Cindy.'

'And she likes him better?'

Josh couldn't help but be flattered by the disbelief ringing in her voice. It was balm to his soul, but he answered without showing the pleasure it gave him, 'They have more in common.'

'Are you sure about that? I thought Cindy worshipped the ground you walked on.'

'That's teenage nonsense. We've outgrown each other. We just weren't meant to be.'

Another wave of silence engulfed them. What was there to say? If Cindy had broken up with Josh because she preferred Solomon, Anna felt unqualified to pronounce judgment either way. Or was it Josh who had broken the engagement? Anna considered the matter too private to ask.

As if guessing her thoughts, Josh said, 'I called our betrothal off, in case you're wondering. I've strayed too far from the moral paths of the honest man. I can't expect Cindy to marry me now. I'd destroy her by dragging her into the mess I've created.'

Ah, Anna thought, *now we're approaching the truth. Poor Solomon has little impact. It takes a professional crisis for Josh to admit wrongdoing.* Concealing her thoughts, she argued logically.

'Don't you think Cindy would understand if you explained your reasons and long-term goals to her?'

'Do you understand it, Anna? Do you?' Josh asked, his index finger tracing the contours of her face.

Oh, Joshua, she thought. That wasn't the question at all. Josh didn't need understanding. That was only subterfuge. His eyes revealed his thoughts more clearly than his mouth. His eyes asked, 'Do you want me?' not 'Do you understand me?' Every gentle caress of his fingers begged, 'Please surrender.'

Surrender? she thought while Josh's hand found its way to her blouse buttons. Give of herself emotionally? How could she? KwaZulu Medical wasn't her life. She was a product of the business fraternity from as far back as her teens when she began helping in her father's office during school holidays. She lived and breathed the world's currencies. Josh might condemn her for it, but didn't the very lack of money cultivate his lawless practices like organisms in the test tubes of his mind? Even a clever professor accomplished nothing without money. Whether Josh acknowledged it or not, her work was an important contribution to the economy.

Offer herself physically? Oh god, yes. It would come so naturally. But she mustn't. She belonged to Hank. How could she stop what was happening right here? Was it too late already to say no? Would Josh be furious and give her a hard time if she backed away? Or would her participation satisfy his curiosity so that he might let her go?

'What are you thinking, my pet?' Josh prompted in a half-whisper, sensing that her mind was engaged more than her body.

'Me? Thinking?' Anna chuckled. 'My mind is a blank. How can I think when your hands are all over me?'

Josh had learned to read her well during the weeks they spent together, Anna noted, but this was a game for two to play. 'Tell me what you are thinking.'

'I am thinking that I became attracted to you from the moment our eyes met at that shareholders' meeting. I want you so much I ache all over. We've waited so long to come together.'

Josh's nearness intoxicated her. She cried out as his fingers found her nipples, squeezing them and setting her alight with a passion all the more intense for being denied.

'Be my woman, Anna, please,' he begged softly. 'Just once, my pet . . . please.'

* * *

William Rosenberg poured himself a whisky in the hope it might help solve the problem that had gnawed at him for the past week or so. Home alone, Melody having gone out with friends, he had time to consider the matter undisturbed by female interjections.

His indecision revolved around KwaZulu Medical who, he had no doubt, were a shady lot. The question was, what to do about it? His duty as citizen and business leader was to inform the police, but what was there to tell? William imagined saying something like 'Captain Broadbent, I recognized the voice of the skinny man at KwaZulu Medical as being the voice of the man who locked me up.' Broadbent would inevitably ask who the man was and what he looked like. Did he know his name? Was it really the same person who shut him in the wine cellar? William heard himself urging, 'Captain, I know I was held at KwaZulu Medical. I counted the steps across the reception area and along the corridor. It all added up. You can believe it, Captain, KwaZulu Medical and the EEM are a joined criminal entity with the same people directing them both.' Was that enough to persuade Broadbent? If asked what he really saw that day, William could only shrug in answer because he had been blindfolded at first and then rendered sightless by the bright spotlight. Identifying the skinny chap's face was impossible.

Broadbent would laugh him out of the cop shop and dismiss his conjecture as circumstantial, a hunch at best.

Yet William couldn't let it rest. Shouldn't every good detective understand the value of a hunch? Didn't some police officers swear by their gut feelings? What was wrong with his own inner promptings? Even politicians wagered on election outcomes based on their intuition.

And weren't there principles to uphold? That bloke, Mtolo, and his cronies running KwaZulu Medical had not been punished. So far, they had avoided detection. Maybe he should talk to his Mineral Enterprises directors and convince them to contract private investigators to watch KwaZulu Medical till he had enough information to satisfy the police.

William mixed another drink and sat in his favourite armchair, the one he called his throne, which he used for quiet contemplation. His thinking chair. Barely had his butt touched its surface when it struck him that the directors—and the police, for that matter— would wish to know his reason for visiting KwaZulu Medical. Would they believe he was only looking up a friend? If so, they would ask who? And he'd better have a good explanation for seeking out such a controversial clinic. Was his seeing Dr Indira Naidoo a professional consultation? They would ask. No, a private call. Just friends.

Melody would be impressed. He anticipated her tirade following that revelation. 'At it again, William? You never did appreciate your home and hearth, did you? I've devoted my whole married life to ensuring you have a cosy home and lack no creature comforts. What do I get in return?' And so she would harp all day and a large part of the night.

He refilled his glass. If he refused to tell the police whom he had seen at KwaZulu Medical, he could come under suspicion himself. Broadbent might visualize a scenario whereby part of the ransom had landed in William's account as reward for his cooperation. He may be seen as an accessory to the crime. After Price's arrest, the reputations of business tycoons were no longer sacrosanct. Lord! What an incriminating situation. Surely Paul, Frank, and Geoff would confirm his version of events.

His whisky tumbler and bottle joined again in spiritual intercourse. He felt compelled to warn Indira. She must part company with that clinic immediately. He wanted her away from Joshua Mtolo and his partners in vice. Would she believe his story about the episode in the wine cellar? She held Mtolo in high esteem and worked happily at KwaZulu Medical. If Mtolo was convicted and the place folded, Indira would be at a loss. The thought lit a lamp of hope in his heart. Indira may still accept his offer to establish her in her own practice, although it was the last thing she wanted.

When the phone rang, it startled William out of his cogitation. His whole body jerked. With no resemblance of majesty, he lifted himself from his throne to answer the intrusive sound. He prayed it wasn't Melody announcing her early return home. It would ruin his impending date with the fashion model doll he had met at a friend's house recently. She was a gorgeous blonde feather in his cap. William laughed at the thought of her. He wasn't so simple or infatuated to fail to see that the lady found his wallet more winsome than his personality, to say nothing of his body. Blondie made a refreshing change from Indira's demanding intellect, which taxed his capacity at times, but if faced with the choice between the two, Indira was still the winner. 'That's my undoing,' he muttered to himself as he headed for the phone. 'I appreciate all manner of women, even Melody.' And the last thing he wanted was having to explain himself to his dear wife.

'Ja, Rosenberg here!' William had reached the telephone.

'Hank, old man, howzit?' he called, surprised. 'What? You want me to come to your place? Right now?' He hesitated. What about his date? Still, if one person could assist him to sort out his dilemma, it was Hank. 'Okay! I'll be there. Man, do I have news for you.'

He hung up, repeating softly, 'Man, do I have news . . . Jesus Christ!' The short spell of sitting in his thinking chair had recharged a battery in William, quickening electrical impulses in his brain. He couldn't believe the thought spreading in his mind. Had Anna been taken to Mtolo's lair as well? He wrung his hands in agitation. Had Anna been holed up in that wine cellar while he talked to Indira? What did Indira know of all this? He raced back to the telephone and dialled her number. No answer. She wasn't home. 'Shit!' William calmed himself with another whisky. No point jumping to conclusions. Evidence was needed. It was police business, but that Broadbent guy worked so slowly. 'Oh Christ, poor Hank,' William mumbled, tipping down his drink.

'Joshua Mtolo,' he fumed through his alcohol. 'I knew there was a reason why I disliked the fellow.' At the time of the anniversary ball, he had been so taken up with Mtolo's possible effect on Indira that he'd failed to give any thought to the man's behaviour towards Anna. He couldn't recall hearing them converse or seeing them dance together. Anna had danced with that headmaster chap but not with Mtolo. Apart from his medical colleague, Zak Elbenstein, who happened to be Hank's specialist, few people greeted Mtolo. 'Oh brother, does the plot thicken!' he exclaimed, still trying to come to grips with the image his mind conjured. He reached for the glass again, knowing full well he was getting drunk. 'Poor Hank,' he belched. Could Broadbent have a point after all when he suggested Anna may have left with another man? The fact that Mtolo and Anna had ignored each other deliberately at the ball was just as telling as if Mtolo had been all over her. And he, William Rosenberg, an expert in infidelity, believed he recognized such acts for what they were. Repressed desire. A fatal attraction. 'Poor Hank.' William shook his head. No, this was inconceivable. He was drinking too much. Anna wouldn't go with any other guy, no matter how sexy he looked. Besides, Hank cut an impressive figure himself, William admitted with a little envy.

He ran his hands over the stubble on his chin. He had to shave before setting out for Hank's house. One never knew who else might be there. While scraping his cheeks with the razor and thinking—he rarely did the two together—William determined that he owed it to Hank to inform the police about the events at KwaZulu Medical. If Broadbent took him seriously, both the EEM crimes and Anna's abduction mystery might be solved in one shot. If he was mistaken, he would look foolish, but he had the satisfaction of having done his duty.

* * *

'Well, I must say! Have we swapped rooms now or something?'

Wasn't that Barbara Mkhize calling? Anna stirred, reaching consciousness in slow motion. No, that silly, whining remark had not issued from Barbara. Her housekeeper didn't sound like that. Anna endeavoured to shake off her sleep-induced stupor.

'Do you find this bed more inviting? Isn't it a little too hot and steamy for you?'

There was that shrill, grating voice again. *Oh, bloody hell,* Anna thought, becoming fully awake while Margo set Josh's breakfast tray down with a bang. Her poison-arrow tongue, tipped with sanctimonious moral authority, hit Anna below the belt. She took instant offence.

'Piss off!' she snarled in her fiercest tone. 'Get out of here till you're called.'

There, that should fix the old bag. She couldn't be bothered with courtesies in the face of Margo's overblown righteousness. 'Piss off' was easier to say than 'Margo, I request that you leave this room.'

A journalistic rule of thumb she remembered from uni was never to use eight words when two would do.

'Oh my god,' she groaned. 'What am I doing in Josh's bed?' The more pointed question was, what had she done in Josh's bed?

'Christ! Hank will kill me,' she muttered, distressed. Guilt manifested itself like a hangover after a night of excesses. And what a night it had been! Stretching from around 1800 hours, with a short break for a meal and a shared bottle of wine at about 2030 hours, to heaven knows when they finally fell asleep.

Where was Josh anyway? Probably doing the rounds of the wards already. Before breakfast? Conscientious workaholic. Anna swung her right leg out of bed. The left one followed more slowly. She sat up with a moan, looking around for her clothes. They had been discarded rather hurriedly, flung away somewhere. Moaning again, she reached for the nearest item on the floor, her panties.

'Holy mackerel!' she observed. 'I haven't felt so sore since I lost my virginity during the first year at uni.' She staggered to the shower. Her breasts were swollen with nipples oversensitive to touch when she washed. She dabbed at them gingerly with a towel. 'Bugger.' She winced, but the generic curse was not aimed at Josh while she wrapped herself in one of his shirts for the few steps back to her room.

While attending to the daily renovation of her face and hair, she hummed a tune, knowing she was in top form. Or would be, if it wasn't for the now very urgent need to persuade Hank that she still loved him. In consternation, she wondered if she had to convince herself as well.

'No!' she told Zavier sternly. 'We're getting out of here. Back home to Johannesburg. Back to Hank, to where we belong. What, Zavier? Do I hear a neigh of disbelief? I have a plan, my little animal. I'm not telling you, though. You can't keep secrets.'

Pulling another hated cotton and denim prison uniform from the wardrobe, Anna produced sufficient willpower not to dwell on the magic of the previous night. She had gasped at Joshua's raw strength but had soon fell into rhythm with him. She mustn't think of that now, however. It had been blissful heaven for both, and her hope that Josh would find her uninspiring and let her go was quashed. Last night's events gave every indication of their growing addiction to each other unless she took decisive steps to leave.

Yet almost immediately, a new, niggling thought stimulated her emotional turbulence. From fearing that Hank would never want her back, her mind changed to wondering why it had been left up to her to find an escape route from prison. Why wasn't she being rescued? Wasn't anyone looking for her? By now, the police should have stormed the place. They couldn't possibly be so clueless. Of course, she realized, Joshua probably had the local cops in his pocket, irrespective of their political stripes. If the cops were IFP guys, they would see only the benefits of Josh's endeavours and turn a blind eye to his felony. ANC supporting officers would look the other way too because the clinic had been established with ANC funds.

'The situation looks hopeless from every angle.' Anna sighed. Could there ever be an efficient investigation into her abduction, given the overall improbity of her case? How was Hank coping? What was he doing? Did he still care?

'All right, Mr Zavier Stripeybum. I hear you telling me to summon my faith and not get depressed. That's easy for you to say, but nothing ever happens unless you make it happen. That's why we're leaving. Liberty ahoy!'

It was high time for her civil disobedience campaign to begin. She had tried talking matters over reasonably with Josh, munificently offering him more money than he dreamed of to let her go. She had attempted to help him in many ways, but he refused to see her position. Numerous times, she demonstrated that Josh was doing himself the greatest disservice by not freeing her. What could she do to further his interests here? Sweet nothing, apart from sharing his bed. That, she suspected, was at the core of his obduracy. Negotiation and diplomacy had thus failed. A higher level of operation became inevitable.

An accidental glimpse in the wardrobe mirror brought a frown of dented pride to her face. Her skin was drying out, and her hair was misbehaving. 'My hair looks like your mane,' she told Zavier. Josh hadn't paid for her skin and hair care lotions, or maybe Felicity didn't know where to buy them. All she eventually received were some nondescript underwear and a pair of cheap, flat-heeled sandals. 'If my friends saw me now, they wouldn't recognize me,' she complained. On the other hand, the worse she looked, the greater the likelihood that Josh would tire of her and dismiss her.

Surprised at her mood swing from the contentedness of sublime sexual satisfaction to crestfallen self-pity, Anna admonished herself for emotional indulgence. There was no way she'd wait till Josh agreed to let her go. She was leaving today. Would ill-conceived plans made on the run bring her freedom? Everything had to be played by ear, but unless she moved now she'd be here forever.

Her planned coup d'état required three steps. The first entailed monitoring Josh's and Sipho's whereabouts every minute of the day. The second was to act normally. Be friendly and helpful like every other day. The third was the hardest. Intercepting Mark, Felicity's cousin, was bound to be tricky. He came to collect the hospital's laundry in the evening twice weekly and returned it the next morning. It was his part-time job while studying law. He drove the laundry firm's van, and Anna figured the young man would not be averse to giving her a ride in return for a cheque to cover his textbooks and a little extra.

She expected that Margo was displeased with her behaviour and would consequently omit the delivery of her breakfast. She was being starved as punishment. Too bad, she could find her own food if it came to that.

It was undeniable, though, that her enjoyment of last night's transgressions had disfigured her sober image. It weakened her ethical standards in her own eyes. 'But', she opined, justifying her conduct to Zavier, 'I hardly find myself in a perfect world, do I?' Zavier did not look up from his drinking bowl. 'Technically, that man raped me, Zavier. I put it to you that I'm under Joshua's roof against my will. I can therefore rightly claim that I was coerced—under duress, so to speak—into having sexual relations with him.'

Anna sighed deeply, allowing that she had given the truth the widest interpretation possible. She broke into ribald chuckles. 'I tell you, Zavier, I'd make a damned fine lawyer if I put my mind to it.'

Hunger prodded her towards the kitchen in search of edible produce of her own choosing. Fresh fruit and yogurt were a welcome change from what Margo normally dished out. She carried a bowl full out behind Fernando's shed. Josh wasn't about, and she ate peacefully, sitting on a garden seat Fernando had been instructed to build especially for her use.

The longer she lingered there thinking about her escape, the more nervous she became. What if her preparations went awry? Perhaps she should wait another day or two. Think about it more fully. Where was Josh now? What if he guessed her intention?

Unable to sit still, she returned the dish to the kitchen while Margo laboured, dragging a canvas sack through the back door towards the children's ward.

'Do you want a hand with that?' Anna called, expecting a condescending grunt of refusal.

'Yes.' Margo pointed to the other end of the bag.

'It's not heavy, just awkward to lift.'

'What's in it?' Anna ventured to ask, taken by surprise when Margo replied with more than one syllable.

'A snake,' Margo giggled, watching Anna's reaction with sinister amusement.

'You're having me on,' Anna said, examining the sack doubtfully. She lifted her end of it with care. Her hesitation brought raucous laughter from Margo.

'You are teasing me. The bag's not heavy enough for a snake, either dead or alive.'

'You'll see, you'll see.' Margo still cackled like a wicked witch.

'Besides, you wouldn't take a real snake over to the children. Tell the truth,' Anna insisted. 'What is it?' Carrying her end with increasing confidence, she helped to transport the sack into the kids' ward.

'Mamba! Mamba! Mamba!' The kids clapped and chanted on seeing the canvas bag. Fernando was already in the ward, busy with numerous tools, suspending a warrior's shield from the ceiling over the boys' beds on one side of the room. Earlier, he had fastened hooks above the beds on the other side, which he pointed out to Margo.

'Help me with this,' Margo demanded while slicing the bag with a pocketknife she produced from her apron. Anna stood back, not wishing to be on the receiving end of the operation. She waited till Margo tucked the knife away, then grasped her end of the sack and pulled. The kids cheered as the snake's head appeared, seemingly born from a canvas womb. It had big button eyes. Its mouth was open, showing a forked, velvet tongue reinforced with wire so that it jutted out without drooping. Its body was a patchwork of fabrics in varying colours and textures drawn over a skeleton of chicken wire. Fernando had fashioned the structure with bends and curves to resemble a live snake. Margo and Felicity sat up most of the night sewing the covering. Anna's silver-bell laughter bubbled at the sight.

'This is unreal. Whose idea was this?'

'The kids thought of it,' Fernando said. 'They were inspired by the story of the Mamba Warriors,' he continued while placing a ladder under the hooks in the ceiling. 'They took sides. One half wanted to be Mamba Warriors and the others King's Guards.' Fernando climbed the ladder. 'Can you hold up the snake's tail please, Anna?' Margo took the head with one hand and supported the one-and-a-half-metre-long body in the middle with the other. Anna did likewise with the tail. Fernando soon had the snake hanging exactly right. He came down again whispering to Anna, 'We thought the youngsters needed lots of things to take their minds off Mary.'

An immediate demonstration of what Fernando meant commenced when the boys began verbal battles with an exchange of colourful insults.

'Mambas are low. They slither in the dust.' This was announced by a strong voice from the King's Guards side of the ward.

'King's Guards are cocky. The Mambas will bite off their heads before they swell too much.' The Mambas' resounding retaliation provoked protests from the girls.

'Not so loud, stupids!'

Margo and Fernando had brought life into the ward, but Josh wasn't there to witness the transformation. Anna checked if his car was outside. It wasn't. Maybe Sipho knew where Josh had gone, but the tokoloshe guardhouse was shut. Josh had to be about; otherwise, Margo would not have brought his breakfast. If Josh was here, Anna puzzled fearfully, why was his car gone? Did he lend it to Peter or Tom? Or was he called away on an emergency? She waited anxiously for Sipho's appearance. He would know what was happening.

* * *

Anna had not much time for precise planning that evening when she attempted her dash to freedom. She hadn't seen Josh all day. That in itself was nothing unusual. His car was still not in its customary parking area. Peter and Tom had arrived in their own vehicles. Anna deemed it safe to think that Josh was out. She refrained from asking Sipho too many questions. He would become suspicious.

'Sorry, Zavier, I don't think you can come along this time. I might be able to fetch you at a later date.' Anna looked at the zebra, wondering whether to leave him or take him with her. Practical considerations won the toss, and Zavier remained put because she wanted to leave her room looking as if she still occupied it. Removing her purse and cheque book from her handbag, she left it, together with her briefcase, standing in their normal spot under the table. Her clothes stayed in the wardrobe as well. She would depart in her prison uniform.

How far would she get? Her knees trembled at the thought. Young Mark was to be her liberator. If he could take her into Vryheid, she would stay in a hotel and either rent a car tomorrow morning and drive home or call for help. Josh wouldn't dare follow. Even he realized that creating a fuss exposed him to unwanted attention. He had every reason to shun the limelight.

From the day Felicity had introduced Mark, Anna had often watched his arrival as he opened the gate with a key card Sipho had given him and then parked the van right in front of the steps leading to the double glass doors. He wasn't carrying those laundry bags any further than necessary. Usually he ran inside and emerged shortly afterwards with a bag slung over each shoulder. She had studied his movements as he threw the linen into the vehicle, slammed the door shut, sat behind the wheel, and drove out again. Here, she felt, an almost foolproof escape presented itself. Mark was always in a rush, and that suited her purpose very well.

This evening Mark arrived later than normally, adding to Anna's tenseness. She had waited till Sipho locked the front office and retired to his quarters. After that, she commenced her wait for Mark, keeping an eye on the gate but never straying far from the kitchen. If someone saw her, she could go and pretend to make coffee. In agitation, she patted her jeans pockets for the umpteenth time. Yes, her chequebook and purse were there.

When he finally came, Mark pushed through the door faster than ever.

'Hi there, Anna,' he called in passing.

Briefly she wondered if she should stop him and ask for a lift but decided against it. She had no idea if Mark knew anything of the circumstances surrounding her. If he did, he certainly wouldn't oblige. It was better not to give him the choice.

She waited till Mark vanished through the back door before running to his van, stepping in and hiding under the passenger side of the dashboard in a curled position. There, she thought, she could remain till Mark returned. Hopefully he wouldn't become aware of her in the darkness till he was already on his way out the gate.

Now that she had taken the plunge to free herself, Anna thought the process had been quite simple, really. Too easy, almost. She pondered why self-preservation had not driven her to act sooner. Was she overconfident?

Only the small matter of her diamonds needed to be addressed later. Josh had suggested that she lock them in his safe for security.

He gave her an envelope and the combination of numbers to open the thing and deposit the jewellery there if she wished. He wasn't going to touch it, he insisted, lest his suggestion be misinterpreted as robbery. 'I may be a bit of a villain,' he said with a laugh. 'But I'm not a thief.' Evidently, a subtle distinction existed between robbery and extortion. Anna grinned. 'Contrariness par excellence,' she giggled softly in the darkness.

She would retrieve the diamonds later because—apart from Josh's office being locked—she wanted to create the impression that she was still on the premises. If the diamonds were there, she hoped Josh and Sipho would think she too was present. It might delay their possible pursuit of her by some hours.

What was keeping Mark so long today? He was always in and out like a flash. Anna's legs began to stiffen and tingle with pins and needles. Maybe the time seemed longer because she was uncomfortable, anxious and impatient to be off.

'Come on, Mark,' she whispered, not daring to lift her head and look. 'Where the hell are you?'

'Ah, at last,' she breathed with relief when she heard footsteps on the stairs. The van's hatch was opened and the laundry bags thrown in. *Bang*! Mark closed the van. His hand on the door handle, he stopped. A second set of footsteps ran lightly down the stairs.

'Mark, can you take me to Bonga's garage please? My car was booked in for a service. I haven't got around to collecting it yet. Hope they're still open.'

'No worries, Professor.' Mark agreed amiably.

For a moment, Anna's system blacked out with shock. She heard Josh's voice as if she was already in another realm, looking down on herself, detached, viewing her predicament with indifference.

Shaking off the inertia with a revolting curse, her first instinct was to climb over the seat and hide among the washing.

Too late. She had squandered precious seconds. Josh opened the passenger door, hesitated in surprise, and then pulled her out roughly by the arms. Her legs, still numb with pins and needles, buckled, and she fell to her knees. Josh yanked her up with a mean grip, pulling both her arms up behind her back. She swallowed a groan. She wasn't about to provide him with extra entertainment by letting her pain show while he pushed her towards the stairs. He hadn't said a word, and his silence was dangerous.

How dare he treat me like that, Anna thought, pain and desperation mingling within her. Josh walked a fraction behind her, and she kicked backwards, hitting his shins as hard as she could to make him stumble and relax his grasp.

'Hellcat!' he hissed through his teeth in agony but held on. He pulled her arms higher still.

Convinced her bones would snap, Anna shrieked, 'Let me go! Damn you!'

Betrayed, Anna heard Mark, her saviour, drive away while Josh marched her inside.

Long before they reached her cell, she wanted to cry with pain and anguish. Beg Josh to please let go of her before he broke her arms. Josh showed no mercy. His lack of compassion steeled her resolve to fight, despite knowing she wouldn't win.

Josh still had not spoken, and Anna needed all her energy to struggle against him as he pushed her into her room, slammed the door, and ripped her clothes off her. Momentarily freed of his harsh grip, she defended herself tooth and nail, literally. None of her strategies and war plans included hand-to-hand combat with a brutal enemy. How she wished she had taken Franz's advice and learned self-defence. She thought briefly about the gun in Josh's safe. Tempted to remove it when she put her diamonds in, she had had second thoughts. It wouldn't have taken long for Josh to miss it and realize where it had gone, but now she needed it sorely. Franz had urged her to practice shooting, although she never felt comfortable with firearms. *I was wrong and Franz was right*, she thought, wishing he were here to assist her.

Her mental call for help cost her a fraction of a second's concentration. Enough for Josh to overpower and throw her on the bed, thrashing her with his trouser belt like she had never been beaten before. This was not the game she played with Hank. This was serious assault. Josh was beside himself and intended to hurt.

Anna bit into her pillow. If she let that madman hear one cry or see one tear, she'd die of shame. Unable to ward him off, she endured the lashing, hoping that Josh's anger would soon be spent. The torture seemed to last forever with her inability to escape her attacker. His earlier abuse weakened her arms too much to enable her to scramble off the bed and run.

The explosion of Josh's fury finally died as suddenly as it had erupted, but as with explosions generally, acrid smoke still hovered. Breathing heavily and pulling himself together, he threw the belt aside.

'Let that be a lesson to you,' he growled.

Anna had only one wish: to get the hell out, but she simply couldn't move.

'Did you hear me, woman?'

'Anna!' he shouted when she wouldn't reply. 'I'm talking to you.'

Seeing her refusal to respond as sheer provocation, he pulled her onto her red-raw, welted back by her already sore arms. She gasped with pain as much as shock because Josh had shed most of his clothes and she guessed what was coming.

No way, she thought. She kicked, aiming her heel at his chin. It nearly worked. She almost struck him but not quite. He was faster, knocking her foot down and forcing her legs apart.

Incensed, Anna screamed, 'No! Don't you dare! Musa-bo!' she added in Zulu to ensure the message penetrated his insensitive skull. 'Not one thrust! Damn you!' A white-hot rage consumed her. It masked her pain and confusion, giving her more strength and resourcefulness. The screwdriver! Suddenly she remembered Fernando's screwdriver still hidden under the mattress for occasions just like this. She managed to wriggle closer to the edge of the bed and reach for it. Josh grasped her shoulders to hold her down, but this time he was too slow. Cold steel against his genitals brought him to a halt.

'I said not one thrust and I mean it.'

Josh's eyes sparked with anger and disbelief. For a moment Anna thought he would punch her, but he restrained himself. *Just as well,* she thought. *I'm buggered. I can't lift a finger to protect myself from another blow.* Josh held her wrist and shook till the screwdriver dropped from her numb hand. She heard it roll under the bed.

'You unbelievably wicked woman,' he said. 'Fernando was looking everywhere for that. You wouldn't happen to have my key card as well, would you? Would I find it here if I searched?'

'No,' Anna lied.

His madness finally exhausted, Josh released Anna at last, and she hoped her ordeal had ended. Sitting on the edge of the bed, Josh shook his head, bemused, as if returning to reality from an alien world.

'If you're quite finished, will you get out!' Anna hissed at him.

'I thought you loved me,' he said with utter dismay. Had he really thought her settling into the clinic's routine, helping out, and being kind indicated she no longer wished to escape? He had dwelt in a sense of false security—that much was obvious.

'How can I love a man who beats me?' she screamed in his face. 'You're out of your mind!'

'That's quite possible when dealing with you,' he answered quietly despite his annoyance. One of them, at least, had to remain calm during this crazy debacle. 'You'd drive any man to insanity,' he stated, adding with a leer, 'especially in bed.'

'Listen, Joshua,' Anna snarled, humiliated by the beating. Josh's tasteless quip compounded the injury with insult. Indignation gave her voice a threatening edge. 'Don't add rape to the list of your crimes. You asked me to be your woman once. I granted your wish once. That's all. No more.'

'Let's be clear about this now.' Josh took a breath to preach. 'You disobeyed me attempting to escape. You took your punishment, and I don't hold grudges. As far as I'm concerned, we're still friends.'

'Like all bleeding hell we are!' Anna shouted, exhausted and close to tears. 'Get out! Leave me alone! Black witch doctor!'

Shocked, he stepped away from the bed. As he left the room, the shattering of Zavier's drinking bowl against the closing door sounded like an unmistakable confirmation of Anna's wrath.

Hell hath no fury, Josh thought, dragging his leaden feet towards his office. He needed to work. It was the best distraction from this latest crisis. He adjusted his jeans as he went. The belt was still in Anna's room. Retrieving it was out of the question. He counted himself lucky to have avoided castration with the screwdriver. And had he not exited quickly, Zavier's bowl would have crowned him.

'Hellcat,' Josh muttered to himself. In some respects, the incident might have afforded him a warped amusement, but his soul failed to see the humour. Two sharp words repeated in his mind like a gramophone needle stuck in a groove, scratching painfully: 'Black witch doctor!' Was that her real opinion of him? She had said it with such derogatory intonation. Granted, she had reacted under extreme stress, but unguarded situations often revealed the truth. 'Guess I can't expect political correctness from her during such trying moments,' he conceded, still grumbling. But the emotional stab wound she had inflicted smarted somewhere deep inside. Would she kiss the ache away if he attempted to make good? 'Yeah, right,' he mumbled under his breath. 'Like to see you try, man.' She would be thorny to approach after this.

Naturally, he hadn't intended hurting her so much. The whole sordid event had gotten out of hand. Something in her brought out the worst in him. The fault had to lie with her. She was wilful, wayward, and obstinate. Yet he admired her for those characteristics. She displayed iron discipline too. Not one tear or sound escaped her throughout the lashing. Anna was no mouse. How could he love and resent her all at once? Why was he so confused?

'Why ask questions when you know the answer?' Josh scolded himself when he sat down at his desk without touching a scrap of the work awaiting his attention. Only to himself and only on rare occasions did he admit that Anna made him feel uneasy because she reminded him wordlessly of his misdemeanours. Her mere presence acted as a catalyst to produce a gnawing anxiety within him. No matter how much he tried to disregard it, it remained dormant in the back of his mind. The dreaded stirrings of guilt.

Sighing, he abandoned work and headed for the dispensary. 'What have we?' He searched the shelves. 'Painkillers . . .

anti-inflammatories . . . Valium.' Pocketing enough pills to last a day, he returned to Anna's room, his heart pounding. Falling in love with her inevitably caused problems, but he had expected to manage them better than his performance hitherto. He had gained neither her affection nor her money. The exercise was a waste of nervous energy just like Sipho predicted.

He knocked softly on Anna's door, his usual brashness tamed by contrition. Her silence squeezed his heart. There wasn't even a sob from her in reply.

'Anna!' he called, knocking again.

Nothing.

'Are you okay?' Why wouldn't she answer? Was she being stubborn or was she seriously injured? He didn't think he'd hit her that hard.

'Anna, please say something,' he beseeched with unaccustomed tremors in his voice. Her lack of response dispirited him, giving rise to a growing fear.

'If you don't speak, I shall assume you are ill and come in anyway.' He turned the knob. The door gave about half a centimetre before resisting. She had placed the latch across it.

'Anna, do you need help? If I ask the sister to see you, will you let her in?' He held his ear to the door.

'This is the last warning,' he called with mounting panic. 'If you don't respond, I'll break the door down.'

'Leave me in peace.' Her voice was barely audible but Josh heard.

'I've brought analgesics for you.'

'Stick you muthi up your . . . !'

'Hallelujah!' Josh laughed with relief. He didn't catch her last word. He didn't need to. His heart felt so light he was dizzy. Her robust outburst lifted a crushing weight from his conscience.

'I'll leave the tablets beside the door,' he called. 'I wrote instructions down for you.'

He returned to his office in a calmer frame of mind. Anna would be okay. She'd come around eventually. He was wrong.

* * *

In the weeks that followed, nobody caught a glimpse of Anna. If she left her room, she did so furtively, going mostly to the kitchen to prepare food and return quickly to her cell. It perturbed Josh, who wanted to apologise but couldn't face her. Everyone noted the professor's touchiness. He found accusing fingers pointed at him. Sipho, who loved talking to her, was vexed because he had relied on her help more than Josh realized. The children were disappointed when their bedtime stories ceased abruptly without explanation. Margo complained she couldn't get into Anna's room in the mornings but later found the kitchen disorderly because Anna had marauded through the larders for ingredients.

'For goodness' sake, Margo, use your brains,' Josh admonished when painted into a corner by their combined criticism. 'I know exactly what you've been serving Anna. I wouldn't want that slop either. Why don't you take notice of what she chooses for herself and offer her more of the same in future? I strongly suggest you improve her fare. I know you don't like her much, but there's no need to starve her.'

Fernando was the only contented man. His best screwdriver had reappeared in its proper place.

* * *

While Josh had cause to count his blessings as his incessant work rewarded him with the gratification of professional success, he sat counting his troubles instead. Featuring foremost among them was Anna, of course. Her withdrawal from the clinic's daily routine needed reversing, but he had no means to bring it about. Normalizing their discourse seemed impossible when she avoided and mistrusted him more than ever.

Sipho too showed his disappointment at every opportunity because together with Anna, he had taken the first cautious and hopeful steps towards a stock market listing for KwaZulu Medical.

Anna's help was tantamount to the venture's positive outcome, but she no longer cooperated, and the project stalled.

'Well, man,' Josh sighed, his head and heart aching. 'Start all over again.' If he could but approach her and convince her of his remorse, he would make a new beginning by taking her out somewhere to help her relax and forget. An excursion away from the clinic was the only temptation he could proffer, which she might find attractive enough after her long incarceration.

'Believe me, lady,' he muttered, thinking aloud, 'I'm eating humble pie with a crust scarped from Margo's dustbin.' Anna, he knew, occupied all the moral high ground, and he could do little if she accepted his invitation and used the chance to make her escape. It would test the fabric of their intricate bond, for tied together, they were in a perverse imbroglio.

His other difficulties were no less significant. He noticed that his clinic was surrounded by a number of curious eyes. Were the mysterious observers police? Were his days of brigandage numbered at last? He didn't think so. He figured police investigators would have moved in to arrest him by now. More likely they were private detectives sent by either Hank or William. Their threatening presence could derail his plans to escort Anna out of the clinic's grounds. If those guys saw him with a white woman, they'd quickly draw correct conclusions. What's more, Anna must be prevented from making contact with them if she became aware of their regular vigils.

Unfortunately, he had nobody to positively identify the lookouts who watched from their cars on the other side of the street. C5, his most reliable and accurate informant, had gone underground. Instead of C5 assisting him, Josh received a message from C4 asking that he might extend his influence to help C5 out of a tight spot. The request brought Sipho's comments about the Caprivis back to Josh as he sat, elbows on desk, fingertips together under his chin, mentally constructing a rescue mission for C5. Sipho, he recalled, had warned that the Caprivis led a politicized existence and often had misdeeds wrongly placed at their door. C5 was accused of murder and promptly disappeared.

'It's not the accusation that bothers him,' C4 explained, upset and angry. 'He can prove his innocence. He's most concerned about the threatened harassment of his ageing parents should he refuse to sign a document stating the princes of the royal house instructed him to do the killing. We are all taking it in turns now to watch over the old people.'

'Take a deep breath and tell me exactly what happened. Talk slowly.' Josh tried to calm him.

C4 controlled himself a little before continuing emphatically, 'It isn't true!' It was all he could do not to shout. 'The princes gave no such orders, and our pal murdered nobody. He's being framed because he's resisting the pressure to sign a false statement.'

'Give me some details,' Josh coaxed patiently.

'The local ANC branch secretary was gunned down outside his house as he was about to get into his car,' C4 reported, still speaking rapidly.

'So why do they say our friend is responsible?' Josh probed.

'It was a drive-by shooting, and the vehicle used was the same model and colour as his,' C4 explained as if Josh were dense.

'That proves nothing.'

'Let me finish, man.' C4 became irritable again. 'The perpetrators stole his number plates and fixed them to their car, which just happened to be the same model and colour. They switched the plates, you understand? The poor guy didn't even notice his number plates had been swapped for a different pair. Honestly, man, how often do you look at your number plates?'

C4 talked like a machine gun. Josh had trouble urging him to think more and say less.

'Rather lackadaisical for a man of our friend's reputation, wouldn't you say?' Josh argued. 'I would have given him credit for more caution.'

'Don't be unfair, man. It's bad enough that nobody believes his story. They reckon he could have switched the plates himself to confuse the police, although I can't see what that would achieve.'

'Do you think he did? You said he's innocent. What's his alibi?'

'The murder took place in Umlazi, but our pal was seeing medical specialists in Cape Town on the day of the shooting.'

'What ails him?'

'Liver . . . drinks too much.'

'Can't he see a doctor in Durban?'

C4 chuckled quietly for the first time. 'He prefers Cape Town because that's where a particular lady of his lives. She's a nurse, and he can go spending time with her as well. Kill two birds with one stone, as they say.'

'It's the same old story,' Sipho said when told of the conversation. 'The ANC wants to see prominent IFP leaders arrested and hopes to coerce people into telling the necessary incriminating lies to justify it.'

C5 was an integral link in Josh's contentious operation. Without him, he felt handicapped and vulnerable, a scary experience he didn't much care for.

* * *

Chapter 10

The Plan

'Oh, my goodness, how time drags!' Anna sighed as she looked out of her window at the flowering shrubs. They were so close she could smell the perfume.

For the last week, she had helped Fernando work in the garden. Once he finished pruning the roses at the farthest end of the property, there would be nothing else for her to do. She simply could not bring herself to seek indoor activities because there was no guarantee she could avoid Josh.

She remembered her first evening here when, sitting by the window, she had determined not to act like a victim. The thought that Josh might have won, keeping her cooped up like a depressed recluse, prodded her out of her glumness and into the sunshine with Fernando. He taught her many a useful trick, like cutting the thick scrub along the fence. He gave her gloves to protect her hands from scratches, showed her the right tools for the job and where to find them, and handed her the spare key to the shed so that she could work whenever she wished.

Josh had not sentenced her to solitary confinement. She had withdrawn because he had chipped a chink off her soul, which wasn't healing. Physically she wished she were mending faster too. Her back still showed faint bruising and hurt with particular movements while gardening. Every twinge of pain reminded her it was high time to think about the armed struggle she planned to wage at the beginning of her imprisonment. Could she get the gun out of Josh's safe after all? If only he didn't keep his office locked when not seeing patients. She imagined pretending to retrieve her diamonds. Instead of taking the jewels, she would grasp the gun and point it at his head. He said it was always loaded. She did not intend to shoot him, of course, just threaten him enough to . . . what? Let her go? If she walked out and hijacked his car, could she point a gun at him at the same time? It might work if Sipho weren't there to immediately disconnect the power from the gate. Getting Josh out of his office at gunpoint, making him stay close till she scrambled into the car while holding onto the gun then roared away to the gate—she still had the key card. Could she manage that? Wouldn't Josh have more than enough opportunity to overpower her and take the gun away during all that time? It needed so much planning without help from a third party. There must be other methods. What was it Winnie Mandela had said about matches? Burning the place down would be another option. If it got out of control, however, other people would be endangered. How could this hopeless situation ever end?

Josh, she admitted, tried to coax her out of her gloom, but did not do so personally. Other people delivered his peace offerings. Margo dumped a cardboard box on her table one morning containing the make-up, shampoo, and skin lotions she had wanted weeks ago. The other day, a pair of elegant sandals appeared beside her bed. Yesterday, a fairy godparent brought a lovely dress and a blow-dryer and brushes. Still, the wounds did not close. One simple five-letter word would act like a soothing balm: *Sorry*! But it hadn't come.

This morning, Anna felt her mood change miraculously. As with a fresh south-west wind that raised the barometer, her mind cleared, uncluttered and hopeful. Just before waking, she dreamt her favourite recurring dream again: Sydney Harbour in streaming sunlight, with *Coomelong* gliding majestically through the waves under full canvas. She saw it as a good omen, which brought a new idea.

Helping Fernando could be a cover for her next escape. Every day she'd cut a little of the scrub away from the fence till the wire was exposed. After that, bolt cutters, which were now readily available to her, were just the thing to take for nightly workouts till little by little, she had a hole big enough to slip through. *Bingo!* The new plan made her laugh, and she broke into song.

Quietly at first, she sang a few bars from *Madama Butterfly*'s 'Humming Chorus', progressing to the melancholy 'Solveig's Song' from *Peer Gynt*. Unable to control her new emotions, she burst forth with 'Libiamo' from *La Traviata*. Her fortissimo threatened to lift the roof. 'Libiamo ne' lieti calici, che la bellezza infiora,' she repeated.

Baffled, Josh looked up from his files. Had someone turned his stereo on full bore? He left his office, following the sound.

'Sipho, who is singing?' he asked, looking into the bean-counting house as he passed, expecting to find a radio there.

Sipho shrugged. 'Nice voice,' he commented without looking up.

Josh bounded to the end of the passage to see who was in his quarters. As he turned left, the full volume hit him, but it wasn't coming from his door.

'Anna!' Although her room was closed, her voice carried as if she sang in a concert hall. He stopped to listen. It dawned on him that this was her way of conquering the torment she suffered at his hands, a cathartic experience. Now they could perhaps move on.

Her singing kindled feelings of happiness within him as well. He began a musical dialogue. Lifting his voice, he sang, 'Give me your hand, my sweetheart . . .'

Anna stopped. *Shame,* he thought. They rarely talked about music, and he had no idea that she, if he could judge her performance at all, had operatic training. *Another interesting facet of her personality,* he mused.

Did he hear a giggle? Her door opened a crack.

'And you will most certainly descend into hell one day, Joshua Mtolo.'

'Come out, Donna Anna, my little boardroom diva.'

He means b-o-r-e-d room diva, she thought. She came into the passage, introducing herself as Mimi. 'Mi chiamano Mimi,' she sang for a few more bars. 'Aren't you going to delight me with the catalogue aria?'

'No,' Josh laughed. 'I don't kiss and tell. But you sound great. Why haven't I heard you before? You should be on stage.'

'As a teenager, I had visions of being an opera singer. But my parents wanted a *real* job for me. Arts were fine for a hobby but not a profession. So my singing languished. What about you? All Zulus can sing. It's in your DNA. You're a cut above the rest, though.'

'I had a friend at Harvard. His name was Bertram Pratt-Jenkins. He was nuts about opera. He came with me to see some productions and encouraged me to sing. He was a good pianist as well and roped me in whenever he felt like accompanying someone. I learnt a lot from him. Unfortunately we lost touch after graduating.'

'Professor, can you please come?' The sister rounded the corner, beckoning, and Josh followed at a trot.

'Excuse me, Anna. I'll talk to you later.'

Don't bother, she thought but said nothing while vanishing back into her cell. She had not spoken one word to him for the last six weeks and chided herself for singing so loud, thereby attracting his attention.

He seemed intent on renewing friendly relations but had not apologized. His next step would employ humour, drawing her out by making her laugh. He had nearly succeeded just then with his light-hearted singing, catching her off guard when she wasn't expecting him. Or was she relieved to see him? Somehow she could never resist his courtly wit and charm when he chose to display it. Nor could she be dogmatic and inflexible enough to see only his bad characteristics. There was much in him that was good, making it all too easy to forget he was a formidable foe. The inevitable truth, she came to realize, was that she could—perhaps already had—drift into a tempestuous love affair.

By evening, the monotonous inactivity of the day dimmed the glow of her enthusiasm. There was nobody to talk to, and she was hungry.

Her thoughts were so absorbed with fence wire and freedom that she failed to hear footsteps behind her as she cut tomatoes and chives for a salad to eat for dinner. Margo's objections to her culinary experiments in the kitchen ceased when she promised to clean up afterwards.

Two strong arms wrapped themselves around her waist from behind, squeezing gently.

'That looks so tasty. Would you make some for me please if I ask nicely?'

She gasped in sheer surprise.

'Margo is a good cook, but I love a change once in a while.'

She turned around, a knife still in her hand.

'Do put that down!' Josh took it from her. 'I doubt you have sufficient surgical skill to wield that.'

'You're right! A meat cleaver wouldn't be sharp enough to penetrate your hard heart.' She continued with her salad.

'Hard heart? Not mine, surely.' He kissed the back of her neck. 'We shouldn't quarrel, my pet. You haven't talked to me in weeks since you cocooned yourself into voluntary exile. I've been thinking you might like a change from Margo's cooking too. How would you fancy coming to the Zebra with me? Sipho always raves about the place. I thought we should try it—tomorrow evening maybe. Agree?'

'Aren't you worried I might run away from you?'

'No, I'm too irresistible,' he replied without the laugh she expected.

In truth, she didn't find it amusing either. 'I could leave, you know. And there's absolutely nothing you can do to prevent it.'

'I am aware of that, but it's the only olive branch I can think of you might appreciate. Do with it what you will.'

Did that mean he was letting her go? It was too much to hope for. What was his stratagem now? Drive her along some lonely road, kill her, and throw her body into a ditch? He could just as easily end her life right here, couldn't he? Or was he so ashamed of beating the daylights out of her he was prepared to give her the choice of leaving or staying with him?

'Where do you want your salad?' she called after him when he turned to go.

'In my office please. I've got so much work piled up—there's no rest for the wicked.'

'In that case, you'll work till you're a hundred! Without a break!'

'Oh, my pet, what have I done to deserve your love?'

Sarcasm will get you none of it, she thought while filling his plate.

* * *

Josh ate his salad alone. Anna walked away, in no mood for further conversation. Whatever hope he had of winning her affection was ruined when he had lost his temper and assaulted her. Couldn't she see how much he regretted his action that day? How much longer would she punish him, depriving him of her company? Now would be a good time to take her out without being observed. The spies who watched the gate from the other side of the road had finally given up and departed. But inviting her to the Zebra could prove a flop. She had neither accepted nor declined the offer. With all likelihood she would leave him anyway. How could he win her heart? He'd failed miserably up till now. Whenever he thought her resistance had crumbled a little, he unwittingly said something silly to upset her again.

He yawned and stretched. Sitting thinking about the frustrating woman wasn't getting his work done. And it had to be finished because tomorrow he wanted the day off. Benny was meeting him in Vryheid in the morning. They planned to go to the IFP's electorate office and sign up for membership. After that, they'd lunch somewhere and catch up on all the news. The evening could hopefully see him at the Zebra with Anna. That would be a good end to a fine day if she didn't abscond.

Tired, he closed his eyes for a moment, rubbing them. As he did so, he saw Anna's green traffic-light eyes glowing in his mind. Emeralds! That was it! It is the perfect expression of remorse. Would she accept an emerald ring from him? Could such a gift entice her to stay? Most likely not. He could never afford the magnificent jewels Hank showered her with. She would only smile at his humble offerings, he knew, but he had to try. Eventually she must understand how he felt. It was only a matter of time.

What a softie he had become since her arrival. That had never been in his plan. He had intended to be firm with her, not unkind but determined not to be influenced by her allure. Now the wretched woman had him all but begging on his knees to be her lover. How the hell could he have let that happen? The USB had destroyed him. If she walked away from him tomorrow, he was annihilated.

* * *

Anna felt that burning kiss on the back of her neck throughout the night. She woke a number of times, alone, touching the empty space beside her.

Gliding back into dream-filled sleep in the early hours, she raised her head reluctantly just before nine, feeling hungry. Margo had made a futile trip to her room with a tray of food she couldn't get in to deliver. Anna was surprised she had slept through the racket Margo created when thus frustrated.

Speaking of racket, she thought, *what on earth is all that whining of machinery?* Sounds like cement mixers and joiners' saws. She parted the curtains but couldn't see anything.

She showered, dressed, and wandered to the kitchen for something to eat. Margo gave her a dagger look, but she took no notice, asking instead, 'What the hell is all that clanging out there today?'

'Something to do with the building,' Margo grunted. 'Jangles my nerves.'

Hearing Anna's voice, Josh came in for his morning coffee break.

'Professor, that din, it drive me insane,' Margo grizzled.

'What's happening out there?' Anna too questioned unhappily. 'It woke me up.'

'It's your own fault,' he laughed at her distracted face.

'Why?'

'It was your suggestion we make use of surplus space. Sipho has a dentist moving into the area behind Casualty. We're extending it to make room for a small pathology laboratory as well. We need plumbing, electrical fittings, and whatnot. So you have to grin and bear it, my pet. There'll be noise for about a week or two.'

He motioned for her to bring her drink into his office. 'Here's the plan.' He unrolled a drawing and spread it on his desk. It showed where light switches, power points, sinks, and the dentist's chair would be. As he rolled the sheet up again, he said, 'Go and have a look if you like.'

He finished his coffee. 'I have to be off now. I'm meeting with Benny in Vryheid. We're going to sign up for Inkatha membership. Sipho's decided to come too. I'm not certain when we'll be back—somewhere between three and four this afternoon, I guess. Tom will take care of things here.' He locked his office.

'Joshua, is that what you really want to do? Are you sure about this?'

'Sure about what?' He looked into her eyes, surprised to find a hint of concern there. Her voice was warmer than normally too, but traces of doubt rang in it.

She came closer to him. 'Remember our first dinner at Benny's when you told me about the extent of political violence in KwaZulu Natal?'

'Yes, Anna.' She wasn't worried about him . . . ? That was impossible.

'A man like you can't fail to attract attention. It won't take you long to rise to significance within the IFP. You may become a target.'

'Anna, my pet,'—he placed his hands on her shoulders—'I'm not a politician. I'm only a doctor. What can our good comrades do to me?'

'You are sure to be nominated as the IFP's spokesman for health and be drawn into the political quagmire with all eyes upon you.'

Josh laughed at her, hoping to banish the genuine fear he imagined he saw in her face. 'Sweetheart, I'm far too busy to get that deeply involved. I'll just be doing what I can and that's it.' He gave her a quick hug of comfort before turning his head, calling: 'Are you ready, Sipho?'

'Oh, and another thing,' he came back to her. 'Margo and Fernando are cleaning out Sandile's cinema. He won't need it anymore. We're turning it into a conference room, like you said. I think the furniture for that arrives today too.'

Goodie, Anna thought. *Maybe I won't be so bored today. Who knows what might happen?* But her heart was uneasy as she watched Josh swagger confidently to his car and drive away with Sipho.

She examined the spare room. Margo parked a floor polisher outside the door and busied herself with bucket and mop. Fernando brought a ladder. They gave Anna an unrelated stare to say she wasn't needed. Too bad, my dears, she thought. I'm joining in. She soon had window cleaning equipment in hand and took possession of the ladder. Fernando was about to protest but had to go and see to the furniture, which arrived at that moment. He stored it in the foyer near the useless telephone. Returning with a long, rectangular parcel, he cut the string and tape around it, unpacking new blinds. Requesting his ladder back, he set about hanging them before cleaning the light fittings.

Anna walked out to check the furniture. It wasn't grand but practical. There were ten items in all: a table, eight chairs, and a sideboard containing a drinks cabinet. She gave them a polish before Fernando and a volunteer brought them into the room.

'It still looks a bit empty,' she remarked to Fernando. He shrugged.

'Can't we put a vase of flowers on that table? Look at the bare wall. It's just crying out for a picture or some kind of ornament. We want glasses, crockery, and cutlery for the sideboard too so we don't have to take those items from the kitchen.'

This time, Margo nodded agreement. 'All my stuff, it mostly for the children,' she commented.

Anna gazed at the bare wall for a long time. Suddenly she remembered an advertisement in a local newspaper. A gallery called Flametree Art Lodge, only about ten kilometres from the clinic, offered paintings and pottery.

'Fernando, can we go to that Flametree Art Lodge place? We could look for some nice pieces there to make this room attractive.'

Fernando's face wrinkled with doubt. 'I don't know,' he said. 'Don't think I'm allowed to take you anywhere.'

'Oh, come on! Don't be a stuffed shirt. I want to see Josh's face when he comes back and looks in here. He'll be so surprised.'

'We can't buy anything. We got no money.' Fernando hoped to throw a wet blanket on her inspiration.

'I have,' she said, giving him a look, which silenced further argument.

'Well, come on. We'll have to go in the van. It's the only vehicle available right now,' he consented unhappily. Still, what could possibly go wrong? he argued with himself while Anna ran for her handbag. She was only a woman. Surely he could keep her under control.

Flametree Art Lodge turned out to be a cooperative studio shared by about a dozen people. Anna lost herself in their shop, looking at everything critically. For a little while she forgot her prison, revelling in a feeling of liberty and awe as if the whole world was brand-new. She had so much fun she forgot there was a time limit. The room should be finished before Josh and Sipho returned.

'We have to get back soon,' Fernando urged.

On her second round, evaluating the goods, she selected a mounted landscape photograph featuring the White Mfolozi River with a village and hills in the background. From the potters she bought a vase, its colouring blending with the blinds Fernando installed. She chose a traditional beer pot to go on the sideboard. The glass-blowers tempted her with delicate brandy balloons and whisky tumblers. Cups, saucers, and plates came from the china painters.

It took some time before she was satisfied. Following close at her heels, Fernando kept an uneasy eye on her and his wristwatch. She paid for her purchases with a cheque, and Fernando drove her back to the clinic, relieved. He hung the photograph in exactly the place she wanted. Margo filled the vase with flowers brought in from the garden and set it on the table. She washed the glasses till they sparkled and the china gleamed. The effort was worthwhile. The room looked good.

Josh and Sipho returned quite late. Sipho noticed the spare room was open and couldn't resist investigating. He whistled at what he saw.

'Hey, Josh, come and see this!' he called out.

'The room's ready, is it?' he queried as he approached.

'Is it ready! Just take a look!' Sipho grinned broadly. 'KwaZulu Medical has seen a touch of corporate sophistication.'

'By Jove!' Josh was astonished. He gave Sipho a quizzical sideways look. 'I know the furniture is paid for, but the other ornamental stuff, I wonder? Did anyone ask you for extra money? You didn't fork out for all that, I hope. You've already contributed way too much,' he commented while admiring the photograph.

'Don't know. Got no idea where that came from.' Sipho shrugged. 'It's arranged with cultivated taste. Now who could have done that?' He smirked.

Margo waddled towards them, carrying a full coffee pot and the new cups.

'Do you like it?' she asked, pouring out the coffee and passing them a cup. 'Fernando took Anna shopping, and they came back with all these lovely things.'

'That answers my question,' Josh sighed. He wasn't able to hold Anna captive much longer. This little act of defiance was her new tactic. She was trying the incremental approach to liberation. Short trips out, come back with gifts for which she paid with her bank card or cheque to leave a money trail, going further afield each time till one day she was gone.

He recalled his dinner booking at the Zebra. He still wasn't sure if she would come. And if she did, would she stay or disappear? Why hadn't she left Fernando for dead at the art gallery? Wouldn't that have been a good opportunity? She could have taken the van and driven off. Or was she saving that privilege just for him? Was it giving her satisfaction to stand him up in a public place? Negative thoughts pulled him back into the old trap of paranoia.

'You're back!' The longed-for silver-bell peal of laughter dispelled Josh's dark thoughts as Anna came to stand beside him.

'You've worked a miracle here,' Josh smiled. 'Thank you very much. It's exactly what this place needs—a lift, something bright and decorative.'

'Are we still going to the Zebra?' Anna asked with hope in her voice.

'Yes, if you want to come. I've booked for seven thirty.'

'I better get changed then.' She took off towards her room.

When she reappeared, she looked more like her old self. Her favourite cosmetics, the quintessential little black dress that had appeared out of nowhere the other day, and the new sandals all helped to rejuvenate her. Josh too looked amazing in good clothes. She couldn't hide her admiration.

* * *

The lights were dimmed at the Zebra. New Orleans jazz played at low volume. Diners talked quietly as Mr Bollard showed Josh and Anna to their table. He had no idea who they were but disguised his curiosity politely. New patrons were always welcome.

'I think my eyes are crossing,' she said as they sat down. 'Sipho sure is right about everything being black-and-white-striped. It's like shimmering heat on tarmac. It confuses me.'

'I wonder if the food is served on black and white striped plates?' Josh pondered with a chuckle.

Both felt the tenseness about them, as if this evening represented a turning point in their relationship, although neither knew in which direction fate would rotate them. The reading of menus and wine lists provided a welcome topic for conversation while choices were made.

Anna glanced about for the fire escape or any other exits. Josh watched her face and noticed the direction her eyes had taken. They had become quite dark again. He had since learnt it meant Anna's brain was working overtime, seeking to derive the best possible advantage for herself from any given situation. She was thinking of leaving, he felt certain. His appetite plummeted. But by the time dessert was served and coffee and brandy arrived, she was still there, talking cheerfully. The traffic lights were switched back on, and Josh relaxed.

'I'm glad you brought me here,' she said. 'It's so different from any other place I've seen.'

'I'm pleased you came, my pet. I am in debt to you for all your help around the clinic and more than that, I owe you the biggest apology.'

He took her hands in his. 'Anna, can you ever forgive . . . ?' He couldn't finish the sentence. There was too much he sought pardon for to compile an inventory. He slipped the emerald ring on her right hand.

'This black witch doctor loves you, Anna.'

A rare blush coloured her face, and she looked down at the tablecloth.

'You know I didn't mean that,' she said, gathering courage to lift her head again.

'Perhaps not,' he looked at her, pressing her hands between his. 'I wasn't at all sure when you said it,' he replied with a voice echoing mischief and a gleam in his eyes. 'It sounded bad. You will have to be very penitential in future, otherwise I will always have doubts.'

Her eyes flashed. She gave him a Mona Lisa smile. 'I will,' she whispered, blowing him a kiss across the table.

'You will be called to repent again and again and again . . .' he smiled, 'till the message sinks in. I can be pretty thick at times.'

Her silver-bell laugh escaped again. Josh's spirit soared. People at other tables turned to look.

Among the heads that swivelled to stare was one topped with a tall black-and-white-striped chef's hat. Freddie Bonga caught sight of the couple as a waiter took food to other guests.

'Thank you for the emerald, Josh. It's very beautiful. I don't have any emeralds.'

'That's surprising given the colour of your eyes.'

'My eyes?'

'Yes, they're fascinating to watch. I can just about tell your mood by their colour. When they're opaque and dark I have to be careful because you're scheming. When they glow brightly like traffic lights, all is well.' He chuckled as another thought struck him. 'In ancient times emeralds were worn as an aphrodisiac.'

'Aphrodisiac . . . ? You're joking!' Uncontrolled mirth surfaced in her voice. 'And traffic lights?' She couldn't stop laughing. 'I wonder if that's a compliment?'

'Rest assured it is,' he nodded earnestly. 'Not the attributed aphrodisiac, though. I'm 200 per cent certain you don't need that.'

Freddie Bonga took a second look, then walked to his locker and pulled the photocopy of Anna's picture out of his jacket pocket.

'It's her!' he muttered. *That dude she's with is Cindy Khumalo's fiancé.* She had introduced him the day he had first taken his Yamaha for a run. Wary of going straight to the police because of his bike gang membership in the past, Freddie contemplated his next step. First thing in the morning, he would phone Nkosinathi and Cindy

Khumalo. If they came to the police with him, maybe everything would work out right.

* * *

With that gesture that had infuriated Cindy so much, Josh left the Zebra, his hand resting on Anna's shoulder.

'What a lovely night.' Anna looked up at the stars. 'Tonight, tonight, the world is full of light,' she sang softly as they walked to the car. Josh held her closer and joined in.

'Tonight, tonight, it all began tonight.' They reached his Corolla.

'No, it didn't,' he said as he kissed her, opening the passenger door. 'It all began at a very complex and unromantic shareholders' meeting.'

'The world is full of light,' Anna sang on.

'I've got that tape somewhere.' He searched the glove box till he found it.

They returned to the clinic well after midnight and walked quietly to Josh's room. He closed the door.

'Tonight, tonight . . . there's only you tonight.'

* * *

Hank lived in a world of his own with mood swings ranging from fury at his failure to get his wife back to feelings of alienation from her. Anna's absence wore him down. He didn't mind admitting it. Franz and Maurice found the change in him disturbing. He spent less and less time in the office. For the last three days, he hadn't come in at all. Even the domestic staff were filled with foreboding. Barbara Mkhize secretly saw Dr Elbenstein, asking what they could do for Hank.

Dr Elbenstein arranged for a nurse to stay in the house in case the medical emergency he had foreseen struck sooner rather than later. Hank dismissed her.

'What do I want her for?' he complained. 'I have a whole house full of people already. Franz and Maurice are here most evenings. Anna's father is staying indefinitely. The domestics fuss over me like nothing else. Clients come to visit, offering help. I can't get away from all their well-meant attention.'

Everything changed, though, with William Rosenberg's arrival.

'Man, do I have news for you! Stop feeling sorry for yourself, old boy. Now listen to me.'

The men crowded around him as he talked about visiting Indira.

'And who's Indira? Do we know her?' Franz teased with a cheeky wink.

'She's his latest paramour. What else would you expect? You should have seen the fantastic gold watch she gave him for his birthday,' Maurice chimed in.

'Which is now broken, thanks to the EEM thugs. That brings me to my point. The EEM and KwaZulu Medical is one and the same crowd.'

Hank looked up, his lethargy disappearing visibly. 'You know, I've been thinking that myself. What does your Indira do there?'

'She's the surgeon. She showed me around the place, and that's when it all came together in my mind and the connection clicked. That's where those EEM guys took me. I even recognized the voice of the bloke who locked me up. He looks to be the administrator there.'

'Sipho Gwala?' Hank asked, bursting with eagerness to have his own suspicions confirmed.

'Don't know his name. Although I didn't see her, it's my bet Anna is there too.'

'Doesn't Indira know?'

'She hasn't worked there for long. She's part-time only and doesn't live on the premises.'

'Well, dammit, that's the best lead we've heard so far.' Maurice jumped from his chair. 'What are we waiting for? Let's go and get Anna!'

'Bloody oath, yes!' Franz readied himself for action. 'Even if we don't find her, there's no harm in looking.'

'If you're right and we locate Anna, I'll never be able to thank you enough, William.'

'Don't mention it, Hank, old boy. Let's make a plan. The place isn't easy to get into and even harder to get out of, by the way. My car was rather conspicuous when I called on Indira. Business suits draw unwelcome attention too. That little bone sack of an administrator recognized me. If I show up there again, we'll never get in. We'll all have to go together, wearing our oldest clothes and driving the crappiest van we can get hold of. One of us will have an arm in a sling, pretending to be injured and wishing to see a doctor. Once we're in, we disperse and search the place through and through. I can't imagine we'll meet with much resistance, but we will each carry a revolver, just in case.'

'That sounds like a good day's work,' Franz reflected. 'Maurice, you book us on a flight to Durban. I'll call Gerhard to meet us at the airport with some shitty chitty bang-bang he can pick up from somewhere, and after that, we'll play it by ear. What do you reckon, Hank?'

'Count me in!' Hank could no longer sit still either. 'Just let me get my hands on Mtolo. I'll teach that bastard to steal my wife.'

* * *

'Wake up, my pet.' A gentle kiss and soft, seductively spoken words roused Anna. A wave of urgent desire engulfed her before she even opened her eyes. She moaned as heat spread through her body.

'Sakubona isoka,' she whispered back. 'Good morning, sweetheart.'

Josh held her in his arms, indicating it was going to be a very good morning indeed. Could she walk away from this man with whom she experienced the joys of heaven? He thrilled her, injecting life into her till she both laughed and sobbed in ecstasy. Her body reacted independently of her mind, each tremor of response urging Josh to new heights too, ending in a shattering volcanic eruption.

She wished the loving would never end, but common sense, as clear as the new morning, demanded she face the facts. She couldn't stay. She was Hank's wife, not Josh's. Life with Hank was her destiny, not KwaZulu Medical. She couldn't have both. With guilty delight, she banished the thought, took two imaginary painkillers to deaden the ache of being torn between two men, and welcomed the new day.

'Come out to dance,' Josh invited when they finally rose from the bed.

'But it's raining now,' she protested, peeping through the curtains.

'So what? It's no different to having a shower.'

'I've heard of singing in the rain, but dancing?' She stepped back from the widow as Fernando came into sight, pushing a wheelbarrow loaded with fencing wire and tools. *Oh, no*, she thought.

'Song and dance go together, my pet. Come on.'

She hurried, naked, to her room and flung the bathrobe around her while Josh looked for his boxers. By the time they reached the lawn behind the tool shed, the rain had stopped and the grass glistened in sunshine.

Josh allowed only twenty minutes for dancing. Usually by about seven in the morning he was already busy checking the wards. Today it was nearly eight, and the time had to be made up somewhere along the line.

Before going back in, he insisted on a walk around the perimeter of the garden to cool off and wind down from the energetic exercise. Reaching the spot where Fernando was repairing the fence, he stopped and pointed.

Turning to Anna, he said, 'Isn't it odd? You know, we sometimes see baboons jump over the fence to get in. Now they have become inventive. They appear to be using bolt cutters to make a hole. I suppose they're getting lazy. Why jump when you can cut a hole at ground level?' He looked sternly at her. 'I've been thinking maybe it wasn't baboons but kangaroos.'

'There are no kangaroos here,' she replied with an uneasy laugh.

'I'm looking at one.' He shook his head with a sad smile. 'I was wondering about your sudden interest in gardening. Anna,' he sighed, 'why do you do it?'

'We've been through all this before, Josh,' she replied with uncharacteristic fearfulness. 'Please, let's not spoil what we shared lately.'

'I don't understand you. You could have left me at the Zebra. Why the hole in the fence?'

'I started cutting it last week, before you invited me out. I'm still here, so can we forget it, please.'

He knew she was right. One more word from him on that topic could destroy their ceasefire. He laid his hand on her shoulder, turning her away from the fence. 'I better go and do some work now.'

Sipho too was already pottering around his office when they passed.

'You're up early,' Josh greeted him.

'Yes, couldn't sleep much.'

'Why? Feeling crook?'

'No, no more than usual.' Sipho grinned. 'I just can't afford midnightly *West Side Story* gala concerts, no matter how melodious the singing.'

'Oh, hell! We apologize profusely,' Josh replied, embarrassed.

'It won't happen again,' Anna promised.

They walked to their respective rooms to shower and ready themselves for their daily tasks. In Anna's case, that was nothing. She determined to start helping Sipho again.

Margo slammed her breakfast tray down as usual. The quality of her meals had been upgraded substantially of late, a fact that irked Margo and she showed it, her attitude becoming more pugnacious than ever.

The dancing made Anna so hungry she ate the toast and drank coffee, the good Kenyan brew, before showering. While scanning the *Natal Witness* headlines, she smiled, surprised at her good temperament. For a moment it had been touch-and-go when Josh had talked about the fence. She had expected renewed strife, but he had held to his promise not to become angry. Had she won him over? Could she begin new negotiations about the ransom and then get home? Did he understand at last that if he let her go without rancour they could be friends, whereas if he remained acrimonious, all hope of generosity and tenderness in future was wrecked?

It was a relief not to be fighting with him—quite the opposite, in fact, Anna thought. She was amazed how agreeably they functioned when they put their mistrust aside. Maybe that was the key to it. She had not walked out on him, giving him a chance to feel less culpable, as if they had buried the hatchet, like making up after a tiff.

Burying that hatchet was a misconception, unfortunately. She still wasn't home and feared the weapon would be exhumed soon enough. She had to get back to Hank. Would Josh accept her decision to walk away, saying 'Sala kahle, goodbye, I'm going now'? Not likely. Should she even try to return home? Hank would never want her after such a long absence during which she had willingly given herself to another man. It wasn't the first time her thoughts ran along those lines, reaching a dead end each time.

She turned on the shower. By now she was accustomed to its lack of water pressure. It didn't stop her from singing while washing her hair. Without giving much thought to what she sang, she began with *Samson and Delilah*, that most seductive of arias which lured Samson to his demise. If there was a subconscious prompting in her choice, she hadn't noticed. She continued with scattered bars from Bizet's *Carmen* while rinsing the conditioner out, then resumed with *Samson and Delilah*. Examining her body critically in the wardrobe mirror, she gave a disappointed sigh at the lack of choice of clothing. She hadn't yet worn that calf-length denim skirt. 'Might be worth a try after all,' she contemplated and continued singing. To her surprise, the skirt was a good fit, making her look and feel fresh.

* * *

In the tokoloshe guardhouse, a sizeable parcel addressed to Josh awaited collection. He picked it up, whistling cheerfully as he carried it out.

'What's that? Where are you taking it?' Sipho's curiosity stirred. Josh appeared to have regained his better humour over the last week, and although he could guess the cause, Sipho wanted to know for certain if Anna was behind it. If those two had kissed and made up, as all signs indicated, Anna might come to help him again.

'It's a stereo.'

'You've already got one.'

'This one's for Anna. I had no idea how much she loves music.' He headed for his quarters, wondering what tapes and CDs he had that might please her.

'Not too much choice here,' he admitted. And then he found it. He hadn't played it for ages. An old tape on which he had recorded Bertram Pratt-Jenkins playing Liszt, *Hungarian Rhapsodies* numbers 1 to 3, and the *Mephisto Waltz* number 1.

Heaving the box on his shoulder, he was about to present it to her when he heard her warm, silky mezzo voice. It wrapped every part of his body in a shawl of gossamer, teasingly soft yet firm as steel.

He groaned quietly. 'Just when I thought the USB couldn't possibly get any worse.'

He stood listening to her Delilah, convinced no opera star could give it more expression. He wanted her to sing, sing while he undressed her, sing while he ran his hands over her body, sing as she trembled with anticipation of his love. He turned away, shaking with longing. If he entered her room now, he wouldn't come out, and the backlog of work would become unmanageable.

Unaware of the emotional blizzard outside her door, Anna sang on, creating her own mental hurricane. Hank loved her singing, especially when she accompanied herself on the piano. *Wouldn't it be nice to play music again?* she thought wistfully. Although hers was a far cry from a professional act, Hank and his friends assured her it was a treat to hear. She missed her baby grand, which stood in a corner of the large entrance foyer because the acoustics were perfect there. When they hosted parties, the foyer became a mini concert hall where she offered entertainment. Some of their friends played instruments too, bringing them along to perform chamber music concerts.

Singing projected images of home before her eyes. She missed everything about her Johannesburg life. She worried about Hank. His disappointment in her didn't bear thinking about and wouldn't improve his well-being. Her conscience protested sharply when she probed her soul, asking if she could visualize herself in bed with Hank again. Scruples tethered her heart. There was a time when she knew nobody could hold a candle to Hank. Of course, she still felt that way, except . . .

Except what? her mirror image demanded. *Come on, say it,* it goaded. *Be frank. It's only you and me who will hear. Who do you prefer?*

'I don't know.' She slapped her mirror image, leaving traces of hand cream on the glass. 'I love them both for their individual qualities.' She gave her mirror an evil eye. 'If you must know, sex with Hank is like a Strauss waltz. It's joyous, exuberant, romantic—at least it was before the haemochromatosis affected his libido. That's not his fault. He's still the wonderful man I married.' The mirror was subjected to another whack so fierce it might have cracked.

'Josh is a different person. His lovemaking is like a landscape. Harsh at times, like all of nature, but also beautiful, stirring, and compelling. I know well how to appreciate both, so sue me.' She poked her tongue at her mirror image. 'Condemn me to hell for all I care.'

She sat down at the kitchen table to escape her reflection, although she could still see it out of the corner of her eye, which threatened to moisten with a tear. She had come to the dead end again. The ethical battles she fought almost daily sapped her strength. They should be totally unnecessary if she let her principles prevail. She told Hank long ago marriage was forever, and so it must be. She wouldn't break her word. However, while she was here . . . *You naughty, miserable devil,* the mirror accused again. *You're weak, weak, weak!*

'I'm human,' she snarled back at it. 'Do you hear? Human—human and fallible!'

Convinced she was going crazy, she left the room to look for Sipho. His figure work settled the mind. It provided law and order in her brain.

She found the stereo outside her door with a note attached in Josh's writing. 'Have fun, my pet.' Delighted, she took it inside, thinking they should unpack it together after dinner.

* * *

Captain Broadbent scratched his ears thoughtfully—first the left, then the right. After many months of following confusing leads, Anna De Bruyn had been discovered, safe and sound, dining in a restaurant. By heck! He still had her on the missing persons list and feared the puzzle surrounding her disappearance may never be solved.

His next pressing question was, why was she in Joshua Mtolo's company? That chap ran KwaZulu Medical and was, according to Rosenberg's allegation, the founding father of the EEM. The two had not met till Anna De Bruyn had introduced them at their anniversary ball. How could Rosenberg be so sure when he had never seen the guy before?

Question 2: Did Mtolo abduct De Bruyn, or was he the 'friend' she had taken off with? The hunch that the whole episode was nothing more than a domestic matter between a married couple taking each other for granted was reinforced in his mind due to lack of information pointing to the contrary. Of course, Hank De Bruyn said his wife would never leave. That reaction was to be expected. He was, after all, the man tipped to be the next Stock Exchange Council president and had high standards to uphold. Anyway, whether Hank spun the financial world on its axis or not, the police had insufficient manpower to investigate without good information to justify the outlay of resources.

Question 3: Was the hint he had been given yesterday correct? Cindy Khumalo was Mtolo's betrothed in the past. Did she harbour resentment which coloured her story? Was she perhaps intent on causing trouble for Mtolo? Another silly domestic squabble very likely.

As she explained, her former students had combined their efforts to help find Anna De Bruyn, and young Freddie Bonga, an apprentice cook, had recognized De Bruyn from a press photo. Unlike Rosenberg, Bonga had met Mtolo earlier. Khumalo had introduced them while still engaged to Mtolo.

Bonga—that name rang a bell, something to do with bike-gang crime. *Must look into that*, Broadbent thought. Was the young bloke a reliable witness? Either way, he would have to make a statement at the Vryheid police station.

Question 4: Did Mtolo abduct the other executives, or anyone at all? Was he, in fact, the recipient of the ransom payments their companies made? If so, where was the money?

Nuisance factor A: The funds in the Swiss account, where did they come from? The bank clamped up, revealing only under Interpol pressure that it belonged to nominees—the Economic Equity Movement, presumably. The address they gave grudgingly was a vacant block in Piet Retief, close to the Swaziland border. Brilliant!

Nuisance factor B: The KwaZulu Police Service—could he rely on their cooperation?

The questions multiplied, depriving the answers of breathing space. Perhaps it was time Mtolo was hauled in to explain a few.

* * *

'Anna, come and have dinner with me,' Josh called in the passage.

'No, you eat with me. We have a parcel to unpack.' She opened her door, beckoning.

He walked to her room. 'Haven't you done that yet? I thought you would have been playing music all day.'

'I've helped Sipho all day. Where have you been?'

'Preventing prospective young medics from fainting at autopsies.'

'Ugh.' She wrinkled her nose.

'They were only looking at brains. It's nothing to be squeamish about.'

While looking through the CDs and tapes Josh had left with the stereo in the morning, she discovered the Pratt-Jenkins tape. 'Oh, this is your friend playing Liszt, of all things. *Hungarian Rhapsodies*—gee, he must be good! I struggled with those no end. I still can't get them right.'

'What, do you play too?' He looked at her, astounded. 'Is there anything you can't do, woman?'

'I can't fly a plane,' she laughed, 'and I can't heal people.'

'I'm not sure about that. Sipho reckons you did a good job transforming me. He tells me I'm not nearly as grumpy as I used to be.'

They set about opening the stereo box.

'Got scissors?' He walked to her bed, lifting the mattress. 'Or a screwdriver?'

'That's not funny, Josh.' She gave him a nasty look but laughed, clawing his shirt playfully.

'By the way, I still have something which belongs to you.'

'Yeah, I know. My key card.'

'No! It's in the drawer.' She pointed to the bedside table. Josh opened it with a strong pull because it was stuck. Zavier fell over.

Curled like a snake, his belt lay in the left corner. He recoiled, unable to touch it. A Zulu swear word fell from his lips. He closed the drawer quickly, trying to hide his momentary weakness from Anna.

'I'll get the scissors,' he said. 'You choose some music.'

He returned with scissors and a box of chocolates as well.

'I nearly forgot these,' he confessed, handing them to her. 'With all the excitement over the conference room, it slipped my mind. Sipho did a great deal of shopping in Vryheid, and I forgot we bought these.'

'Oh, thank you.' She smiled. 'That's marvellous to share.'

He operated patiently on the packing tape around the box. 'You know,' he said while snipping, 'it's been great holding a staff meeting in the conference room. You should have been there. Why didn't you come?'

'I'm not staff. What do I know about running a hospital?'

'You're a money person like Sipho.'

'Sipho's specific designation is hospital finance director. Here he is administrator as well. He has special knowledge.'

'You should have seen how everyone relaxed and talked more freely. When they're all cramped into my office, squatting or perched on the edge of my desk, they're only thinking of getting out again as quickly as possible.' He grinned at her. 'I'll send you a gilt-edged invitation to our next meeting. How's that?'

The stereo was soon freed from its cardboard and foam restraints, plugged in the power point, and playing splendidly.

Margo heard the music and laughter from Anna's room and took the evening meal straight in without asking questions.

'Oh, that smells just wonderful,' Josh praised. 'It calls for a drop of wine. Stocking up on drinks was another of yesterday's achievements. What shall we have with this beef? I'll get a couple of reds, and you can pick.'

Anna quickly changed into the captivating animal-print nightie, which she could easily have worn as an evening gown—it looked so graceful on her. She ran a brush through her hair, altering her coiffure from the two-comb version to a loose French roll, with wispy strands of hair softening her high forehead and cheekbones. Josh preferred this, claiming it looked less corporate and severe.

He returned bearing bottles and glasses. Stopping in the open doorway, his eyes feasted on her from head to toe. 'Bewitching,' he murmured. He set everything on the table and closed the door.

'We don't want to disturb Sipho again.'

Anna perused the labels on the bottles.

'Which one first?' he asked, brandishing a corkscrew.

'That one.' She held a bottle out to him. He uncorked it, poured, and they clinked their glasses, each with an arm around the other.

It was an expansive meal despite the sparseness of its ingredients and the simplicity of the setting. She may now have a stereo, but her room was still little more than a cell.

They ate slowly, making each bite count, letting the music penetrate their consciousness and the sexual tension mount.

Anna rose to take the dishes away when they finished, but Josh stopped her.

'Come, my sex slave,' he beckoned, giving her a look that ignited her instantly. She melted in his arms, his nearness making her tremble as he slipped the nightie's straps off her shoulders.

Aroused, he played with her body. Only a short time ago, she would have reacted angrily to the 'sex slave' comment. Now she didn't care. She scarcely heard him.

'Oh, Joshua, please, I need you.' Her voice was half whisper, half sob.

'Delightfully wild woman.' He picked her up, carrying her to bed. Who was whose slave was debatable, he thought. She had him eating out of her hand. There was nothing he wouldn't do for her.

Another sobbed plea for his attention told him she was a living inferno. He was no fireman to extinguish it. He plunged in, happily dying in the heat.

As they lay blissfully in each other's arms, he wondered briefly what the right term for their relationship was if she wasn't his sex slave. Ruefully, he remembered it was the role he had envisaged for her initially, but something different had happened. What were they? She wasn't his wife, although he wished it were so. Theirs wasn't a business partnership either. Heaven forbid! He never needed to pay for sex. But their interaction had gone way beyond normal friendship. They were lovers and something more, deeper—soul mates? Kindred spirits? No, more than that. They had come to see each other not with eyes but with their hearts. *We each gained an understanding of the other's world*, he thought. And the process was still a work in progress. It could only lead to a firmer, more binding union, he hoped.

'You're my sweet little pet,' he whispered while her body shuddered with the aftermath of their climax. Once she had taunted him mischievously about pets that bit and scratched. *She's used to the nickname now*, he thought, smiling. *I succeeded in taming the little hellcat, and I love her, claws and all.*

* * *

The stockbrokers' equivalent of an SAS contingent assembled in the entrance of the De Bruyn mansion, waiting for a taxi to the airport. Their luggage was already stacked on the portico. Hank, Franz, Maurice, William, and Albert Cumberland, Anna's father, were all kitted out in frayed jeans, old pullovers, and windcheaters.

Like new recruits, they talked about the battle ahead with eager anticipation.

'I hope Gerhard has managed to get an old van for us,' Franz remarked.

'He never called back to report difficulties. He'll be there,' Hank assured him.

'Can't wait to see Indira.' William smiled. 'I want her out of KwaZulu Medical too,' he said.

'We can take her with us if she wants to come,' Maurice promised.

Hank looked happy. He thought they were like gallant knights of old, going to rescue damsels in distress. The phone rang in his study. 'What now?' he muttered as he went to answer it.

'You'll never believe this!' he exclaimed when he returned. 'That was Nkosinathi on the phone. His friend saw Anna and Mtolo having dinner in the restaurant in which he works as apprentice cook. It's called the Zebra. They phoned Cindy Khumalo, and she contacted the police.' He rubbed his hands together, laughing. 'Looks like we might have law enforcement help when we get there.'

'Not only will we take Anna home, but we'll also make a citizen's arrest and transport Mtolo to the police. I can see us having shiploads of fun,' Franz chortled.

'Not before I've dealt with him, please,' Hank reminded him while the taxi rolled around the circular driveway. 'Nobody is depriving me of my satisfaction. I want my pound of flesh out of the bastard with the blood still in it.'

* * *

Chapter 11

The Reckoning

Anna settled into a new routine. Early mornings of love with Josh, dancing on the grass, showering, breakfast, and helping Sipho began to resemble an ordered life. Lunch she usually ate alone, after which she sat at the computer to tackle Josh's teaching modules and other correspondence. She had the luxury of background music now to help her concentrate. When Josh finished his last round of the wards for the day, he joined her. After dinner, they discussed issues concerning the hospital or matters like his offering help to the IFP, organizing first-aid stations at their rallies. After a cup of coffee, he returned to his office, attending to paperwork. Anna began editing his children's stories, sorting them into book format.

Everything was going too smoothly, she feared. Josh presented himself from his most thoughtful and generous angle, seeing to her comfort, bringing little gifts, and keeping her company at night.

'This place has drawn me into itself like a bog,' she sighed. She felt as much part of the furniture here as at De Bruyn's, except that she was free there—coming and going unhindered, able to make decisions on what affected her, the household, and the staff, free to be herself.

The clinic's restrictions, dictated by Josh and his fear of losing her, were suffocating and intolerable. It guaranteed more attempts to escape, resulting in renewed unpleasantness. Josh couldn't accept the fact that she needed to be her own person. She wasn't his property. He couldn't own her, even if she chose to live with him voluntarily. Not even Hank owned her.

She wondered, not for the first time, *Why didn't I break free when the possibility presented itself?* Fernando could not have stopped her, and Josh had handed her the chance on a silver platter. Was it that despite her iron will not to become a victim she was precisely that? It wasn't unusual for abducted persons to identify with the wrongdoers eventually. Or was she too soft-hearted to inflict the bitterness of parting on him? On herself? Were subconscious ties of reciprocal sympathy and tenderness holding her back? Josh appeared to have learnt that kindness and consideration were more effective bonding materials than his previous preaching and punitive measures.

Was it possible her reluctance to return home stemmed from not knowing what awaited her? What would Hank say? How much should she tell him about the time spent here? Could he still trust her when she did? Would they restore their old harmony or be like strangers? These were uncomfortable questions without answers.

Waking up early and lying in bed thinking about affairs she preferred not to dredge from the back of her mind was torture.

Carefully so as not to wake Josh, she reached for her watch. Quarter past five, nearly time for him to get up anyway.

Oh, crap, she thought, *what about breakfast?* Josh said Margo and Fernando had two days off. Who was cooking? She rose quietly to see if Felicity was preparing food for the children. Finding the kitchen empty, she began arranging trays for Josh and herself.

Sipho—what did he eat in the morning? She should have asked Josh about Sipho's diet. Did any of the children need special nourishment? Wasn't there a notebook somewhere with a record of who was fed what? She searched the drawers, hoping to find instruction sheets. The sister appeared with a friendly 'good morning'.

'Looks like I'm chief cook and bottle washer today.' Anna smiled.

'Oh no, Felicity should be here any minute.'

'Well, I'll make a start getting something ready for the professor and myself. If Felicity hasn't arrived by then, I'll take over. Do the kids need special meals?'

'No, they all eat the same.'

'What about Mr Gwala?'

The sister took a folder of laminated sheets from a shelf and checked through it.

'Here we are.' She passed it to Anna. 'Just a cup of tea to take his tablets for now. He'll have a bit of fruit later.'

The tea urn was switched to low. Anna cranked it up to make coffee for the sister. Fried eggs on toast and grilled tomato might be good for Josh and herself, together with a little fruit salad and yogurt. She felt hungry just looking at the sizzling pan. An appetizing aroma wafted around the kitchen.

Felicity was still missing by the time she had Josh's tray ready.

'What have you been up to?' he asked when she appeared with breakfast. 'You don't have to do that! Felicity should be here.'

'Something has held her up, I think. I'll cook if she doesn't come. I just have to know if anyone needs special diets.'

She headed off to fetch her own tray, by which time a breathless Felicity dashed through the door.

'I'm sorry,' she gasped. 'My car wouldn't start.'

'Let me know if you want help,' Anna offered, taking her tray.

'Thanks a lot,' she said, already clattering with pots and pans. 'I hate getting behind. It won't do. Mum would be cross if she knew.'

Anna set her own provisions on the table. 'I'm surprised we have any unbroken trays left the way Margo bashes them about,' she commented to Josh.

He laughed. 'What a wonderful change it is to have breakfast brought by a beautiful smiling woman. The only thing missing to make the morning perfect is a kiss. Will you oblige, my pet?'

'No, I'm too hungry,' Anna pouted.

'Please, sweetheart, just one.' He propped himself against a pillow, holding his arms out to her.

'All right, just one.' She laughed when he pulled her on top of him, and one kiss became four or more.

'Sleeping with you is a bad idea,' he lamented while recovering his breakfast from the bedside table where Zavier had been pushed aside. He looked at Anna's watch. 'I don't get up early enough anymore. I have five minutes to eat.'

'Hope eggs on toast is what you want. I don't know how to feed people here.'

'It's great, Anna, thanks. I told you I appreciate variety. But you don't have to do this. It's not your job. You're not a domestic helper.'

'So?'

'I'm thinking that's why I like the feel of your hands on me so much,' he explained, his eyes leaving her in no doubt about his meaning. 'They're so gentle and smooth. Why ruin them with kitchen work?'

'Oh dear,' she giggled. 'You have no idea what work these hands have done. You still have a totally wrong impression of me. I may come from Rose Bay, one of the more salubrious parts of Sydney and be married to a finance guru but it doesn't make me a princess.

The foundation of my psyche is still to jump in and help where assistance is needed. I've been here so long now, but you still don't really know me.'

Josh looked at her thinking, *She accuses me of preaching. What have I just listened to?* However, he smiled provocatively, saying, 'No man knows a woman fully. They're too mysterious a species.'

'In my experience, few men try hard enough,' she retorted.

'That's not fair!'

Anna smiled at his vacant expression. 'But I am trying,' his eyes seemed to say.

'Eat your breakfast, and then it's time for you to start work, young man.' She used her uncompromising voice, accompanied by a no-nonsense look.

'Hell,' he grumbled, 'you sound like the formidable, old matrons when I was an intern just out of uni.'

'Oh, I think I may have an advantage over them, wouldn't you agree?' Loosening her bathrobe a fraction, she posed coquettishly, showing a perfectly shaped thigh and breast.

'You're seduction personified. Fancy arousing a man so early in the day!' He shook his head in mock rebuke.

'Just eat.'

'I will, I will. I could devour you for breakfast, lunch, and dinner and still be starving.'

* * *

Anna helped Felicity till lunchtime. Once the kitchen was cleaned and preparations for dinner made, Felicity took time out to get her unreliable car to a garage. She gave Anna a list of guidelines.

'Just in case I'm not back in time, would you start dinner for me, please?'

'Sure,' Anna agreed. 'No need to rush back. I'll manage.'

She ate a late lunch and, ensconced in her room, busied herself with Josh's material. A knock on her door made her jump. It opened slowly.

'Traitor!' The tokoloshe pulled an angry face.

'Sipho, you startled me. Come in.'

'What's the big idea of spending so much time with Felicity?' he asked with indignation, pretending to feel jilted.

'She was late this morning because her car broke down.'

'That's no reason for you to help her instead of me.'

'Yes, it is. You want your meals, don't you?'

'Yeah, but . . .'

'No *yeah buts*, Sipho. I was already up cooking breakfast while you were still asleep. I might have time for you after dinner, though.'

'Okay, I forgive you,' he grinned and vanished in tokoloshe fashion.

Anna turned the stereo on. Josh had given her a CD of James Galway playing Bach just before lunch, and she couldn't wait any longer to hear it.

By ten to three, her eyes needed rest. It was time for coffee and chocolate biscuits, which she was about to fetch, when a cacophony of voices sounded from the foyer.

'What the devil?' She frowned, listening. Her heart missed a beat. She turned the stereo down to hear better. Were those voices familiar? No, couldn't be. Sipho must be having a dispute with the builders. Forgetting about coffee, she raised the music volume again and concentrated on work.

* * *

'Slow down a bit, Maurice. We're nearly there.'

Acting as navigator, William sat in the back of the rusty, scratched, pale blue van, hoping to escape detection. He wasn't easy to recognize with a baseball cap, washed-out denim jacket, and black corduroy pants.

In the front passenger seat, Albert Cumberland had his arm in a sling and a moth-eaten brown cardigan draped over it.

Hank, Franz, and Gerhard sat in the middle. The three looked like aged hippies in open-necked shirts, which hung creased and untidy over worn-out jeans. Windcheaters tied around their waist by the sleeves covered their guns.

'Turn your left indicator on now and follow that ambulance. The bone sack will open the gate for it, and we'll slip in right behind.'

'So what do we do once we're in there?' Hank queried.

'The ambulance will turn right, but we will head straight for the main entrance. I will stay in the van, ducked down, out of sight at first. All of you go in and distract the bone sack. Ask him any questions you like. I suggest you turn left when you pass his enquiries window. Look for a door to the right near the kitchen with steps going down into a cellar. Meanwhile, I'll check the outpatient area and persuade Indira to come with us. I'm not quite sure what lies to the right of the public phone, but it's worth exploring. Indira never showed me that area. Don't think she knows much about it. Also, look for the back door, which opens onto a courtyard. It provides access to the new buildings.'

'The place is rather outstretched and rambling. It might take more time than we thought to search it.' Hank craned his neck as the gate came into view.

'Can't see any police cars here yet. Wonder what's keeping them?' Franz remarked, looking ahead.

'Would Broadbent have much authority with the KwaZulu Police?' Gerhard wasn't surprised by their absence.

As William predicted, the ambulance turned right, and Maurice charged ahead towards the steps, bringing the van to a halt outside Sipho's window.

'I think one of us should stay in the van to be prepared for a quick getaway.' Hank expanded William's plan. 'My intention is to get Anna away without delay the minute we find her. Goodness knows what state she will be in if she has been locked into a cellar all this time.'

Albert felt for his gun. 'The thought of that makes me wild, mate,' he grunted. 'Can you imagine her mother's anguish? I have to find her for Vera's sake.'

Maurice took a good look around as he pulled the hand brake. 'This might sound strange,' he said, 'but the place doesn't look unappealing.'

The others gave an irritated *what?* by way of reply. 'Well, look at it,' Maurice continued. 'It's colourful, flowers blooming everywhere, neat lawn, clean and tidy pathways, clearly marked parking areas. Looks like a tight ship is run here, friends. We might be in for a surprise.'

'Yeah, Mtolo will get the biggest surprise of all,' Hank threatened darkly.

Gerhard drew the short straw to stay in the van. Albert made an awkward attempt to open his door, alighting clumsily. Maurice rushed around to help him. It was a convincing performance.

Hank and Franz climbed out, stretching and yawning. They kept their backs to the window.

'Now whoever finds Anna, keep her away from me and Mtolo. I might just rough him up a bit. She shouldn't have to witness that.'

'He might ruffle your feathers instead, brother.'

'He's welcome to try,' Hank scowled fiercely.

Franz looked at him, surprised at his uncharacteristic display of macho confidence.

'The best thing'—Hank turned to the others—'is to escort Anna to the van immediately and, if necessary, drive away. Don't worry about the rest of us. You can pick us up later when you've got her to safety.'

'Right! Onward, Christian soldiers!' Maurice muttered, leading them in while William slunk behind the van and headed for Casualty.

Unnoticed by the group, Sipho watched them from the minute they arrived. They were strangers to him, except for William sneaking behind the van. He didn't like the look of the team, identifying Albert and Maurice's pantomime for what it was and detecting their guns too.

'I may die tomorrow,' he whispered, 'but I wasn't born yesterday.' Picking up the internal phone, he gave a warning ring in Josh's office.

Hank overtook Maurice on the way in. 'Where's Mtolo? I want a word with him!' He slammed his fist on the counter at the enquiries window. Albert stepped beside him, his arm free of the sling. 'Where's Anna? I want my daughter! *Now!*'

Sipho came to the window, a deceptive smile on his face.

'Gentlemen, please . . . this is a hospital, not a war zone. I must ask you to take your guns back to your vehicle. Concealing them under clothing isn't good enough.'

'Ah, bullshit,' Albert exploded. 'Don't take any notice of him,' he said to Hank. 'Come on, let's go. You turn left like William said, and I'll go right.' Franz and Maurice disappeared through the back door.

Hank turned left, walking into Sipho's domain. 'Am I talking to Mr Gwala?' he asked, looking him up and down.

'You are!' Sipho stared back.

'I thought so. We have spoken on the phone in the past. I'm Hank De Bruyn. If you'd kindly tell your professor I'm here to see him, I'd be obliged.'

'Did I hear my name mentioned?' a soft, slightly menacing voice sounded behind him.

Hank turned, coming eye to eye with Josh. They stepped towards each other. Hank's narrowed eyes and clenched fists were the briefest warning Josh had of imminent danger.

'That's for taking my wife!' The first right-handed blow landed on Josh's face before he had time to think. 'And that's for what you did to her!' Hank's ambidextrous left slammed on Josh's nose. He reeled backwards against the wall with blood streaming from his face like a ruptured water main.

'Shit, man, take it easy,' he managed to splutter.

'Don't tell me you don't deserve any of this!' Hank came closer, shouting.

'No, I won't . . . but it's a small price to pay for the pleasure.' Had Josh not been in so much pain, he would have laughed.

Taking the flippant comment as a slight to Anna, Hank's right fist rose again, but Josh managed to deflect it and the next left as well. The failure to land more punches fired Hank's meat-axe madness. Josh's refusal to lash out in return poured petrol on the blaze.

'Well, come on! Don't just stand there insulting Anna! Fight, you coward!'

Josh drew his sleeve across his face in a futile attempt to clean off the blood.

'Get this, man!' He staggered towards Hank. 'Anna is an honourable lady. I would never degrade her name in any way.' He gave Hank a bruising thump on his upper arm, which almost unbalanced him. 'I would fight you for her happily if it was an even contest.' He wiped more blood away. 'Unfortunately you're not a well man, Hank, so it's not much of a challenge. Besides,' he said, giving Hank's other arm a sickening twist when he raised it to throw another punch, 'I'm a doctor. I'm not permitted to kill you.'

By this time, Sipho alerted Casualty and Peter and Tom came running to assist.

'Okay, you two! Cut it out!' Authoritative voices spoke. Competent hands grasped Hank's and Josh's arms, increasing the distance between them. Tom removed Josh for treatment. Peter cast an eye over Hank's hands.

'Those knuckles are swelling fast,' he said. 'Better let's have a look at them.'

'No, thanks,' Hank refused ungraciously, exiting through the back door.

'Very well, have it your way.'

* * *

Anna sat up alert once more, listening to what sounded like doors being kicked open—first Josh's, then Sipho's. The empty unit next to hers wasn't spared either. *How weird*, she thought. *Margo isn't here today.*

Her own door opened with a civilized tap as if the person entering did not wish to distort the music of Bach with crashing boots.

'Dad! What are you doing here?' She flew into her father's arms with a shriek of joy.

'Looking for you, girlie.' He embraced her with a relieved sigh. 'Now I can ring your mother and tell her we found you.'

'We?' she puzzled. 'Who else is here?'

'The whole bloody army, just about . . .' Albert laughed for the first time in weeks. 'Franz, Maurice, William, Gerhard, and Hank of course.'

'Hank! Oh, good heavens,' she gasped. 'Where is he?' She sprinted towards the door to find him.

'Ah, not so fast, girlie,' Albert held onto her. 'By now he'll be having one of those typically male conversations with Joshua about a lady they both know.'

Her eyes widened, horrified. 'You mean fisticuffs?'

'Yep! That's the intention.'

'Oh no! They're not fighting over me? That's ridiculous.' She headed for the door again.

'No, Anna, leave 'em to it.' He restrained her. 'Let them knock their madness out of their systems.'

He pulled a chair to the computer where she worked when he entered, taking a look at the screen.

'Don't tell me you're studying medicine,' he joked.

'No, I'm not that bright. It's course material for uni students. I'm only copy typing. It passes the time. Things get pretty boring around here otherwise.' She shut the computer down.

'How did you find me, Dad?' Anna turned her chair towards him with a brilliant, happy smile. 'I've been here so long, I thought everyone had forgotten me.'

'Don't ever say that, girlie. We've all been going crazy without you, not knowing what really happened to you. Your mother is beside herself.'

'Well, how did you hit on this place?'

'Ah,' Albert grinned, 'it was William. He was so convinced he was imprisoned here.' Albert chuckled. 'In a wine cellar, would you believe! He persuaded us after paying a call on Indira Naidoo . . .'

'The surgeon from here . . . ?' Anna interrupted, stunned.

'Sure, she's his latest lady-love, I'm told. She encouraged him to take a look around. William fancied he recognized Sipho's voice too. Even that Broadbent fellow with all his logical questioning couldn't rid him of the idea. So we decided to come and investigate because William thought you might be here too. Just before we left Johannesburg, the young boy—what's his name?— Kosi something . . . rang Hank to say his friend Freddie saw you having dinner with Joshua at that Zebra place. Not knowing what to do next, the boys phoned Cindy. She reported the sighting to the police. You were still on the missing-persons list.'

Anna was flabbergasted. Indira? William's girlfriend? Josh couldn't have known that. And Cindy talking to the police! There was vengeance for you! Josh was coming unstuck rapidly. Where would it end?

'I'm happy to say you don't look like you've lived in a cellar. You appear in good shape.'

'It hasn't been easy, Dad, but I enjoy some conveniences in this gilded cage.'

'Why didn't that professor bloke send a ransom demand to Hank?' Her father was placing his finger on the trigger, she thought.

'That's still in abeyance,' she replied carefully. 'Now might be the time to sort it out if I can get everybody together.'

'Sort it out? You're kidding, aren't you? Now that we found you, Hank wants you home. There won't be any money for the likes of that professor.'

'Dad, please listen.'

'What, don't you want to come home?'

'Of course I do, but I have unfinished business here.' She smiled sweetly at her father, reminding him of his wilful little girl who usually got her own way. 'I'll start with the simple things like getting my diamonds out of the safe. After that, I'll change my clothes. The ones I'm wearing aren't mine. They're prison clothes.'

'Who cares what you wear? Getting you home is what's important.'

'Come with me,' she beckoned. 'You can phone Mum while I retrieve my diamonds.'

She sat her father down at Josh's desk, pushing the telephone towards him. His fingers trembled with jubilant triumph as he dialled home.

'Hip hip hurrah! We've got her!' he told Vera, excitement raising his voice. 'Yeah, she's safe,' he reported, elated. 'Anna, talk to your mother!'

She took the phone. 'Of course I'm all right, Mum. Things aren't as bad as everyone feared.'

Having reassured her mother, she gave the phone back to Albert and opened the safe for her diamonds. She laid them around her neck, fastening the chain at the back. Without prompting, her memory rushed to the other evening when Josh had closed the clasp for her before their Zebra dinner.

'We woke your mother up,' Albert chuckled merrily as he replaced the receiver. 'She doesn't mind, though. Before I left her, she said she'd kill me if I didn't tell her immediately when we found you.'

'Feel like a coffee, Dad? When did you last have refreshments? I bet you've been on the go for a good many hours. So have the others. Where did they go?' It was time to round them up, time to face Hank.

Glancing through the kitchen window while switching the urn to boil, Anna saw Franz standing on tiptoe, peering into the shed. Hank and Maurice headed for the children's ward. *Drat*, she thought. *They shouldn't be there. They're sure to cause upsets*. The wind blew Maurice's windcheater, flipping it up to reveal his pistol.

'Did you all bring weapons?' she asked her father, dismayed and disappointed in their judgment.

'Yeah, we did. William advised it. We had no idea what to expect.' He saw his daughter's disapproval clearly.

'Dad, that ward is full of traumatized kids who have suffered horrors no child should experience. Seeing to their psychological welfare is what this place is for. They don't need disturbances like this. And they don't need guns.'

She quickly made a pot of coffee and took it and her father to the conference room, excusing herself momentarily.

'Enough is enough,' she muttered while following her men into the ward. They talked quietly to the sister without noticing her entry.

'Coffee, anyone?' she called cheerfully. They turned around, gaping at her before coming to their senses.

'Anna!' Hank swallowed hard. 'Oh, my love.' He rushed towards her, holding her in an embrace she thought would never end. 'Where did you come from? Aren't you supposed to be locked in a cellar?'

'Nonsense', she laughed, adding, 'but I'm glad you've come. I'll never get out of here without your help.'

'I feared you'd be so incapacitated I'd have to carry you out.' Hank smiled, holding her closer still. 'You look well, my love.'

'For a prisoner,' she sighed.

'Well,'—Hank nodded his thanks to the sister—'let's get you home ASAP!'

'Hank, what have you done? Look at your hands!'

'They are a little worse for wear, I know. It's of no importance. Let's go—quickly.'

'We don't need to rush. Come and join Dad for a coffee.'

'I am thirsty,' he admitted. 'I'd rather not linger, though.'

'Maurice might want a drink.' She winked at him before they too embraced.

'Great to see you, Anna,' he said with relief. He still blamed himself for her abduction although Hank never reproached him.

Franz entered. 'Hell's bells!' he exclaimed, looking at Anna open-mouthed. 'Where did you spring from? You're supposed to be underground! I've searched every possible hole in this place.'

Anna hugged him. 'You were right telling me to learn self-defence. In future I'll take firearm practice more seriously.'

'You're all right, I hope?' he asked, holding her away from him and examining her thoroughly.

'Yeah,' she grinned. 'I'm tough.'

'We'll take you home.' Waving his arm to the others, he took Anna's hand, heading for the door.

'Let's gather in the conference room for coffee,' she encouraged. 'Where are William and Gerhard?'

'Gerhard's waiting in the van, so we can head off quickly. As for William, he's got his head in a cloud about a woman called Indira. Can't think where the hell he's got to.'

'He'll turn up when he's ready. If not, we'll just leave him here,' Anna laughed as they walked back to the administration building. 'Tell Gerhard to come in. He must be bored sitting out there wondering what's happening. I'll replenish the coffee. I think we've got a drop of brandy left too.'

'I sure am glad we found you, Anna,' Gerhard said when he came in while she poured coffee for the others. 'I feared we'd made a huge mistake when you still hadn't fronted after I finished reading two newspapers.'

She held the brandy bottle up for him to see. 'Want some?' she asked with an amused smile.

Gerhard sat down with one of the delicate brandy balloons from the Flametree Art Lodge, which he placed on the table. The men talked among themselves, and Hank's hands became a topic of interest.

Anna took the opportunity to slip away to her cell and change into her own clothes. She gathered her handbag and briefcase, ready to leave. As she walked past Sipho's room, Tom and Peter rounded the corner, supporting Josh between them.

'Oh, gracious me! *Joshua*!' she cried.

He was a mess. His shirt and jeans soaked with blood, his eyes swollen all but closed, he barely raised a hand to acknowledge her presence as they saw him to his room.

'We fixed him up,' Peter said. 'He'll feel better when he's got clean clothes and swallowed some painkillers and such. It's only a broken nose.'

'My private army is downing brandy in the mess,' Anna said, her voice ringing with irony. 'Join the party if you wish. Sipho should come too. I'll help Josh.'

'Brandy! Great! We need it after dealing with him.' Peter pointed at Josh, tossing a packet of painkillers on the coffee table.

'He's a dreadful patient,' Tom chuckled.

While assisting Josh into a shirt, perfectly ironed and starched by Margo, Anna talked to him urgently.

'Listen Josh, you're likely to have a call from the police. They will question you, me also later on. They still have me recorded as a missing person. We have to collaborate to be sure we both tell the same story.'

'What's going on?' he asked, still dazed and slightly concussed.

'We were seen at the Zebra. Freddie Bonga, the apprentice cook there, recognized me from a newspaper photo and you because Cindy introduced you.'

'Yeah, I remember that. He was so darned proud of his motorbike.'

'Freddie was shy about informing the police because he once belonged to a bike gang so he phoned Cindy. She reported our whereabouts to Captain Broadbent at the Criminal Investigation Unit.'

'Cindy?' Josh asked, not believing what he thought he heard. 'Vengeful woman! I'm glad I didn't marry her.'

'Joshua, *you did not abduct me!* Do you understand?' Anna said with emphasis. 'You offered me sanctuary here because I was stalked by a man in a yellow VW Golf. That's the story I'm sticking to. As far as I know, you never held business executives here for ransom. The cops will get the three-monkeys tale from me.'

Josh wanted to laugh but couldn't. 'Has it come to that?' he commented, seating himself on the couch and leaning his head back. Thinking was beyond him. It hurt too much.

'You would be obstructing a police investigation and perverting the course of justice, my pet,' he mumbled at last. 'It's called misprision, concealing knowledge of a crime.'

'Only if the prosecution finds enough evidence . . . which they mustn't,' Anna proclaimed, at her conspiratorial best.

She handed him a glass of water and opened the tablet pack. 'How many?' she asked, looking at him with pity although she agreed he had deserved every thump Hank had delivered.

He swallowed two. 'Yuck!' he complained, laying his head against the couch's backrest again, closing his eyes.

Sitting with him, running tender fingertips over his bruised face and kissing his swollen eyelids, she murmured, 'Poor darling.'

'That's a more effective analgesic than any other ever manufactured. Do that again.'

'We don't have time. I have to join my warriors of righteousness. I must drill them to support my plans. You need to be there to hear what is said.'

Josh wouldn't move till she kissed his eyelids again. 'I'm ready now,' he said, flexing his muscles. 'It's not Daniel in the lions' den. This time it's Joshua.' Offering her his arm as if escorting her into a function room, they proceeded along the corridor.

Anna giggled all the way, finding the situation eccentric and absurd. Her rescue team heard her long before she appeared. Conversation ceased, and Josh was subjected to stares of silent misgiving.

When Franz looked at Josh's face, he too began to laugh. 'Good job, Hank! Pity I wasn't around to see you do it.'

Josh growled, not enchanted with jokes from Anna's unlikely heroes. 'Must say, for an ailing man, you pack quite a punch.' He fixed his swollen-eyed attention on Hank who looked at his knuckles, grunting something unintelligible.

The room became crowded with the three De Bruyn men, Albert, Maurice, Tom, and Peter occupying the chairs. The one at the head of the table was vacant, and Josh led Anna towards it. Sipho rolled in with two office chairs for Josh and himself. Anna moved slightly left to make room for Josh beside her. It brought her closer to Hank and her father next to him.

'A rose between two thorns,' Albert muttered to himself, impatient to be out. He couldn't see the need for discussions. The brandy was good, though.

A look around the room showed Josh only one man he didn't know, an approximately sixty-five-year-old chap. He appeared tall and wiry, with the pale, watery, horizon-seeking eyes of a mariner. His gaze rested on Anna with obvious love as he spoke.

'I told your mother to get herself on a plane and come here. She's dying to see you.'

'That's wonderful, Dad. I can't wait!' She clapped her hands.

So the guy is Anna's father, Josh thought, seeing the strong resemblance in their smiles as they conversed.

With the course of events unfolding so differently to what they expected, the men looked rather bewildered. Anna clearly needed to explain herself. Satisfied for now with her state of fitness, they allowed the brandy to mellow their fury. Their level of hostility towards Josh would be adjusted either up or down according to her account.

'Well,' Anna sighed and shrugged when they all looked her way. 'Thank you for coming to my aid.' She nodded at each man in turn as she said his name. 'You have no idea how it feels to think yourself forgotten by those you love.'

'You never left my mind, Anna, you must believe that,' Hank interrupted.

'How could we forget you?' Franz laughed at her. 'Blotting out your personality is impossible.'

'I tried escaping,' she continued hesitantly. 'It didn't do much good. I needed a third party's help, and here you are!' She smiled, lifting her hands as if to bless them.

Hank addressed Joshua with rage. 'Why the hell didn't you send a ransom demand and let Anna come home instead of keeping her and alienating her affection?'

Josh was still slow to react. The painkillers were sleep-inducing. Anna answered for him.

'Josh paid me quite a compliment,' she grinned mischievously. 'He thinks I'm worth half a million US dollars.'

'Good lord,' Hank said, staggered. 'You're priceless, my dear! The fact is, though, we can't pay it. We'd be ruined.'

'I know,' she agreed. 'I had to talk him out of it. I proposed he accept US $800,000 over four years, coupled with a guarantee that no legal action against him will ensue. He's still thinking about that offer,' she added, grinning at Josh provocatively. With an imploring look at the others, she said, 'I don't want to go back on my word.'

'De Bruyn Brothers doesn't negotiate with criminals,' Gerhard said sharply. Like Albert, he couldn't see why money should be paid at all.

Anna's face became earnest. 'My answer to that is threefold. Firstly, I feared I was negotiating for my life. I am sure you know how real criminals operate. How would you react to receiving one of my fingers in the mail with a demand for a million dollars? If you ignore it, you are sent another digit, and so it goes till I am dismembered. I wanted to come home as quickly as possible in one piece. Might I just add, Gerhard, that although I'm grateful you are all here I can't help but wonder what took you so long.'

Hearing Anna's spitfire note of discord, Josh emerged from his stupor, mortified. 'You hurt me, Anna. Did you seriously think I would harm you?'

'Initially I did not know what to expect, Josh. You were a dangerous stranger, and I felt I had to be prepared for anything. Now I realize my apprehension was unfounded.' She gave him a soothing smile.

'Secondly,' she continued, 'I would use the word *criminal* cautiously. What is insider trading?'

'Ha ha.' Franz pointed a finger at Gerhard. 'She's got you there!'

'Thirdly, in your discourse, you might like to exchange *criminality* for *desperation*. When a person has exhausted unsuccessfully every legal means to obtain the necessary funds to help the vulnerable, what's the next step? You don't just admit defeat when it comes to helping defenceless children overcome their enormous difficulties. The children here are ill, traumatized by violence and orphaned in some cases. They have nowhere and no one to turn to. Are we going to abandon them?'

The explanations left the men looking at each other quietly. When a collective sigh sounded from them, Anna rose, heading for Josh's office.

'What are you looking for, pet?' he called after her.

'The file with the correspondence from the NGOs.'

'Sipho's got that. It's in the cabinet by the window, top drawer.'

Hank's face became flushed. *Pet*, he thought. *That's what that incredible rat bag calls Anna. Pet! I'll show you some pets, man.* An idea took shape in his mind. Josh had deprived him of what he loved most. Now he would turn the tables by removing what Josh valued highest: his hospital. It was Maurice's remark about the neatness and order of the place that sowed the seed. As it germinated, he found Maurice was right. The people here worked hard, taking much pride in their achievements. Their approach was disciplined and diligent. Given time and financial backing, this fledgling enterprise would thrive, but Josh would be little more than an employee.

Anna returned with the file. She passed it to Gerhard. 'Take a look at this.'

As the folder progressed from hand to hand, she walked around the table topping up coffee and brandy. Josh was silent, not at all himself, although the painkillers were effective. She placed a concerned hand on his shoulder.

'Are you all right?' she whispered. 'Are you sure you wouldn't like a cup of coffee?'

'No thanks, Anna. I'll get a glass of water.'

He half rose, but she held him down. 'I'm going to the kitchen. Do you want ice?'

'Yes, please . . . and thanks.' He watched her walk out.

Hank felt a stab in his heart observing the exchange between them. He hadn't come a day too soon to fetch Anna home.

She returned with iced water and two glass trays piled with chocolate biscuits. Placing one at each end of the table and handing Josh his iced drink, she sat down again, her face drawn and worried. Her eyes, Josh noticed, were like black cherries. There was no trace of green in them.

Hank, who was last in line to see the correspondence, closed the file and handed it back to her. She turned to Josh.

'Do you think now that you could take up my long-standing offer if Hank approves it?'

He leaned forward, looking more alert after sipping the water. 'As you said before, Anna, one can't just give up. I must keep this place functioning, and I need every cent I can get to do so. The money would be very welcome.'

Hank leaned towards Josh. 'Like Gerhard, I maintain that we do not make deals under strained circumstances, nor do we simply give money away. However, there are ways to solve the problem.'

His eyes, colder than icebergs around the Titanic, penetrated Josh's shell, but he spoke softly, smiling. *Reminiscent of a crocodile*, Josh thought.

'At present there are four partners here, you included. If you like, we'll be the fifth to provide financial backing. Take it or leave it, Professor Mtolo. You'll get nothing else.'

Josh looked at Sipho who snorted dismissively. 'That's not a partnership. It's a takeover!'

'My sentiments exactly,' Josh concurred.

How often in the past had he wished for the financial involvement of white business interests? Here was Mr Moneybags with tempting proposals, but he wanted it all. He aimed for control. He would override everybody else's vote by sheer pecuniary bullying.

On the other hand, the million-dollar man had overlooked one crucial point: Anna. Josh smiled inwardly. A partnership meant ongoing contact with her. He may forego a little control over his business but still exercise influence over and through her. Was that worth a gamble? He needed time to hear Tom and Peter's opinions as well. Indira would have original ideas too.

Josh rose, turning towards the door. He signalled to his partners and to Sipho to follow him out.

'Excuse us please,' he said. 'We'll be in Casualty for about . . .'— he looked at his watch—'twenty minutes. I'm sure Anna will see to your comfort in the meantime.'

This was the moment of decision, Josh thought. What if Hank was false and wouldn't pay? Did he merely seek to fool him into relinquishing his beloved hostage? When he first captured her, he imagined this type of situation taking an entirely different turn, like a cheque laid before him while he held a gun to her head. Now he could not frighten her in his wildest dreams. He'd be miserable without her, but a partnership, if Hank was genuine, allowed for flexibility and a chance of at least talking to her occasionally.

The front door slammed. Forcible arguing with agitated, sharp words raged loudly.

'William, I will not have it! You are not going back to the police!' Indira's determined voice bounced off the foyer's walls as they entered before Josh and the others came near the exit.

'This is my livelihood you're jeopardizing. I like this place. I enjoy working here where I can make a difference. I will not have you disrupt my life or that of my colleagues. If I hear of you talking to the police once more, it will be the end of our friendship.'

'Don't be a drama queen, Indira.'

'I mean it, William!'

'Can you come with us please?' Josh pulled Indira away.

Hearing conversation from the meeting room, William found his way in. He looked at Anna with a surprised but satisfied smile.

'Told you so!' He hailed the others. 'I knew Anna would be here.' He threw his arms around her, kissing her on both cheeks. Eyeing her closely, he said, 'It's amazing! The wine cellar hasn't had much effect on you. You look great.'

'Wine cellar?' Anna played dumb. 'What wine cellar?'

'The one here, just past the kitchen.' William indicated the end of the passage.

'I don't know of any wine cellar, William.' She laughed at him. 'If there was one, you would have drunk all the wine, I bet.'

William's face creased in concentration. He addressed the others again. 'Where did you find her?'

'Anna was in her room, listening to Bach while typing medical reference material on a computer. Can you believe that? After all our anxiety, worrying about her?' Albert grinned, pleased with himself for finding his daughter before the others did.

'Are you saying'—William turned to her, outraged—'you got preferential treatment here while poor old me was left to rot in that wine cellar?'

'Left to marinate, more likely.' Maurice couldn't help himself. He laughed out loud.

'I don't know what you're talking about. The only wine we have is in the drinks cabinet over there. Did you want some? I'll get you a glass.'

'Yes, thank you. You can do that, and while you're at it, I'll come with you and show you my dungeon. You must have seen it. There's a pantry there too.'

Anna dissolved into a fit of giggles again. 'Lead the way, William.'

'This I have to see,' Franz said, joining the procession.

William knew where to go. Second door past the kitchen, he stopped. 'Here,' he turned the knob, only to find it locked.

'I'll get the key,' Anna offered.

William unlocked the door. He couldn't find the light switch. so she flicked the neon tube on for him. He looked around the narrow room, his confidence evaporating. What revealed itself was a storage area for disposable equipment like boxes of gloves, specimen jars, bandages, ice packs, and spare bed linen.

Not giving up, he pointed to further stairs going down to a second door. 'There, did you bring a key for that door too?'

'Sure, come on down.' She opened the next door. William and Franz followed.

'Where's the wine, William?'

'It was there, screwed to the wall, next to the toilet door. There was a bunk opposite and a table with two chairs in the centre.'

'And what do you see now?'

'A hospital bed and storage shelves where the wine rack was. What's the room used for?'

'It's the isolation ward.'

'What's that?'

'It's for highly infectious cases, you know, like Ebola.'

Franz and William turned on their heels instantly. Anna followed, laughing and locking up.

'That's not at all amusing, Anna. What did you bring us down here for?'

'You wanted to see it. Don't worry,' she said, suppressing her mirth, 'it's cleaned and decontaminated. I thought Indira would have told you about it.'

Taking wine glasses from the kitchen, she conducted the men back to the meeting room.

'William, you must be getting confused,' she said while uncorking a bottle. 'You see, in its previous life this place was a farmhouse many of which have similar layouts. Goodness knows where you were taken, but it couldn't have been here.'

'How come you're here then? What precisely are you doing here if the EEM isn't holding you for a ransom?'

'They're not, and this isn't EEM. You're at KwaZulu Medical. I do believe we are about to become the financial partners in this new venture. That way they can continue caring for sick and disturbed kids. You must admit this couldn't possibly be your place of incarceration, so be a good boy and do as Indira asks. Don't go back to the cops.'

A sly glint of understanding crept into William's eyes. He knew when he was led by the nose. He called it a Melody trick. Anna had pulled a Melody trick, but why?

Before William said any more, Hank looked at his watch impatiently. 'It's about time Mtolo and company were back,' he remarked. Nearly forty minutes had elapsed since they retreated. 'If they're not here in five minutes, we're leaving.'

The front door clanged. 'Here they come.' Franz nodded in the general direction. 'Top of the class for punctuality.'

The partners filed in, finding seats where possible. Josh positioned himself behind Anna's chair, placing both hands on her shoulders.

'What's your decision? Are we in agreement?' Hank questioned brusquely. Were his hands not so swollen that he could barely close them, he would have attacked Josh again. A good interpreter of body language, he understood the challenge Josh extended by standing close to Anna and touching her. He was laying claim on her. Rearranging his face failed to curb the man's impertinence. Nothing had changed for Joshua, except a slight shift in focus from (a) Anna or ransom to (b) Anna and diminished control of the business. Oh yes, he thought, he could exercise financial dominance over KwaZulu Medical, but that predatory witch doctor would strive to retain leverage over Anna's heart. He had won the battle, but the war was just beginning.

A squeal and tapping of running feet turned everyone's attention towards the door.

'Come back right now, Nozipho!' Sister Miriam ran after her as the child entered, sheltering timidly behind Josh.

'I'm sorry she's disturbing you,' she stammered.

'It's not a problem, let her stay.' Josh's calm voice soothed Nozipho till she looked up into his ruined face. She burst into tears.

'What happened to you, Doctor Josh?' she sobbed. She sidled closer to Anna, unable to brave the sight of the damage.

'It's all right, sweetie,' Anna comforted, hugging her. 'Doctor Josh had a little accident, that's all. He'll be fine.'

'Who are all these people?' Nozipho asked through sobs. 'Are you leaving us, Nkosazana?'

'One question at a time, Nozipho. Would you like a biscuit and a glass of milk?'

She nodded, and Anna reached over to pull the biscuit tray closer. Indira fetched the milk.

'Are you leaving?' she repeated.

'Yes, Nozipho, I'm going home.'

'Why?'

'Because my job here is finished.'

Nozipho's tears flowed again. 'I want you to stay.'

'I'm sorry, sweetie, I can't do that.'

She was quiet for a time, her eyes flirting with the biscuits. Eventually, she asked her burning question: 'I thought you were going to marry Doctor Josh.'

'What gave you that idea?' Anna laughed. 'I can't do that either.'

'Why?'

'Because I'm married already. See the man next to me?' She turned Nozipho to face Hank. 'That's Mr Hank De Bruyn. He's my husband. The man next to him is my father. Do you want to know who the other visitors are? I'll introduce you.'

Anna left her chair. Walking around the table, she acquainted the little girl with everyone.

'I wish you would stay,' Nozipho repeated. 'Why can't you have two husbands? I know men who have more than one wife.'

Everyone laughed except Hank and Josh.

'Funny you should say that, Nozipho. I remember asking the same question when I was your age. Why can men have more than one wife but women may only have one husband? Doesn't seem fair.'

'If you could have two husbands, would you marry Doctor Josh?'

'It never occurred to me because it isn't possible.' Anna chuckled while Hank and Josh looked uncomfortable. 'I'm thinking, though, you're young enough to do something about advancing marriage equality for women. You know what to do?'

Nozipho shook her head.

'When you're older and through school, you go to university and study law. If you do well at that, you have yourself voted into Parliament. That's where they make all the laws, you see. You can work towards having unfair regulations overturned.'

Anna smiled indulgently at Nozipho. 'I can see it already,' she laughed. 'Nozipho Nkomo's Private Member's Bill to have marriage laws amended.'

Nozipho hadn't a clue what Anna meant and why everyone laughed. She retreated into bashfulness.

'It's all right, sweetie, they're not laughing at you. They wouldn't do that to a clever kiddie like you.'

Turning to Hank, Anna said, 'You shouldn't have gone into the children's ward. We're in trouble now. Nozipho's DNA is pure curiosity. She should be at school, but she has nowhere to go. AIDS has wiped out her parents and other adult relatives. At present she occupies a bed which a sick child should have. She has to leave this place, but she's reluctant. It's the only home she's known for the last twelve months.'

When Josh tried unsuccessfully to capture the girl's attention, Anna asked, 'Would you like to do me a favour, Nozipho?'

She nodded. '*Yebo*, Nkosazana.'

'Do you know where my room is?'

She shook her head.

'Turn left when you go out and then left again. The last door along the passage is my room. Go in and take Zavier from my bedside table and look after him for me. You will find my handbag and briefcase in the passage too. Do you think you could bring them to me, please?'

The child departed with a skip.

'Nozipho is a typical example of the children Joshua and his colleagues aim to help. Unfortunately, KwaZulu Medical's staff will never be unemployed because the waiting list is endless.' Anna looked at her menfolk to ascertain if her message had taken hold of their thinking.

'Can you please tell us your decision, Professor,' Hank demanded, ignoring Anna's words temporarily. 'Are you and your partners agreed on accepting financial help from us?' He drummed his sore fingers on the table irritably. Pain told him it wasn't a good idea.

'Yes, we think it may be a way forward. My colleagues anticipate a greater scope to provide services for patients.'

'I'm so glad,' Hank said sarcastically, noting not a word of welcome to the partnership was spoken. They looked at him with stone faced neutrality as if to say, 'Let's see you prove your worth, man.'

'Good, we can finally get home,' he said when all De Bruyns readied themselves for departure. 'You will hear from our lawyers, Waterman and Bruce, within the next fortnight. Mr Gwala, you will keep me informed please and let me know who represents you. Don't hesitate to ring me at any time.'

William heaved a sigh. 'I'm glad that's done.' He was happy to go home with Indira, taking her hand to lead her out.

'I wish you wouldn't go.' Nozipho brought Anna's belongings. She almost cried again as she clutched Zavier to her chest.

'I have to go, sweetie.' Anna bent down to hug her. 'A thought just occurred to me! Do you want to come with me to Johannesburg? . . . Maybe just for a holiday at first . . . to see whether you like it. If you do, you could stay and go to school there.'

Her eyes widened. She opened her mouth to reply, but indecision plagued her. She looked at Josh for guidance.

'Do you remember a lady called Cindy Khumalo?' Anna asked.

'She was my mama's best friend.'

'I know where she lives and teaches now. We could ask her to help find you a good school. Would you like that?'

Nozipho looked at Josh again, still unsure about a daunting future in a big, mysterious city.

'Ask Doctor Josh if you are ready to be discharged from his hospital.'

The child turned away, suddenly shy again.

'Shall I ask him for you?'

Nozipho nodded, and Anna said with a smile, 'Doctor Josh, is Nozipho fit enough to come with me? She knows she can't live in a hospital forever.'

'I have no objection. Nozipho may leave.'

'There you are, sweetie. You can come.'

'Go and fetch your things, Nozipho,' Josh said quietly.

Anna looked at him with forbearance. Her heart bled for him, although the others thought justice was served. He was physically and emotionally wounded, losing two people he loved, and it showed in his demeanour. He had instead gained the promise of money from a new, domineering partner who would be difficult to handle. He felt uncertain whether the compromise was worth the agony.

Before Anna's liberation squad took her to the van, Felicity entered, passing a sprig of violets to Josh.

'Look what Felicity grew in the garden,' he said, smiling at Anna. His cut lower lip bled anew with the stretch. He wiped it away quickly before pinning the blooms to her lapel and embracing her. 'Welcome, partner,' he whispered.

'Oh, Joshua, thank you!' She wanted to add, 'What a lovely thought' but failed. Tears stung her eyes. She felt the others' uncomprehending stares. None said a word of farewell to the doctors.

'Are you coming?' Franz called from the steps outside.

'Don't cry. I mustn't cry, not with all of them watching.' She anesthetized her emotion.

Nozipho joined her, carrying a small plastic bag containing her worldly treasures.

'Mhlawumbe ngizobuya masinyane,' Anna said, hoping the others wouldn't hear and pressure her for a translation. 'Perhaps I will return soon.'

'Be a good girl. Don't give your Aunty Anna trouble.' Josh squeezed Nozipho's shoulders affectionately.

Hank and Albert approached impatiently, one taking Anna's handbag and the hand that held it, the other doing likewise with her other hand and briefcase.

'Come on home, my dear,' Hank said, his face compressed with resentment.

* * *

Chapter 12

The Partnership

Anna couldn't walk quickly. Her heart was a dead weight of mixed emotions dropping to her feet and retarding her steps. Nozipho fell back too, turning to wave to Josh. The others had already gone inside.

Gerhard took a turn at driving. His house in Durban was to be their first port of call. Maurice jumped in the passenger seat beside him. Franz and Albert stretched out in the back while Hank, Anna, and Nozipho claimed the middle seats. Nobody spoke as Gerhard turned the key, reversed, and pulled away. The gate was closed when they reached it.

'Crumbs! I still have Josh's key card,' Anna remembered. She pulled it out of her handbag, passing it to Gerhard. He rolled the window down, leaned out to insert the card, and the gate moved slowly, still reluctant to release her, she thought.

'Oh, it works now,' she marvelled when Gerhard handed it back. 'How weird! I stole it off Josh because I thought it would aid my escape, but it never worked for me. I wanted to take his car and drive away before anyone could stop me.'

'It's probably controlled by a little computer. You only need to delete the card number from the memory and you get no further.' Franz chuckled in the back. 'Can't imagine you would get very far in that Corolla of his anyway. It looks on its last wheels to me.'

'I was desperate.'

'We never made that citizen's arrest I was so looking forward to. We should go back and do it now.'

'Forget it, Franz. We're partners now. The last thing we need is a big scandal.'

'Hm.' Anna nodded. 'It's not a good look for the new council president to take up his post already dogged by dubious happenings.'

'How do you know about that?' Hank shot her a surprised look.

'I read the editorial in the last *Dividend Magazine*. They suggested it was a foregone conclusion Hank De Bruyn would take over when Michael Tripp retires.'

He smiled, kissing her tenderly. 'I might, now that I have you back.'

'I hope William keeps his mouth shut too. I don't want him visiting Broadbent, gloating how he found out about EEM when the police couldn't. That's why I tried so hard to confuse him about that wine cellar business. I'm not sure I succeeded. We'll have to hope Indira holds more sway over him.'

* * *

Despite its age and outwardly decrepit condition, the van sped smoothly towards Durban, carrying its silent occupants home. Nozipho fell asleep leaning against Anna's shoulder. Hank sat, twisted a little uncomfortably, allowing Anna's head to rest on his chest. He yawned and rubbed his sore knuckles.

'I'm as hungry as a lion,' Gerhard complained. 'Can't wait to get home.'

'Yeah, I could eat an elephant,' Franz agreed.

As they came closer to Durban, their drowsiness fell away. Albert stirred slowly, pulling a page torn from a boating catalogue out of his back pocket. He passed it to Anna.

'What do you think of that?'

'Wow!' She smiled, studying the picture of a Griffiths-designed eighteen-metre steel cruising yacht.

Albert chuckled in the back. 'A sister for *Coomelong*.'

'Big sister, you mean!' Anna read the description, commenting as she went, 'Gardner 6LXB 150-horsepower engine, 4,500 litres fuel tanks, sails for the balmy weather: Main, Spinnaker, Topsail, Mizzen, and Genoa, built to survey—that's always good. Enough safety and electronic navigation gear too . . . she'll cost as much as a house, I bet.' She turned to look at her father, who had a mysterious but contented expression in his eyes.

'Oh,' she laughed. 'I know that look. You're going to buy her, aren't you?'

'I already have. I'm calling her *Anna*.'

'You can't rename a ship, Dad. It's bad luck.'

'Not this time, girlie. Finding you was the biggest stroke of luck to outweigh all else.'

'How did you come by the boat?'

'An Aussie expatriate is selling her. He's a researcher and used her for scientific expeditions. He's retired now and can't afford the upkeep any longer. He's let the survey lapse too, so I bought her at a reduced price.'

'You won't be sailing her home alone, will you? I'd love to come along!'

'You're welcome, girlie, if Hank can spare you. Gus and Oscar have offered to join as deckhands. They're very excited.'

Gus and Oscar were Albert's favourite nephews. As officers in the Australian Navy, they were keen and exceptionally good sailors.

Anna's heart sank. She saw herself relegated to the galley if her cousins and their teenage sons came aboard. Also, would Hank let her go? He wasn't saying much. He should be adept at functioning without her by now. Otherwise she would be imprisoned all over again . . . in a more luxurious goal, granted, but with annoying restrictions all the same.

She turned back to her father. 'I know what Mum will say when she hears of this. "Boys and their toys!"'

'She wasn't exactly intended as a toy when I bought her—rescue vessel more like it. We wanted a means of emergency transport out of the country for you if that became necessary. It was another alternative to get you away quickly and back to Australia in case you had trodden on the government's sore toes. Remember, we had no idea of your circumstances or what lay behind your disappearance.'

'Have you taken her out yet?' Anna asked eagerly, hoping there would be enough time for her to sail with her father before her cousins arrived. 'You must take her to Cape Town and give Gogo a little joyride. She would be so thrilled. I'll come too. We'll pick a calm day and take Gogo with us. Ever since I told her about you entering *Coomelong* in the Sydney to Hobart race, she's been enchanted with the idea of being at sea. Have you had time to visit her?'

'Gogo was on the phone every day, coaxing, cajoling, and urging me to come. I promised to see her as soon as we found you.'

'We should have a big dinner party for William once we're home. Without his single-minded determination, we'd never have known where to find you, Anna.' Hank spoke without any indication that he had listened to Anna's conversation with her father. 'Also, I have to talk to young Freddie. I offered a reward for information about you, and he told Nkosinathi where he'd seen you. Till then we were only speculating as to where you might be.'

Gerhard turned into his driveway. Nozipho woke when he switched the engine off.

'In you come, all of you,' he invited jovially. 'We need food.'

Julia, his wife, came out and embraced Anna.

'So glad to see you safe. Are you all right?'

Anna nodded and smiled. The 'Are you okay?' question was becoming tedious to answer, but she'd have to suffer it for a while yet.

'And who have we here?' Julia noticed Nozipho.

'Nozipho will be our guest in Johannesburg for a while. We'll try and find her a school there,' Anna explained.

They drank coffee and munched sandwiches in the biggest, most sparkling kitchen Nozipho had ever seen. She hadn't the slightest idea what at least half of its gadgetry was for. The phone rang, and Gerhard waved to Anna.

'It's Jakobus, he wants to talk to you.'

'Marvellous to have you back, Anna! I'm kind of jealous and upset I couldn't participate in the rescue. What we can do, though, is feed you and your liberation army. Fiona's got dinner ready. Get back in the van and come around.'

Everyone boarded the shabby vehicle again except Gerhard and Julia, who used their own car. Anna drove the short distance to Jakobus' house.

'Come in! The bubbly's on ice,' he called out. His grounds man garaged the ugly van behind the villa, out of sight. It had served its purpose and would very likely be pensioned off.

Anna breathed deeply. 'The sea.' She smiled at her father. 'It's so good to smell sea air. It opens the heart valves . . . figuratively speaking. I'm beginning to feel free.'

They were led to a dining table set with so much food Nozipho's eyes popped.

A little girl appeared at the door. She looked around, sizing up Nozipho with a curious glance.

'Say hello to Auntie Anna, Monika,' Fiona admonished her daughter. 'Do I have to remind you of your manners?'

'Oh, you grow so fast, Monika,' Anna laughed. 'I haven't seen you for a long time, so I can really tell the difference.'

Monika grinned. She liked nothing better than being told how fast she grew.

Anna placed a hand on Nozipho's head. She stood close by, looking insecure and overwhelmed.

'This is Nozipho, Monika. She's coming to live with us for a while. I hope she will like Johannesburg.'

Monika was a year older than Nozipho, taller and more confident. Quietly she sneaked around the table, gathering goodies on a plate, and waved to Nozipho to follow her to her room.

Fiona shook her head. 'It's good of you to cater for your new friend, Monika, but ask Nandi for food instead of robbing the table of all the best delicacies. This wasn't intended as your personal smorgasbord.'

Monika giggled impishly, and the children disappeared.

'That poor kid is all alone in the world,' Anna said with a pitying sigh. 'She's got nothing but the clothes on her body. She's an AIDS orphan. Lucky for her she's not HIV-positive herself, but her parents perished along with other adult relatives. Her future is bleak unless someone offers her shelter.'

Fiona studied Anna's face closely. She knew her brother-in-law's wife as the life of any party, but now she was so staid and grave. Her sense of humour seemed to have flown. Perhaps she was tired. She would keep an eye on Anna.

Everyone sat around the table with the men giving the food their undivided attention after toasting Anna's return to the De Bruyn fold.

'What the hell made you go into partnership with Mtolo?' Jakobus shared Gerhard's opinion, who repeated no money should be wasted on a scoundrel like that professor.

'I was inclined to agree,' Albert joined in. 'But just think, that "scoundrel" could have killed Anna, in which case we wouldn't be sitting here in comfort enjoying a meal. I'm damned thankful he treated her well enough.'

'You're right, Dad. Joshua isn't all bad. Give him credit for some redeeming qualities.' She smiled, but the strain of the previous months showed on her face. 'The partnership was Hank's idea,' she said, 'but I hoped he would see my point.'

'And your point was . . . what?' Jakobus questioned her continuously, not knowing what pacts were forged in his absence.

She explained at length how the children, the employees, and the community, even the medical students, would be affected adversely if KwaZulu Medical ceased to operate.

'I can see the economic argument, but I still don't understand why you bother,' Jakobus grunted. 'Anna, you're usually so astute and such a tough nut to crack. You're going soft on us.' He refilled her glass while giving Hank a puzzled look.

'What was I supposed to do?' Hank asked hotly. 'How can I disagree with Anna on the one side and her deeply distressed father on the other? And we mustn't forget Indira's performance,' he reminded.

'Indira? Isn't she William's sweetheart?'

'Yes, she threatened to break off the friendship if he breathed another word to the police. She claims the place is her livelihood and wants to see it prosper. I understand her reasoning.' Hank found it easier to imply he had been under moral pressure from all angles than admit his deliberate intention to bring Joshua down a peg or two.

Jakobus shook his head. 'I don't go along with William's conduct either. If he must have his affairs, he should provide for the lady.'

'I believe self-respect and ambition drive Indira to seek independence from William. Does that strike you as odd?' Anna smiled wryly at Jakobus, wondering if one verbal cuff around the ears was enough to quieten him.

Hank sought to close the topic, saying, 'The hospital is Anna's project now and she's responsible to me if it falters.'

'It will do just fine if I am given a free hand,' she replied with a glow on her face, which wasn't all wine. Hank gave her a displeased look, wondering if her words had a second meaning under the surface.

It had been a long and demanding day for everyone. Weariness caught up as the comfort of food and wine took hold. The bonhomie was running out. Gerhard looked at his watch.

'It's time we called it a day,' he remarked to Julia. 'Who's staying with us?'

Franz rose from his chair slowly, his hands on the table for support. 'Julia offered me a bed if that's okay still,' he yawned.

'Right, you better come along then. What about the rest of you?'

'I've booked rooms on Marine Parade to please our seafarers here,' Hank said. 'They should feel at home in the Edward. That only leaves little Nozipho. I had no idea she was coming too.' He looked around but couldn't see the child.

'Speak of the devil,' Fiona said as Monika and Nozipho turned up together.

'Mum, can Nozipho stay with us till she has to go to Johannesburg?'

'*Please*, Mum!' Fiona again corrected her daughter's approach to asking favours.

'Please, Mum,' she repeated dutifully. 'And can she have some of the clothes I grew out of? She's got none of her own.'

'Yes, of course, dear. Now go back up to your room, both of you. I'll be with you shortly.'

Exhaustion was claiming Anna too, but the worst part of her day was still to come. To be alone in a hotel room with Hank scared her. What could she say to him?

At the Edward's reception desk, she stayed close to her father. Hank spoke to the clerk, and when Maurice and Albert received their keys, they said 'Good night' and settled in the bar for a nightcap. Hank took Anna's arm. 'Up we go,' he smiled as he pushed the lift button.

'My dear,' he said when the door to their suite closed behind them, 'I haven't had a minute alone with you to tell you how glad I am to have you back.' He embraced her, silencing her reply with long, drawn-out kisses while pulling her closer.

'I feared you wouldn't want me any longer,' she said with a catch in her voice. 'So much has occurred that should never have happened.'

'If we dwell on that, we won't have another happy day in our lives.' He kissed her again. 'I admit, though, I was worried you wouldn't want to come home.'

'I would not leave you. I told you that before.'

'I know, but we have no inkling of what's around the corner. Life offers many challenges and surprises. It can foil our best intentions.'

'My intention is not to desert a wonderful husband.' She kissed him for being so understanding, but his next question shook her spirit.

'So can you tell me honestly that you do not love Joshua Mtolo?'

'No, I can't,' she said in a whisper after looking at the carpet for a long time.

'You took a while thinking about that.'

'That's because he's chauvinistic, reckless, and self-absorbed. Further, he has a temper at times, which he reserves for "obstinate" and "disobedient" females. I had more rows with him than I can count on my fingers and toes. Much of what he does and says I can never approve. Yet he has a winning charm. He's a good enough man deep down, but no sensible woman would leave her husband for him.'

To her surprise Hank laughed heartily. 'That's probably why Cindy is marrying Solomon next week. Did you know?'

'Cindy and Josh broke their betrothal some time ago. He was dismayed about Cindy calling the police when Freddie told her he'd seen me. I don't know what he expects after stringing her along for years . . . but that's Joshua for you. Women only have feelings so men can disregard them.'

'I think you're saying all this just to make me happy.'

'I can say flattering things about him too. He's conscientious and exacting about his work. He has much empathy with patients, especially children. They thrive when he's there and fret when he's not. He takes their well-being to heart and even writes stories to cheer them when they're low. He lost a young patient while I was there and grieved as if she was his own child. He enjoys communicating with people and can be very generous. Sipho is a typical example of his unstinting desire to help. He wouldn't be alive now if it wasn't for Josh's importing medication for him from the USA and paying for it too.'

'That's enough,' Hank cut in. 'I'm sure you can list all his excellent points, but I don't want to know.'

'Good,' she sighed with a wicked grin. 'You won't ask me any more awkward questions then? I'm getting too tired to answer them.'

She opened the balcony door and stepped out. Hank followed, placing an arm around her, drawing her close while she absorbed the nighttime atmosphere.

The traffic never stood still on Marine Parade, but on the top floor of the Edward, the noise was muffled. Colourful illumination glowed in every lane of Funworld, the amusement park opposite. Music and people's laughter drifted up to her. The Indian Ocean rolled in, its waves hissing hypnotically on the sand. She counted seven cargo vessels standing out to sea, waiting to enter the port. Their lights blinked a greeting through the warm, embracing darkness.

Sensing her dreaminess, Hank fetched two glasses of champagne. 'To us,' he toasted.

She smiled and kissed him. Perhaps they could refresh the closeness and familiarity of their marriage. All was not lost, surely.

'It was thoughtful of you to accommodate us here. Thank you so much, dear. I love it.'

'Your father does too.'

'Sometimes I wish we lived here. Don't get me wrong, our Illovo house is great, but I miss the sea at times.'

'Why don't we buy an apartment along here? We could use it as a weekend getaway. It would help you combat your salt-air withdrawal symptoms, and we'd see more of Gerhard and Jakobus' families. It's the perfect investment too. Couldn't possibly go wrong.'

'Are you serious, Hank?' She hugged him.

'Of course I mean it. I wouldn't say it otherwise. You more than deserve it, my love. Whatever happened in Vryheid, your negotiating skills averted a financial disaster for De Bruyn Brothers. Although we don't show it, we are all in your debt.'

Draining their glasses, they walked back in, and Hank caught sight of himself in a mirror.

'Christ, look at me!' he exclaimed, repulsed. 'Some suave guy I look in these ragbag clothes.'

Neither he nor his brothers bothered to change out of their disguises before dining at Jakobus's house.

'You're perfectly fine from where I'm standing,' Anna grinned. Did she hear an excuse for Hank to take his clothes off and head for the spa? He'd expect her to join him.

* * *

The six o'clock wake-up call on the telephone roused them from their slumber the next morning. Hank stepped out of bed, stretching. Anna surveyed him sleepily from under the lashes of half-closed eyes. He had to have been working out. His whole body appeared more vigorous, and his face bore a healthier colour. He threw a bathrobe around himself and came to her side of the bed, gathering her in his arms.

'I have to be off, my dear. Maurice, Franz, and I are booked on an early flight home, but you and your father can follow later.'

She gave him a morning kiss. 'That means I will have a chance to see the boat,' she said.

'Yes, I'll let you know your mother's arrival time. You could both get on a plane that reaches Johannesburg at much the same time so you'll meet her there.'

'Great idea.' She kissed him again. 'I must see Fiona to check on Nozipho. I owe Fiona thanks too for sending up that case of clothes for me. It saves me running to the shops for extra gear.'

'Sweetheart, I hope you don't mind, but I'm taking your diamonds home. They're going in the vault. You can wear the replicas I've ordered.'

'Aaww! I'll feel incomplete without them.'

'I've been far too slack with your security in the past. A repeat of what has happened to you must be avoided. I don't want to see you get killed for those stones.'

'Replicas? How awful!' She winced as if stung by a bee.

'You can still wear the real ones for special occasions when I escort you.'

'But Dad is here. I'll be with him.'

'And that's another thing . . . I don't want you out and about unaccompanied from now on. You are not to go anywhere alone.'

'What? I'll feel imprisoned all over again.'

'That's regrettable, but how do we know there are no copycats prowling out there?'

'I think you are overreacting.'

'Don't imagine I haven't searched my soul after you vanished. I came to the painful conclusion I should have looked after you better.'

'Hank, I have to be able to lead a normal life. In any case, men get abducted too. Once you are Stock Exchange Council president, you will be an obvious choice for any rogue with a monetary grudge.'

'And your danger level will double, my dear.' Suddenly he laughed.

'What's tickled you?'

'I need bodyguards for you, and the best chaps I can think of are the ones who took William. They have to be experts.'

'I don't know them, but Sipho does. I doubt he'll tell you who they are.'

'We'll see.' He stepped into the bathroom.

Anna flopped back on her pillow. Hank was worried for her. Unfortunately, his concern meant her movements would be monitored. She'd be like a teenager again, having to report where she was going, when, and with whom and told what time to be back. *I might as well have remained at KwaZulu Medical*, she thought.

Gerhard arrived, taking Hank, Maurice, and Franz to the airport. Anna rang her father's room to hear his plans for the day. He had hired a car, he said, and was happy to take her anywhere she wished.

'Can we go on the boat?'

'How did I know you would ask that?' He laughed. 'Of course we shall go. Phil Bush, the previous owner, wants to come when I take her out next. I think he's very sorry to part with her.'

'I have to see Fiona and make sure Nozipho is happy. After that, I'm free to sail all day.'

'Come down and we'll have breakfast before I ring Phil.'

Anna showered quickly and, rummaging in the case of clothes Fiona dropped off, chose garments with a nautical character. Navy pants, a red T-shirt, and a white blazer created a sporty look. She found white sneakers in a plastic bag.

Monika and Nozipho couldn't contain themselves when the possibility of a boat trip beckoned.

'Can we come? Please, please, please!' Monika jumped around the kitchen with excitement.

'You're going to school, my girl,' Fiona said sharply.

'How about we leave the sailing till after school? I want to ring Phil next anyway. If we don't yet have children's life vests on board, I have to buy those first.' Albert calmed the kids. 'We want food for the trip too, don't we? All those arrangements take time, so if we go after school, that should be perfect.'

* * *

Anna loved the cruiser. She took the helm most of the time as it would be her only chance to do so.

She complained to Albert. 'I bet as soon as I return to Johannesburg, I will be immersed in money deals. There will be no time to enjoy the wonderful sense of freedom I derive from working a boat.'

A little before dinnertime, they dropped anchor and Phil attempted to fish. The kids climbed down the side via a steel ladder for a swim.

'Stay close to the boat, girls. You don't want to be shark bait,' she warned while scanning the water with binoculars.

Handing the glass to her father, she busied herself preparing a chicken salad for everyone. The kids were called back on board when it was ready, and they ate with an appetite enhanced by sun and sea.

They returned home well after dark, pleasantly relaxed and drowsy.

'The youngsters just need a bath to get the salt out of their hair,' Anna said to Fiona.

Monika was sent to the bathroom first because she still had a little homework to finish.

'Sailing was fun,' Nozipho commented to Anna while taking her turn to wash. Within an hour, both girls were fast asleep.

Jakobus returned from work. 'Oh, good to see you, Anna,' he smiled. 'Hank rang to say your mother will be here in three days. He'll call you at the hotel later with more details.'

'Fantastic!' She squeezed her father's arm. 'I'll check for flights as soon as I can.'

Jakobus poured drinks and slumped in a big chair. Albert regaled him with an account of their boat trip and how much Monika enjoyed it.

'She's a very good swimmer too,' Anna added. 'You could have a professional in the making.'

Father and daughter soon returned to the Edward, where Anna phoned Hank for news about her mother.

'We'll have a sumptuous dinner party when we're all together again,' Hank insisted. Franz and Rosemary are coming. So is Maurice and his girlfriend. William is guest of honour of course. He's bringing Indira because Melody is in Chicago visiting her brother. You don't mind, do you?' he questioned with enthusiasm. 'That's ten people including your parents.'

'How's Pompom, by the way?' Anna changed the subject, attaching more importance to her cat than to dinner parties.

'She's fine, although she's exhibiting weird habits since you've been away. I have some empathy with the animal. I've behaved strangely too due to my missing you.'

'I don't like the sound of that. What have you both been doing?' Anna's voice rang sternly in his ear although it was underscored with affection.

'Forget about me, but Pompom's been doing her Turkish Van thing, swimming around the fountain and coming in, wet as a floor mop, to jump straight onto your piano. She never did that before.'

'No, she mustn't! She'll ruin it!' Anna's voice rose to a shriek, causing Hank to cover the receiver's earpiece with his hand.

'Barbara shoos her off. She draped a heavy rug over the lid to minimize any damage. So far everything is still okay.'

'It's time I returned to reintroduce standards of proper behaviour in the household.'

'The sooner, the better, my dear.'

'For the next three days, I shall make the most of my sailing time, though.'

'Good, it will lift your heart and past experiences should fade.'

Fade? Anna thought. She couldn't wipe the past months off the slate and pretend they never existed. For Joshua to become a distant, non-invasive memory would take years. It wasn't likely to happen now that she and Hank had become partners in Josh's business. They were welded together, no matter how obstinately Hank refused to see it.

Pushing the thought aside, she said, 'We still have to find time to see Gogo. We can't disappoint her.'

'Let's arrange something after the party.'

* * *

'Mum! Yoohoo! Mum!' Anna called loudly across the arrival lounge, pushing her way through the throng of waiting people. Albert and Nozipho followed hard on her heels. Suddenly Vera spotted them and waved a green-and-gold scarf in their direction.

'My darling girl,' Vera cried. 'This is the happiest day in my life.'

'Did you have a good flight, Mum?'

'Come on, love,' Albert smiled broadly at Vera. 'Let's get your luggage into Dumisani's jeep and go home. I expect you're weary after so many hours flying. It gets tiring, even in first class.'

'Home,' her father said. Did Illovo feel like home to her now? Anna wondered as they crossed the portico while Dumisani Mkhize helped with their baggage.

The doors stood wide open, and she entered the vestibule feeling like a dream had transported her back through indefinite time.

Pompom was the first living creature she saw, sitting upright and alert, tail around paws, on the piano.

'Pompom . . . meow . . .' she called softly. 'I'm back, kitty.'

Pompom surveyed everyone from the lofty heights of the baby grand's lid before stepping down lightly onto the keyboard. A graceful leap landed her on the stool. She found the crowd of humans entering her abode disconcerting. After another encouraging 'meow' from Anna, the cat approached, purring a welcome around her legs.

'Hello, my pet,' Anna found herself saying with a start as she picked Pompom up to cuddle her.

Barbara Mkhize rushed through the dining room towards her.

'Mrs De Bruyn, thank God you're home safe and sound!'

Anna sat Pompom on the piano stool before embracing her housekeeper.

'It feels like I was gone for years. Now I have to acclimatize to home again. Where is Hank?'

'Mr De Bruyn is still at work. He will be home soon. Is everyone eager for dinner? It should be ready in twenty minutes.'

Maurice turned up next. 'Hank's on his way,' he smiled at Anna who sat him down, offering drinks.

'You are staying for dinner, I hope.'

'Yes, Hank suggested I should. He wants to fill me in on a couple of deals he struck.

Albert took Vera's bags to their bedroom, and she showered before dinner.

Nozipho sat forgotten on the piano stool, patting Pompom.

'Oh, you've made friends with her already,' Anna said, dashing from lounge to dining room to kitchen and back, ensuring the table was set for the correct number of people and chilling the right wine.

'You've won her heart otherwise she would run and hide. She doesn't like too many new faces in her house. You realise', she added with a laugh, 'this is not my house, it's Pompom's. Everything in it is Pompom's too. Cats have a possessive attitude.' She thought Nozipho showed signs of discomfort, sitting with her arms folded tightly around her. 'Are you hungry? We'll eat dinner soon, and then I'll show you around. Are you worried about sleeping alone in a big room?'

She nodded.

'We'll see what we can do about that. Let's feed ourselves first.'

It occurred to her that borrowing Monika during the upcoming school holidays would be the best way to ease Nozipho into her new world.

Franz arrived unannounced, and another place was set at the table.

'Can't stay long,' he said, 'but I thought I'd bring you a "welcome home" present, Anna.' He offered her the parcel.

'It's not gift-wrapped. I feared the contents might jar with any sort of pretty covering. You won't even like it much, but it might be useful.'

Anna laughed at him. 'Don't think your negative comments reduce my curiosity.'

She took the package to a sideboard and opened it.

'Oh, fair dinkum, Franz!' she exclaimed, lifting the lid of a leather case containing two Glock semi-automatic pistols, deadly toys in red velvet. Their convenient size felt comfortable to hold. They were made for a lady's self-defence. She replaced them carefully.

'Promise me you will always carry one in future,' he urged. 'And learn to use them well.'

'You know I'm a good shot. You said so yourself.'

'With training you will be even better. You will practise regularly?' he beseeched.

'Yes, I promise—faithfully. You have no idea how much I wished for just such a piece during the past months. I had more than enough provocation to use it too.'

He looked at her with an expression of horror, realizing she may have been more frightened than she admitted while away.

'Not shoot to kill, silly, but to intimidate. I would at least have looked like a woman who meant business.'

Hank arrived and eyed Franz's startling present with approval.

'That's exactly what you need, Anna.'

'Does that mean we can discard the bodyguard idea? Pit bulls make me nervous.'

'We'll review that later. Let's eat, I'm starving.'

Even after a good meal, Nozipho looked a little glum, and Anna feared she was homesick.

'Nozipho, would you like to phone Doctor Josh and tell him all about your sailing?'

Her face brightened instantly.

'Come, you can use the telephone in the kitchen.'

After a quick crash course in the operation of the device, Anna left her to talk. Her excitement bubbled forth in a stream of rapid Zulu, which even Barbara had difficulty following.

'I might have trouble settling her into a bedroom,' Anna whispered to Barbara. 'She's not accustomed to sleeping alone.'

'I can help,' Barbara chuckled. 'My son is bringing the grandkids later this evening. The cottage will be full of children for the school holidays. What's one more? Nozipho can share with them.'

'Doctor Josh says hello,' Nozipho relayed the message while skipping across the kitchen to where Anna and Barbara stood by the stove talking quietly.

'Mrs Mkhize will show you your bed now, Nozipho.'

'Where will that be?'

'In her cottage, just past the swimming pool. Follow her and you will see.'

Barbara noticed the girl directing uncertain looks at Anna.

'You better come too, Mrs De Bruyn.'

'Very well.' She took Nozipho's hand.

Fitz, the Mkhizes' poodle, squeezed out of the cottage door, bounding towards them barking, intent on an introduction to the new little human coming to visit. Priding himself on his efficiency as a super alert watchdog, he heard them coming as soon as they opened the back door. His clumsy offer of friendship, jumping up and licking, brought smiles to Nozipho's face.

'Does he play with Pompom?' she asked, patting him.

'Oh, no!' Anna and Barbara laughed together. 'There is no love lost between them. He has a healthy canine disrespect for cats.'

'What's his name?'

'Fitz! Down, Fitz,' Barbara scolded. 'Nozipho doesn't want to be licked like ice cream.'

They almost reached the Mkhizes' door when a low growl sounded close by. Pompom and Fitz eyeballed each other, Cold War style, across a boundary determined by themselves, which neither dared to breach.

Albert and Vera came out for a stroll in the garden before bed.

'What did I hear Barbara call that dog? Fitz? What an ugly name for a cute dog.' Albert loved all animals.

'The Mkhizes didn't name the dog,' Anna said. 'They inherited the little pest together with his title.'

'They could have changed it into something that sounds similar but more endearing . . . something like Fipps perhaps.'

'He belonged to Dumisani's friend, but he didn't christen the poodle either. That was done by the breeder in this instance. To Pompom's disgust, Dumisani brought Fitz home after his owner died. The critter's full name is Fitznothing.'

'Fitz what?' Albert laughed.

'The breeder wedded Fitz's mother to a particular male with whom he thought a litter of especially sweet puppies would result. Fitz's mother refused to consummate an arranged marriage. By devious means she managed to enter another enclosure where her true love was housed. The four puppies born from that union were thus illegitimate; bastards. The disappointed breeder gave them silly names with the Fitz prefix. Fitzwhatsit, Fitzwhatever, Fitzsomething and Fitznothing.'

'The poor dog!' Vera's infectious laugh set them all off as they walked back inside.

'Pompom,' Anna called. 'Where are you, Pompom? It's bed time . . ., come on.' She carried her cat into the house.

Hank poured drinks for all while Anna tidied the dining room.

'Sit down, Anna,' he said. 'Where are the kitchen maids?'

'It's getting late, Hank. I sent them home. It was high time Barbara knocked off too. I'm sure a grotty dining room and kitchen is the last thing she wants to see tomorrow morning.'

'What's the point of having domestic staff when you do the work?'

'They can't cut themselves in half. If your business finishes late, delaying dinner, they might have to work in shifts.'

'Good point, we'll look into that,' he said, handing her a glass. 'This is your first evening at home. We should be celebrating, not working.'

He took her hand, leading her into the lounge, where Albert and Vera enjoyed their last drink. Pompom sat beside Vera but, on seeing Anna, ran to her, meowing.

'Have you been fed, *my pet*? Let's check your bowl.' Pompom's equipment was in the laundry, where with a slight tremble of the hand, Anna refilled the cat's dishes. Would she ever call Pompom *my pet* without perceiving the echo of a seductive voice?

When she returned, her parents embraced her and retired. Hank saw Maurice out. While setting the burglar alarm, he said, 'Bring your drink, dear. We might as well go to bed too.'

Anna followed that suggestion readily. She had enough for one day and was surprised at Hank's stamina. Quite often he had gone to bed before her but not tonight.

'About tomorrow . . .' he said while watching her brush her hair, 'I have to see Michael Tripp, and I have no idea how long our discussions will take. If you want to keep your parents company, you don't have to come in.'

'I might as well pick up the old routine soon.' Seated at the dressing table mirror, she smiled, meeting his eyes in the reflection.

'Broadbent wants to see you at your earliest convenience.'

'Did you tell him I'm home?'

'Yes, but he didn't seem surprised. William came with me and explained that he had another, more thorough, look around KwaZulu Medical and was no longer certain it was the place he was taken to. He withdrew the allegations against the clinic's management.'

'Good man! He deserves his dinner party. Tell me exactly what you reported to Broadbent so I don't contradict you.'

'I told him it was all a misunderstanding. We thought Malcolm Price planned a vendetta against you. When that Darren Thompson chap followed you, you took fright and vanished.'

Anna continued brushing, wondering if Broadbent believed she had lost her nerve so easily.

'What do you think of Franz's welcome-home present?'

'Chilling but appropriate.'

'I have a gift for you too, dear, one that you will like better.'

He produced a small box from his dressing gown pocket and held it out to her. When she reached for it he pulled back.

'Kiss first!' He looked at her longingly.

Laughing, she jumped up, hugging and kissing him.

'Now you may open it.'

'They are absolutely beautiful,' she beamed, lifting Marquise diamond drop earrings out of their snap-lid box. 'Am I allowed to wear them or are they to be mothballed in the vault too?'

'You can see they didn't come from my father's mine, but I was impressed with their design. The gems are not flawless, but an untrained desperado's eye would still feel temptation at their sight.'

Anna resumed her seat at the dressing table, exchanging the studs she wore all day for the attractive present.

'They look great! Thanks, Hank. I really would like to wear them.'

'I guess it's all right at work where familiar people surround you,' he consented, knowing full well there was no purpose in giving her jewellery only to have it sitting in a safe.

She kissed him again. 'They are so lovely.'

Pulling her closer, he undressed and kissed her with urgent possessiveness. She yielded, surprised. He hadn't been so vivacious for the longest time.

'Absence has made the heart grow fonder, has it?' she questioned, bewildered.

'Not only the heart, my dear . . . other appendages too.'

Her silver-bell laughter filled the bedroom.

'Oh, sweetheart, I haven't heard you laugh like that for so very long. It's a surefire remedy for my glum feelings during your absence.'

She completed her undressing while he watched intently.

'Tell me,' he asked suddenly without explanation, 'why have you never initiated sex? In all our years of marriage, I don't recall you ever making the first move.'

'I'm timid and inhibited,' she whispered with a raunchy sideways glance at him, her glowing eyes rebutting her claim.

'Really? I wouldn't have thought that.' He stepped forward, grasping her. 'Let's see if your reserve can be overcome.'

* * *

The rising sun streamed into the breakfast room. Its sliding doors leading to the swimming pool were opened wide, letting in the morning air.

As was her custom before her abduction, Anna rose early with Hank. Together they ate fruit and yogurt and discussed their plans for the day. This morning, Albert and Vera joined them.

'What would you like to do today, Mum?' Anna asked while sipping coffee.

'I'd love to see De Wildt's Cheetah Farm and then perhaps continue on to Pretoria.'

'Good, take my car. I'll go to the office with Hank. With any luck I can get that unpleasant interview with Captain Broadbent done today so I'll have free time to spend with you tomorrow. I know you love the shopping malls.' She winked at her mother.

The Mkhizes' grandchildren raced out squealing for joy as Dumisani rolled the cover off the pool for their morning splash. Nozipho was with them.

'Good morning, everyone,' Anna called, stepping out to watch the fun. 'Did you sleep all right?' she asked Nozipho, who nodded cheerfully.

'Why do you have a cover over the pool?' Nozipho asked, her curiosity restored by sleep and breakfast.

'So Fitz and Pompom don't come to harm,' Anna laughed. 'Pompom is a Turkish Van, and they don't mind getting wet,' she explained to the kids. 'At one stage she had a penchant for walking around the edge of the pool, eyeing the water. One day Fitz chased her. She slipped into the water and swam away. She didn't know dogs could paddle.' Anna chuckled as the kids' faces broadened into grins. 'Fitz jumped in and pursued her, trying to nip at her tail. Pompom panicked, and frightful pandemonium and splashing ensued. Fearing both animals would drown, I leapt in after them, just like you see me now—already dressed for the office, make-up applied, hair fixed—and pulled them out.' The kids laughed uproariously. 'After that, Fitz and Pompom signed a treaty. The front of the house with the fountain is Pompom's leisure area, while Fitz remains master of the back garden and pool, which we keep covered to avoid further disasters. If either animal violates the agreement, there's hell to pay, and I need to act as judge and jury to keep the peace.'

Unfamiliar with the story, Anna's parents joined in the laughter. 'I would love to have seen you,' Vera giggled, unable to imagine her well-groomed daughter looking bedraggled with a wet cat under one arm and a dripping dog under the other. 'Talk about a drowned rat.'

* * *

Whistles, cheers, and clapping sounded as Anna stepped from the lift into the De Bruyn Brothers reception area. Her office resembled a jungle with every variety of flowers decorating all corners and spilling over into Maurice's room. Staff members greeted her with well-wishes, expressing relief at seeing her.

'Smorgasbord dinner and drinks for all in the conference room today!' Hank invited happily. 'Everything will be back to normal now,' he announced. To prove the point, he sat down at his desk and, as before Anna's misadventure, left his door open for people to enter and discuss their problems.

When an acceptable level of industriousness returned to every section, Anna settled at her desk too. Broadbent's interview played on her mind, and she telephoned to arrange seeing him later in the morning. A staff huddle in Hank's office followed informing her about matters which arose during her absence.

Her telephone rang as she walked back to her desk carrying an arm full of files. Occasionally, Hank's extension rang together with hers, and they picked it up as one.

'Anna De Bruyn speaking!' Hank listened in.

'Anna, thank goodness I've got you.' Sipho's worried voice carried to her.

'You sound distressed. Is something wrong?'

'The police took Josh away at a quarter to six this morning. He's arrested under suspicion of kidnapping and extortion.'

'No! How could this happen?' Her heart pounded. 'William has withdrawn his accusations.'

'But Paul, Geoff, and Frank haven't. Josh's lawyer is working on a bail application, but I know I won't be able to raise the money. I think we're looking at something like R35,000. The police department seems determined to make things hard for him.'

Anna breathed deeply to steady her voice. 'Someone in the police service is playing guessing games. William has seen KwaZulu Medical and admits he is not sure if he was imprisoned there. How can the other three who haven't set foot in the place continue pressing charges against persons unknown? Like William, they saw nothing.'

'The cops are on a fishing expedition. They have to be seen doing their job.'

'Wish they'd go and catch real criminals,' Anna growled with disgust. 'I'm seeing Broadbent later today. Maybe I can get some sense out of him. Where have they taken Josh? Is he in Vryheid?'

'Yes, so his lawyer tells me.'

'Okay, leave it with me. I'll call you back as soon as I come up with a practical solution.'

'Don't you dare bail him out!' Hank came over, pointing a determined finger at her. 'Let him stew for a bit.'

'Fine, fine,' she agreed, agitated and aggrieved at his dictatorial stance. Her rebellious nature came to the fore. Why shouldn't she bail Josh out? What exactly had he done that was earth-shattering? He hadn't killed anyone. Nor had he exploited the poor. He didn't deal in drugs or smuggle arms. His only iniquity lay in lifting money from four fat cat business executives in order to relieve the suffering of disadvantaged children. The dough didn't even come out of the guys' own pockets. Their companies had forked out, and they could afford it. It represented small change to them. If their insurances didn't cough up to cover the loss, they would probably deduct the sum from their profit and pay less tax, thereby recouping part of the money anyway.

Anna leaned back in her chair. The more she thought about it, the angrier she became. 'Can't think of a more direct method of wealth distribution,' she muttered when Hank retreated. At least this way, the money was going straight to where it was needed without countless administrative or corrupt hands dipping into it first.

As soon as Hank and Maurice left the office for their meeting with the Stock Exchange Council, she picked up the phone.

'Could I speak to Mr Benny Shanks, please? It's Anna De Bruyn calling . . . yes, it is urgent.'

* * *

'Ah, Mrs De Bruyn! Good to see you. Please, take a seat. Coffee?'

Captain Broadbent's overwhelming friendliness distracted Anna. She mistrusted him, wondering what pitfalls his mind had dug for her and which direction his questions would take.

'I hope you can clear up one or two points for me.'

'I'd be happy to, if I'm able.' If only she knew what story Josh had spun at his end. She prayed silently their tales would tally.

'You were Professor Mtolo's financial advisor?' he began.

'Still am.'

'Some confusion exists about KwaZulu Medical's Swiss bank account. Can you tell us anything about it? For example, when was it established?'

'I don't know.'

'What do you mean you don't know? You oversaw his investment portfolio.'

'The account already existed when Professor Mtolo approached De Bruyn Brothers for advice.'

'Who helped him before he came to you?'

'He came to us from Pale and Gibbs. He didn't tell us why he wanted to make the change, and we don't ask. It's his prerogative to choose who buys and sells shares for him.'

'And were his financial affairs in order at that stage?'

'As far as I could ascertain . . . yes.'

'KwaZulu Medical is still repaying a loan from the ANC?'

'That is correct.'

'Where did Professor Mtolo live before the clinic was founded?'

'I don't know,' she answered truthfully but Broadbent looked at her with a frown. Her replies contained too many 'I don't knows' for his liking. Anna thought it was time she threw a question on the table.

'Captain Broadbent, what is this about? Is Professor Mtolo accused of misdeeds? You see, I shouldn't be discussing his affairs so freely. It is confidential. This is not a murder investigation, surely.'

'Would it surprise you to know we have him in custody for extortion? Kidnapping as well.'

'I'm speechless!'

'You spent a good while at KwaZulu Medical. Did you notice anything untoward during that time?'

'Good heavens, no!'

'What did you do there?'

With a sigh, Anna wondered if her replies were adding up in Broadbent's mind. Would her next answer see her tumbling into that pit of his?

'I worked with Sipho Gwala, the finance manager. We hoped to cross all financial t's and dot the i's in preparation for a stock market listing. That is a long way off, though.'

'Why didn't you tell your husband where you were?'

Did she hear the mouse trap snap just then? It felt like something had hit her.

'Captain, you are aware of the Malcolm Price scandal. You also know about our man in the yellow VW Golf and the possible connection there. If Price planned revenge and if certain cabinet ministers became sufficiently nervous, how could I risk telling Hank where I was hiding? The knowledge would endanger him too. I didn't want to return home to a dead husband.'

Broadbent sighed and drank his coffee. He knew he'd been told a sob story, but how could he prove it was false?

'What made you select KwaZulu Medical as a hiding place?'

'Coincidence, I suppose.' She shrugged. 'Professor Mtolo was working at the academic hospital, where I met him to discuss the Swiss account among other things. He gave me a lift back to where I parked my car. While driving, I told him about the yellow VW following me. He offered me sanctuary at his clinic, thinking I should stay out of Johannesburg for a while to keep safe.'

Broadbent's mind clicked, but he couldn't grasp the elusive thought. Was there something in this? Either his earlier hunch about her leaving Hank was correct, or Mtolo had used the opportunity to abduct her on the spur of the moment. But Mtolo, if he was EEM, never sent a ransom demand. What did that make it? A domestic dispute? A love triangle? He remembered Hank's bruised knuckles when talking to him last. His explanation was that he was working out and the punch bag had taken revenge on him. He had bought boxing gloves now. That was true enough. He'd just come from a sporting shop and still carried the parcel and receipt when he turned up for his talk. He also looked healthier than previously, so there might be a grain of truth in his story. However, when Mtolo was arrested, the report said his face was badly bruised and his nose broken. Did Hank thump him and get his wife back? Of course, Mtolo formulated a quick excuse about attempting to break up a shebeen brawl. The warring parties took exception to his interference, he said.

Broadbent let none of his thoughts show, sipping more coffee very slowly and smiling.

'That Swiss account again,' he said at last. 'Why did you need to talk about that?'

'The interest derived from the funds there wasn't recorded as income. It looked like tax evasion, but it was quite unintentional. I took immediate steps to rectify the matter.'

'And was it corrected?'

'Oh yes, straight away.'

Broadbent changed the subject abruptly. 'William Rosenberg was abducted by a group calling themselves the Economic Equity Movement. With time, he became convinced he was held at KwaZulu Medical. He insisted Joshua Mtolo was the mastermind behind everything. He withdrew the accusation recently. Did he truly think he erred or was he leaned on to alter his story?' Here Broadbent gave her a mystified look. She felt uneasy, exposed to his scrutiny. She hoped her face wasn't betraying her.

'Did you ever see Mr Rosenberg while you were there? Why should he change his statement?'

'No, I did not see Mr Rosenberg. That's not surprising, though. The place is quite big, and my accommodation was at the back of the staff quarters.'

'Who persuaded him to change his opinion, Mrs De Bruyn?' Broadbent's voice had a 'don't mess with me' ring to it.

'You mean *what* persuaded him?'

'I said *who*?'

'Didn't he tell you?'

'I want to hear your ideas.'

This was the mother of all awkward questions. What explanations had William invented for changing his mind? Had he confessed his friendship with Indira? There was no way around this.

She would have to answer as frankly as she could. She hoped her smile convinced Broadbent even if her words didn't satisfy him.

'As I said, I didn't see Mr Rosenberg at KwaZulu Medical. If I had, I could have assured him there was nothing sinister about the place. However, I believe Dr Indira Naidoo, the surgeon there, is a good friend of his. My theory is she may have shown him around the premises whereupon he realized his mistake.'

* * *

After Broadbent, Anna's next pursuit was lunch at Benny Shanks' Bistro. Arriving almost an hour late thanks to the captain's verbosity, she hoped Benny might offer her a stiff drink and a good meal. She needed both, and he did not disappoint her, insisting she ate before they talked business.

'So what's the trouble with Josh?' he asked, bringing her a cappuccino and sitting down to listen.

'Joshua is in jail,' she said, sounding sullen.

'Yes, you said that on the phone.' He was surprised to see Anna looking downcast. Could it be *that* important to her?

'Hank won't let me bail him out. Sipho reckons we'll need about R35,000. I can't take that out of my account here because Hank sees the statements, and getting the money from my Australian investments may take too long. Josh doesn't have that time. His patients need him. The students rely on him. The IFP has rallies coming up where Josh promised to organize first aid stations. He can't be stuck in custody for long—it's impossible. He's too much in demand.' Her hands fluttered in all directions as she spoke, energized by alcohol and caffeine.

'Could I prevail on you to be my proxy?' She gave Benny a pleading smile. 'Would you offer bail for Josh in my stead? When my Australian funds come through, I will reimburse you, that goes without saying.'

Benny chuckled, his inquisitiveness tantalized by the fact that Hank refused his assistance. His radar perceived a delicious scandal in the offing.

'I'd do anything for Josh, you know that, but why was he arrested?'

'It's a long story, Mr Shanks . . .'

* * *

What a day! Anna reflected. It seemed to lack its full twenty-four hours, or was her watch on the blink? Her intention was to reach the office before Hank and Maurice. The celebratory smorgasbord dinner would lose its significance without the guest of honour present. She stepped on the gas. The motor whirred in tune with her brain, which was in overdrive due to Benny's coffee.

Benny, she thought, would do whatever it took to free Josh from the jaws of the law. Yet she was unhappy. A peculiar feeling of dejection, which overcame her all too frequently of late, stalked her again. She cursed the necessity to take action behind Hank's back. She should tell him about Benny's involvement. She wouldn't rest easy till she did.

Was her marriage unravelling? She felt a twinge in the region of her diaphragm at the thought. Since when was she deliberately deceiving Hank in this way? The little white lies, darker-coloured ones too, multiplied like compound interest. In time, his confidence in her would shatter. That would spell the end. Was that what she wanted? The answer was a resounding no! *Oops . . . red light! Watch it, woman. You'll kill yourself!* She hit the brake just in time.

Heartily sick of the spin doctoring and schemes her life required these days, she wondered when the half-truths, twists of facts, and excuses would explode in her face. Now that he had a hold of Josh, how deeply was Broadbent digging to find evidence that would stick in court?

To distract herself from the emotional indigestion, she let her thoughts drift to her parents. Were they having a good time? Hopefully they wouldn't be late for the smorgasbord. Barbara's thankful smile when told nobody would eat at home today was a sight to behold. She could spend the day in her cottage with the grandkids. Nozipho was unlikely to miss her. The Mkhizes were as close to a family as she had been for a long time.

Anna progressed smoothly through the traffic and arrived early enough to retouch her make-up and check the messages on Hank's desk. None were urgent. Nkosinathi walked past, looking for Maurice.

'He hasn't returned yet,' she told him, wondering why he appeared so serious when everybody else gave her jaunty and supportive smiles.

'Can I help you, Nkosinathi? You look concerned.' Judging by his hangdog posture, she expected him to confide girlfriend troubles.

'I'm worried about Freddie Bonga's mother. The comrades burnt her house down,' he replied, looking near to tears at the thought.

'Is she all right? She didn't get hurt?'

'Luckily she wasn't at home, but now she has nowhere to live, and she lost her job too.'

'That's bitter.' Anna pointed to the visitor's chair at her desk. 'Do you know any details? Would you like to sit and talk about it?'

He sat down with a sigh. 'The comrades threatened to torch her house when she wouldn't observe the rent and rates boycott. That was some time ago, and she's been a target ever since. Last Tuesday, she witnessed a hit-and-run accident in her street. Only it was deliberate. A motorist had knocked a pedestrian down, meaning to kill him. Mrs Bonga noted the car number and told the police when they asked questions. The comrades subsequently accused her of being a police informer and set fire to her house.'

'Where's Mrs Bonga now?'

'With her brother in Vryheid.'

'What went wrong with her job?'

'Her employer thought the comrades would come looking for her at work and possibly burn down his shop too, so he sacked her.'

'Charming.' When Anna shook her head without saying any more, Nkosinathi stood up to return to his desk.

'Wait,' she called. 'Does Mrs Bonga have new employment yet? What was she doing in her last job?'

'She was shop assistant. It might take a while before she finds new work.'

Anna scribbled on a phone message pad. 'Can you get in contact with her?'

'I think so. Freddie doesn't come to Soweto on weekends now, but I can ring his uncle's workshop.'

'Tell Mrs Bonga to phone Barbara Mkhize. Here's the number.' Nkosinathi pocketed the paper, which she passed him with an uplifting smile.

'Mrs Mkhize is my housekeeper, and she needs help desperately. We have spare accommodation for Mrs Bonga too. It might solve a problem for her.'

'Thank you, Mrs De Bruyn. I will let her know.'

'One good turn deserves another,' she said, earning herself a broad grin from Nkosinathi.

Hank and Maurice arrived soon after, followed closely by Albert and Vera.

'Dinnertime . . . come on, everybody!' Hank called them to gather around the conference table.

* * *

How automatic old routines were, Anna thought, pulling the covers over Hank and herself. They nearly always waited till bedtime before reviewing the day's events under four eyes. It wasn't a particularly sexy thing to do, and she made a mental note to change their schedule to avoid the practice in future.

'Did you enjoy the dinner, love? You didn't appear to be your sparkling self. Something not right?'

She had already told him about Mrs Bonga while they sat in the spa. *Now for the hard part*, she thought, sighing.

'I'm sorry about Joshua's bail,' she said turning towards him.

'What's there to worry about? He'll have time to think about his stupidity in the lock-up.'

'You told me not to bail him out. I didn't, but I persuaded a good friend of his to do so.'

He looked at her strangely. She couldn't tell if he was cross.

'I'm sorry to be so devious,' she said earnestly. 'But Josh has too many patients relying on him, and we have to eliminate the makings of a scandal, Mr President.'

Hank said nothing. It was rare when she couldn't read his expression to gauge his reaction. Was he hiding something?

'Are you angry with me?'

'Yes and no.'

'Please don't give me an ambiguous reply. I'm too worried. I hate crossing your intentions like that.'

'I did something behind your back today too,' he said sheepishly. 'You're not going to like it one bit.' He looked at her with a half-smile. 'At least you have the courage to be open about your machinations.'

'Oh, hello! What do you have to tell me?'

Relieved he was taking the matter in his stride, she became playful. Wrenching the bedcover back off him, she said, 'Tell me this minute, or else!'

'Or else what?'

Within an instant, she was on top of him. 'This is your inhibited woman who never initiates sex,' she whispered, her mouth close to his ear. 'You will tell her your secrets fully or burn in erotic purgatory.'

'What, with you on top?' he laughed. 'Bring it on, darling. The more, the better.'

'You will be only too happy to divulge all by the time I finish with you.'

* * *

Chapter 13

Reflections on Water

When the bow dipped, the water crashed on board. Swishing and foaming sternwards, it ran off through the scuppers as the boat lifted, climbing the crest of a new wave. From behind dark clouds, the sun watched the sea's turmoil. Briefly, a searching beam touched Anna's face while she braced herself, straddle-legged, at the wheel, anticipating the next onslaught of wave power.

'Wow!' she called to a passing gull. 'Where did that come from?' Weather predictions had been favourable when she had set out early this morning—and now this!

Nature caught her unawares, jolting her out of her reverie and directing her concentration to the sea and distant coastline. It had not begun raining in earnest when she found herself plunging and ploughing in increasingly poor visibility towards Richards Bay. With one hand, she switched the clear vision window on, while with the other she grasped her spray jacket. A visual check of the deck assured her all equipment was secured. She stepped to the radio, calling Richards Bay, alerting other small craft to the deteriorating conditions. When she ventured out of the wheelhouse, the wind whipped her French plait across her shoulders like a cat-o'-nine-tails.

Anna's thoughts were miles away, but now she summoned them back, and like homing pigeons, they returned to their centre of creation. Unless this squall subsided soon, there was no estimating her arrival time at Richards Bay. Joshua waited for her there. Her mind's eye saw him clearly—agitated, pacing, fearing for her safety.

But Anna felt free in body and spirit. The *Island Gypsy* cabin cruiser was hers and hers alone. Nobody would dare touch or lay claim on it. She had bought it after her parents returned to Sydney. It wasn't the latest whiz-bang model, but it was sturdy with reliable 120 hp Twin Ford diesels. At a ten-metre length, it was small enough for her to work single-handed, but roomy, offering every comfort. She named it Vera for her mother and hired the Wilson's Wharf berth her father had used in Durban as its permanent home.

Alone in the wide open sea, she could think. She revelled in the meticulous seamanship the capricious conditions required because it disciplined her, helping her to take life cautiously. Here she could face her emotional difficulties without blowing them out of proportion.

On the telephone, she had discussed her craving for aloneness with Josh, saying she felt like a snail seeking non-stop shelter in its shell. 'Does that mean I can't cope? Or is it just my introvert nature?' she asked him warily.

'Who ever heard of Anna De Bruyn not coping?' He laughed but couldn't disguise the concern in his voice. 'You are inclined to hide away, but that doesn't mean you can't deal with pressure. It's more like refreshing your resources to battle on because really, there's not much of the introvert in you.' He spoke lightly, but there was more to come. She listened to his opinion carefully.

'I think you may be a little depressed, my pet. Make a list of everything that troubles you, and work on each issue one after the other till they're resolved and eliminated. I can't suggest any more, Anna, because we are too close. Our emotions will get in the way. There's a chap in Johannesburg you can see if you wish. Dr Damien Winter is excellent.'

Josh sounded worried, almost guilty, but he had hit the nail on the head. Too unyielding to acknowledge depression, she avoided consulting Dr Winter but realized the truth of Josh's words as she drew up her list of bugs. Writing down her grievances was the easy part. Dealing with them may prove impossible while she was angry and disappointed with Hank.

Fault lines emerged in their marriage big enough to make the earth sway beneath her. *No, silly woman, that was just the heaving deck.*

Should she divide her page into two columns? One side for petty injustices, the other to record serious irritations. As she wrote, she found that the petty and serious merged into one when neglected little annoyances festered and grew. *Forget the columns*, she told herself. *Treat it like a human interest story.*

When did the first crack appear? Who was to blame? What irked her most? Sitting in her study, patting Pompom on her lap, she allowed time for thought. What could she have done better? Could Hank have responded differently? Joshua? 'We all made bad decisions which are almost impossible to revoke,' she wrote.

Did it start with Hank's hiring of retired Major Ernest Mortimer as her bodyguard? He knew she was dead set against the idea. Perhaps the rot had set in with something as insignificant as Hank taking her diamonds away. It left her questioning whether the jewellery ever was her property. Maybe it belonged to the De Bruyn family? Did Hank really present it to her or was he viewing it as a company asset from Walter De Bruyn's mine, which she was merely allowed to borrow? He never clarified the matter. As she received no recompense from the firm for her work, she saw the gems as her remuneration. Hank De Bruyn giveth, and Hank De Bruyn taketh away, it seemed. Was he always ambivalent like that? Had she been too besotted all these years to see his less-flattering materialistic traits?

The greater blow had probably been Hank's handling of the bodyguard affair. She had come into the office late that morning after visiting Vince Lewis in hospital. When Hank called her into his room, she was confronted by a tall sixty-year-old stranger.

'Come in, dear,' Hank said. 'Meet Major Ernest Mortimer. He's taking charge of security for us. He has a team of three men to keep an eye on our vehicles, alarms, cash, and related matters. One of his young colleagues will deal with IT security.'

How she kept her temper that day she couldn't say.

'Ernest's a nice chap,' she joked despite her fury when he left. 'He's very much like my dad.' Looking askance at Hank, she added, 'You have a knack for picking the right people for jobs.'

'Of course I have, sweetheart. Look at the wife I chose!'

She picked a paper clip from his desk and chucked it at his chest. It pinged softly as it bounced off his gold tiepin.

'Eh, watch the missiles, lady.'

Retreating to her office, she showed her displeasure by closing the door. It was the last she saw of Hank for that working day. Maurice popped in quickly to say they were off to a meeting. Hank didn't bother speaking to her.

The relinquishing of her car to Ernest twisted the knife in her wound. He was to drive her when and where she wished. The vehicle was De Bruyn Brothers property, but she wasn't giving it up without a fight.

'My car!' she demanded explosively when Hank had a moment to listen. She had never addressed him in that commanding tone. He looked at her, shocked.

Trying to calm her, he explained reasonably, 'Women driving alone are not safe from hijackers, dear. And what's more, if you don't drive yourself, you have extra time to read and prepare for meetings. That has to be an advantage.'

'It's all right for you,' she countered facetiously. 'You bought your new Porsche Targa Sports to match your council president's hat.'

'You can use the Mercedes if you need transport urgently.' He tried placating her, seeing the rage in her eyes.

Since when had they been so at odds? Had Gerhard's comment about De Bruyn Brothers not negotiating with criminals been the catalyst? She understood it to mean she wasn't valued. Her life and well-being had been of less consequence than half-a-million US dollars in De Bruyn's accounts. When she touched on that sore point in passing conversation, Hank glossed it over replying, 'Gerhard didn't think deeply enough before speaking. He does that at times. I doubt he grasped the implications at that point. His gaffe didn't dawn on him till your father spelt it out.'

Hank was snowed under with work while settling into his new role at the Bourse. Much of his time was spent in meetings with the finance minister and his director general, reserve bank officials, treasury bosses, and captains of industry. He had little chance to deal with anything other than business. Oh, but he did have sufficient leisure to choose his new car.

What about his promise regarding the Marine Parade apartment? He had not lifted a finger in that direction nor had he given her the go-ahead to deal with the matter alone.

Well, Anna thought, *he can forget it*. She no longer desired it. She had her boat now, which was indisputably hers. She had paid for it herself, and as the De Bruyns were no sailors, it was unlikely to see them on board. The apartment would have been available to all and sundry, community property without privacy. She recalled feeling let down when Hank said it was a good investment in the same breath as suggesting he wanted to please her. It was to have been her reward for keeping financial rogues from De Bruyn's door.

Unlike Hank, Benny Shanks always had time to help friends despite being fully occupied running his restaurant chain. He visited Josh in jail and deposited the bail money with his lawyer. Josh was released after surrendering his passport. Anna hoped the court would find there was no case to answer.

Benny again drove out of his way to call at her office one afternoon with the good news he had heard that Josh's case may be thrown out for lack of evidence. When she insisted on giving him the bail money back, he ran to the lift, hurriedly pressing the Down button.

'Bye!' He waved with a laugh and was gone.

He left a flyer lying on her desk announcing the date and time of the next IFP rally at the Jabulani Stadium in Soweto. Josh had plans to man two first-aid stations there with the help of colleagues from Johannesburg.

The flyer became the focus of discussions at home. The Mkhizes wanted to be at the rally punctually. So did Mrs Bonga, who had joined the household recently. Nozipho, always alert, had wind of the activity already and was excited about seeing her dear father figure, Doctor Josh.

Nkosinathi and Cindy Khumalo-Mataka made arrangements to go till she heard Josh would be there and changed her mind. She later accompanied Solomon when he agreed to come, promising to steer clear of the first-aid tents.

Although she hated crowds, Anna was tempted to join in. She saw the Inkatha leader on television almost daily and wanted to hear him speak in person. However, Major Mortimer had other business that Saturday and couldn't escort her.

'But I'll be with a whole group of people,' she argued in vain.

Hank put his foot down, firmly stopping her leaving the house. When she tried giving the situation a positive slant by suggesting they have a quiet afternoon together instead, Hank announced he had a dinner to attend with clients. He returned late at night, finding her still playing the piano and refusing to go to bed with him.

He climbed the stairs slowly, shaking his head. He'd have to sleep alone once more. Hadn't he had enough practice at that lately? Weariness threatened. The extra responsibilities demanding his attention had recently stopped him giving his physical fitness priority. He would have to make time for it or he wouldn't conquer the workload. He'd neglected his diet as well. *Can't afford that.*

Sleep just wasn't happening. Each tick of the clock sounded like a cymbal crash. By two in the morning, he was still awake, tossing about. Anna hadn't come. He threw the blanket aside and went in search of her. The lamp beside the piano was still burning, as was the lounge light. Music books and the keyboard lid were left open too.

He found Anna on the couch, fully clothed, sleeping curled up as tightly as the cat at her feet. Wet tissues lay bunched on the carpet. Should he wake her?

There was never so much discord between them as now. Both were unaccustomed to handling disputes because they rarely arose. He couldn't even blame Joshua for it. The bastard had been in jail. Not long enough unfortunately, but the court case was still to come. Paul, Geoff, and Frank stuck to their guns, wanting justice. The witch doctor might get his comeuppance yet.

He decided to make a pot of herb tea and wake Anna when he had it ready. While waiting for the kettle to boil, he wondered, dismayed, what scuttled his resolve to do fun things together with Anna and make her happy. Time was his worst enemy right now. It was alleged to be equal to money, if the old saying was true, but now it slipped badly out of kilter. Money flowed in, but time dissolved like sugar in coffee.

Their interaction worsened by the week. He wasn't imagining that. At the time of the dinner party for William, Anna was almost her normal self. Her parents were still here, and she played music to please them. It was quite a performance with Maurice and his girlfriend, Gill, bringing their instruments and William lugging his cello in. They formed an enjoyable group with Anna on piano and sometimes singing, Maurice playing oboe, and Gill violin. The food was to die for. Barbara excelled herself now that Mrs Bonga helped her. It became a very late night for everyone.

The next two functions were big gatherings to see Michael Tripp into retirement and welcome the one and only Hank De Bruyn as the new president. Anna, as usual, outshone the other women present. She looked refined and dignified, playing on that instinct for elegant simplicity she always applied to her choice of clothes. He noticed men stealing discreet glances at her long black skirt and the split up its side. A cowl-necked white blouse drew inoffensive attention to her bust. He let her wear the diamonds for both occasions. At least that was one promise he managed to keep.

The farewell dinner for her parents was a riot. Anna's cousins had arrived by then, and their teenage sons teased the Mkhize grandkids without mercy. They threw balls for Fitz, making him dance on his hind legs, and raced the youngsters in the pool, letting them win occasionally.

Once they departed, Vera flying, the men sailing home, the house became quiet again, and Anna turned morose. Was she missing her family? Perhaps she was homesick. Their prearranged trip to Sydney was a non-starter, thanks to Joshua's intervention. 'That character has much to answer for.' Hank swore like a trooper.

He made his way to the lounge carefully, not wanting to upset the tea tray. Resting it on the coffee table, he tiptoed to the piano to stack the sheet music and close the cover. His movements roused Pompom, who resented his intrusion just so his desire for tidiness was satisfied. She crouched, belly to the floor, sneaking behind him and leaping on the keys. The discordant clang startled him and woke Anna.

'Pompom, what the hell? Oh, it's you!'

'I'm sorry, my dear. I didn't want to wake you so rudely.' He came to join her. 'Pompom was helping me sort your music. I've made you some tea.'

'Thank you, I can do with that.'

Hank looked dreadfully tired, she thought, watching him pour her drink. She shouldn't have been so hard on him. It plagued his mind, causing sleeplessness. For a moment she felt guilty but recovered quickly on seeing the pile of wet tissues accumulated beside the couch. He was unduly harsh with her too. Why were they undermining all chance of a harmonious life?

'Shame you weren't at that dinner with me. I met very interesting people there.'

'You didn't ask me.'

'No, I should have.'

She looked at him wordlessly.

'Watch out, that's quite hot,' he warned, passing her a cup.

He could think of nothing else to say without starting arguments. *What a poor show we're making of this*, he thought. He should sit beside her, holding her in his arms. Fearing he wouldn't be welcome, he racked his brain for ways to dismantle the invisible barrier between them. He found that apart from work, they had nothing to talk about. When he looked at it clearly, he admitted that was nearly always the case. It had certainly been standard practice long before Joshua came on the scene. Had their nearly eighteen-year-old marriage been a life side by side rather than together as one?

'Your father forgot his boat catalogue,' he said, picking it up from the arm of the chair where Albert had left it. He handed it across to her, trying to catch her eye.

While she flipped listlessly through its pages, he made another attempt at conversation. 'You know that bulk carrier crowd, Oreship?' He watched her till she looked up. 'We've had a huge order from them for Mineral Enterprises shares. A representative of theirs was at the dinner, urging us to snap up any available stock we could find, no matter what price. I smell another corporate raid. I'll have a quiet word to William about it. He'll be spitting chips.'

'Oreship tried pushing into Billiton as well. They're aiming for a monopoly to transport raw materials, I'd say. It's the best way for them to get it. Buy enough mining stock to get inside the industry; place their own man on the board and control who ships what and where.'

Anna had spoken at last. Even if it was about shares, it was communication. He had not expected her to be informed about the latest stock market shenanigans, but she was on the ball as always.

'Aren't you going to Durban on Monday?'

'Yes, I want to check out the boarding school Solomon recommended for Nozipho.'

'Do you think you have time to look in on Oreship and see what they're up to? You know your way around shipping.'

'I should manage that,' she said, her voice level and businesslike.

Damn! She's stuck her nose into that brochure again, he thought when she cast her eyes downward, concentrating on information about a particular boat. She should be smiling at *me!*

He finished his tea and rose with a yawn. 'I'm going back to bed, are you coming too?' He put the empty teapot and cups on the tray.

'Yes,' she answered. 'I'm so tired I feel like a wrung-out dishrag.'

'That's not a very enchanting picture of a beautiful woman.' Maybe flattery would help, he hoped.

She took no notice. Her sense of humour lay buried under the wet tissues. Returning the tray to the kitchen and tossing the boat book onto the bureau in her study, she followed him to bed.

* * *

Anna nearly missed her plane home that Monday afternoon. More than satisfied with her day, she sat strapped in, smiling while the aircraft taxied to the runway.

To her horror, Major Mortimer set out with her in the morning, boarding behind her and sitting two seats away.

On landing in Durban, she phoned Julia and Fiona, arranging to meet for lunch. She collected her hire car and drove to the boarding school. It was a former Model C school, meaning a state school located within a previously 'whites only' area. Parents contributed heavily in school fees to see such top-performing schools continue operating. Anna was happy with the school's curriculum and amenities, but how would Nozipho feel?

Major Mortimer, meanwhile, followed and waited in his vehicle reading a paper till she came out. *What a waste of time and money,* she thought, sending a look of disapproval in his direction.

Her next stop was Oreship. Mortimer hung about while she discussed shares with their finance team till lunch. By that time, he needed sustenance too and entered the same bistro the women chose for their get-together. He sat munching at the other side of the room.

Anna was determined to lose him after the meal. Not only was it an irresistibly amusing exercise to confuse him, but she also didn't want him reporting he'd seen her talk to a boat dealer. This was going to be her affair entirely. In her father's discarded catalogue, she had spotted the perfect vessel for herself and became hell-bent on buying it. The boat would be her private refuge when, upset with the restrictions on her movements and resulting feelings of inadequacy, she experienced a compulsive desire to withdraw.

Ordering more wine for Fiona and Julia, she hoped they wouldn't draw attention to their table with noisy objections to her departure. 'Please excuse me now. It was lovely seeing you, but I still have other obligations. We must have these pleasant lunch dates more often.'

She exited quickly, power-walked to her car, and drove away, hoping Ernest hadn't noticed. And he hadn't. Arriving back in Johannesburg in a black mood an hour after her flight, he swore to resign. That was fine with her. She was happy, the proud owner of a boat. She hit on the idea of acquiring a car for herself as well. Her own, independent of De Bruyn Brothers so nobody could deprive her of it.

The next day Sipho called, telling her he sat on legal papers to do with the partnership. Signatures were needed urgently. Could she come? This necessitated a visit to Waterman and Bruce's Durban office too.

'I was there only yesterday,' she complained. Lowering her voice considerably, she whispered, 'It's not so straightforward for me now that I have a bodyguard hanging around. He monitors my every step, and I mustn't deviate from his preferred routes.'

Sipho laughed merrily. 'You sound so exasperated, Anna. Don't worry, we'll sort the guy out for you.'

Two days later, she arrived at KwaZulu Medical with Mortimer driving her BMW. Joshua wasn't there to welcome her, but Sipho ushered her into his bean counter's domain with cheerful smiles. He stationed Ernest in the room next to hers and left him to hang up his jacket.

'Blast,' she complained to Sipho. 'I won't be able to play CDs at night now without disturbing the pit bull.'

'I bet that won't be the only sound keeping him awake,' Sipho chuckled.

'You haven't lost your wickedness, Sipho.'

'Why should I? It's all I have left.'

She shook her head. She'd only been here about half an hour and already she was laughing. Sipho still had the ability to cheer her.

Joshua wasn't expected till late but telephoned soon after her arrival.

'Is everything all right?' he asked. 'Margo was supposed to give your room a spruce-up.'

'All is well,' she assured him. 'Thanks for the new curtains, by the way.'

'Sipho says you brought your bodyguard. That's very wise, my pet. You will need him.'

'Yes, he's sure to get the gist of everything that happens here.'

'No, no,' Joshua chuckled, causing her heart to skip at the sound. 'I will be the generous and obliging host. You will see. I shall personally make him the nicest cup of tea he ever drank.'

'Joshua!' she warned, giggling. 'Are you thinking what I imagine you're thinking?'

'Oh, trust me, he will sleep like a log.'

'That would solve a slight problem,' she agreed.

'I can't wait to see you, Anna.'

'Come as soon as you can . . . please.'

He hung up, and she busied herself with the material Sipho spoke of. Reading through the legal jargon was most time-consuming.

She noticed Mortimer wandering about getting his bearings. He wouldn't know what hit him if he got in Margo's way. *I should stick him in the wine cellar and throw away the key*, she thought resentfully.

* * *

Hank and Maurice were rarely in the office before noon now. Hank wore his Stock Exchange Council president's hat till about lunch, after which a change of millinery transformed him back into plain Hank De Bruyn, stockbroker. Both men breezed in at about 1430 hours, said a quick 'Hi, Anna,' and buried themselves in more work. Neither of them had much time for the daily running of the place. Hank relied on Anna for that. He often wondered how she managed, never seeing her greatest strength: the ability to delegate. His talent in human resource management was choosing the right people for the right jobs. However, it was Anna who ascertained what the applicants Hank hired were capable of. She divided the work according to what people could handle. Nobody felt overwhelmed by the volume or nature of the material landing on their desks.

For all that, they were notoriously understaffed. Anna cast a worried look at Vince Lewis as she passed his pigeonhole of an office. He had not been long out of hospital and ought not to be here. She shouldn't listen to his protests of boredom at home, she thought, stopping by his desk and looking over his shoulder at his computer screen.

'As soon as Hank and Maurice arrive, you go home,' she ordered. 'You're not ready to work a full day.'

Max and Brad, the traders, nodded agreement. 'You tell him. He's stubborn, thinks he's Superman.'

'I'm keeping my eye on you, Mr Lewis,' she reminded him as she returned to her desk.

She began sorting and reading information she brought back from Oreship. Mineral Enterprises were nervous about Oreship's aggressive purchases of their shares. 'Something needs to be done about it,' William said to her the other day. 'We might go into a trading halt. That should slow them down.'

Her phone rang. 'Professor Mtolo wishes to see you. Shall I send him in?' Penny, the receptionist asked.

'No, he does not have an appointment,' she laughed, jumping off her chair and racing to the front desk.

'Joshua! I had no idea you were in our neck of the wood. How are you? Come with me.'

He held a sprig of violets and a box of chocolates. Passing them to her, he said, 'I'm right in the thick of it, seeing AIDS patients.'

They entered her office, and she pushed the door shut with her foot while her arms embraced him. Carefully she let her fingers glide over his face again.

'My god, I'm glad you're so much better now.'

'I'm battle-hardened, my pet. And you look as fetching as ever.'

'Time for coffee?'

'No thanks, sweetheart, not today.' He pinned the violets to her dress.

'I might be free for lunch at Benny's tomorrow, though. What say you? Yes? No?'

'What time?'

'Twelve-thirtyish?'

'I'll be there,' she smiled. 'Come hell or high water.'

'Can you shake the major off?'

'I'll shoot him!'

A shout of alarm, and a thump wiped the smile off her face. She heard feet running, muffled on carpet. Josh opened the door to see what happened.

'It's Vince,' someone called. 'He's collapsed!'

Josh ran towards the group crowded around Vince. 'Excuse me,' he said. They backed off, recognizing authority.

'Quick, get my bag!' He threw his car keys to Anna who dashed away.

By the time she returned Josh had Vince sitting up with Brad supporting him. Someone brought a glass of water, and Vince was pumped full of pills and an injection. It took a good half hour till he could stand.

'I'll drive him to hospital,' Josh said quietly.

Anna thanked him, handing his car keys back.

'Well done, Doc,' Max called out. 'Take care of him.' The staff awarded Professor Mtolo hero status from that moment.

'I think I just solved a personnel problem,' Anna told Mrs George. 'If Vince insists on working till he drops, he can work at Josh's clinic. Sipho needs help, and if Vince is unwell, at least he's in the right place for immediate attention.'

* * *

Hank hadn't had the stomach to tell Anna about his forthcoming travel plans. The arrangements for attending conventions in Hong Kong, New York, London and Frankfurt were made while Michael Tripp was president. With his retirement, it fell to Hank to represent Johannesburg. Hank was adamant he'd use the opportunity to arbitrate for the complete lifting of economic sanctions. Maurice was to accompany him to gain greater insight into international monetary systems.

Anna was deeply wounded when she heard of it from Mrs George.

'Why are you punishing me, Hank?' she asked when they, still adhering to old habits, discussed the day's progress in bed.

'Come again? What?'

'Will you please explain what I'm doing wrong?'

Hank looked at her, puzzled and annoyed. His patience with her problematic moods was wearing thin.

'You start by telling me in what way you think I'm keelhauling you and why.'

'All right. You took my diamonds away.'

He rolled his eyes to the ceiling. 'I told you it's because—'

'Let me finish. You set that pit bull, Mortimer, on me. You made me give my car to him. You're not letting me take a step without him.' She swallowed a sob. 'You no longer trust me, so why don't we just end this blasted farce and divorce?'

Hank's irritation turned to alarm. 'Anna, for goodness' sake! Mortimer isn't there to spy on you. It's not his job to tell me where you're going and who you see. He's only meant to stay near you and shield you from harm. It's done for your security. I thought I'd made that clear enough.'

'I carry a gun for security.'

'So you should.'

Once the floodgates were opened, Anna couldn't stop the surge of bitterness.

'You don't take me anywhere anymore, and as for keeping promises like the purchase of real estate on Durban's Golden Mile . . . forget it.'

'I'll get around to it. What else is on your mind? Come on, spit it out.' This was crazy. Anna was always so contented. He never heard such a string of complaints from her. What was her problem?

'I also want clarification as to whether those diamonds are actually mine or whether they are family property, which you only lend me at times.'

'Don't be daft, woman. Of course they're yours.'

'Thank you.'

'Do you want that in writing?'

'While we're at it, let's talk about your upcoming international trip.'

Hank's bluster disintegrated. Who told her about that? 'What of it?' he mumbled.

'I have never been to Hong Kong. It would enhance my understanding greatly if I could come with you to familiarize myself with their modus operandi.'

'You can't come, dear. I need you here.'

'You're taking Maurice.'

'That's right.'

'Why take your personal assistant and leave your wife at home? Maurice can stand in for me while I go with you.' She took a deep breath. 'Who's ever heard of a stockbroker who hasn't been to Hong Kong?'

'Let me remind you, Anna, I'm the stockbroker.'

'And what am I?'

'You're my right hand, dear.' He took her right hand and kissed the fingertips, hoping to stem the flow of accusations, which weren't all figments of her imagination. It didn't work.

'What have I been to you all these years? The times you were unwell and I ran the business for you? I was good enough for that. Am I suddenly incapable? Unfit to be taken to international summits?' She turned away from him.

'Anna, it's not like that at all.'

Tears stung her eyes. She bit them back.

'You will be in Hong Kong on my birthday. Did you think of that? It's the one day in the year we always reserve strictly for ourselves.'

'I had no say in the dates. They were confirmed on Michael Tripp's watch, and I'm stuck with them. You can still have a party. Invite anyone you like or arrange a bash in a hotel somewhere.'

'It won't be the same without you,' she lamented. 'Please let me come with you.'

'I'm sorry, love. I don't think it can be done this time, so just take it like an adult and stop acting like a spoiled little rich girl unable to get her own way.'

As soon as he said it, he wanted to take it back, but she left the bedroom.

In the morning, she appeared late, chewing absentmindedly on toast when Hank entered the sun-drenched breakfast room by the pool. She didn't look at him. He came to stand beside her chair.

'I'm sorry about last night,' he said hesitantly, kissing and stroking her hair. 'I said horrid things.'

'I did too.'

'I've been thinking it's probably too late for you to join me in Hong Kong, seeing that's my first stop. We could meet in New York, though. Would that suit you?' he asked when she remained silent. 'We might see *Aida* at the Met.' He remembered his intention to share quality time with her.

Did he expect she'd jump for joy? she wondered, reaching the conclusion that after yesterday, she cared little about travels with him.

'It's Hong Kong I'm interested in,' she said, speaking in a manner more to herself than him. 'When I say I haven't been there, I mean I never focused on their stock exchange and affiliated money markets. All my previous dealings concentrated on Hong Kong's shipping industry.'

'So you don't want to come to the other cities?'

'No.'

'Oh well.' He shrugged. 'It was just a suggestion. Don't say I didn't offer a compromise.'

* * *

Another wave assailed the Vera, first lifting then dropping her into a trough. Anna adjusted her steering towards Richards Bay. She was nearly there. Thirty minutes more and she'd be tying up at a little pier used by recreational craft like hers. She made out Joshua's silhouette on the jetty, his shoulders hunched against the wind. He waved his arms when he saw her. She lowered the fenders over the side.

Calling to him, she tossed him a line to catch. 'Slip that over the bollard, please, love.' When he did, she tied up deftly. Laying an aluminium gangplank across for him to board, she said, 'Welcome aboard MV *Vera*!'

'Oh, Anna, Anna! You crazy damned woman! What are you doing out there in this weather?' He embraced her, holding onto her as if she were drowning, her wet weather gear soaking his clothes.

'The weather forecast was wrong. It was beautiful earlier. The wind will die soon. Come below into the cabin. I'll heat up tomato soup to warm us.'

Josh wasn't listening. 'You could have killed yourself out there. What makes you think an amateur seaman can master rough conditions like this?'

She laughed out loud. 'You should try it too. Pitching your wits and strength against nature's force is the greatest thrill. It teaches humility too. You realise how little you matter in the vastness of the universe.'

'Don't talk to a doctor about combating nature's wiles.'

She chuckled again, kissing him tenderly.

It did not still his concern about her foolish overconfidence. 'You lack the training to be out there on anything but the calmest of days,' he scolded, becoming upset when she remained unimpressed. 'It's not amusing, Anna. It's dangerous.'

'Look at this,' she smiled, escaping his grasp. Handing him a laminated document detached from a clipboard, she asked, 'Does that calm your fears?'

He read for a minute while astonishment widened his eyes. 'Anna Christina Cumberland, second mate? You? You mean like deck officer? On a container ship? I wouldn't believe it if I wasn't reading it. Does Hank know about this?'

'Of course. After our wedding, he came with us the only time I sailed on a commercial voyage working together with my father. Hank joined as supercargo. A very seasick supercargo, might I add.' She grinned, remembering the time. 'We didn't have much freight on the trip, so Hank was in charge of mostly ballast. It turned out to be a hairy ride from Sydney to Perth. We didn't stop in Melbourne as we had no boxes to unload there. There was a strike at the Sydney docks, which broke out before containers for Melbourne were loaded. The vessel was consequently not quite as low in the water as she could have been, and boy, did we feel it!'

'So how did you come to sail with your father?'

'The folks in Perth wanted their goods, strike or no strike. Also, Dad needed the berth for another vessel so as not to clog up the harbour with waiting ships. It was one of those strikes about employing Australian labour on vessels trading in Australian waters, and the dock workers joined in sympathy.

'Dad drummed a skeleton crew of scabs together and took her out in the middle of the night. "I'll deal with the unions later if they have anything to say to me," I remember him commenting.

'Alternating watches on the bridge with Dad, twelve hours on, twelve off, we got to Perth feeling very tired. They threw a party for us there in appreciation of our feat. The weather had not been kind to us. Hank was only too happy to fly back to Johannesburg. He's not much of a traveller. Dad handed the vessel back to the owners and flew home too.

'And now you know I have my tickets, you can rest easy. You might even place your life in my hands coming to Durban with me.' She passed him a cup of soup, enjoying his dumbfounded silence. Sitting opposite him, blowing over her cup to cool it, she explained why she had gone to sea in the first place.

'I told you I wanted to be an opera singer, remember? When my parents objected, I fell back on my next favourite activity and opted for a career at sea. My father was over the moon with approval. I worked myself up to second mate—not on vessels my father commanded, mind you. No nepotism involved here.

'It was tough going because I was also enrolled at university for a BA. When Mum had a close shave with cancer, Dad and I tossed up who would stay home with her. In the end, we decided we'd both forsake the sea and look after her together. That's when Dad built up the export–import business he had going on the side. He added the shipping agency and, apart from a brief spell as harbour master, more or less washed the salt out of his hair. I did too. Modern container ships aren't all that romantic. And now you see me in my diminished role as a stockbroker's wife. Quite a demotion, eh?'

'I thought you liked your work. You seemed so passionate about it,' Josh said, surprised.

'I do, but Hank thinks I'm burnt out. Maybe he's right.'

'Did he say that?'

'Not in so many words, but I can read his mind.'

'Do you think that's the cause of your depression?'

'A substantial part of it. Hell,'—her voice rose—'why do you think I bought this boat? It symbolizes freedom. I can't bear restraints. I had you keeping me confined for months. Now Hank restricts me, giving my car to that Mortimer and setting him on my tail ostensibly to ensure my safety. It deranges my emotions. You can't expect any other result than rebelliousness.' She shook her head about to loosen her French plait.

'Let me refill your soup cup, pet,' Josh said, rising from his seat. It had finally come, he thought. The repercussions from Anna's anxieties and uncertainties over the past months had congealed into an explosive plastic consistency, which she strove gallantly to keep from igniting. Should she fail, she would be hurt badly. He must help her.

'You didn't see Damien Winter?'

'No, I don't give in to depression, and I'm not swallowing bottles of pills for artificial cheer. That's why this wild weather is good for me. It cleans the mind like nothing else.'

He should have known she would find her own measures to counter destructive influences. It was just a matter of guiding her to avoid relapses. Because he no longer saw her as an enemy, she appeared to feel no resentment towards him. She had stopped accusing him of disrupting her life or wrecking her marriage. At least his attempts to support her wouldn't be rebuffed.

He stood behind her, gently untangling her plait.

'That hairstyle doesn't suit you, my pet.'

'I know, but it's practical for life aboard. If I don't pin it back, the wind blows it everywhere and ties it in knots. If you'll excuse me, I'll have a shower and wash the salt spray out.'

'I might join you.' His eyes gleamed.

'Have you seen the size of the shower? If we both fit in there, we will have broken a world record,' she roared laughing.

It wasn't the silver-bell variety. That was rarely heard now, but it sounded like a new spirit entering at last.

'All right, you shower and I'll have a look at your bits and pieces.'

'I beg your pardon?'

'Up there,'—he pointed to the narrow companionway—'your engine control console, compass, and all the electronic bits and pieces you have there.'

* * *

What a wonderful, glorious time they had spent, Anna reminisced, sitting at her desk back in Johannesburg.

Tied up at the jetty for the night due to the wild sea, they had relaxed utterly, absorbing each other's love. The morning dawned bright and sunny, allowing her to get under way after a late breakfast. She wished they could sail around the world together. But this wasn't fairyland. It was reality, and she took Josh to Durban from where he planned to return to Vryheid and she was to fly back to Johannesburg to keep the office shipshape. Hank mustn't find fault upon his return. Not that he was due at home soon. He would be away for three weeks at least.

From the airport, she headed straight for the office, still wearing her boating clothes—white jeans, white halter-neck top, and navy blazer. The garments fitted snugly. Max and Brad wolf-whistled when she entered. They had never seen her look so sporty.

'All right, back to work, you lot,' she laughed. Throwing her duffel bag into her room, she accepted a cup of coffee from Betty and called all staff into the conference room.

'Is everyone well?' she asked, looking around. 'How about you, Vince? We'll have a little chat later.'

She opened her work file containing notes reminding her which jobs she had left with whom before she took off on the boat.

'What's new?' She smiled at them all, looking up. 'Any gossip? Pity.' She shrugged when nobody produced anything of interest.

'What's happening with Oreship and Mineral Enterprises, Max?'

'They've slackened off a bit. William Rosenberg's still unhappy, though.'

'I'll call him later. Has anyone succeeded in getting hold of the manager at Golden Studio?'

'Tried four times to call him,' Brad explained. 'No go. I think they've gone bust.'

'That wouldn't surprise me. They owe money everywhere.'

And so the meeting continued, question after question till Anna saw where they were at and issued follow-up instructions. The staff responded to her easy, laid-back management style. Hank never admitted productivity had increased since she had returned from KwaZulu Medical.

Everything was in good order and condition at De Bruyn Brothers, and Anna settled down to a number of routine jobs. She was in top gear. Was it the sea, or was Josh's company responsible for chasing her blues away? Depression was only a bad memory— for now anyway.

'And I will have a birthday party!' she whispered to herself. *If my dear husband won't let me share his activities, he can't participate in mine.* 'Tough cheese, Mister President.'

While thinking she might invite the whole office to Illovo for the celebration, Penny entered, carrying a package.

'It's just arrived via international courier,' she said, placing it on Anna's desk.

'What is it?' Betty and Mrs George came in too.

'Has Major Mortimer seen this? He's supposed to vet all parcels and bigger items of mail,' she reminded them.

'Yes, he passed it to me,' Penny confirmed.

'Let's see.' Anna opened the courier satchel. Full of bubble wrap and tissue paper, the contents took some unravelling.

'Oh!' they all exclaimed when an elegant gold-clasped crocodile-skin purse appeared out of one wrapping and an embroidered silk shawl out of the other.

'That's so beautiful.' They admired Hank's birthday gift for his wife. It came with the cutest card featuring a basket full of kittens. Anna displayed the enchanting picture prominently on her desk.

The four women chatted, all laughing at once, discussing what garments were most suited to the fine accessories.

A loud cough at the door quietened the hubbub. Ernest Mortimer entered with the air of a general. He surveyed the women as if they were unruly privates. His eyes and sideways jerk of the head indicated he wanted them to leave.

Anna stared at him in disbelief while Penny and Betty headed for the door. Mrs George was about to exit too when Anna pointed to the chair opposite her desk.

'Do sit down, Pamela.'

Anna arranged herself comfortably, carefully rewrapping her presents and keeping Mortimer standing. Her office was no place to pull rank. He had to learn, the hard way if necessary, that in Hank's absence, she was the boss. Slowly she lifted her head. 'Can I help you, Major?'

'I need to speak to you in private.'

'Indeed, Major, I expect you wish to discuss security matters.'

'In private if you please,' he repeated testily.

'Security does not necessarily mean secrecy, Major. Not here anyway. We're a fairly transparent lot. No doubt you heard Mrs Pamela George is headed for promotion. She will work in tandem with Mr Van Buuren. Therefore, Major, she needs to be aware of all issues affecting De Bruyn Brothers.'

'When is Mr De Bruyn due back?' Mortimer asked with the barest courtesy in his voice.

'Not till the end of the month at the earliest.'

'It's only the fourth today,' he muttered.

'Maybe I can assist if you have a problem.'

'You *are* the problem!' he blurted, his dander up.

'Oh, come now, Major.' Anna chuckled. 'Let's get you a chair and a cup to tea and see what we can thrash out.' She pressed the intercom. 'Betty, could we please have a pot of herb tea . . . the most calming stuff you can find. Major Mortimer appears a little tense.'

He glared. 'Not as calming as the brew I was served at KwaZulu Medical, I hope.'

'Didn't you like it? Do you have a preference? Betty can make whatever you wish.'

'You know perfectly well what I mean. When a naturally alert and active man suddenly sleeps like a baby? I call that extraordinary.'

'The place is very quiet, Major. The main gate is locked after 2300 hours, and no ambulances come shrieking in because the hospital is on bypass at night unless disaster strikes. It's hardly like a Johannesburg suburb. That's why you find it relaxing.'

He gave her a frigid look while tossing an envelope before her. 'That's my resignation, effective immediately. Seeing Mr De Bruyn is unavailable, you can have it.'

'Thank you, Major.' Anna read the letter and laughed.

Ernest rose to go, his eyes projecting total antipathy. Betty blocked his way out with the tea tray.

'Here we are, Major.' She smiled, showing him the brand on the teabag tag. 'Nothing but the best.' She poured him a cup.

Anna took a sip of hers as well, saying, 'Don't misunderstand, Major. I'm laughing because I agree with every word you wrote. I accept your resignation. There's just one question. What about your colleagues? Are they happy to suddenly find themselves unemployed?'

'I have other situations for them.'

'Very well, I respect your decision. I just want you to know this is nothing personal. I'm sure we could enjoy perfect cooperation under different circumstances. As it happens, you are unfortunately wedged between my husband, who understands the need for security, and me. I am a maverick, intolerant of the straitjacket effective protection imposes.'

The phone rang, and Anna picked it up, a clear signal of dismissal to Mortimer.

'Hank! How's everything in Hong Kong? Are you well? Thank you for the lovely present, it's gorgeous. The ladies came to admire it too. We had a great fashion talk till the major came and broke us up. He tried taking command—gesticulating and, with body language, ordering them out of my office. Can you believe that? The cheek of him.'

She gave Mortimer a mocking grin. 'I'm switching to speakerphone. The major is here. He's just resigned with immediate effect. He can't stand me a day longer.'

'Anna, what have you done to him?' Hank half laughed. 'I guess I'll have to teach him how to deal with difficult women.'

'Yes dear, I love you too.'

'What reasons did he give for resigning?'

'He says he can't carry out his duties efficiently due to lack of collaboration and conformity on my part.'

'Tell him to hang fire with that abdication of his till I get back. I'm sure we can work something out.'

'Of course we can. Just leave me out of his job description so he's not responsible for me. That way, we'll both be happy.'

'Put the call through to my office and I'll talk to him in there.'

Anna pointed to Mortimer and then to Hank's office. She switched the call over and poured more tea for Pamela and herself. 'Now where were we with those accounts of Maurice's?'

* * *

Anna saw the golden opening immediately. Ernest Mortimer's resignation restored her independence. She could drive to Vryheid now to hear Shenge address a rally there in compensation for missing the earlier Soweto meeting. Vince might join her. It was time to show him the ropes at KwaZulu Medical. With any luck, he may agree to work there in future.

Her burgundy BMW would again be her company car. On inspection of the vehicle, however, she found it reeking of pipe tobacco. Pooh . . . no, she'd take Hank's Mercedes and leave it there to replace Josh's Corolla. 'One day, that old bomb will draw its last breath and Josh will be stranded. A doctor needs a fast, reliable, and comfortable car,' she coughed, shutting the BMW's door quickly.

'No time like the present.' She smiled at Vince. 'Do you feel like coming to KwaZulu Medical with me? I intend making it a weekend trip, which lets me observe the IFP's rally in Vryheid.'

Vince nodded enthusiastically. 'I've talked to Sipho Gwala on the phone quite often. I'm curious to meet him.'

'He'll be very happy to familiarize you with the accounts. Don't let him cook any books, though.' She laughed, shaking her head. 'He takes creative accounting to new heights.'

'Sounds like a guy worthy of attention.' Vince's pale face coloured with his smile.

'I'm guilty of . . . eh . . . adjusting the books myself so Joshua can have the Mercedes—when I find the keys. His Corolla is clapped out. The Mercedes is a company car. We are in partnership with Josh's clinic, therefore I can't see why he shouldn't make use of it. Fair dinkum, where are those blessed keys? You knock off now, Vince. I'll see you tomorrow.'

She crossed to Hank's room, checking through his desk. Nothing. 'Must be at home,' she hoped.

It was foul play of the worst sort. Anna's anger rose quickly. Hank said she could use the Mercedes if she needed urgent transport but had deliberately hidden the keys, or so it seemed. She fingered through every pocket of his jackets and trousers without finding as much as a parking docket. 'Damn, I bet Mortimer still has them.'

When a cup of coffee and chocolate biscuits rebuilt her faith in mankind, she remembered Dumisani Mkhize had a spare set.

'Goodie!' She hummed a tune, throwing the keys he gave her into the air and catching them. 'My dear Hank,' she laughed to herself. 'You are so unprepared for what will confront you on your return. Let's see how you feel when the boot is on the other foot.' She giggled softly. *I will teach you how humiliating it is to be deprived of one's car as if driving it were a privilege no longer deserved.* He had his Porsche, of course, but would nonetheless find Josh's possession of the Mercedes abhorrent.

* * *

'This is a delicious lunch, William. Thanks for inviting me.' Anna savoured the 1979 Bollinger he ordered.

'I would love to see you at my birthday party too. It's at home, and most of the office will be there. Bring your cello.'

'I thought you were about to say "bring a lady,"' William laughed. '"Bring your cello" sounds so bourgeois and tame.'

'Of course Melody is invited too.'

'She's still with her brother. I'm secretly hoping she'll stay there.'

'Don't be awful. You miss her dreadfully.'

'You know, I really do. Home isn't home without her there.'

'If Joshua has time to come, he can bring Indira so you will have someone to talk to.'

William drank deeply and sighed. 'What are we going to do about Oreship? I thought we could bounce ideas off each other.'

'They are bad news, but you might come away having the last laugh.'

'We can't stay in a trading halt for too long.' William looked worried, the wine glass never far from his hand.

'No, it's not fair on other, more genuine investors. The pension funds need the constant trade to accumulate wealth for their stakeholders.'

Anna toyed with her own wine glass, which William refilled instantly. 'If you were to discourage people from selling their Mineral Enterprises shares right now, the value would rise due to the lack of available stock. Oreship would then face a drought of your shares on the market, and the few they picked up would become so dear they would have to stop buying. Hank has already advised them Mineral Enterprises shares are few and far between. Eventually they will realise it's not quite so, but by then, other pressures may come to bear on the situation.'

William nodded slowly. 'I could ignore the dealings because Oreship doesn't want a takeover. They just need a representative on the board. They want their preferred man in there. That's the annoying part I can't countenance. I can't let them own such a large stake in the company.'

Anna chuckled while a sinful little smirk broadened her face. 'Hank could send the auditors to Oreship with a "please explain". How is it they have so much spare cash to buy such a volume of Mineral Enterprises stock? With any luck, the auditors will unearth faults to make their investors shiver. After that, it's easy to initiate rumours of corruption. Oreship shareholders may not be impressed to see what should be their dividends pumped into inflated Mineral Enterprises shares instead.'

'That's a dirty trick, but I like it.' William ordered another bottle, smiling with delight. 'I forgot Hank can do that now.'

'How many shares do you still have at your disposal? Enough to swamp the market to such an extent that Oreship would suffer a debilitating loss if the price collapsed?'

'You are a murderous lady with devilish ideas, Anna. Once the price has crashed, we can buy them all for a peppercorn and, later, when we deem the price to be at an acceptable level again, throw them back on the market. Yes, we'd very likely have the last laugh then.'

'To Oreship.' William raised his glass.

* * *

'Here's our most popular DJ!' Max called as Nkosinathi helped Vince carry a box of CDs into Anna's lounge. Nobody dared discourage him from officiating as master of ceremonies at her birthday function.

The foyer was cleared for dancing, with the occasional table and two chairs pushed aside. Even the piano was wheeled closer to the window. Coloured lanterns hung suspended in all rooms.

Many of De Bruyn's staff had already assembled to sing 'Happy Birthday,' bringing flowers and gifts. Franz and Rosemary entered together with William plus cello.

'Can't stay long, the kids are sick,' Rosemary apologized.

'I'm glad you could come anyway. I've made your favourite snack, devil on horseback. Help yourself to food and drink.'

William looked around, forlorn. 'Where's Indira?'

'Coming later,' Anna replied, passing him on her way to the kitchen for more platters of food. She nearly collided with Nozipho, who insisted on staying up to see the presents and talking to Doctor Josh when he came.

When Cindy and Solomon arrived, Nkosinathi begged them to demonstrate their excellent ballroom dancing. Vince chose Strauss waltzes because Anna favoured them. Nkosinathi, Anna noticed, brought a girl with him.

'I haven't met your friend yet,' she prodded him for an introduction.

'Mrs De Bruyn, meet Suzanna Tsedu,' he smiled with self-conscious formality.

Anna said, 'No other learners in the computer classes have exceeded your results yet. You were to have the next traineeship, Suzanna.'

'Nobody has said anything about that so far,' she answered with a note of disappointment.

'That's not good enough.' Anna turned away with purposeful strides. 'Excuse me a minute.' She would not see Suzanna ignored simply because she was a girl.

Cindy and Solomon had stopped dancing, refreshing themselves with iced drinks. Anna welcomed them warmly.

'Nkosinathi brought Suzanna Tsedu here this evening,' she told them, pointing in the youngsters' direction.

'Where are they?' Cindy's eyes lit as she stood on tiptoe surveying the guests. 'I haven't seen Suzanna in months.'

'By the way,'—Anna edged closer to Solomon—'what's happening with Suzanna's traineeship?'

'We couldn't find anyone to take her on, although Cindy was certain William Rosenberg promised sponsorship.'

'Let's tackle him,' she urged, waving across to William. Laying a hand on his shoulder when he came over, she said, 'I heard a whisper a while ago you promised a Mineral Enterprises traineeship for Suzanna Tsedu. Is that right?'

'Ahh, y-e-s . . .' He nodded to Solomon and smiled at Cindy, trying to remember where he had met her. 'Of course,' he laughed suddenly, recalling his risqué dance with her at the anniversary ball.

'Suzanna is the next candidate if you are still prepared to sponsor a student.' Anna called Nkosinathi, and he brought Suzanna to chat with their former teachers. She ushered the group into the dining room to work out the broader details of the scheme, modelling it as closely as possible to the agreement Hank had reached with Nkosinathi. Suzanna would not be disadvantaged due to her gender.

Dumisani Mkhize approached slowly. 'Mrs De Bruyn, you have more guests arriving,' he announced with a lordly flourish.

Anna crossed to the foyer just as Vince changed from Strauss to Tchaikovsky waltzes.

'Joshua!' They rushed towards each other. Picking her up as easily as a ballet dancer lifting his partner, he swirled her around in greeting.

'Happy birthday, my pet.' A gift and accompanying card protruded from his inside jacket pocket.

'I'm so glad to see you. Have some refreshments,' Anna said breathlessly when he stood her on her feet again.

'I need to go back to the hospital for a while but thought I'd better deliver Indira promptly. She was becoming restless.'

Joshua, who couldn't stop being a doctor for even half an hour, steered straight towards Vince, asking how he was mending.

Although a little too weak to dance, Vince was in fine fettle. With an exuberant grin, he dived into his DC crate, surfacing with African dance music recordings.

After the stylish drawing-room atmosphere, the contrast was stark and immediately introduced a different colour and liveliness to the night.

Nkosinathi whooped, running into the middle of the floor with Suzanna and Nozipho. 'Township jive!' he called and waved his arms, persuading everyone to join. 'Come on, Mrs De Bruyn! You don't need to know the steps. Just pretend you have no bones.'

Unrestrained laughter sounded from Max and Brad, who moved like they were born township dwellers. They chuckled at William who, in his brown shirt and red tie, resembled a big teddy bear pulled from a child's toy box, while Indira beside him was the delicate doll in a sari. Cindy and Solomon entered into the party's changed spirit looking as though they had drunk more than mineral water.

When all guests were comfortable, enjoying the celebration, Anna unwrapped Josh's birthday tribute in the privacy of her study. He had left the house shortly after talking to Vince and Nozipho.

A little gold box contained emerald stud earrings to complement her ring. The card expressed an enticing invitation to taste forbidden fruit.

I am staying at Benny's tonight. Please come when your visitors depart. I should be free also by then.

* * *

Chapter 14

The Rally

Anna drove like the wind, aiming to spend as little time as possible on the road. Beside her, Vince closed his eyes. He couldn't bear to look ahead, only mustering courage to see where they were when she slowed passing through towns.

At Ermelo, she asked, 'Do you want to stop for a coffee and something to eat?'

'P-l-e-a-s-e!' he moaned.

'Oh, you are awake! I thought you'd dropped off.'

'Can you drive a bit slower? You scare the devil out of me.'

'All right, I'll stick to a hundred from now on.'

'Anna, you promised!' he protested when after their Ermelo break she stepped on the gas once more, overtaking a Greyhound bus.

'Sorry, but the quicker we reach Vryheid, the sooner we can both relax.'

'If we get there in one piece?'

'You're just a pessimist. Go close your eyes again.'

Vince, Anna thought, displayed characteristics that should enable him to harmonise with Sipho Gwala. She could almost hear herself having a similar conversation with him. In their own way, both men were calm and humble, yet each had an unmistakable streak of boldness and plucky self-assurance, garnished with a sense of humour. And both were top-rank professionals, knowing their work inside out.

'I hope you will like KwaZulu Medical,' she said as they approached the clinic and Vince returned to full consciousness. 'There are just two things to remember. Don't be afraid to make adjustments to your living conditions if you see the need, and keep out of Margo's way. When you meet her, you will know why. She's the domestic Girl Friday around here and takes her responsibilities way too seriously.'

Vince stepped from the car, looking about him. Stretching and stamping life back into his feet, he tossed drowsiness aside like a dog shaking off rain.

'Also,' Anna continued, 'you don't have to remain here if you don't feel it meets your expectations. You can return to Jo'burg any time you wish.'

Fernando came down the steps to help with the luggage. Sipho followed, and Anna introduced them to Vince.

Sipho said, 'Welcome, Vince, let's get you settled. Your room is between Anna's and mine.'

'No Major Mortimer?' Fernando asked, his voice rising a pitch in surprise.

'He quit,' Anna explained with a chuckle.

'What a shame. I looked forward to talking to him again—great bloke.'

'He doesn't like me. He even made diplomatic mention of the fact in his resignation letter. However, he had a long phone chat with my husband, and I wouldn't be at all surprised if Hank talked him into staying on. I'll enjoy my reprieve for as long as it lasts,' she laughed. Then a new thought came to her. 'Is anyone going to the IFP rally on Sunday?'

'Peter and Tom will. They're assisting Josh,' Fernando smiled, grasping Anna's duffel bag. He ran an eye over the Mercedes. 'That is some car you've got there,' he commented as he walked through the glass double door. The vehicle made an impact parked outside Sipho's window. Josh's Corolla was absent, meaning he was very likely working at another hospital.

'Yes, I'm leaving it here for Josh to drive. A doctor needs reliable transport. Josh travels so much, and the Corolla is just about dead on its wheels.'

'He'll be delighted,' Fernando agreed, heading for the staff quarters, where he stood her duffel bag and briefcase on the kitchen table in her room.

Yes, that table was still there in all its dilapidated ugliness together with the other mismatched furniture. Only the curtains were new. Much improvement was called for if she was to work here more frequently, Anna thought, overcome again with disturbing memories. It was then she noticed little romantic, welcoming touches. A big vase of flowers stood on the bedside table. More CDs and chocolates were placed near the stereo and a new, colourful, feminine robe hung from the hook in the bathroom.

'Come on Vince, I'll show you the important things first.' Sipho pulled him in the direction of the kitchen. 'Food,' he grinned. 'It's surprising Anna hasn't worn out the linoleum with her frequent marches along here for coffee and biscuits. What's your favourite snack?'

'Cheese,' Vince replied, rubbing his tummy. 'I don't eat much of it, though. Too fattening. My diet is sadly restricted. I wonder if the doctors here are as firm as their Jo'burg counterparts regarding comfort food?

'You'll meet them shortly. You can size them up for yourself.' Sipho smiled reassuringly. 'Trust me, they understand human failings.'

As always, Margo's sixth sense for intruders in her kitchen was switched to full alert.

'Here she comes,' Sipho whispered. 'We're ambushed.'

'Who . . . ?' Vince's stunned expression said it all. He found her beyond description. He wondered what she had eaten to become so overweight. Her noisy, tinkling ankle bracelets mesmerized him. The enormous, brightly painted wooden beads around her thick neck appeared to choke her.

She looked him up and down insolently. With her usual bluntness, she honked, 'So you're the new guy!'

'This is Mr Vince Lewis,' Sipho said gravely, giving a dignified nod to Vince. 'He'll be here for a while helping me. And Margo . . . go easy on him. He's a bit unwell, so do your best to fuss over him. He will appreciate it.'

'Fuss over? Did I hear "fuss over"? Are you mad?' Her eyes bulged with indignation. 'Haven't I got enough work already without bothering about sick adults?'

Sipho nudged Vince. 'See what I mean? She's a witch.'

'I thought Anna's warnings about her weirdness were just good-humoured exaggerations,' Vince remarked, perplexed.

'That's the understatement of the year,' Sipho muttered.

Margo turned on them. 'I suppose the Lady Anna De Bruyn is here too?' Sarcastic, hoity-toity accents rang in her query. 'Or has she become Mrs Anna Mtolo in the meantime?'

'Don't be so disrespectful, Margo. Anna can sue you for slander and defamation. She can sack you too. Remember that in future if you value your job. Now go home and leave us to eat in peace.'

'It was only a question,' she grunted disdainfully but with less emphasis.

'It's the wrong question.' Sipho turned away in disgust. 'Come, Vince.' Embarrassed, he led the way to his office without another word.

Their verbal stoush echoed across the passage where Anna dropped the Mercedes keys on Josh's desk. She sat for a while, looking through the papers and files he worked on but knew there was nothing she could help with. Apart from invoices for medicines, which she could pass to Sipho, she wouldn't know A from Z about his operations. But what a vast difference existed between the present and the past, she thought. From a scared hostage sitting quavering, fearful, and suspicious beside this desk to—as Sipho just said—having the power to hire and fire in the clinic, even though she wouldn't dream of exercising her prerogative to do so. Nonetheless, she looked at her life with a degree of incredulity. The tables had turned to her advantage. 'That's the power of money,' she sighed.

'Sipho,' Anna called as she entered his office, waving the invoices and seeing the two men already huddled at his desk. 'I thought I heard you tell Margo to go easy on Vince. You're draining his energy with work before he even had a meal. A slave driver couldn't be more demanding.'

'It's just our private "getting to know you" session,' he explained defensively. 'Isn't it, Vince?'

Joining the banter, Vince chewed the end of his pencil in absorbed concentration. Squinting at the computer, he wailed, 'I'm earning my pay by the sweat of my brow.'

'See?' Sipho pointed a ruler at him. 'He's not working, he's play-acting. Anyway, all three of us need to look at this stuff tomorrow.'

'Forget tomorrow. When's dinner?'

Sipho checked his watch. 'As soon as our professor gets here, which should be in half an hour.'

'Can Margo manage the extra heavy duties?' Anna added a snide remark of her own.

'She better! Lazy old bag,' he mumbled sideways to Vince.

'Are we all eating together in the conference room?'

'I think that's the idea so we can welcome Vince into our midst.'

'I'll set the table. Who's coming? Tom, Peter, Vince, you, me, Josh?' She counted, touching her fingers. What about Indira?'

'It's her day off.'

'Isn't she only part-time?'

'Ha ha, very funny! She's been here constantly since Josh dwelt in government accommodation. We've been so busy lately part-time work is out of the question.'

'Spoken with the conviction of a dyed-in-the-wool dictator,' Anna grinned, nodding at Vince. 'Don't let him get away with these tactics.'

Anna followed through with her intention to see to catering matters. Fernando came to the kitchen, drawn by the delicious smells of Margo's cooking.

'Yummy,' he sniffed. 'That's mouth-watering. May I eat with you lot today?'

'Certainly! It saves you preparing dinner at home, I guess.'

'Home cooking . . . ? What kind of luxury is that?' He looked at her, amazed at the absurdity of the question. 'I live on takeaway meals most nights.' He looked yearningly at Margo's bubbling pots.

'I promise to wash up afterwards. I want Margo in a personable mood tomorrow.'

'Since when does her attitude matter?'

'When you need to beg favours, it pays to let consideration flow both ways,' he answered with calculation in his eyes. 'The builders have finished the rooms for the dentist and the pathology lab. I have to paint both areas before the tenants move in. It necessitates borrowing Margo's cleaning agents as well as her helping hand—both hands, really.'

'I'm happy not to be in your shoes,' Anna replied with the look of a fellow sufferer.

Suddenly two hands held her eyes shut from behind. The familiar, melodious voice asked, 'Guess who?'

'Joshua,' she giggled, turning around. 'It's good to see you.'

'Likewise, my pet.'

'Are you hungry?'

'You bet! I've had the busiest day. I skipped lunch.'

'Go and join the others. Fernando's assisting me here. We'll have the food dished out in no time.'

'Don't tell me Margo is letting you take charge in her kitchen?' Josh couldn't help but laugh at that anomaly.

'She had no say in it. Sipho dismissed her with mean threats. She went home in a disagreeable state.'

'One day, those two will come to blows.' They heard Josh prophesy on his way out. 'I fear for Sipho when that happens.'

Dinner was a convivial affair. If Vince had doubts about staying at KwaZulu Medical, they were dispelled.

Peter and Tom, however, were not quite as jovial as expected. Either they were tired, missing their evening meal with their families, or something weighty pierced their normally placid nature. Josh noticed the silent wrath clouding their faces. He asked, 'How are your children bearing up, Peter? Are they still going to that school?'

'Yes, for now. And so is that dog of a teacher, but I won't rest till he's dismissed. Even if my kids end up going elsewhere, that bastard shall not remain here to molest others if I can help it.'

How long had Peter bottled up his revulsion? Anna wondered, listening in horror. Venom rushed from his words like a rain-swollen river.

'That filthy dog knows I blew the whistle on him. He sent me death threats for my troubles.'

'We need to fix him before he gets you,' Fernando swore under his breath. 'We can't have teachers who beat boys and sexually molest girls. He's not fit to live.'

Josh turned to Anna. 'Do you think Major Mortimer could help? It looks like Peter needs protection.'

'Mortimer quit, unless Hank persuaded him to tear up his resignation. What about C5 and friends?'

'Yes, it's just possible they might be free. Sipho, will you please contact them? We can't have anyone menace our staff. It's intolerable.'

'Don't mind if we go home.' Tom stood up to leave. 'It's best we are with our families right now.'

'Very good,' Josh nodded. 'Don't come tomorrow, Peter. Don't come at all till we can get a protective network organized around you. I'll let you know what's happening.'

'Let me drive you home and pick you up in the morning,' Fernando offered. 'My bakkie is bulletproof. It's ex-military.'

After the grimly, sinister end to their dinner, everyone dispersed. Sipho conducted Vince to his room before making a number of phone calls in his office. Anna began the washing up as Fernando drove Peter and Tom home. In a sensitive and helpful mood, Josh joined her, offering to deputise for Fernando.

'What's on your agenda tomorrow?' he asked, curious to know how she filled her day.

'I'll be in conference with Sipho and Vince in the morning. Following that, I'd like to join you when you head off to the IFP rally. I'm determined to hear Shenge speak if only once.'

'Great! I have to leave early to set up our equipment. You can assist with straightforward stuff like the paperwork.' He busied himself drying plates as he talked. 'You brought a swanky car here today.'

'Yes, it's for you to drive,' she said, both arms submerged in dishwater. 'The keys are on your desk.'

The cup Josh dried all but slipped from his hold. 'That's insane . . . I can't afford a prestige car!'

'It's not your personal property, sweetheart. It's a company car belonging to the partnership. Any one of us could drive it, but as you are most in need of conveyance, you're the one who gets it. Face it Josh, your Corolla's had it.'

'Yes, but a Merc? I'm not going to drive that around here. It sends the wrong message and asks for trouble.'

'Use it for the long trips. You will find it more satisfactory.'

'Undoubtedly . . .'

She smiled at his bewildered face while he hugged her. 'It's good of you to think of my convenience, pet. Thank you.'

'Don't worry about drying these.' She pointed to the pots. 'I'll finish it if you still have other work.'

'Yes,' he chuckled. 'It will take me till about midnight.' Smiling disarmingly, he asked, 'Dare I hope you may stay up for me?'

'I'll be curled up in your bed, purring like a cat,' she promised seductively.

* * *

Josh breathed deeply and smiled. 'This is wonderful,' he said during a break from their morning's dancing behind the toolshed. He raised his arms to sun and sky. 'It feels as if we never parted. We always continue from where we left off previously.'

'We're not really separated, Josh. We still manage to see each other frequently even while working at different locations.'

'You better believe it, Anna, my pet. You are the mainspring of my existence. Without you, I'm only a robot going through the motions of living.' He held her so tight she barely breathed.

'I had no idea lack of sleep inspires romantic declarations,' she laughed when he released her.

'Admittedly, another hour of proper sleep would be beneficial, but it can't be done.' A look of simulated martyrdom insinuated it was all her fault.

After ten more minutes of dancing, they came back inside to shower.

'Eh! That new bloke, Vince . . . what does he have for breakfast?' Margo glowered at them as she passed with a string bag of oranges in each hand. Signs of happiness as displayed by Anna and Josh were not permitted in her presence.

'Same as me,' Anna called back cheerfully. 'And top of the morning to you too.' Giving Josh a quick hug, she danced along the passage to her room.

To her surprise, the shower gushed with refreshing force. The builders had renewed the plumbing, she thought with a grateful sigh. A few bars of song escaped her till she remembered her neighbour. Vince needn't be woken so early on a Sunday morning. Using the blow-dryer was too noisy. She'd dry her hair after breakfast. In the meantime, it felt great to slip into casual clothes that weren't made of denim. She couldn't face the prison garments in the wardrobe and toyed with the idea of giving them away. Dreadful memories clung to them like the electronic tags used in clothing stores that shoppers can't remove. Opening her duffel bag, she pulled out camouflage-print cargo pants and an olive-green T-shirt. Wouldn't Hank laugh if he saw her in this get-up? She chuckled, picturing his stupefied face. Having promised Franz to always carry a gun, the cargo pants were ideal because of their big pockets. And who knew what challenges the day would present?

At that moment, it brought a thump and crash. Margo entered with the breakfast tray. Some routines never changed. At least the food was tasty, made with fresh ingredients and accompanied by aromatic coffee, of which she only drank half a cup. She ate slowly although she always found herself hungry after the morning's dancing exercise.

Briefly she thought about pleasing Margo by returning her empty tray to the kitchen. Margo had encouraged such assistance unsuccessfully in the past. She would be deprived of joy today as well because the Lady Anna De Bruyn was about to demonstrate she was not above petty vengeance. She collected Vince's, Sipho's, Josh's, and her own trays and placed them on the bench—spread out, higgledy-piggledy, leaving no room for other implements. Margo would be forced to stack everything before she had enough space to prepare more food. 'Just let her dare complain,' Anna congratulated herself shamelessly while entering Sipho's office.

All rooms were left unlocked now. 'What a surprise,' she quipped, but nobody heard. She turned the computer on and opened the main gate for Fernando when he arrived. He brought Tom with him. Together they loaded his bakkie with gear for the first-aid tents. Josh finished his round of the children's ward and dashed to Casualty, where he conferred at length with Indira. It was a morning of frenzied activity for the doctors, and Anna was glad to be tucked away with nothing but journals and ledgers for company.

Vince and Sipho's appearance disrupted her peace.

'You should still be sleeping,' she greeted them sternly. 'It's Sunday, for goodness' sake.'

'I bet we had more sleep than you,' Sipho suggested with accurate estimation. 'Dancing on the grass at five-thirty this morning . . . really!' He clucked, shaking his head with a knowing expression when Anna gave him a sharp eye.

He broke into an amused, self-satisfied smile. It wasn't often he had her on the back foot. Fearing to dwell too long on his hard-won advantage, he handed her a file of legal correspondence.

'Can you look through this, please? We need to know exactly where we stand with the title for this place. If there's the slightest loophole, the ANC may muscle in on our affairs. They're resentful about our success. The more influence we gain, the greater the likelihood all their miserable secrets will leak out to the rank-and-file membership. Their loan to us was supposed to remain hush-hush.'

'It should be above board,' she replied, taking the file. 'The ANC advanced the loan. You used the money to purchase the homestead outright. No mortgage from banks is involved. The title came straight to you. If the loan repayments are not in arrears, I can't see any problems.'

'That's what I would have thought. It's not that I mistrust our legal eagles, but I'd like another opinion to be a hundred per cent certain.'

'I'll ask Mr Waterman to check and make sure nothing's been missed.'

Sipho had work for Vince too. Sunday or not, he wasn't slackening the pace.

'How does this Oreship kerfuffle affect our dividends from the Mineral Enterprises shares, Vince? Perhaps we should diversify our portfolio further.'

Many more such questions occupied the bean-counting trio almost till lunch when Anna called a halt. She looked up at Sipho and asked innocently, 'What's the brand of shoes you're wearing?' Her wink towards Vince told him Sipho was about to be hit with retaliation for his comments about sleeplessness.

Wondering what prompted a question so out of context, Sipho asked, 'What do you mean by brand? They're nothing special.'

'May I see, please?'

He raised one foot to chair level.

'I knew it!' she shouted gleefully. 'They're Bossy Boots.'

Sipho guffawed, swinging his arms as if marching. 'These boots were made for walking' he sang. ' . . . and that's just what they'll do . . .' – 'All the way to the kitchen for sandwiches.' He took Anna's hand. 'Are you coming to make drinks?'

Josh sneaked fruit, maize cakes and coffee into his office. 'I'm nearly ready to leave for the rally, Anna. Are you through with your morning's work?'

'I will be with you,' she called back, running to her room. She plaited her hair and slipped the Glock into the deep pocket in the right leg of her cargo pants.

Josh stood beside the Corolla when she joined him. Man, he thought, she has her hair in that ghastly plait again. Just look at those graceless, unshapely pants. The T-shirt clings to her nicely, though. Today her face bore an unusual glow. It was already noticeable when they exercised this morning. She wasn't drinking as much coffee either, he noticed. Concealing his musings, he opened the passenger side for her. 'Let's go!'

The gathering was to take place on vacant Council land on the outskirts of town. Josh approached the area slowly till, held up by three busses, he came to a standstill.

'I don't like the look of this,' he said when men in ANC T-shirts alighted, assembling by the roadside. 'They are organized for trouble.' He watched them doubtfully. 'They don't appear to carry weapons, but I'd swear their busses are loaded to the roof.'

Anna glanced around, uncertain. 'What now?'

Josh tried shrugging off his anger and impatience. This wasn't getting his first-aid tents up. 'Unfortunately they have a democratic right to be here, but they should respect that right by not dressing provocatively in ANC T-shirts. It inevitably incites resentment. If we did that at their meetings, we'd be evicted without apology. What's the bet they'll heckle and interject as soon as Shenge starts speaking?'

The ANC supporters formed a noisy, unruly group who blocked the whole street as they moved towards the meeting ground, singing at the top of their voices.

'I can't understand their words.' Anna listened a while. 'What are they on about?'

'It's one of their outdated inflammatory struggle songs,' Josh explained. 'It's called "Awuleth' Umshini Wami". It means "Bring me my machine gun".'

'A clear revelation of their intentions, I'd say.' Anna's misgivings about the crowd grew with the song's crescendo.

'Look,'—Josh turned to her—'this is no good. It could get rough. It's no place for you.'

'I see numerous women here,' she pointed out.

He emitted an exasperated sigh. 'Anna, for once do as I say. I'm walking the rest of the way. You drive back to the clinic and stay there. Tell Sipho of the potential for violence here. He should lock the gate and let nobody in unless they're half dead. There's sure to be unrest later.'

'Will you be all right? How will you get back without your car?' Anna felt the contagion of apprehension about her.

'Fernando has his bakkie here. I'll be fine.' He climbed out, watching her execute a U-turn and drive away.

'Damn!' she cursed, wondering if she would ever hear Shenge's oratory. Fate seemed to plot against her. She drove on for two or three kilometres when her oft-deplored obstinacy asserted itself and she turned back towards Vryheid. 'I'll get to this rally if it's the last thing I do,' she promised herself.

With difficulty, she parked close to the centre of action. The area became crowded. The throng of ANC followers had melted away, infiltrating and blending with the IFP members. The white and red first-aid tents were visible in the distance. She avoided them, fearing Josh's endless recitation of reproaches for placing herself in what he deemed to be dangerous situations.

Wanting to be near the speaker's dais, she took off quickly in that direction. A path trodden by thousands of feet provided a course towards her goal. Dry grass crunched under her feet. The odd skimpy bush and tree, growing at intervals, offered little shade from the afternoon sun. Already she heard the loudspeakers being tested.

A man armed with a knobkerrie walked some distance ahead. Another fellow holding an AK-47 approached from the direction of the bus parking lot. Josh was right, she thought, they do have arms in the busses. The machine-gun bearer hollered at the man ahead. When he turned, she recognized Peter Shabalala, who raised his knobkerrie threateningly. It was no greeting among friends.

The men began a serious argument, shouting swear words in Zulu and English. With limited success, she tried interpreting what was said. Not only was it all in rapid Zulu but the microphone's reverbs screeched and echoed all around. She caught two words, though: *abantwana* and *esikoleni*. 'Children' and 'at school'. Realization hit her like a blow. The AK-47 carrier was the schoolteacher Peter wanted removed from his post. As if in a bad dream, she watched the teacher raise his gun.

In the months that followed, she could never explain adequately what happened next. She was on autopilot.

Cover—she needed cover. The nearest bush would have to do. The distance between her and the teacher was still a fraction out of range of her Glock. That couldn't be helped. It was a risk she'd take.

She ran and squeezed herself into the bush, aiming through its foliage. If she could hit the teacher's hand before he pulled the trigger . . .

The men still shouted insults. Neither took notice of their surroundings. The teacher's body became taut with concentration as he adjusted his aim.

Now! She fired. The microphone's reverbs still whistled. With a relief that brought black spots to her eyes, she watched the teacher's gun drop. His left hand held his right elbow. Blood flowed through his fingers.

Shaking uncontrollably, she knelt in the bush, trying to compose herself. The Glock's range was a little out, which probably accounted for her hitting the teacher's elbow instead of his hand, she figured. Or mayhap she was too nervous to aim well. She had fired at a living person for the first time. But was she to remain inactive while that creature was about to cut Peter's head off with a sweep from his AK-47? Peter was a friend, the father of three children. What would they do without him? What would KwaZulu Medical be without him? Her emotions turned topsy-turvy. Target practice was fine, but she had hit a living being. What if her aim was so unsteady that she killed him? She didn't want to think about that. How could soldiers shoot to kill? No wonder so many suffered PTSD.

Disregarding his Hippocratic Oath, Peter walked away while the teacher called his friends for help. So the prick had backup, she thought, while Peter strolled about in blissful ignorance with nothing more than a knobkerrie. Although, when wielded in strong hands, these sticks proved lethal, it was no defence against a machine gun.

The teacher's friends were a long time coming. In fact, they didn't turn up at all. Instead, he found himself disarmed none too gently by two uniformed officers, who hauled him off to a police van. Two inspectors stayed behind to survey the scene. She knew she had to get away. They would work out where the bullet came from and find her. Still shaking helplessly, she tried rising while keeping an eye on the pair.

'All right, lady, that's enough of playing with your popgun.' In shock, she sank back onto one knee. 'You better come with me now.'

She was extracted from the bush and supported to keep upright.

'Mrs De Bruyn? What are you doing here?' He hadn't recognized her in her casual clothes till he came close enough to address her.

'I could say the same to you, Major Mortimer.' It was hard to know who was more surprised. 'Don't tell me,' she said, 'Hank talked you into staying with us. He can be very persuasive.'

'Well, I came to think we should both try harder to cooperate in future,' he said with a self-conscious grin.

'Perhaps,' she sighed, and they shook hands. Hers still trembled.

'Unless you want to answer a host of silly questions, you had better come away from here quickly.' He placed his arm around her. 'We'll pretend we're boyfriend and girlfriend. We saw nothing, heard no shots, and were enjoying a day out,' he explained when she looked set to protest. 'We're so engrossed in one another the rest of the world doesn't exist. Come on . . . you can act, can't you?'

'Wait,' she stopped. 'Wouldn't it look odd to be leaving when the rally is just beginning? We should be going the other way.'

'I would prefer to vanish,' he said, looking dubious. 'But you could have a point.' They turned around.

'Keep clear of those first-aid tents,' she begged. 'Josh will skin me alive if he sees me here. He thinks I've driven back to the clinic.'

'You take him for a simpleton.' Ernest chuckled a little, giving her a pitying look. 'Of course he knows you're here. He saw the Corolla when he went looking for Peter. Peter didn't arrive punctually, which rang alarm bells, and he went searching for him with Fernando.'

'You've seen him then?'

'Yes, my coming wasn't unexpected. Vince rang me last night explaining the problem with the teacher. I set out at four this morning, and it's just as well from what I see.'

'Vince? Have you kept in touch with him even though you resigned?'

'Oh yes, we've become good friends, didn't you know?'

'Ernest! Ernest Mortimer!' A man came towards them.

'Blow me down,' Ernest laughed. 'If it isn't . . .' He seemed uncertain what to call the man or if mentioning his name constituted a security breach.

'It's me, Gideon,' he puffed as he hurried along. 'It has to be about six or seven years since we last met.'

'Good heavens, yes,' Mortimer replied, delighted.

Gideon turned to Anna. 'You must be Mrs De Bruyn. I've heard much about you. All of it good,' he added when she looked at him, puzzled. He saw her glance quizzically at Mortimer, wanting an introduction.

'Just call me Gideon,' he smiled.

It didn't take much imagination to see Gideon was a man of dark masquerades, although he had an open, friendly smile, which she couldn't help but like.

'You better go to that tent over there,' Gideon pointed. 'It's a good vantage point for seeing and hearing what's happening. Josh and Peter are there. The one on the opposite end of the ground is manned by Doctor Dlamini and Sister Miriam.'

Gideon departed with a 'See you later.' To Ernest, he added, 'Let's have a drink some time. We have much to catch up on.'

Still entwined with Anna, Ernest left her no choice but to head towards Josh's tent with him.

'Look who we have here,' he announced, pushing her inside.

Josh and Peter ran towards her with open arms. 'You are the most worrisome female alive,' Josh scolded while both hugged her. 'Not a day goes by without my wishing you were my wife, although I should be relieved you're not. Heaven bless your courage, Anna.'

'Or foolishness,' Mortimer grunted aside. 'This little skirmish could easily have gone wrong.'

'Who was that chap we talked to before?' she asked Ernest when Josh exhausted his breath lambasting and praising her simultaneously.

'An acquaintance from long ago,' he answered vaguely.

'Do you know him, Josh?' She turned away from Ernest, feeling he was being secretive. She'd had enough mysteries for one day. 'He's a tall man, a little on the corpulent side, wants to be called Gideon. He seemed to know me, but I've never seen him before.'

'Gideon? Yes, his friends call him Giddy,' Josh laughed.

'Yes, but who is he?'

'C5,' he confided in a whisper with his hand held to his mouth.

'Really? That's why he knew about me. I've never met any of his contentious unit.'

'He and his colleagues are here on legitimate duties protecting the VIPs. Being the good friends they are, they also kept our schoolteacher's South African Democratic Teachers Union accomplices otherwise engaged. I reckon Tom may have a number of them in his care right now. It's hard to believe that horrid teacher holds a senior position in SADTU.' Josh rubbed his hands excitedly. 'When Giddy came in telling us you hit the kingpin, we couldn't believe it.'

'He didn't see me do it, surely?' she asked, astonished and certain nobody else was in the vicinity.

'Nothing much escapes Giddy, my pet.'

She continued interrogating Ernest. 'What's your connection with him? Come on, 'fess up!'

Reluctantly, Ernest admitted, 'I was his commanding officer when he was just a young smart aleck.'

'Shenge is here! They're starting!' someone called outside. According to police estimates, the crowd numbered around thirty-five thousand, but it could have been nil—so quiet did they become. As yet, nobody required medical attention. Peter and Josh had time to stand outside listening to the presentation. Ernest joined them, carrying a chair for Anna.

Shenge stepped on the podium to roars of approval. He started his address with a prayer and a minute's silence in respect for recently assassinated IFP members.

'Dear friends,' he began. 'Believe me when I say fundamental changes in South Africa will come through negotiation around the conference table, not through armed struggle. However, even after the destruction of apartheid, we will continue the all-important struggle for economic empowerment. We must work towards becoming a truly African and yet truly modern state.

'To achieve this, the IFP looks to liberalizing our social and economic dynamics to help unleash our country's potentials. We cannot afford a government that controls nearly 60 per cent of the economy. The IFP believes privatization should be constitutionally mandated and implemented by an independent privatization commission.

Derisive howls sounded from the ANC T-shirt wearers. Shenge continued without acknowledging them.

'The IFP will promote the privatization of all parastatals, including public utilities. Privatized assets will be returned to free market competition so we do not pay more for them here than what is charged for similar services in other countries.

'To enhance direct empowerment, broad-based public ownership of shares in newly privatized enterprises will be encouraged. Broad-based black economic empowerment should not be of benefit to the well-connected only but become a support for the masses of the poor as well.'

'Did you hear that?' Anna whispered, pulling at Josh's sleeve. 'You're too well-connected. Acquaintance with the president of the Stock Exchange Council lifts you above the ranks of the poor,' she commented, tongue in cheek.

'Yes, I have a Merc for a company car to prove it,' he grinned. 'I'm corrupt and busy improving my socio-economic status. Now I want to see the parents of my little patients share in this South African economic miracle.'

* * *

Anna and Ernest's pact for a smoother working harmony was subjected to empirical testing immediately after the rally. Assuming authority as if by divine right when the dais cleared of dignitaries, he said to her, 'Okay, that's it. I'm taking you back to Johannesburg now.'

'You are?' She smiled, but her darkening eyes emitted warnings.

Josh turned away, amused. He saw the signals. Fernando too knew enough to agree the major skated on thin ice. He couldn't resist offering a helpful hint. 'Careful, Major,' he grinned. 'This lady, she don't take no shit,' he said with deliberately broad inflection.

'You could earn my gratitude for a lift to Durban tomorrow morning, Major. In the meantime, Professor Mtolo needs all hands on deck to dismantle and pack the tents and equipment.'

'Surely Fernando can do that.' Ernest couldn't help but issue orders.

'Today should have been Fernando's day off. It was generous of him to offer assistance and the use of his vehicle.' Her eyes flashed angrily at Mortimer. 'I do not take such a show of goodwill for granted, Major. Can you manage to remember that?'

'Don't argue with him, Anna.' Peter came forward. 'I can help Josh.'

'Thank you, Peter, but no. You've had a bad day, and if we all lend a hand, the task will be completed quicker. Major Mortimer must realise we are not his platoon to command.'

At the clinic, Felicity's very late but substantial afternoon tea settled tempers to fair on everyone's mood barometer. Tom, Peter, and Fernando departed for home. Anna sought Vince, finding him in the kitchen flirting with Felicity.

'You look like you're here to stay,' she said, her lively imagination conjuring pictures of Margo's reaction to this occurrence. 'I'll be leaving in the morning. If you encounter problems, phone me.' She gave him Jakobus's home phone number as well as information about reaching her on the Vera. 'That's where I'll be for the next couple of days if you need me.'

Without Margo, Sipho felt happier about entering the kitchen. 'Did I hear you say you're going tomorrow? Already?' His face showed disappointment.

'Yes, I have to go. I know I can rely on you to make Vince feel at home. You've always done your best for me in the past,' she added, meaning every word.

Mortimer wisely booked himself into a Vryheid hotel. Anna called him into the conference room before he left. She poured him a glass of wine. He raised it, saluting her.

'We nearly started off on the wrong foot again,' he laughed. 'Please pardon my barrack square conduct.'

'Rest assured, had I not given you my handshake on future improvement of workplace relations, I would tell you nothing about my plans.'

A look of irritation crossed his stern countenance, but another sip of wine relaxed his facial muscles again.

'I must congratulate you,' he said, trying his hand at unaccustomed humour while indicating the wine. 'This beats Joshua Mtolo's cup of tea.'

'Oh.' She was all concern. 'Did you want one of those? I can ask him to make it.'

He still did not know her well enough to be certain if this was a joke but laughed, saying, 'Not on your life, lady.'

'That's better,' she approved. 'You're a handsome man when you laugh.' She gave him a daring smile. 'Only Margo is licensed to be crusty here.'

Her teasing reminded him sobriety was needed. He asked quietly, 'So what are you doing tomorrow?'

'I need to set out at a reasonable time, maybe about nine. First stop is Jakobus' house. Fiona has a new proposition she wishes to discuss regarding Nozipho's school. Secondly, my mother-in-law is staying with Jakobus as well. The poor lady gets lonely in her Cape Town house. She won't need much persuading to come home with me. Hank hasn't seen her in such a long time. Thirdly, give me three days to see to the Vera. I'll let you know which homeward flight we're booked on so you can fetch us from the airport. That's about it.' She ran through her mental checklist. 'You have all necessary phone numbers in case of hassles or emergencies, so you should be right driving back to Jo'burg as soon as you have dropped me off.'

'I'm afraid it's not that easy. My brief is to be near you at all times. I can't be in Johannesburg and leave you in Durban.'

'I'm sure that instruction wasn't meant for when I'm in Jakobus's house.'

She always has a counterargument, he thought, nettled but hiding his temper. 'What about the boat?'

'Hank doesn't know about that and nor did you until today. You must have eavesdropped on my conversation with Vince.' Her darkening eyes, rapier sharp, cut him down, but he ignored the admonition.

'Now that I have found out,' he said, consciously making an effort to be patient, 'I feel responsible.'

'And what would you do on the Vera? Stick your head in the bilges to see if a bomb is planted there?'

He laughed without humour.

'Nobody gets near me when I'm underway, unless you know of pirates frequenting South African waters.'

'Stranger things can happen.' He looked at her, awaiting more argumentative commentary.

'All right,' she sighed. 'You can come if you observe my three shipboard rules. One, I'm the owner and skipper. My word is law. Two, no alcohol while at sea. Three, no smoking.' She hoped Ernest would think twice about boarding when deprived of his pipe and whiskey.

'Done!' he agreed much to her regret.

* * *

'What an appalling day,' Anna groaned, collapsing onto the patient's chair beside Josh's desk.

He took her hand. 'I've seen better ones too. You should go to bed and relax. I'll make you my Mortimer tea, and you will feel fresh and alive tomorrow.'

'I've never shot at a person before,' she said, distressed. 'I can't just brush that off like lint from my jacket.'

'You did what was necessary.'

'He'll never use his right arm again.'

'That's his problem.' Josh pushed his paperwork aside and rose, rolling his chair back.

'Come, pet.' He pulled her up. 'It's time to concentrate on ourselves.' They left the office. With a comforting hand on her shoulder, he led her to his quarters and seated her on the couch. 'Want to listen to music?' he asked, watching her closely. She nodded wearily, and he selected her favourite Bach disc to revive her spirit.

'I'll make that mug of tea for you now, but don't worry . . . it will only be a quarter of the strength I gave to Mortimer . . . just enough to ease the tension.'

'That blighter has discovered my boat,' she said, piqued by his prying into her life. 'Now he wants to sail with me. Big Ears must have overheard me telling Vince. In future, I have to be careful about what information I give Vince. The two have struck up a friendship and, no doubt, exchange news quickly.'

When Josh brought the tea, she sipped hesitantly but smiled, delighted with the flavour. 'It tastes good. Thank you.' She downed the rest with relish.

'You can stir honey into it if it's not sweet enough.'

'It's great as it is. I like it. I should learn to make it myself.'

'No,' he grinned, 'the ingredients are a witch doctor's secret.'

He sat down beside her, placing an arm around her shoulders. They listened to the music in companionable silence. Her head rested against his upper arm, and he thought she would soon be asleep.

By the end of the CD, she was still awake, though, the tea being either too weak or her stamina too great.

'Is there something you need to tell me?' he asked softly, noticing her restlessness.

She gazed straight ahead. Had she heard him? It wasn't like Anna to remain so still, he thought. She was not an African woman, so failing to look at him could not be interpreted as a respectful gesture. Anna was always direct. *She's thinking of a reply*, he imagined, *but taking a long time.*

'No?' he asked when she appeared to swallow her response back down. A small, expectant smile played on his face. 'Then let me tell you something. I think you are pregnant.'

That brought her to face him in a flash. 'Joshua,' she said, caressing his face lovingly, 'it's too early to be certain.'

'Anna, it's a miracle,' he affirmed. 'I've wanted a child for heaven knows how long. It never eventuated with Cindy. I suppose she took contraceptives until such time I agreed to marry her. But now!' He stood up, leaping over the coffee table. 'May the ancestors be praised,' he shouted. 'I'm going to be a father!' After changing the CD, he came back to the couch. With growing anguish, he wished she shared his joy. Why was she so non-committal?

'Are you unhappy about it?' he asked presently, fearing her possible indifference.

'I'm as thrilled as you, Josh, but I have a big problem. It's called Hank. What do I say to him?'

'I shall speak to him,' he said with his consulting room voice.

'You are a glutton for punishment,' she chuckled. 'You better let me deal with it my way . . . when I think of one.'

A note of panic entered his voice. 'Please don't even dream of having the baby in Sydney. I can't follow till my passport is returned to me.'

'I wasn't thinking that far ahead, sweetheart. I shall take each day as it comes, I guess.'

'Anna, darling, you're a gem.' He held her in his arms, saying her name over and over with enchanted rapture till she fell asleep, a smile still on her face. Unable to let go of her, he lifted his feet onto the coffee table and settled for a long night, embracing the mother of his child.

* * *

Ernest Mortimer telephoned just before nine. Could they leave for Durban in the afternoon instead of the morning? he wondered. Expressing his wish to lunch with Gideon, he asked if Anna wanted to join them.

'The afternoon will be fine,' she assured him. 'It gives me extra time to work with Sipho and Vince. You go and enjoy your meal.'

Josh had already left for Empangeni Hospital, and she missed him. At some time during the night, he carried her to her room and put her to bed. Who said the tea didn't work? She had no idea the change had taken place till she awoke at about seven, finding herself in her own bed and alone with the sun penetrating the curtain. A note, weighed down by the vase of flowers on the bedside table, explained his early departure. He wrote that he would be tied up with more rallies for the next two weekends but hoped they may meet on the third. Reminding her to seek medical attention, he added the name, address, and phone number of a renowned obstetrician. A wrapped present, which looked and felt like a book when she poked it, was left beside the note. She opened it quickly.

'Oh, great!' Josh's children's short stories were published. The volume was called *Mist in the Valley*, a collection of short stories for children by Dr J. B. Mtolo. Hearing Sipho's door opening, she threw her new bathrobe around her and followed him to his office.

'Sipho, look!' She held the book out to him.

'Yeah, I know.' He grinned broadly at her. 'Good, isn't it?'

'After all my slaving over the editing, you mean to say you knew about this but kept it quiet? You sneaky old tokoloshe.'

He laughed as if it was the best joke out. 'Josh wanted to surprise you and swore me to secrecy.'

Casting a quick glimpse out of the window, she saw the Corolla left behind and the Mercedes gone. 'I knew he'd find it irresistible,' she said, drawing Sipho's attention to the switch.

'I have another revelation for you,' Sipho said, employing both arms to dig for a file on his paper-strewn desk. 'I'll need a front-end loader soon to push some of this unnecessary stuff away.' After diligent investigation beneath five folders, he caught hold of the hidden material.

'Shall I tell you or do you want to read it?' he cackled with excitement.

'You're itching to reveal your riddle, so go ahead,' she encouraged.

'Indira, bless her heart,' he began, 'prevailed upon William to drum up enough support for us to go public. And he did it too. Have a look.' He handed the file to her. 'Mineral Enterprises will discharge our loan to the ANC in return for shares once we're trading. That's great, as it adds to our capital. Two health funds, the health workers' union, and even the mine workers' union are contributing funds towards our venture. In time, there may be more. At least we have five subscribers we can rely on to begin with.' He smiled with satisfaction.

Anna looked at Sipho's papers. 'That's fantastic, Sipho. It means, though, control of this place is slipping further away from Josh's grasp. Have you discussed it with him?'

'He's so busy with the medical side he doesn't have much time for anything else. He will be a director, of course, and I hope you will agree to serve in that capacity also. William and Indira will too.

'Indira insisted William and Hank get their heads together to work on the details. She's very keen to see the clinic become a public company.'

Pleased but disturbed by a perceived lack of transparency, she asked, 'When did all this happen? I had lunch with William recently but we only talked about Oreship. Hank took off on his tour without a word about any of it to me.'

'You must have been sailing the seven seas at the time,' Sipho said.

Hank had told his brothers responsibility for the hospital project rested with her. He should have informed her of his change of heart.

Suddenly she laughed out loud. The irony tickled her fancy. William, the first VIP prisoner, exerted his muscle to ensure the place flourished. Indira was a staunch ally and would be better placed to manage the clinic's affairs, bringing both medical and business expertise to the job. If in time the court's verdict turned against Josh, Indira could step in immediately, filling the void. Continuity was thus guaranteed.

* * *

Chapter 15

The Hard Landing

Hank jerked upright, woken from a shallow slumber when the 747's wheels hit the runway. He was home, whatever that meant these days. Would he find Anna waiting for him in the arrival lounge? Surely she wasn't still incensed about being left behind to run the office. She made no attempt to see him off when he left, claiming a heavy workload. That was true, but it would not have stopped her once.

The captain's voice sounded over the speaker system, instructing passengers to keep seat belts fastened firmly because they were crossing a live runway.

'In this fog? Great!' Hank remarked to Maurice beside him, who looked out of the window into solid grey.

Wasn't that precisely how he felt about his marriage? Bumpy, with no indication where he was heading. He must try pulling it out of its nosedive before the inevitable crash landing.

It was up to him. He had many flying hours of thinking behind him to realise his attitude hadn't helped Anna one iota. Hang on, though, how was a man supposed to respond when his wife loved another? He thought he'd just about won her back before her parents left, but it was an illusion. It took more time and effort than he would have dreamt possible to overcome the estrangement looming over them. He had to curb his impatience.

A careful choice of words was important when talking to her. She was sensitive, and her emotional radar registered feelings he didn't know he had.

'Why are you punishing me?' she asked during their last horrible discussion. He wasn't! What for?

'Yes, you are, Hank.' The answer came from deep within: *it's for her intimacies with Joshua*. It didn't matter that she may have succumbed because she had no option, but succumb she did. He couldn't disregard it. It nagged like a toothache, intensified by her refusal to call it rape. Yet given his state of health, did he have the right to expect her to live without physical love? Bluntly put . . . without the vigorous sex she craved?

She forgave everything Josh had done and didn't conceal her fondness for him. She was too damned scrupulous for that. Yet for all her candidness, a part of her remained private. She hinted at their dreadful rows but never said what caused them, other than pointing to differences of opinion regarding the ransom and vexation due to her escape attempts. He never pressed her for details, hoping she would confide more about this warfare as time passed, but she shut the memories away.

Why had he behaved so beastly towards her? Wasn't she affectionate and caring? supportive in the business? enthusiastic in bed? She was, but he believed he noticed a difference in her manner without the ability to articulate the exact cause. Perhaps the change was in him, not her. Was he being an ass? Why would she try to escape if she loved Josh so much? How could he peel away the complexities of this case and arrive at the truth?

The truth! The word caused emotional reflux. Where had she been the last four days when he failed to raise her on the telephone? Nobody knew. Mrs George said the entry in her diary for those days read 'AWOL!' With Mortimer in stinking humour, he couldn't engage him to check either. Had she returned to KwaZulu Medical? He hadn't the gumption to phone there, fearing they thought him a feeble excuse for a man who couldn't keep his wife in check.

Nobody controlled a headstrong woman like Anna. One cooperated with her. One discussed, debated, negotiated, reached agreements, and compromised. *I with her, she with me.* That's how the marriage had always worked, with neither party enforcing their will on the other.

She had been honest and apologetic about Joshua's bail. And what happened next? He had employed a bodyguard without telling her, with the full knowledge she would be upset. Adding insult to injury, he gave her company car to the man. Was he straightforward with her about this trip he'd just touched down from? Leaving her behind. If that didn't drive her into another man's arms, what would? Yes, he was the biggest fool alive.

'Maurice! Maurice!' Gill ran towards him, kissing and hugging him when both men emerged from Customs. 'I'm glad you're back. I missed you. This trip was too long,' she declared, out of breath but smiling.

Where was Anna? Hank looked around. Perhaps she had driven back to the office because the plane was late. *Oh,* he remembered, Mortimer had her car. Couldn't one of his security team have driven her? What did he employ them for? Maybe talking the major out of resigning was a mistake. The mood Anna was in would convince her of a conspiracy against her. Had the two reconciled their differences yet? he wondered.

'Gill can take us to the office,' Maurice suggested.

'No, man, you go home. It's Friday in our corner of the world if I'm right. You go and have a good rest. I'll see you Monday morning.' Picking up his bags, Hank searched for a taxi. He felt pain in his heart. *The sort pills can't fix,* he thought miserably.

'Let us at least drop you off at home.' Gill sought to help.

'No thanks . . . you're kind, but I want to check in at the office before I head home.'

He found everyone working quietly in the House of De Bruyn although it was nearly closing time. The atmosphere seemed strangely relaxed. He couldn't think why. He was tired and sore of spirit.

Vince Lewis wasn't there. Poor bloke must be in hospital again.

He walked towards his office, acknowledging greetings from staff members as he went. Passing Anna's closed door, he stopped, puzzled. Why was a smell of pipe tobacco wafting through the cracks? He pushed the door open with considerable apprehension.

'It's good to see you back, Hank.' Ernest rose from the chair and desk normally occupied by Anna.

For a moment, Hank doubted his sanity. The room now held four medium-sized desks back to back. The vase of flowers Anna kept on the little table by the window was missing. Her Tom Roberts paintings had vanished too. *She's left me!* he thought, his heart pounding like a jackhammer. With a greying face and unsteady voice, dreading the answer, he asked: 'Where is Anna?'

'She's at home,' Ernest smiled. 'She's brought your mother here for a visit.'

'How thoughtful of her,' Hank managed to say, his mind still reeling. 'I have a guilty conscience whenever I think of how infrequently I see the old lady.' Was it too early to feel relieved?

'You might find some changes here,' Ernest grinned.

'Alterations indeed; like what the heck you are doing in my wife's office?'

Mortimer saw fatigue and uncertainty in Hank's eyes. During the past month, he came to appreciate Anna as a tough, resolute, and determined lady, doubtless a little too much for Hank to handle.

'Mrs De Bruyn decided to rationalize office space, kindly making room for my team. It saves the cost of renting another floor in this building. As you and Mr Van Buuren do not spend as much time here now, she has moved in with you, and Mrs George is sharing with Mr Van Buuren.'

Nkosinathi approached as Hank crossed to his room. 'Shall I go and lock your luggage into your car, sir?'

'Yes, please, that's very good of you. Where is Vince?' he asked quickly before Nkosinathi's exit.

'Mrs De Bruyn sent him to work with Sipho Gwala. She said it cuts down on her travelling and Vince benefits from instant medical attention should the need arise.'

Hank's disposition improved remarkably at this news. Anna didn't want to go to KwaZulu Medical, a propitious sign.

'And who does Vince's work here?'

'Mrs De Bruyn said I should do so. She was waiting for your return before making it official.'

'My office looks very different,' Hank said, not realizing Nkosinathi had left.

There was plenty of room for two desks. Anna arranged them at an angle so they faced each other at a slant creating a triangle, with the small table and its vase of flowers forming the base. She matched the furnishings perfectly to the existing décor, with Regency bookcase, shelving, and a new drinks cabinet, all manufactured from oak and dark walnut. New curtains were of the same forest green as the leather top on both desks as well as the chairs. There was no sign of the paintings. She may have stored them in the vault for now, Hank thought.

Maurice's room received a similar makeover. It too was spacious, comfortably accommodating two workers. Anna repeated the triangular positions of the desks and matched new curtains to the rusty brown leather of their tops. Hank wondered how Maurice would react to being reorganized in his absence. It was presumptuous of Anna to shift everything without prior consultation, but at least she was still here. 'Be thankful for small mercies,' Hank advised his inner self, seeing clearly that this was her revenge. It was payback time for flying away without her.

More surprises awaited him at home. The first thing he saw was a new BMW in the garage. Wondering whose it was, he walked around it, admiring its rich deep-blue colour and light-grey upholstery. He couldn't imagine his mother owned it. There must be other guests in the house.

He found Gogo sitting in the lounge sipping sherry, with Pompom curled beside her.

'Mother!' he called out. 'Welcome!' He laughed, placing his arms around her affectionately. 'Developed a taste for alcohol?' he ribbed her mischievously.

'It's Anna's influence, you know,' she giggled back at him. 'You've no idea what she encourages me to do.'

'It's good to see you enjoy her company. Where is she anyway?'

'She was called to the telephone . . . ah, here she comes.'

Hank turned about, walking towards her. She stopped under the arched door frame, leaning against it, eyeing him with a parody of a smile.

'The return of my prodigal husband, I see,' she said, her voice reproachful.

Ignoring the verbal stiletto in his chest, he smiled broadly. 'Reunited with my sweet wife!' Disregarding her remonstrance, he embraced her, holding onto her till she had no choice but to kiss him.

'That's more like it,' he grinned. 'You're not still angry?'

Barbara's announcing dinner saved her answering the question. With Gogo in the house, the small talk at dinner was best kept pleasant. Hank escorted his mother to the dining room. 'It's good to have you here. What have you ladies been doing?'

'Oh, you'll never believe it. Anna bought a boat!' Gogo's excitement knew no bounds. 'She took me sailing. I even slept at sea for two nights. I've never had such adventures. To think I'm enjoying little cruises at my age!'

'Bought a boat?' Hank questioned, looking challengingly at Anna. 'Whatever for?'

'Because I miss the sea. Didn't I tell you? It's preferable to an apartment on Marine Parade.'

Ouch! Hank felt the stab. Anna threw darts again, hitting him fairly in the eye. Trying to change the subject, he asked, 'Who does that spiffy blue BMW in the garage belong to?'

'Me,' she answered sharply. 'And it's not a company car. I paid for it. There'll be no allocating that one to security personnel.'

God, since when was he married to a porcupine? Afraid to ask more questions, he addressed his mother again.

'Do you want to look in on Franz and Rosemary tomorrow?'

'I certainly do. I haven't seen the new baby since her christening. I'm here so rarely. When Anna suggested I should visit, I jumped at the chance.'

'Do you have your maid with you?'

'No, Ivana is in Durban with her sister. She wanted extra time off, so I came here.'

Anna ate sparingly. The wine in her glass was all but ignored. Hank avoided her gaze while he engaged Gogo in conversation.

Neither of us is prepared for the awkwardness and pain of a floundering union, Anna thought. Their marriage had fallen through the safety net they had attempted to spread when he brought her home from KwaZulu Medical. If only he had noted her appeals for renewed togetherness. His entire concentration centred on nothing but work. He expected her unquestioning support at all times but rarely acknowledged her help. That's how it always was. Why had she not seen it earlier? It took the ructions Joshua created to show her she was taken for granted. She should pack her bags and leave. Her pregnancy sounded the death knell for the marriage anyway. There was no saving it now. It was mortally wounded.

Gogo soon became sleepy as the wine added its mellowness to the previously downed sherry. She excused herself, with Mrs Bonga helping her to her room.

'Before you go,' Hank said, 'I have something for you. I'm glad I can give it to you personally instead of mailing it.' He pulled a silk pouch from one of his bags, which still awaited transport upstairs. It contained a shawl similar to the one he sent Anna for her birthday.

'It's so soft and smooth,' Gogo smiled, delighted she hadn't been forgotten.

'And what about you, my lady?' Hank turned to Anna when his mother left the dining room. 'I can see you still feel my trip without you was an affront to your self-worth. Can we let bygones be bygones?'

'I guess so,' she shrugged.

'The charm of your welcome is overpowering, my dear.' With a pleading look he added, 'Tell me what I should do to make good, because at the moment I feel as if I'm married to a cactus with an abundance of prickles.'

He was being smart, she thought, trivializing her feelings. She said, 'Cacti have beautiful blooms.'

'I know,' he laughed, 'especially the ones which open at night.'

She could do without his double entendre, but her sullen attitude was pointless. It achieved nothing. Both had overhauled their outlook on life, and neither he nor she was totally guilty or innocent in the process. She couldn't shut Hank out of her life. If he eventually retreated when she told him about the baby, that was his choice. She would do nothing to further increase the rift between them. He could even sail with her if he managed tearing himself away from work. *The JSE won't collapse without him*, she thought with a slight smile.

'You're grinning,' he said, taking her hand. 'We'll turn over a new leaf, you and me.'

Mentally, Anna shook her head. He was so sure of himself. He would be surprised to find she no longer tolerated being seen as a useful piece of furniture. From now on, his interests would not enjoy priority.

'I notice you wrote your dissatisfactions down to release your frustration with me. Couldn't we have talked about it?'

She took a sharp breath, ready to berate him for his indiscretion and snooping.

He raised a hand, knowing her admonition would follow. 'I wasn't spying,' he cut in quickly. 'Barbara wanted to see last month's butcher's account to compare it with the current one, which she thought excessively high. I helped her find the bill and saw the piece of paper on your desk. You left it there open for anyone to read.'

Anna regarded him silently. She thought she knew this man, but it appeared every aspect of their marriage had to be reappraised—when he had time to talk matters through.

'Interestingly,' he went on, 'I wrote my thoughts down also after your abduction. Would you like to read it?' He reached into his jacket pocket, pulling out three sheets of notepaper. 'I'll show you mine if you show me yours,' he quipped.

'I'm not really amused, Hank,' she said, sounding indifferent.

'You're right. There's nothing remotely entertaining about it, but unless I try to introduce a little humour, I shall go crazy.' He looked at her for a long time before continuing. 'I feel as if I'm losing you, Anna, and I don't want that—ever.'

'I don't want us to be like Fitz and Pompom either, Hank.'

'Now who's talking gallows humour?' he countered with a laugh. 'Come into the lounge, dear. We might as well be comfortable while we thrash out what to do in future.'

* * *

The fountain splashed hypnotically. Pompom lay stretched contentedly beside it, never twitching a whisker when stray droplets from its jets landed on her fur. Anna and Hank sat on the portico in the morning sunshine, sipping fruit juice and looking through financial magazines. It was a peaceful Sunday with little traffic about.

'See this?' Hank asked her, pointing to an article reporting on Mineral Enterprises. 'Their shares have risen again while Gold Corp is stuck in the doldrums. William will be cock-a-hoop.'

'It's good for KwaZulu Medical too,' Anna agreed. Glancing towards the wrought-iron gates in the distance, she watched a car passing slowly and reversing as if to park at the curb. She continued reading the story Hank showed her.

He looked up keenly when he saw Captain Broadbent and Major Mortimer approaching the gate. 'What the hell do they want on a Sunday morning?' He rose, opened the gate with the remote, and walked towards the visitors. 'Good morning, gentlemen, what can we do for you?'

Broadbent stopped some paces away from the portico, waiting for Hank's approach. 'We're here on a sad mission, Mr De Bruyn,' he said solemnly.

'Well, come have coffee,' Hank invited. 'It always eases awkward news. What is it?'

'No, thank you. We're here to tell you the senior partner at KwaZulu Medical was shot dead at yesterday's Inkatha rally.'

Hank's mouth opened wordlessly. He looked at Broadbent with disbelief.

'Professor Mtolo was coordinating first-aid stations. An IFP official was the gunman's intended target. The professor was killed while trying to assist the victim who was still alive at that stage.'

The men heard Anna's stifled scream. 'Oh my god!' Hank ran to her.

She sat, her right hand in her mouth, biting her knuckles, trying to swallow her cries. Blood ran over her emerald ring, dripping on the magazine and tablecloth. He stopped short, helpless when confronted with such discomposure. He waved the men away with a quick thank-you. Wrapping his arms around Anna, he attempted to stop the mutilation of her hand. She wouldn't move. He might have tried touching a marble statue—she was as stony and white.

The housekeeper came running, realizing something was wrong. 'Mrs Mkhize, please, quickly . . . bring a cup to tea for Anna. Hot, sweet, and black. Tip a splash of rum in it too. She's in a kind of shock.'

Unable to budge her, Hank pulled his chair close to hers. He had never seen anyone so distraught. Even Gogo had not reacted with such heartbreaking pain when his father had died.

'Anna, my dear . . . here, drink this,' he said when Barbara came with the tea.

With a robotic motion, Anna took the cup Hank held for her. Staring straight ahead, she sipped a little but put it back when it became smudged with blood. She looked at it in wonder. When Hank tried cleaning her hand, she became aware that the blood was her own. Her head sank onto Hank's shoulder.

'Oh god,' she sobbed. 'Why? Why Joshua? Why now?'

Hank sat still, letting her cry. He figured that was what Josh would have done—let her cry it out of her system, however long it took. He endeavoured to calm her, kissing her hair, wiping her eyes with the serviette Barbara brought with the tea, and talking soothingly.

'Come inside, my dear. We need to bandage your hand.'

She rose slowly. Hank placed an arm around her middle. She still felt like a statue to touch, he thought, but at least she was moving, although she leaned on him for support.

In the bathroom, Barbara helped to bandage Anna's knuckles, only to see her convulse with the force of hysteric weeping when taking the emerald ring away for a thorough cleaning.

'Sweetheart, come, you need rest.' Hank tried consoling her, leading her to a two-seater couch in a sunny spot of the lounge room. He sat beside her while a kitchen maid brought more tea. For a while, she was quiet but tense. Hank pulled her close so she could rest her head on his chest.

'We've suffered many persistent ill winds of late . . . and now this catastrophe!' Her thought, once spoken, provoked more weeping.

'It's not your fault, love. Self-reproach will only hurt you more. The binding spell you endured is broken now. You are free to be yourself again.'

Her tears flowed faster.

'Sweetheart, do you think we are the only well-to-do household to have ever lived through the consequences of a kidnapping? Many weren't as lucky as we are. They lost their loved one. At least you are safe and we are together.'

She said nothing. He continued, 'We are strong people, you and I. We will get through this.' She remained unresponsive, and he thought she must have fallen into exhausted sleep.

He should be relieved today. His nemesis had bowed out at last . . . but it gave him no comfort. Josh's death was a despicable act. No man should die while helping others to live. It was a senseless crime committed in the name of unitary power for the ANC. South Africa saw far too much politically motivated violence, which remained unquestioned, uninvestigated, and unpunished. The pitiless savagery of self-interest dominated. The innocent were left behind mourning the mutilation of their society.

Presently, Anna rose and walked to her piano. She sat on the stool, lifted the lid, and began playing and singing haltingly, her voice trembling with tears.

'Ach, siehe mich vor Wonne beben.' *Samson and Delilah.*

Hank quietly lowered himself into a chair on the opposite side of the foyer, listening. It pained him to see her in such a soul-destroying condition. He felt unable to help and began fearing for her sanity.

Suddenly she gave a cry and ran to the window. Startled, Hank followed. 'What is it, dear?' he asked when she talked in a whisper so soft he couldn't hear. 'Why did you stop singing?'

'Didn't you see Josh standing at the piano?' She smiled through tears.

Hank froze in panic. Her mind really was going.

'He smiled at me and said *Ngiyabonga*!'

'What does that mean?'

'Thank you.' She returned to the piano. 'He's letting me go. I am free.'

'Anna, you need rest.'

She laughed suddenly, a haunting sound, which shook him more than her claim to have seen Josh.

'Don't look at me like that. I'm not mad.'

'Please, Anna, you need to rest. You've had a dreadful shock.'

She shook her head at him. 'You know me. I'm the daughter of a master mariner and a sailor at heart. Seafarers are a superstitious lot. I can't explain it, but I feel easier now.'

Her fingers danced over the keyboard. She sang again—'Solveig's Song', about a woman waiting for her lover forever. It was another of Josh's favourites and confirmed her whispered promise to him at the window. 'I will wait for you, wait for eternity.'

When she stopped, she looked at Hank, sitting in the chair, his drink beside him neglected. She knelt at his feet, resting her forehead on his knee. Not looking up, she spoke so quietly he had trouble hearing.

'I'm expecting Joshua's baby.' More sobs came in wild gasps. 'I'm so sorry he died without seeing the child he wanted so dearly.'

Hank got to his feet, lifting her, and carrying her upstairs to bed. 'You are going to rest now, no arguments! Before you do, though, there are things I should tell you too.'

'Confession time,' she gulped, blowing her nose.

'I've had plenty of time to think about us. I've done little else lately,' Hank began, watching her carefully for any signs of misery or fatigue.

'I know Josh had you in thrall from the moment you clapped eyes on each other at that shareholders' meeting. Even though neither of us knew what was to come, I began wondering if I had neglected you somehow—unintentionally, of course—anyway, you know all that. Remember what happened when we went to bed that night after the meeting? Wasn't anything to shout for joy about, was it?'

'That's not your fault,' she cut in immediately.

'It made me think, love. I began to wonder about Zak's treatments. He means well and, in theory, does the best he can, but was his approach right for me? You read it all in the notes I made at the time I showed you.' Hank coughed, embarrassed. 'Here comes the confession part, dear. I paid a couple of glamour pussies to let me practice. I wanted to be sure my health regime was working. I couldn't bear to disappoint you.' He looked at her, head to one side, gauging her reaction.

'I can't talk,' she replied with a shrug. 'Although'—she tilted her head as well, imitating him provocatively—'the notion rings a bell like Big Ben . . . doing the wrong thing in order to do good. I've come across it before, I think. People who say two wrongs don't make a right are not always correct.'

Hank drew her closer to him. 'There is a chance the baby you carry is ours,' he whispered in her ear, his voice raw with a new emotion. 'It's a slim chance but not totally impossible.'

Anna kissed him like she hadn't done in a long time. 'Oh, Hank! No matter how minute the chance, let's clutch at the hope.'

* * *

Author's Note

Welcome, dear reader, to the world of my wild and hyperactive imagination.

None of the key characters in this story exist in true life. Nor do their businesses and pursuits.

Occasionally, though, you may stumble across a name you recognize. Or you may identify a string of facts tying this parcel of fiction together. For you, I include a list of background reading to help you detect where the string around the package may have snagged.

Ubuntu aims to illustrate the futility of politically motivated violence and the difficulties rich and poor citizens face when thrust together to create a new beginning.

Background Reading

Buthelezi, M. G. (1991). 'Remarks by Mangosuthu Buthelezi, President, Inkatha Freedom Party, Royal Hotel, Durban, 29 January 1991'.

de Klerk, F. W. (1998). *The Last Trek: A New Beginning.* New York: St. Martin's Press.

De Kock, W. (1986). *Usuthu! Cry Peace! The Black Liberation Movement Inkatha and the Fight for a Just South Africa.* Cape Town: the Open Hand Press.

du Preez, M. (2013). *A Rumour of Spring: South Africa after 20 Years of Democracy.* Cape Town: Zebra Press,

Forde, F. (2014). *Still an Inconvenient Youth: Julius Malema Carries On.* Johannesburg: Picador Africa,

Gumede, W. M. (2005). Thabo Mbeki and the Battle for the Soul of the ANC. Cape Town: Zebra Press,

Harper, B. (1999). *People of Heaven.* Sydney: Pan Macmillan,

Inkatha Freedom Party (1996). 'Submission to the Truth and Reconciliation Commission', sections 2–5.

Jeffery, A. (1997). *The Natal Story: 16 Years of Conflict.* South African Institute of Race Relations, Johannesburg.

Jeffery, A. (2009). *People's War: New Light on the Struggle for South Africa.* Johannesburg: Jonathan Ball Publishers (PTY) Ltd.

Johnson, R. W. (2009). *South Africa's Brave New World: The Beloved Country Since the End of Apartheid,* London: Penguin Books Ltd.

Mandela, N. (1991). 'Opening Address by the Deputy President of the African National Congress at the ANC/IFP Summit, 29 January 1991'.

Renwick, R. (2015). *Mission to South Africa: Diary of a Revolution*. Jeppestown: Jonathan Ball Publishers.

Sparks, A. (2003). *Beyond the Miracle: Inside the New South Africa*. Johannesburg: Jonathan Ball Publishers (PTY) Ltd.

Temkin, B. (2003). *Buthelezi*. London: Frank Cass.

Wentzel, J. (1995). *The Liberal Slideaway*. South African Institute of Race Relations, Johannesburg.

Woods, J. (1984). *Special Payments*. London: Arrow Books.